Everybody in the
Church Ain't Saved

Everybody in the
Church Ain't Saved

Patti Trafton

www.urbanbooks.net

Urban Books, LLC
78 East Industry Court
Deer Park, NY 11729

ISBN 13: 978-1-60162-361-4
ISBN 10: 1-60162-361-5

First Mass Market Printing August 2012
First Trade Printing October 2008
Printed in the United States of America

10 9 8 7 6 5 4 3 2 1

Distributed by Kensington Publishing Corp.
Submit Wholesale Orders to:
Kensington Publishing Corp.
C/O Penguin Group (USA) Inc.
Attention: Order Processing
405 Murray Hill Parkway
East Rutherford, NJ 07073-2316
Phone: 1-800-526-0275
Fax: 1-800-227-9604

Prologue

Steam rose from the plate Patrice Russell balanced in one hand, while she filled a glass with sweet tea with the other. Although she'd secretly nibbled on crackers and M&M's whenever she thought Pastor Short wasn't looking, she was hungrier than a newborn baby past its feeding schedule. She slid into a booth by the window, mumbled a few words thanking God for the fried chicken, macaroni and cheese, and mixed greens she'd piled on her plate, and then dug right in. Lorene McCall and Regina Holloway were taking too long for her to wait on them.

As she bit into her chicken, her eyes scanned the restaurant for her two friends. Lorene looked as if she was giving the hot bar attendant a piece of her mind, the way her head swiveled on her neck, while Regina stood at the salad bar, her nose turned up at the food items offered. Minutes later Lorene practically slammed her plate on the table, clearly irritated, and took a seat beside Patrice.

"Who you done cussed out now?" Patrice asked as she stirred four packets of sugar into her glass with her straw.

"That stupid-ass girl gon' tell me it's gonna be another ten minutes before some more chicken is ready. They know it's Sunday, damn!"

Regina took a seat across from her two friends. "We ain't been out of church for a hot five minutes and there you go. Lo, how do you get up singing God's praises week after week then cuss people out in the next breath?"

"Don't start, Regina. 'Cause, last I checked, the Bible says we all have sinned, so don't try to act all holier-than-thou. I'm tryin'a get myself together, but every time I try to live right, here come somebody to mess it all up."

Regina disregarded Lorene's comment. "Anyway, do y'all remember my cousin, Jean?"

They both nodded.

"Well, she started a community choir."

"For real?" Patrice asked.

"Yeah, they sound good too, chile. They did a concert last night and had everybody shouting. Did anybody bless the food? Never mind—I don't know if I want y'all praying over my plate," Regina joked.

Lorene and Patrice silenced themselves, respecting Regina's quick prayer, but dove right back in as soon as she lifted her eyelids.

"When do they rehearse?" Lorene asked.

"I think, every Tuesday and Saturday. I have to call her to find out for sure."

"Well, find out quick, because I sure do miss singing out," Patrice said.

"I'll check and see if we can go sit in on one of their rehearsals this week," Regina offered. "Then if we like it, we can join."

It had been a few months since the young women had sung outside of their own church, At the Cross Pentecostal. They all had been members of the Pentecostal District Mass Choir, but when the choir president handed out what they felt to be an unfair penalty for late arrivals and absences, all three of the women and a host of other fellow church members quit. They'd been told that they couldn't sing at a major church event, due to no fault of their own. At the time, their church van, driven by Hubert Jones, one of the meanest deacons of their congregation, was their only means of transportation. Purely out of spite, he frequently "misplaced" the van keys, or took his time about getting the choir members to scheduled rehearsals.

"I'm sorry, but ain't none of y'all from Pastor Short's church singing in the convocation next month!" Angela Simmons snapped.

The group bustled off the van and rushed through the vestibule doors into the sanctuary, realizing that once again they were all tardy. All of the other choir members were seated in the pews and grouped into their respective voice sections.

Startled by Angela's unexpected and abrupt greeting, the latecomers were speechless. Everyone except Lorene.

"What? Why?" she asked, her tone just as nasty as the one she'd been greeted with.

"Well, if y'all would have been here on time, you would have heard the discussion about people missing rehearsals and coming late. Y'all late every single week, and we done gave y'all enough chances."

"But it don't be our fault," a tenor spoke up. "You know we don't drive ourselves over here."

"And whose fault is that? The whole choir gotta suffer 'cause y'all wanna take your time about getting here?"

"What about the money we just paid for our robes?" Patrice questioned.

"That money is non-refundable." Angela poked her lips forward.

"Well, y'all gone give us our damn robes then!" Lorene shot back, causing gasps to escape the lips of the other members.

"Oh no, she ain't cussin' up in the house of the Lord," someone from the soprano section said, louder than a whisper.

"Lorene, I can't give you no money back, but you will respect this church!" Angela's hands flew to her hips as she demanded reverence in her place of worship.

"And you 'bout to respect this ass-whuppin' I'ma put on you if we can't get our robes!" Lorene charged down the aisle at Angela, but was quickly held back by a couple of tenors who leapt from the pews to calm her down.

"Naw! Let her go. Let her come on up here so I can show her a thing or two. I'ma beat the devil right outta that girl!" Hardly intimidated by Lorene's loud mouth and size four body, Angela stood solid with her stocky, 300-pound frame.

"Let's just go," Regina suggested. "They know they wrong, and God will take care of that. Come on, y'all. They ain't the only choir in town." Regina, the levelheaded peacemaker, was again able to influence them to do the right thing.

After a few more heated words, the group piled back into the van and headed for home, Lorene cussing Deacon Jones out every mile of the way. Patrice, Lorene and Regina made up in their minds that they weren't going to sing in the PDM Choir anymore. Every choirmember at At the Cross made the same decision, with the full support of their pastor.

Faye Wilson, one of the sopranos in the choir greeted Regina, Patrice, and Lorene when they arrived at Jean's rehearsal later that week.

"We were just about to get started. Y'all gone join tonight? We need some strong voices in the soprano section; I hope that's what y'all sing." The words seemed to roll off of Faye's tongue without her taking a single breath.

Lorene smiled. "Well, we're just going to sit in for this rehearsal and see how we like it first."

"Oh, okay, that's fine. Let me know if you have any questions or anything. I think y'all will like it. We're a pretty good group. I'ma check back with y'all later when we finish, but if y'all want to join in and sing, just let Jean know, 'cause she don't let no voice go to waste." Faye chuckled as she walked off.

Right away Patrice and Lorene took to Faye's high-spirited personality, but Regina was appalled by what she saw. There were more men in the soprano section than there were women, sweeter than the peppermints in a little old lady's handbag. A few of the females were dressed as if they were on their way to a rap video dance audition, and the overall hovering aura was chaos and confusion.

Nonetheless, at the end of rehearsal the trio joined anyway, impressed by the choir's talent, and propelled by their own love for singing.

But it didn't take long for Regina to decide that the Love, Joy, Peace, and Deliverance Community Gospel Choir wasn't the place for her. Not willing to deal with the foolishness, she quit before anybody could say *John Jacob Jingleheimer Schmidt*.

But Patrice and Lorene felt right at home.

Chapter One

Although it was the middle of March and eighty-five degrees outside, the combination of the air conditioner and fans made it too cold for the building. Patrice couldn't understand why it is that, as soon as it gets warm out, people immediately turn on the AC. The fans were enough. Her eyes wandered around the huge sanctuary, with its dozens of dropped lightings, and ceiling fans that twirled so fast, the human eye couldn't see the blades, its multi-colored windowpanes, red carpet in the aisles and one hundred and twenty red plush pews in four sections filled with people giving God the praise as the choir sang.

"When all God's children get together, what a time, what a time, what a time," Patrice pushed out from her diaphragm into the mic as she led the church into a shouting frenzy. *"Hallelujah!"* she shouted, swinging her shoulder-length locks, and shuffling into her own fancy footwork. She held her back, and jogged in place, reminding

herself to save some of her energy for later, thinking about which club she, Lorene, and Faye could go to once they were done singing. She had given her life to Lord umpteen times, but at nineteen, there was too much partying to do and too much sex to have.

Patrice's mother, Annie Ruth Russell, would often warn her daughter about her behavior, saying, "Patrice, you better stop playing with the Lord! You keep on letting the devil fool you, you're going end up in destruction. And I ain't gone keep lettin' you live any ol' kinda way under my roof."

The words went in one ear and out the other.

The pastor gave the benediction and dismissed the service.

Patrice thought to herself, *There'll be plenty of time for me to live right, once I get my momma's age, but tonight I'ma party like it's 1999!*

"Lo, let's go to the FNB Club on base," Patrice suggested as they made their way to Lorene's car.

"Girl, you know goodness well I have to go to work tomorrow." Lorene, the most responsible of the three, had a job working in the shipyard as an office assistant. "I'll be tired as a monkey hanging with you."

"Please? We don't have to stay out long." Patrice waved Faye over to join them.

"Where are we going tonight?" Faye asked, a wide smile on her face, swinging her hips from left to right. "It's time to change dance partners."

"Lord have mercy. Not you too. Y'all are not going to worry me to death about going out tonight," Lorene said. "And I guess I'm supposed to escort y'all heifas around in my car, huh?"

"Faye, give her some gas money," Patrice said. Without Lorene's car, the only place Patrice could go was home.

"You give her some!" Faye shot back.

"Chile, please. You know I don't have a job."

"Exactly! So my next question is, how are you going to get in the club without any money?" Lorene's crinkled forehead expressed her frustration with Patrice's freeloading mentality.

"My mom spotted me twenty-five dollars. Shucks, I need to save that. I'm trying to buy me some shoes I saw on sale at JCPenney's."

"You are a trifling somebody. You're too old to be bummin' money off your momma. You need to get a job." Faye sucked her teeth.

Patrice rolled her eyes at the both of them. "Okay, okay, I'll chip in five dollars. Now can we go, please?"

Lo sighed. "All right, but we ain't staying out all night. I was late last Monday, and I'm not going to lose my job, messing around with you two."

"My girl!" Patrice squealed, snapping her fingers and rotating her hips. "That's what I'm talking about."

"Whatever. Get your crazy behind in the car before I change my mind."

Patrice stripped out of her skirt and wiggled into a pair of extra-tight black pants. She purposely bought a size eight, rather than the ten she needed.

As Lorene coasted to a stop at a traffic light, Patrice took notice of two handsome brothers in the car beside them, and used the opportunity to shed her church blouse, remove her bra, pinch the nipples of her double D's, then tied on a red sequined halter, never taking her eyes off the men.

Filled with wild excitement, their eyes bucked.

"Patrice, please don't tell me you back there giving another drive-by peep show," Lorene howled.

"I'm just changing clothes. Dag! How we gonna go up in the club looking like we just finished leading praise and worship?"

"You coulda changed at my house," Lorene snapped. "I'ma stop letting you ride around in my car, before you have some nut following us, with your fast ass."

Thirty minutes later, Lorene circled the crowded lot looking for a place to park. The lot was filled, so they had to park close by the barracks.

The military men gawked and whistled at the ladies when they got out of the car. Lorene was conservatively dressed in a yellow sheared sundress with spaghetti straps and white high-heeled sandals. Faye, a voluptuous size fourteen, was dressed in a black mini skirt with white tube top and black pumps. The girls looked sexy indeed and strutted with confidence through the club's entrance.

A tall, thin, heavily weaved woman stood just inside the entrance with a towering, muscular bouncer checking ID's and collecting cover charges. She said, "Oh, y'all mammies let you come out and play tonight?"

Faye glanced at the others, a confused look on her face. "What's her problem?"

"I detected jealousy. She probably ain't had no ding-ding in weeks." Patrice scoffed.

They all burst into laughter.

Patrice pulled her fake ID from her purse and flashed it, then waved her hand in disrespect. "Check the date, sweetheart."

The woman glanced at their photos, and then looked at the trio like they stank.

Patrice threw her hips extra hard for the bouncer's sake. *Broke-down drag queen!*

As they entered the dance room and found a table, a few brothers turned their heads in their direction. Just as they ordered a round of drinks, a tall, lanky J.J. Evans look-alike approached their table and asked Patrice to dance.

She thought better of it. After all, Marvin Gaye's "Sexual Healing" wasn't exactly the type of song to dance to with a perfect stranger, but she went against her gut and accepted.

He guided Patrice to the dance floor like a perfect gentleman, and then gently swept her into his arms. Moderately, his hips began to rotate seductively against Patrice.

Oh, he want a taste of the nana, Patrice thought as she kept with the flow of his rhythm.

J.J. pulled her closer to him, filling his hands with her behind, and allowing her to feel the solidness of his manhood. His gyrations against her suddenly became harder and more demonstrative.

Although Patrice physically enjoyed the feeling and was turned on by his erotic display, the dance floor simply wasn't the place. Slightly embarrassed, she glanced at his face and nearly burst into laughter.

Eyes shut tight, deep wrinkles on his forehead, J.J. was biting his lower lip and looked as if, any second, he was going to have an orgasm.

Other female dancers gawked at them as they lost focus on their own dance partners, while the faces of the brothers expressed encouragement and envy, as they wished they could be the ones nearing a climax.

Patrice, now thoroughly embarrassed, wanted to pull away from the obviously horny man, but then she had a second thought. She looked at the other dancers on the floor and mouthed the words, "Watch this."

Her lips protruding forward, Patrice snaked her body against J.J., then turned her backside toward him and bent forward at her waist, pressing against him, and adding in the sound effects of a few open-mouthed moans.

After a few wiggles and a couple of shakes, uncontrollable tremors came over J.J., and he began to go into a full-out conniption, signifying he was approaching an orgasm. Just as he reached his peak, Patrice quickly pulled away from him and headed to her seat.

"Where you goin' girl?" he mumbled. "Fool!" she huffed over her shoulder.

J.J.'s eyes popped open to witness a crowd in full-blown laughter as he tried to gain his composure. Patrice couldn't help but laugh herself.

"Did you enjoy your dance, nasty?" Faye asked through giggles.

"Girl, you wish you could put it down like me. Y'all ain't never broke a brother off like that." Patrice snapped her fingers in the air. "I shoulda charged him."

All three ladies burst out in laughter.

Suddenly Parliament-Funkadelic's "She Was a Freak" blared through the speakers.

"Aaaaahhh! That's my jam," Lorene said, bobbing her head from side to side.

Laughter in his voice, the DJ announced, "And this goes out to the lady that just put it on the brother right in the middle of the dance floor."

Before Patrice could join in with singing the lyrics, three brothers were lined up wanting to dance with her. Sizing them all up, Patrice picked the finest of the three. "Sorry." She shrugged at the other two, leaving them at the table with Lorene and Faye. She turned back to the guy of her choice and said, "If you put your hands or your dick on me, I swear I'ma shoot you."

"Oh, nah! I wouldn't disrespect you like that, lady," Glen Pearson immediately replied, hiding his disappointment. He was actually hoping to get a little bit of what she had given her last dance partner. *That's all right*, he thought. *I'll just use my natural charm to get up in them drawers.*

The DJ kept the groove going, mixing in Flashlight, and received cheers of approval from the crowd. Glen showed off his best moves, impressed with Patrice's ability to keep up. She'd been so lost in her steps that she hadn't given Glen much eye contact, but as the music slowed just a bit their eyes finally caught.

Good gracious, he is fine. Patrice's eyes absorbed every inch of his six-foot frame, defined chest, flat stomach, and narrowed waist. Even through the sweat, she could still detect the cool, masculine fragrance of his cologne. The skin on his face was flawless, and beneath the club's lights, his eyes almost glowed in the dark.

They danced through two more songs, but when the music's tempo decreased to a slow jam, Patrice made her move to exit the floor. *There ain't no way in the world I'm going through that mess again.* "Thank you for the dance," she said politely before turning away.

Glen pulled her back gently. "Please don't walk away. No hands, I promise," he said, putting up his hands in mock surrender.

Patrice found it hard to resist the gorgeous eyes staring at her and hesitated for a moment.

It was all Glen needed to continue. "My name is Glen, and yours?" He lightly took her hand and led her into a simple two-step.

"Patrice."

"Patrice," he said slowly.

Patrice felt warm inside hearing him say her name. In her nineteen years of living, never had her name sounded so sexy before.

"It's nice to meet you, Patrice."

It was during Stevie Wonder's "Ribbon in the Sky" that Glen pulled her close to him, and held her around her waist, mindful not to let his hands roam. Seconds later, Patrice draped wrapped her arms around his neck, feeling chills going up her spine. When the song ended, he kissed her hand and escorted her back to her seat.

"We'll be right back. We're going to the ladies' room." Faye stood to her feet and smoothed her skirt with her hands. "Watch our drinks."

"Was it something I said?" Glen joked, moving aside to let Lorene and Faye pass. "Patrice, I just wanted to thank you for the dance. If you don't mind, may I have your phone number so I can call you sometimes?"

"No, not at all. It's 555-1675."

He quickly scribbled the numbers down on a torn napkin. "Actually, I'm getting ready to leave right now. I have to get up bright and early in the morning for work. Are your friends coming back, or will you be needing a ride home?" he asked with suggestive eyes.

"I'm sure they'll be right back, but to be honest with you, I am kind of tired and I'm ready to go right now," she lied. She wasn't tired at all and was hoping that he would offer to take her to a much quieter place.

"If it's okay with you, I'll take you home. Where do you live?"

"I live off of Clare Lane," she revealed, standing to take his hand.

Her conscience was screaming, "Patrice, you are crazy as hell, if you let this man take you home," but Patrice liked to live dangerously.

"Downtown Newport News?"

Patrice studied his face when he asked. She was a little embarrassed to tell him the exact location. Then again, what the hell! "Yeah, the projects."

Chapter Two

"Aw shucks now! Patrice done found her a fine tutey." Lorene leaned over the countertop toward the mirror to examine her makeup.

"Oh my God, did you see that girl on the floor? She can be embarrassing sometimes," Faye said, fluffing her curls with her fingers.

Lorene nodded her head as she applied more color to her thin lips. "Yeah, she can be embarrassing. I feel like cussing her ass out sometimes, but I'm used to her acting like a fool. I've been knowing her ever since we were kids, so I ain't got nothing but love for her."

"Yeah, I love her myself. The girl is crazy, though."

"Girl, I can't believe it's one-thirty A.M. already. I'm going to be all to pieces tomorrow at work. My boss warned me several times about the errors I've been making, and if I don't tighten up I'm out the door."

"For real, Lo? You didn't tell us about that."

"Girl, you just don't know. I have to deal with a lot of shit."

"Well, try to cheer up. It will be all right."

Lorene sighed. "Yeah, hopefully it will. Come on, let's get back out there before she make her way on top of the speakers and start stripping."

Lorene and Faye found their way back to the table and Patrice was nowhere in sight.

One of the brothers who was dancing with Faye earlier came back for another dance. He noticed that the girls were scanning their eyes around the club, trying to find their friend. "If you are looking for your girl, she bounced out of here a couple of minutes after you ladies went to the bathroom."

"With who?" Lorene snapped, mad that first of all Patrice left without saying a word, and secondly, left their drinks unattended. Having heard too many horror stories about stuff getting slipped into drinks, Lorene wouldn't even think about taking another sip.

"I dunno. She was with some cat with his arms around her waist."

"Well, hell, you saw all of that and you don't know who it was?"

The brother frowned. "Look, don't get all huffy with me. I'm just letting you know that your girl is gone."

Faye patted his arm to try to make peace. "We're sorry," she offered. "Thank you, though."

"No problem."

In an instant Lorene's eyes became as red as fire. She quickly got up from the table. "Come on, Faye!"

Lorene was walking so fast, she seemed to be in a race. Faye tried keeping up with her, but she had to trot a bit to do so. "Lo, slow down, girl. You got my heart jumping rope."

"Hurry up then! I'm sick of this shit. Every time we try to go out and have a nice evening, this ho mess it up! I told her about that. She's going to mess around and have someone kill her ass."

When they got to the car another vehicle had just pulled in the parking space beside her. The person on the passenger side swung the car door open so wide that it bumped and scratched Lorene's car.

Immediately Lorene was furious. One thing she didn't allow people to mess with was her car. It was her pride and joy. "Bitch, what the hell is your problem! I just got my car painted."

The girl had on a red mini skirt, white halter-top, and red pumps. Her hair was matted to her head. "Who you calling a bitch?"

"You, you nappy-head heifa!"

"I think you better get in your car and drive away before you get your ass kicked."

Lorene stepped in the girl's face. "You and what army?"

Without warning, the girl shoved Lorene so hard that her back slammed into her car. Like a rubber ball, Lorene bounced back, grabbed the girl by the throat, and began landing blows repeatedly to her face.

"Lo, stop!" Faye tried pulling Lorene off the girl, who was flailing, gasping for air, and trying to find her balance. Faye looked at the other girl, who just stood paralyzed by shock. "Will you help me break them apart?"

The other girl would not move.

Finally Lorene let her go.

The girl in red coughed for air. When she had enough breath to talk, she pushed out, "I'm gonna kill your ass! You better watch your back, 'cuz I'm gonna kill your black ass! Then she landed a large, slimy wad of spit onto Lorene's car.

Lorene started to jump on her again, but this time Faye was able to stop her. "Lo, let's go please. Get in the car," Faye said.

Once they were in the car, Lorene was cussing up a storm. "See, this shit is all Patrice's fault! If she would have kept her fast ass in the building, I wouldn't be going through this shit. She gets on my damn nerve. Wait till I find her. She better hope I don't have enough strength to kick her ass."

Faye gave Lorene a please-spare-me look. "You know goodness well you ain't kicking Patrice's *tass*. That's your girl." Faye was careful not to use actual cuss words.

"Yeah, you're right, but I am going to cuss her out."

They caught eyes with each other for a moment then broke into laughter.

"Girl, you tore that girl's *tass* up."

Lorene and Faye drove the avenues looking for Patrice. While driving, Lorene's mind drifted back to how her nasty attitude started.

When she was in elementary school, kids used to tease her a lot because she didn't have a mother. Her father did the best he could, trying to comb Lorene's hair, but was awful at it. The children would call her "motherless spook baby," "knotty-head china doll," and on and on.

The worst of all was Joanni. Joanni would catch Lorene in the restroom and make Lorene fondle her own breast, punch her in the back until Lorene lost her wind, and after school when Lorene came out to play, she would make Lorene and another female child hide behind a tree and grind each other.

One day at school, Lorene was sitting at her desk, trying to do her school work. Joanni kept pulling Lorene's pigtails very hard. Lorene felt a warm tear strolling down her cheek.

All of a sudden she turned around and swiped her pencil across Joanni's face. Joanni held her cheek as blood dripped on her desk. The children and the teacher gasped. Of course, Lorene was suspended from school, but Joanni along with the other children never bothered her again.

From that point on, Lorene been cursing folks out. Now although she protected herself with a dangerous weapon—the tongue—she still had a lot of hurt inside.

Faye broke her out the trance. "Girl, where in the world could she be?"

"I don't know. Let's go home. Hopefully she would have enough sense to call somebody." Lorene sighed.

Chapter Three

Glen and Patrice stopped at Hardee's Restaurant, which never seemed to close, for a late-night breakfast. Just as any gentleman would do, he asked Patrice what would she like to eat. She mentioned a super-sized sausage platter and a large orange juice.

"After all that dancing I've done tonight I've worked up quite a bit of an appetite." She rolled her eyes and patted her belly.

"You can order what you want."

Glen smiled and thought to himself, *Baby, eat all you can eat, because you're gonna need your strength when I tear that ass up tonight.* "It's all about you, baby."

"And what do you mean by that?"

"It simply means I have been mesmerized by your beauty all night long and I want to make all your wishes come true. So if one of your wishes is to indulge yourself in a large breakfast, your wish is my command."

"Don't even try it. You must think you're gonna get some booty tonight."

I am. "Naw, baby. What kind of a man do you think I am? I would never disrespect you like that."

Once they were seated, Glen reached for Patrice's hand and began to pray. "Father God, we thank You for blessing us and for this time of fellowship. Father, bless the food and the hands that prepared. And, Father, I pray that as we prepare to leave that we would arrive home safely. In Jesus name . . .

"Amen," they both said in unison.

Patrice smiled as she began to dig in. "So, I see you are a praying man."

"Not really, I just give honor where honor is due."

"Do you go to church?"

"No, not anymore. I used to go every once in a while back in my hometown."

"Oh, so you're not from here?"

"No. Trenton, New Jersey."

"Oh, what Trenton makes the world takes," Patrice said, quoting the slogan on the side of the bridge that spans over the Delaware River into Trenton.

"What do you know about that?"

"Let's just say, I get around every once in a while. So you haven't found you a church home here?"

"No. I used to sing in a community choir, but when a lot of faggots started joining, I had to get out." Which made Glen mad as hell. He wanted to screw every woman in the choir but didn't have the chance.

Patrice laughed. "What? You're afraid that one of them might turn you out?"

"Hell no. I was afraid that I was going to beat the hell out of one of them if they tried to get close to me. I'm a pussy man."

Patrice continued to laugh. "You're crazy. What was the name of the choir you used to sing in?"

"Love, Joy, Peace and Deliverance Community Gospel Choir. Mouthful, ain't it?

Oh my God! Patrice almost told him that she'd just joined that choir but thought better of it and decided not to. She didn't want him to judge her, just in case she wanted to spread her legs and give him some. "How long ago was this?"

"About six months ago."

Whew, that's a relief. He probably doesn't know Faye. She just got in three months ago right after Lorene and I joined.

They were quiet for a moment. Then Glen said, "Well, other than you love to dance, tell me a little more about yourself, miss lady."

"You're trying to get to know me?"

"Yes." Glen's real thoughts were. *Hell no. I just want that juice spot in between them gorgeous thighs.*

"Well, really there's not much to tell. I'm what you call a spontaneous person. I do whatever comes to my mind."

"No order, huh?"

"I have order, I mean, to some degree." Patrice suddenly went into silence, which let Glen know that his comment slightly disturbed her.

He used that as an opening to take his prey home. "Hellooo?"

Patrice didn't respond.

"Listen, let's go to my place and we can talk some more."

Much to Glen's pleasure Patrice nodded.

His one-bedroom apartment was nicely furnished with a beautiful cream leather sofa, glass coffee and end tables, and cream lamps. Expensive wall hangings mounted in huge frames, along with an expansive mirror, decorated the space. Against a long wall was an extravagant entertainment center with huge speakers. It was nothing Patrice was used to. She only had a small

boom box with a wire hanger sticking out where
the antenna had broken off. As far as the pictures
on the wall of her mother's house, there was only
a picture of a white Jesus with long, silky, brown
hair, embellished with roach droppings inside of
the cheap brown frame.

"Have a seat. I'm going in the kitchen to fix me
something to drink. Do you care for anything?"

"No, thank you." She seated herself on the
couch, crossed her legs, and started to make herself at home, picking up a frame photo of a little
girl from the coffee table. She was dressed in a
blue tee shirt that read, "Daddy spoils me." Her
thick, long hair was styled in two ponytails on
either side of her head. Patrice noticed she had
a birthmark in the shape of an apple right above
her left eye. She was absolutely adorable.

Glen came out of the kitchen with a half-filled
wine glass in his hand and sat beside her.

"What's her name?"

He grinned so hard, he created a pair of dim-
ples. "Tiffany."

"Ah, she is so precious. How old is she?"

"Five. Yup, January fourteenth, 1979. I would
never forget that wonderful day when my baby
was born."

Patrice was astonished. "Are you serious?
That's my mother's birthday."

Glen smiled.

"So where is she now?"

"She lives in New Jersey with her mother. I try to go see her every chance I get, but I don't want to talk about her because I don't want you to see me start tearing up. Besides, I want to talk about you. How come somebody as sexy as you don't have her man with her tonight?"

Patrice turned her head, pretending to be shy, and shrugged. "Everyone is not spoken for."

Glen stood to his feet and turned on some soft jazz music then pulled her up from the sofa, coaxing her to dance with him.

Hold up, Patrice thought. *He wants to get to know me? You don't learn about someone by asking one question.*

Only after a minute or so, he started to dance his way toward his bedroom, holding her tightly. She tried pulling away from him, but the more she pulled away, the tighter his grip became.

"Glen, I'm ready to go," she said firmly.

He ignored her and kept maneuvering her toward the bedroom, refusing to loosen his hold. Patrice began to inwardly panic as she thought about a conversation she, Lorene, and Regina had about being in a rape situation. They'd reasoned that fighting would do no good because it would provoke the man to become angry and maybe even deathly brutal. Then he would take their coochie anyway. They'd agreed that it was better to be raped and remain alive than raped and end up dead. Although she felt forced, she didn't fight.

Glen laid Patrice on the bed then pulled off her pants before removing his own. She saw a nasty scar on his left thigh, which looked like a stab wound. Her attention was diverted from the scar when he pulled off his underwear. His penis was so long and thick, it scared her to death. Patrice wasn't a virgin by any means, but she tightened herself up because she really didn't want to be there.

Glen had a hard time getting inside of her, but after a few forceful thrusts, he had fully entered her body.

Once he did, she wanted to cry for two reasons. First, Glen was literally raping her. Second, he felt so good.

After he relieved himself, he held her and went to sleep, and Patrice didn't make it home until eight o'clock the next morning.

Chapter Four

Glen was sitting at his desk daydreaming
about last night. He could not get Patrice off his
mind. At first he just wanted to get the goods and
disappear, but after having sex with her, he felt
much differently than he did with anyone else.
He'd remembered getting up to use the bathroom and seeing how beautiful she was while
sleeping. He thought to himself, *I can't do this to
this girl, although she didn't pass my test. Lord,
please help me. Here I am, a twenty-five-year-
old man, still playing these stupid games. I just
want to love someone and have someone love
me back. Is she the one? Well, if it's at all possible, I would like her to be the one for me.* Then
he said to himself, "I got to give her a call when
I get home."

"Patrice," Annie Ruth called from downstairs,
"telephone!"
Patrice picked up the receiver in her room.

"Hello?" she asked, once she heard the clatter of the other phone being hung up.

"What in the hell is wrong with you?" Lorene started right away. "You know damn well you ain't got no business leaving with somebody you don't know. You're so damn trifling. We didn't know where you were or nothing. As far as we knew, you could have been dead! Patrice, do you have any idea how scared we were?"

Patrice was silent. Lorene was right. What in the world had she been thinking? She searched her mind for justification for her actions from the previous night. All she ever wanted was someone to love her. She wasn't thinking about college or trying to find a decent job like Lorene, but she just wanted to fall in love, get married, and live happily ever after. Was that too much to ask?

"Well, Miss Growny, what do have to say about yourself?" Faye chimed in.

Patrice had no idea Faye was on the phone listening on three-way.

"Y'all, I'm so sorry. Lo, you are right. What was I thinking?" She heard Lo breathing hard into the phone's receiver, sounding as if she was about to have a heart attack, which indicated to Patrice that she was mad as hell.

"So, are you going to tell us what happened?" Faye asked.

Patrice gave them full details of what took place.

They both yelled and cussed her out, sure enough then, but finally they calmed down long enough for Lorene to ask, "Are you okay?"

"Yeah, I'm fine. Everything that you're saying, ma has already said. She cussed my butt out for not calling her last night."

"What? Your momma cuss?" Faye exclaimed.

"Girl, in a heartbeat! I can't quite understand somebody that's holy but says *shit* and *ass* in a minute. She claims that it's not cussing."

Faye burst into laughter.

"I told her to say it to her pastor then. As a matter of fact, get up during testimony service and say, 'I thank the Lord for waking my ass up in the morning and placing me in my right mind to go through this shit I have to deal with every day."

Easing more from her anger, Lo laughed. "Girl, you crazy."

"I sure did tell her. Anyway, now she's making me find a job, and if I don't, all the cleaning I do will be my pay for staying here, meaning, she's not going to give me money anymore, talking about I have to start paying rent." Patrice rolled her eyes and sighed very heavily.

"I don't blame her. You too old to be mooching off your mama, and if you can screw and wave your hands all in the air, you can carry your ass to work somewhere—*I said on and a on and on on a on*," Lorene said, singing the lyrics of "Rapper's Delight" by Sugarhill Gang.

Faye screamed in laughter then said, "Tell her again, Lo!"

Patrice asked with sarcasm, "Oh, so now you are a poet?"

"And didn't know it." Lorene snickered.

"I don't see nothing funny, and anyway, these little jobs out here don't pay nothing." Patrice pouted.

"Heifer, they will pay you more than twenty-five dollars," Lorene huffed.

Patrice didn't comment, but Faye broke the silence by saying, "It was probably my fault that your mama went off on you. I kind of called last night and asked to speak to you."

"Faye!" Patrice gasped.

"Don't even try it. Don't be mad at me behind your foolishness. If you weren't going to go home, you should have told us, and maybe we could have covered for you."

"I told you why I didn't come home."

"Yeah, after the fact," Faye said. "But, anyway, I'm sorry."

Patrice smacked her lips and said, "Don't worry about it. What's done is done."

Within in a matter of minutes they changed the subject. Faye started singing, "Jesus on the Main Line."

Patrice asked Faye, "So do you like the way Dwayne revised that song?"

Dwayne, the choir's piano player, was as sweet as potato pie. In fact the LJP&D Community Gospel Choir was full of homosexuals, who felt loved and accepted by the female choir members. The "faggies," as the girls called them, kind of created a brother and sister mix that some of them never had.

"Yeah, girl. We are supposed to sing it this coming Saturday night at Mount Calvary Holiness Church."

"Dag, I forgot all about that. I have to braid someone's hair." Lorene smacked her lips.

Patrice wrinkled her forehead and asked, "On a Saturday night?" It was unusual for Lo to waste a good Saturday night doing someone's hair.

"Yeah, chile, that's the only time she can come."

Patrice sighed. "Well, you're just going to have to reschedule because you know you're the strongest alto we have." Patrice heard a beep on her line and blurted, "Hold on a minute." She clicked over. "Hello."

"Hi, sweetheart" Glen cooed.

She had mixed emotions about his call. A part of her was angry because he had the audacity to call after violating her. The other part of her remembered the pleasure of feeling his body stroke her over and over again.

"Hey, hold on a minute, Glen. I have someone on my other line." She clicked back over. "Y'all, I got to go. Someone is on the line for my mama," she lied. She dared not tell them who it really was. They would have cussed her out again.

In unison Lorene and Faye both said, "Bye."

Once again she clicked back over. "I'm back."

"Who were you talking to? Your man?"

"That's none of your business."

"I thought it was, being that we took care of business last night."

Her coochie started jumping. She had to admit, she did want what was between his legs. *Rapists don't call you, right?* She thought, trying to convince herself that she wasn't raped.

"So, when can I see you again?"

His sexy voice made her womanhood pulse a second time. "I don't know. When do you want to see me again?"

"Right now."

She glanced at the clock on her nightstand. It read 9:00 P.M. Considering the hour, she knew it was nothing but a booty call, but she really didn't care. All she knew was, this brother knew how to put it on her. *I might as well have fun tonight because tomorrow I need to start looking for a job.* "I'll be ready in thirty minutes," she responded, attempting to sound as sexy as Glen.

Hanging up the phone, she sat on her bed for a minute, thinking about the previous night all over again. It was against her better judgment to go over there, but damn, this man's piece was too big to pass up.

She took a quick shower and packed an overnight bag with a red negligee, red low-heeled bedroom slippers, and a Jovan Musk bath set. She also packed a bottle of body oil, planning to offer Glen a massage, wanting tonight to be much different than last. Finally she packed a white tank top, a pair of jeans, and some white "butter cookies" to wear the next day.

"Where are you going this time of night?" Annie Ruth asked when Patrice came bouncing downstairs, bag slung over her shoulder. Her mother was seated in her recliner doing a crossword puzzle.

"Over Lorene's house. She asked me to stay with her tonight because her father is going out of town. She's scared to stay in the house by herself." Patrice could tell a bald face lie so professionally, it was a shame. Her mother hated liars, and she knew that God did too.

Whenever her mother caught her in a lie, she'd say, "In the Bible it says, 'All liars have their place . . .'"

Yeah, yeah, yeah.

This time Patrice had told a half-truth. Lorene's father was going out of town, but Patrice had no intentions of seeing Lorene that night. Lorene was used to being at home alone. Having lost her mother as a toddler, she never had the privilege of having a mother raising her.

"Okay, be safe."

Her mother believed anything when it came to Lorene. Within two minutes, she heard a horn blowing.

"Ooohhh, yes, baby." Glen took his sweet time sliding in and out of Patrice. "Oh, Patrice, your kitty feels so good. Say it's mine, baby. Say it's mine." Changing positions, he held her legs over her head, licking the inside of her thighs. Sweat dripped from his face onto Patrice's tremoring body.

"Yes, baby. Oooooh, yes, this nana is all yours."

He stuck his thick tongue between her coochie lips and licked it like ice-cream, trying to catch every drip.

She squirmed to back away from him, because it was feeling so good that she could not take anymore, but he locked her legs in his arms, to keep her from moving.

Patrice started flowing like a river. "Pleee-aase! Stop! I can't take anymore, baaaabeeeee! AAAAAHHHHHH!"

Turned on even more, Glen ignored her pleading. He then turned her over to her stomach and pulled her to her knees.

Suddenly Patrice felt a surge of pain. His penis seemed much thicker and longer than it did just a few minutes earlier. *Oh my God! What in the world did he do?* Patrice began to cry out in pain. "Glen, Stop! PLEASE! You hurting me!"

He stopped immediately, turned her back around, and saw that she was actually crying. "Are you okay? Baby, I'm sorry. I didn't mean to hurt you." He lowered himself and started kissing her nana ever so softly.

She turned her head and caught sight of what tortured her. This negro had stuck the biggest dildo she'd ever seen in her life inside her.

Glen explained that he wasn't ready to come, because she was rocking his world, so he'd used that for a substitute. "Baby, I'm truly sorry." He crawled beside her and started kissing her tears, and then in the mouth.

His sincere apology began to ease her pain, as he held her in his arms, while she cried herself to sleep.

When she woke up, it was five in the morning. Glen was still sleeping peacefully. She rubbed his chest, waking him up.

He stretched, yawned then kissed her on the forehead. "Good morning, lily," he mumbled.

"Who in the hell is Lily?" Patrice responded with attitude.

"A beautiful flower like you."

"Oh, I started to say—"

"Say what? That you love me?"

"Love you? It's a bit too early for that, don't you think?"

"No, not really. I believe in love at first sight, don't you?

With a sad sigh, Patrice responded, "Well, I guess. It just never happened to me."

Glen noticed her countenance. "What's wrong?"

"Glen, can I ask you something?"

Looking directly in her eyes, searching for her soul, he said, "Yes."

"Last night I felt very uncomfortable at first. When I kept asking you to stop, why didn't you?"

"I don't know. I thought you were saying no but really you wanted it like I did."

Patrice frowned. "Glen, *stop* means *stop*, and *no* means *no*. I kept thinking to myself, *No, this man ain't raping me.*"

"Raping you? Baby, I would never do anything like that. That wasn't my intentions at all. And if you felt that way, I am so sorry. Please don't take it like that. You are absolutely right, *no* means *no*. Please forgive me, Patrice."

Patrice saw the sincerity in his eyes. "That's okay. All is forgiven."

"Baby, I'm serious. I am truly sorry."

Patrice rubbed his cheek gently. "I said it's okay. Don't worry about it. Come here." She kissed him softly.

Moments later they were at it again, but this time without "King Dong."

On his way to work that morning, Glen took Patrice home. Before she got out of the car, he gave her a kiss, and in return she started stroking his manhood.

"You better stop, before I turn this car back around and take you with me."

"We can do that," Patrice said with a sly grin.

"No, we can't—if I want to keep my job."

Patrice pouted and gently rubbed the side of his face. "All right, I'll see you later." She then got out of the car and looked back while walking to the door. She noticed that Glen was watching her butt. "G'on, boy," she said smiling, and he finally drove off.

As she entered the apartment, Patrice thought a lot about what Lorene had said to her about working, so she made up her mind that she was going job hunting. Besides, her mother left her no other options.

Chapter Five

Patrice stood in line at Hardee's Restaurant, trying to decide whether to ask for an application or just order a sausage, egg, and cheese biscuit, and be done with it. She was a little hesitant to ask for an application after seeing how extremely busy the employees were. *I just can't see myself busting my ass for some chump change,* she thought. After noticing that she was next in line, she had to hurry up and decide what she was going to do.

"Good morning. May I take your order please?" asked the older white woman, her uniform covered with flour and grease spots. She smiled at Patrice, revealing five teeth in her mouth that resembled brown sticks, three up top and two on the bottom.

"Yes. I would like the sausage, egg, and cheese biscuit, and a small tea."

"Okay. Will that be all for you today?"

Patrice nodded.

"That will be two dollars and twenty-one cents, please."

As Patrice dug the money out of her wallet, she asked, "By the way, are you hiring?"

"Yes. We sure do need some help. Do you have any experience?"

Patrice shook her head in shame. *Oh well . . . I tried.*

"That's okay. We can train you. It's nothing to it actually."

Patrice was somewhat glad to hear that. However, she was thinking, *I wish somebody had trained you to brush them teeth. Maybe you'd still have some today.*

"Let me get you an application. I know this is a short notice, but can you possibly start today? We are very short-handed," she said with pleading eyes.

"Right now?" Patrice asked in surprise.

"Naw, sweetie. I can give you some time to go home and prepare yourself. I believe I have a uniform that fits you. What size do you wear, small or medium?

"Small." Patrice was so excited that she actually had the job without going through an interview.

"What time can you start?"

"Well, I have to catch the bus to get back here, so I guess around two?" She searched the woman's eyes to see if she was okay with the time.

"That will be fine."

It was actually 2:30 P.M. when Patrice arrived again, ready for work. The same five-tooth woman came strolling out of the office and handed Patrice some forms that had to be filled, signed, and put in Patrice's employee file.

After the paperwork was completed, she guided Patrice to Christina, her best cashier.

"Christina, I need you to show Patrice how to work in drive-thru." She glanced around at Christina's work-station and noticed that there were only a few cups left on the counter. "You need to stock up your area, while it is slow."

"That's what I'm about to do, Millie. Hold your horses."

"All right, smart mouth." Millie turned to go back into the office.

"All right, dookey mouth," Christina spat, causing Patrice to burst out in laughter. "Girl, she can be a witch sometimes. She probably is, with a mouth like that."

"Why would anybody make her store manager, with her mouth all tore up?" Patrice asked, immediately taking a liking to her co-worker.

"Girl, Hardee's don't care. As long as you kiss butt, you can be in any position you want."

"Well, evidence shows she's been kissing somebody's behind."

They both fell out laughing.

"What's your name anyway?" Christina asked.

"Patrice."

"Girl, I'm going to like you." Christina showed Patrice how to clock in on the register, and then moved on to the food and price keys. Patrice's next lesson was on reading the pick up menu screen. Christina discerns Patrice becoming frustrated from trying to consume everything so quickly.

"Don't get aggravated, girl. It will get easier, once you get used to it."

"I sure hope so. I'm about to quit already." Patrice sighed.

"You better not. I'm not training you for my health." Christina rolled her eyes. Then she smiled to let Patrice know she was only joking.

"I'm not." Patrice slightly smiled. "But you better not leave me hanging."

Once it got busy Christina asked Patrice to bag the food, while she took the orders and collected the money. Whenever an order was taken, it would show on the pickup screen. During the rush Christina kept calling back food items that didn't appear on the screen.

"A double cheeseburger, large fry, and a large chocolate shake!"

"A what?" Patrice looked on the screen for the order that Christina had called for over the mike.

"A double cheeseburger, large fry, and a large chocolate shake!"

Patrice hurried and bagged the order and gave it to Christina. She whispered, "Girl, what are you doing? I don't see that mess you're asking for."

"I'll tell you later," Christina whispered back. "What time are you getting off?"

"It is supposed to be six o'clock."

"I get off at six too. You got a car?"

"Nope."

"I'll take you home. Where do you live?" Christina shoved a bag of food out of the window after placing a few dollar bills inside her register.

"In the projects," Patrice answered, referring to a government-subsidized neighborhood in downtown Newport News.

"No problem. I'll tell you in the car."

Shortly after six, Patrice settled into the passenger seat of Christina's little black Chevy.

It smelled like she had just opened a cherry-scented car freshener. As Christina whipped the small vehicle out of the parking lot, she began explaining to Patrice about the extra food items. "Girl, you got to know how to dance, if you going to work drive-thru."

"What does dancing have to do with serving cheeseburgers?" Patrice asked, exhausted from being on her feet for the past four hours.

"That's what it's called, 'Dance.' " Christina giggled at the look of confusion on Patrice's face. "See, this is how it works—I don't ring up all my orders, but I still take the money for them. I got a register in my head. I know exactly how to add up everything that I don't ring up. So when it's time to count my drawer and it's a hundred dollars over, guess what? The money is mine." Christina started moving to the music from the radio, giving meaning to the term *dance*. "That's right, honey."

Patrice gasped. "You lying!"

"Girl, please. Hardee's don't pay enough. I got to get mine. I make four hundred dollars a week, plus my two weeks' pay, which is usually a measly two hundred dollars. Yes, darling, I gets paid."

Patrice thought, *Thank you, Lorene, for telling me about Hardee's.* "Girl, you done told me something. Humph! I'ma do it too."

Patrice stole so much money over the next few weeks, she didn't even mind adding a few dollars to her church offerings.

Chapter Six

I really love the Lord, I really love the Lord
You don't know what He's done for me He gave
me the victory Oh, I love Him, I love Him, I really
love the Lord.

Patrice sang the song so beautifully, she had
just about every eye in Mount Calvary Holiness
Church filled with water. She led one verse, and
Peaches, who had a voice like BeBe Winans, led
the second. Peaches' real name was Peter. (He'd
changed his name, affirming his homosexual
orientation.)

After they ended the song, they heard a
woman in the congregation screaming, "Thank
ya! Hallelujah! Thank ya, Jesus!"

Using that as his cue, Dwayne started out slowly,
playing getting-ready-to-shout music. Keith, the
drummer, accompanied him, tapping on the cym-
bals.

Seconds later, people started jumping to their
feet, giving God the praise. They carried on for

several minutes, jumping, shouting, and hollering all over the church.

Finally, everyone had taken their seats again,
and a young minister came to the podium and
grabbed the microphone. "God is good!" he
yelled, his voice bouncing off the sanctuary walls.

The congregation responded, "All the time!"

The minister placed his hand on his hip and
then rocked from side to side. "I said God is
good!"

"All the time!" they replied even louder.

The minister turned to look at the choir behind him in hot burgundy robes. His eyes quickly
scanned the members in search of Patrice. Once
his eyes rested on hers, he smiled. "Girl, if I had
a woman who sang to me like you sing for the
Lawd, I would give her everything I got. She
would ask me for five dollars and I would give
her fifty."

The entire church congregation started laughing.

"And, young man, you are anointed too," he
added, looking at Peaches.

The minister's comment stayed with Patrice.
She thought he was handsome enough to have
any woman he wanted and wondered if he was
looking for a wife, or at least a lover. After he
made the comment to her, she felt her tunnel

moisten at just the thought of lying beneath his body, and planned on fantasizing about him when she laid her head to rest.

After leaving Mount Calvary, the choir went to Po' Folks, a restaurant specializing in good ol' Southern food. After the group was seated, they started to make conversation about the church service they'd just left.

"Dwayne, you were putting a hurting on that piano," Patrice exclaimed. "Yes, Lord! You tore that baby grand up!"

"He most certainly did. When I heard that piano go *dent da da da, dent da da da*"—Faye played an imaginary piano, moving her shoulders up and down, and everyone else started clapping their hands to her rhythm—"you almost made me catch the Holy Ghost!"

They all laughed.

Then Patrice's mind reflected on the night before, when Dwayne had called and told her some man put a hurting on his booty hole. She gave him a sly look then glanced at his butt and said, "Umph, umph, umph! But that piano ain't the only thing that's hurtin', is it?"

Instantly he recalled the talk they'd had and returned the look. "What? I'm sorry but, Trice, it felt so good, girl, na na, girl, girl, girl!" he exclaimed, recapping his actions from the previous night.

Patrice screamed, laughing at that clown. "Boy, you are so nasty." Patrice gasped.

"Ho, I know you ain't talking. You know more ding-aling than I know letters in the alphabet."

"This is true, this is true." She dropped the conversation right away, not wanting Dwayne to blurt her business out to everybody at the table. She had to think about becoming that minister's wife, and he wouldn't want somebody who'd been all over town. She looked over at Jean, the choir director. "Hand me the salt please."

"Sure," Jean replied.

Jean was as sweet as she wanted to be, but was mustier than two bags full of rotten onions. Every time a straight man joined the choir, she had to do a ding-ding check, to see if it could delight that coochie of hers. Patrice couldn't understand how they slept with her and put up with her funk. They had to smell it. Maybe her beauty overwhelmed the stench.

"Patrice, I heard you got a job," Jean said, her mouth full of food. "I hope it doesn't interfere with our engagements. I need all the sopranos I can get."

"Naw, it's only part-time." As long as she "danced," Patrice didn't have to spend much time working. "I told my manager that I could only work during the day from eleven to three."

"Eleven to three?" Lorene almost choked. "Girl, you ain't gon' make no money."

Lorene did make the engagement, although she was late, making it in time to at least sing the last two selections.

Patrice rolled her eyes and reminded Lorene of her own words. "It's more than twenty-five dollars."

"Okay, you got me," Lorene said, backing down.

Peaches hollered across the table, "Patrice, that minister had his eyes on you." He had no idea that Patrice had banked him in her memory.

"No, he didn't. Stop playing."

"Please. Yes, he did. I know that look when I see it," he said, a wide grin on his face.

Patrice smirked. "And what look is that, Peaches?"

"Oh, girl, don't act like you don't know. He wants to taste that fruit in between them there thighs of yours."

Patrice gasped. "For God's sake, Peaches, that is a man of the cloth."

"Please . . . everybody in the church ain't saved, honey. You of all people should know that."

They laughed.

"Who is he anyway?" Keith asked, sucking the barbecue sauce off his fingers. "He kind of looked familiar."

Jean answered, "That's Bishop Thompson's nephew."

"How old is he?" Patrice asked.

Faye looked at Patrice suspiciously. "Are we interested?"

"No, I just asked. He looks kind of old."

Jean started laughing before answering her question. "That's that old soul hanging around old folks. He ain't nothing but twenty-six."

Patrice dismissed Jean's response with a wave of her hand. "Ain't nobody thinking about that man," she lied.

Patrice looked back at Dwayne. He was chomping away on a pork chop dinner served with mashed potatoes and gravy, black-eyed peas, and hot butter biscuits, his iced tea served in a jelly jar. "Dwayne, you did a wonderful job on revising 'Jesus on the Main Line.'"

"Thank you. But, of course, y'all are the ones that had to sing it. We did a wonderful job together, girl, a wonderful job." He lifted his glass to his puckered lips, to which Lorene began smirking. "Lo, darling, did I say something funny?"

She wiped her mouth with a napkin then looked directly at Dwayne. "Honey, you are a lie, and the truth ain't in you."

With a confused look, Dwayne responded, "What?"

Lorene smacked her lips. "Revising 'Jesus on the Main Line,' huh?"

Immediately Dwayne began to get hot under the collar. "What the hell are you talking about, witch? I worked day and night like a runaway slave on that song for six months straight."

"I'm talking about, you know goodness well you did not revise that song."

Everyone at the table suddenly came to a shocked hush and bounced their eyes between Dwayne and Lorene. Lorene was the type of person that didn't care about folks' feelings getting hurt or not. She would let the truth be known. Dwayne didn't mind hurting folks' feelings either.

Patrice did a double take in Dwayne's direction. The man got two shades darker. Patrice thought, *Lord have mercy, not tonight. Every time we get together some drama starts up.*

"Look, you cracked-lip heifer, you don't know what the hell you are talking about. I don't know if that is ketchup on your lips or blood."

Patrice stopped chewing. "Please don't start him up, Lo."

"I don't give a rat's ass if he does start up. He knew he heard that song off of Jacob Hall's first album. I knew that song sounded familiar when he was teaching it. And just tonight when I was singing it, trying to remember my part, my client start singing it with me. Then she said, 'Girl, that is an awesome song.' I asked her how she knew the song, and she said, 'You know, that's on Jacob Hall's first project he did back in the late seventies.'"

Everybody's mouth fell open wider than the Grand Canyon.

Caught in plagiarism, Dwayne was so embarrassed, he could have crawled under the table. Without saying another word, he got up from the table and went outside.

Right away, the choir began talking about Dwayne, dogging him behind his back.

"Oooh, chile! I'll steal your man, but I can't steal nobody's song," Peaches said, waving his right hand like he was taking an oath. "That's my boy, but I can't get with that."

"Now that don't make no *bam* sense," Faye said with a disgusted look. "How in the devil is he going to claim somebody else's song?"

Jean slowly shook her head from side to side. "Girl, you ain't lying. He had me all proud of him for nothing."

When they finished eating, everybody left a tip and went to the cashier to pay for their dinner.

Patrice said, "Y'all go ahead. I need to put my shoes on."

As soon as their backs were turned, she picked up every dollar the group left as their tip and stuffed the money in her bra, pocketing enough to pay for her dinner and some leftover. Quickly she joined the rest of the group as they all went to their cars.

Patrice didn't have a car, so she always rode with Lorene. As they approached the car, Lorene let out a shrill scream.

Everybody ran over there to see what was wrong, and then stopped with gaped mouths as they looked at Lorene's car. All of Lorene's tires were flat.

Lorene thought about all the drama she'd dealt with in her past, the nights of being alone because her father was on the road frequently, the pressure she's under at her job, and now this. Lorene wasn't the only one fuming; every choir member was as well.

"Ain't nobody did this mess but that fat, nasty, stinking, bucked-tooth, cock-eyed, cock-sucking faggot, Dwayne! I'm going to kill his ass when I see him!" Lorene said, both hands balled up into fists.

Faye looked at the tires then at Lorene. "That is ridiculous. He has lost his mind. Lo, you need to go call the cops on his trifling butt."

"I ain't calling nobody because, I don't want his ass in jail, I want him dead! Maybe I should call the police and report myself, because I'm going to slice that don-of-a-bitch tonight!"

Jean crinkled her brows and asked, "What in the world is a *don-of-a-bitch*?"

Lorene rolled her eyes. "A combination of daughter and son."

Keith, the only one in the choir that tried to live this life how God wanted, rubbed Lorene's back, trying to calm her down. Every time the choir got together to sing, eat, or just play, Keith always prayed before the choir did anything. The boy could preach like Paul. Keith said in a calm, still voice, "Lo, I have triple A. I just called them. They'll be out in just a few minutes."

Patrice stood on the other side of Lorene and asked Keith, "I thought triple A will only work on your car."

He smiled a little. "It all depends on who you know, and I know Jesus."

Keith always had a way of changing the atmosphere from something unpleasant to something wonderful. Whoever he walked down the aisle with would be blessed. Patrice knew it wasn't going to be her. Although she would have loved to have a saved man, she had too much party in her to give it all up right now. She felt as though she was too young to be sitting in church all day. *Keith ain't studying me anyway. He has his eyes on Lo. I don't know why, because the girl can outdo Peter in the Bible when it comes to cussing. But, I must say, my girl is very at*tractive.

Lorene was a woman of high moral standards. She may have had a couple of dates here and there, but she wouldn't sleep with any one of them. In fact, she was still a virgin. Patrice had tried talking her into having sex at least one time, telling her that she would love it, but Lorene would always say, "Girl, on my wedding night, I don't want my coochie asking my husband, 'What do you want? I have seen enough of your kind and I am too tired to deal with you. Please go away." Patrice always laughed at that, but would feel guilty afterwards.

Patrice felt as though it was too late for her. Her well had its first bucket dipped in it when she was thirteen, and she'd been addicted ever since. Sex had become one of her favorite pastimes, but deep in her heart, she longed to settle down with the right one. Every time she slept with a different man, she would swear up and down that he would be the last one. She just wanted someone to love her and never let go, but he would let go, and she would end up giving it away to someone else. Her knight in shining armor had to be out there somewhere.

Once the tow truck arrived and began replacing Lorene's tires, the crowd got smaller and smaller. Finally, no one was left but Lorene, Keith, Faye, and Patrice. Keith told them he would make sure she got home safely. He walked over to the truck that read "AAA at your service" and signed a stack of papers.

Lorene had calmed down a lot, but she had a blank look on her face. It frightened Patrice just a bit, because she had never seen this type of behavior coming from Lorene.

"Now that this mess is taken care of, how are we going to get even with Dwayne?" Faye asked.

Patrice didn't say anything. Neither did Lorene. She was too upset to say much of anything, and Patrice had no plans of messing with that nut, Dwayne. She didn't have a car for Dwayne to slice up, leaving him no other choice but to cut Patrice if he got mad enough. Hell no. She was crazy but not dumb.

Keith had his hands in his pocket, whistling and strolling back over to where the girls were standing. "Well, ladies, looks like everything is cool." He noticed Lorene's expression and said to Patrice and Faye, "Are you two going home tonight, or are you staying over Lo's?"

"I was planning on going home, but we can't leave her like this." Patrice held and rubbed the back of Lorene's hand with her thumb.

Faye nodded her head in agreement.

Keith was relieved. "That's good. I'll take Lo home in her car. Patrice, you drive my car. I'll follow you."

Patrice nodded. "Okay."

During the drive, Faye and Patrice hardly spoke. Faye was as scared as Patrice was, because this was the first time they'd actually seen Lorene in this state of mind. She looked like she was about to have a nervous breakdown.

"Girl, did you see Lorene's facial expression?" Faye asked just above a whisper, as if Lorene was in the back seat and she didn't want her to hear.

"What facial expression? The girl was looking like a zombie. It sent chills down my spine," Patrice responded

"I'm kind of scared for Dwayne a little. He must don't know how crazy Lorene can get."

Patrice yelled, "Scared for him? Girl, please. His faggot-ass is the one that better be scared 'cause, he better believe, Lo is gonna kick his ass."

"That's what I'm saying, Trice. You should have seen when Lo whipped that girl *tass* in the parking lot because she hit Lorene's door and spit on it too. Lo ain't no joke. I'm just glad I'm her friend and not her enemy."

By the time both vehicles pulled up in front of Lorene's house, it was 12:30 A.M. The girls noticed as they climbed out of the car that Keith and Lorene didn't get out right away.

Patrice walked over on Lorene's side and peeked inside.

Keith lowered the window for a few seconds. "We'll be in in a minute. I need to talk to Lo first."

Patrice nodded her head and touched Lorene's shoulder, assuring her that everything would be all right. "Let me know if you need anything," Patrice offered after Lorene handed her the keys to the house.

The girls went inside and immediately called their parents to let them know what had happened, and that they were going to stay with Lorene for the rest of the weekend, since Lorene's father was out of town on a preaching engagement.

Patrice kept peeking out the window to see if they needed anything.

Faye watched Patrice peek out of the front window at least three times. Then she said, "Trice, don't worry. Keith got it. The man is the sweetest thing I know. If anyone can calm Lo down, he can. She's in good hands."

Patrice pulled away from the window and took a seat on the couch. "Yeah, you're right. But you know what? I feel like calling Dwayne."

Chapter Seven

"Lo, are you all right? Lorene, please say something. I don't like when you are quiet like this," Keith said. "Sweetheart, you got to let it go. You and I both know that Dwayne is not dealing with a full deck of cards. You know, Lo, the word of God says, 'Let this mind be in you which is also in Christ Jesus.' Now you know the boy has a reprobate mind."

Lorene remained silent, although she did finally bring her eyes to meet Keith's.

"If you want, we can go fill out a police report on him, but whether you do or not, you're going to have to find it in your heart to forgive him. You just have to. If not, it's just going to fester on the inside. Listen, I know you may not want to hear this right now, but it's in my heart to tell you. Jesus can be your healing balm if you allow Him. He will heal your pain. I, of course, cannot. I can only be here for you for moral support. He is the only one that will deliver you from what you are feeling right now. Lorene, please say something."

Although she spoke no words, finally tears began to flow down her face.

Gently, Keith wiped them away with his fingers. The more he wiped, the more tears streamed, until she burst into full-fledged wailing. He wrapped his arms around her as best he could and held on tight.

"Keeeeith! Ahhhh, ah, ah, ah, ah! Oh, Keeeeith! Ahhh, ah, ah, ah! God, please help meeeeeee! Help me, Looorrd!"

Lorene never showed her true feelings when people really hurt her. Deep inside she would cry like a baby, but on the outside she would fight like a raging bull. This time she couldn't hold it back.

"That's it, baby. Give it to Him. His yoke is easy and His burdens are light. He will never leave you nor forsake you. That's it. Let it go," Keith said to her.

Within minutes Lorene was quiet again, other than softly sniffing while resting her head on Keith's shoulder. He continued to hold her as he moved his lips, speaking in tongues, but only the Lord heard him.

When he felt that he could, he pulled away slightly and looked into Lorene's eyes. "Are you okay?"

She nodded. "Thanks so much, Keith. I felt so much rage within me, I scared my own self. I actually want to kill him. I have never felt like that before. It was like the devil and his demons broke out and had a party in me. I wasn't going to care 'bout who got hurt in the end. I just saw fire." She chuckled a little. "It wasn't the Holy Ghost fire neither. And do you know what the sad part is? After wanting so bad to kill Dwayne, I wanted to kill myself. It was like a war going on inside of me," she said just above a whisper. "On the way home I saw angels fighting for my life. Their backs were turned, and their arms kept going up and down, like they were slaughtering demons on my behalf."

"That doesn't surprise me. Sweetheart, the battle is not yours, it's the Lord's. But I will say this, having your tires slashed is not worth killing yourself. Don't you think that's a bit too extreme?"

"Having the tires slashed was the icing on the cake. No one knows the pain that I go through from day to day. I try not to show it, but I'm tired of being unhappy all the time. I know life got to be better than this."

Keith sighed. "Well, maybe I'm just on the outside looking in. I have no right to judge you, but just remember that we were all born for a reason. We are not destined to go to hell. Hell was made for the devil and his angels, not us."

Lorene dropped her head in shame. "I am partially responsible for all this mess. I shouldn't have said anything."

He gently picked her chin up and says, "Hey, look at me. This is not your fault. Besides, you know whatever is done in darkness will come to light. Don't worry about it. What's done is done."

"In a way I am glad this happened tonight. Now I understand. God will use our enemies to draw us close to Him."

"Precisely."

They sat in the car for another twenty minutes or so. Keith turned the ignition and pushed in a tape that Lorene had in her car. The music played softly, "Your tears are just temporary, your tears are just a relief of the pain the heartaches and grief . . ."

Lorene broke the silence. "I can't wait to go to church tomorrow and give my life to the Lord. That's if I don't fall asleep before they make altar call. Bishop Thompson is long-winded."

Keith broke into laughter first, but then said," You don't have to wait until tomorrow. You can do it right now."

Chapter Eight

"Hello? May I speak to Dwayne?" Patrice couldn't wait until Dwayne got on the phone so she could cuss him out. Faye was sitting across from her waiting patiently for her turn, wanting to give him a few choice words as well.

"Hello?"

"Dwayne, what the hell is your problem? I can't believe you would stoop so low to slice up the girl tires!"

"First of all, I believe you better take that bass out of your throat my dear. You sing soprano. And, second of all, what the hell are you talking about? Whose tires are sliced?"

"Oh, you're going to act like dumb-dumb the duck now, huh?"

Faye's eyes got wider than fifty-cent pieces. "Oh no, he ain't trying to act like he don't know what you're talking about! Give me the phone!" She snatched the phone out of Patrice's hands. "Listen, you *bam* faggot!" she spat wildly. "You better bring your raggedy *tass* over here right now and apologize for messing up that girl's car. You are so *bam* trifling. The only one you worry about is your stinking-*tass* self. You gets on my nerve. You got a lot of nerve, playing for the Lord and acting like a *bucking* devil."

Patrice was holding her stomach, howling with laughter. Faye always cracked her up when she called herself cussing.

"You better check yourself 'fore you wreck yourself! I don't know who you calling yourself getting an attitude with, but I know one thing— you better not try to get one with me. Now I am going to ask you two clonkeys one more time. What in the hell are you talking about? And whose tires are sliced? Is it Lorene's? Put her on the phone, because obviously I don't speak fish!"

Faye's mouth had gotten so wide, and her eyes were now burgundy with anger. She was ready to whip his hind parts.

"What did he say, Faye? What did he say?"

"Girl, he must think we work for Barnum and Bailey Circus, because he called us *clonkeys*, and *fish*." (*Clonkey*, a combination of *clown* and *monkey*.)

Patrice was heated. "That's all right. Hang up. We're going over there and handle this." Patrice snatched Lorene's keys off the table, and they stormed outside.

Just as they stepped off the porch, Keith was opening the car door for Lorene. Lorene had a peaceful glow on her face, and she looked very calm.

Dag, she's looking like Keith's twin, Patrice thought.

"Where are you going?" Lorene asked.

"We're going over Dwayne's house and whup that *tass*."

"No, you're not. Trice, give me my keys."

Now before Patrice went in Lorene's house, she couldn't quite figure out the expression that Lorene had on her face, but she most definitely knew this one. She knew it because she saw it all the time when people left the altar after being born again. *This girl done gave her life to the Lord.* Patrice was happy for her, but it wasn't going to be the same. Who was going to drive them to the clubs? Charlie had three angels, not two.

Faye just did not notice the change that had taken place. She was still trying to go over Dwayne's house. "Come on. He can't whip the three of us."

"Faye, shut up. Can't you see that Lo gave her life to Jesus?"

Faye frowned and was looking back and forth between Keith, Lorene, and Patrice. Then she opened her mouth in shock. When she realized her mouth was wide open, she covered it with her hand.

"What? Oh my God. That's wonderful!" Faye blurted.

Lorene and Keith were smiling so hard, they were showing all thirty-two.

Patrice smiled a little. In the back of her mind she was kind of mad. Lorene was her girl. Now she didn't have a swinging partner. Faye was all right. They were tight too, but Lorene was more fun to be with and knew so much about her.

Lorene said, "Y'all go in the house. I'll be in a minute."

They did as they were told.

Patrice kept looking back at Lorene. She just couldn't believe that Lorene was saved.

"Keith, thank you again for everything. I will pay you back as soon as I get paid."

"No, you're not. I don't want you to do that."

"No, no, no. I must."

"Woman, can you please let me help a damsel in distress? Listen, don't worry about it. I'll need you one day and you will help, won't you?" Keith looked into her eyes for a response.

Lorene smiled and nodded. "Thank you so much."

They hugged each other.

Keith kissed her on her cheek and said, "I better go. Good night, sweetness." He waited until Lorene got into the house. Then he walked slowly to the car, got inside, and said a prayer:

"Father God in the name of Jesus, Lord, I give you all the glory and honor for Thou are truly worthy. Father, I just cannot thank you enough for what you have done and what you are going to do. Please watch over Lorene tonight. Keep her safe from danger seen and unseen. And, Lord, help her true friends that love her dearly. Please let grace and mercy follow them all the days of their lives as they dwell in Your house, Father. And, Lord, thank You for keeping me. You know the desires of my heart. I will not allow the enemy to take control of my life. You are in control, Father. For in Your word You said, it's better to marry than to burn. Thank you, Father, for quenching this fire I have on the inside for Lo. For in due season we shall walk in unity if it's Your will. Let Thy will be done on earth as it is in heaven. Lord, I even pray for Dwayne. Please protect him. Keep him safe. For we wrestle not against flesh and blood but wicked spirits in high places. He doesn't know he was being used by the devil. Bless his life. Lord, when and if You do these things, I'll be so careful to give Your name the praise. In Jesus name I pray. Amen."

Keith wiped a single tear from his eye and looked at the house once again before finally driving home.

Chapter Nine

*"If you live right, heaven belongs to you,
If you live right, heaven belongs to you, If
you live right, heaven belongs to you, Oh
heaven belongs to you."*

Saint James Baptist in Smithfield was packed with folks. Lorene, Faye, and Patrice had arrived a little after the testimony service had started.

As soon as they hit the door, Keith saw them and started grinning like he'd just won the Nobel Peace Prize. All of a sudden he started playing the drums with a burst of energy, fueled by him simply laying eyes on Lorene. He had been inviting her to come to church for quite some time now, but she would always have something else to do. He enjoyed their late conversations on the phone every night, so he was glad that she finally had come.

Lorene was wearing a soft lilac dress with matching pumps, her coal-black hair styled in

Shirley Temple curls. He noticed Faye and Patrice following Lorene to their seats. They looked nice as well, but he could tell by the expression on Patrice's face that she didn't want to be there. *Lord have mercy. I knew Lorene had to pull teeth and nail to get her to come,* he thought.

Patrice sat in the pew pouting, wishing the congregation would put an end to the song they seemed to be going on and on with. She was still tired from partying all night at the club with Faye. She'd tried to convince Lorene to come with them, but now that was mission impossible, seeing that all Lorene was interested in was talking on the phone with Keith all the time. She preferred to be in bed than to be sitting in somebody's church listening to testimonies. She was outdone with Lorene waking her up so early that morning, humming hymns, and lifting the shades, allowing the sun's beams to tear her eyes up.

She cut her eyes over at Lorene, remembering her attitude of praise and worship that forced her out of bed far sooner than she'd planned.

"Mmmmm. Loooo." Patrice moaned. "What are you doing up so early?"

"Girl, get up. This is the day that the Lord had made. Isn't it beautiful?"

"I'm sure He won't mind if I look at it much later. Close the blinds." Patrice pulled the covers up over her head.

"Nope. Get your behind up and wash your stinking butt." Lorene snatched back the covers. "We're going to Smithfield today to worship."

"Keith's church?"

"Yes. Today is Friends and Family day. We're going to be Keith's guests."

"You are going to be his guest by yourself 'cause I ain't going. I have to work tomorrow." Patrice turned her head away from the window.

"Three hours, Trice? And at midday at that? Come on, girl, I need you to help me travel. You know that I have a bad sense of direction. I would get lost as soon as I cross the James River Bridge."

"You better go buy you a map."

"Please, pumpkin?"

Anytime Lorene called Patrice *pumpkin*, Patrice knew that she really wanted something badly.

"After service they are going to feed us some good ol' soul food, and after that Keith's mother invited us to go sailing. Girl, they have a beautiful boat."

By the way Patrice was looking at her, Lorene could tell that she wasn't enthused.

"Come on." Lorene begged.

Faye came strolling in Lorene's bedroom, where Patrice slept, rubbing the sleep out of her eyes. "What's going on?" she asked with a groggy voice.

"Where are we going? is the question. Hurry up and get ready. We're going to Keith's church today."

"Cool." Faye looked over at Patrice and noticed the frown on her face. "What's wrong with you, Patrice? You don't want to go?"

"Naw, she don't want to go, with her lazy tail. See if you can talk some sense in her."

Lorene went prancing back into the kitchen, trying to hurry up and make something to eat before getting dressed. She had already showered and spoken with Keith on the phone before 7 A.M. Lorene really liked him. She'd never had a friend of the opposite sex that treated her with so much respect.

Patrice pulled the covers over her head again and tried to go back to sleep.

"Trice!"

"What, Faaaye?"

"You are a trip. You're always begging Lo to take you to the club, and now you acting like you're going to die if you go to church with the girl. If it was some man with a strong pipe in between his legs, you would be up before the crack of dawn."

Patrice knew she was right. Just last night when she got into bed, she wished Glen or the bishop's nephew were there to fill her up. Instead she had to rely on her middle and index fingers to do the job.

"Patrice! I know you hear me!"

"Okay, okay, I'm up, and I'm going, "cuz I see right now y'all ain't going let me live it down if I don't. Lo! Let me use your car to go home right quick to find something to wear!" She yelled from the bedroom.

"Yeah, right," Faye said. "Ain't nobody gonna let you use their car. Knowing you, you will have some excuse not to make it back in time. Lorene, I'll take her."

Lorene was in the kitchen cooking some oatmeal. She heard Faye laying into Patrice and was glad about it. Everything Faye was saying was true. Lorene always did things for Patrice. She felt for once her selfish behind could do something for someone else, but of course, she wasn't going to throw anything in Patrice's face. She had a new way of seeing things. God didn't throw in her face all the things He did for her. He did it because He loved her, and likewise, Lorene did things for Patrice because she loved her.

An old testimony broke Patrice's thoughts of that morning's conversation. She squinted her eyes at the old, fat woman giving the testimony. She wore a red hat with a purple scarf. Her purple blouse looked too big for her, and her red skirt was jacked up in the back and hung low in the front.

"Giving honor to God, who's the head of my life, pastor, saints, and friends. I thank the Lord for being here. I thank the Lord for waking me up this morning, starting me on my way, and placing me in my right mind. I thank Him for the activity of my limbs and the blood that is running warm in my veins. I thank Him for another day's journey, and I believe I'll run on and see what the end is going to be. And for those of you that know the words of prayer, pray my strength in the Lord."

Patrice looked at Faye and Lo, and immediately they all started giggling at the woman's words. They had talked many times about how folks gave the same ol' testimony.

What do they do? Patrice wondered, *After getting saved, does the church secretary give them a manual and say, 'Now go and learn this testimony by heart'?*

In Patrice's peripheral vision to the left she saw a fidgety little girl sitting beside a young woman, probably the child's mother, wearing a too tight, low-cut blue blouse, and a black skirt that had a split that went all the way up her right thigh. Patrice looked at the woman's bad weave and laughed to herself. Then she turned her head back at the little girl and watched for a few seconds as she tore the corners of the church bulletin piece by piece. She was so cute. She had on a pink lace dress, white tights, and black patent leather shoes. And her hair was styled in a lot of little ponytails with pink, white, and black barrettes.

"That little girl looks familiar. Do we know her from anywhere?" Patrice whispered, turning to Faye.

Faye peered down at the child. "No."

Certain that she'd seen the girl before, Patrice looked a second time.

The mother took notice of her staring and raised her eyebrows as if to say, "May I help you with something?"

Patrice smiled and silently mouthed, "She's cute."

"Thank you," the woman mouthed back.

Trying to make the best of the service, Patrice began clapping her hands and singing a praise song along with the rest of the congregation but couldn't help intermittently glancing at the child. She knew her from somewhere, but just couldn't put her finger on it.

It finally dawned on her, once she got a little sleepy and went in her purse to find something to nibble on, to keep from closing her eyes. She pulled out a piece of peppermint and tried to be discreet when opening it, which was very hard to do. She couldn't figure out why candy-makers put candy in hard plastic paper that made a lot of noise, knowing that every time someone hears the familiar rattling they'd ask for a piece. Not that she didn't mind sharing, but she didn't want everyone to look her way now while opening it.

Sure enough, the little girl approached her and asked if she had any more.

Now that the child was right in her face, it was clear to Patrice who the child was. "Oh my God! This is Glen's daughter."

The little girl whispered loudly, "Mommy."

The young woman looked at her.

"Can I sit here?"

She nodded her head.

I thought Glen told me that she was in New Jersey with her mother. That lying son-of-a— Patrice caught herself, looked toward heaven and whispered, "Oh excuse me, Lord. Please forgive me." Patrice couldn't understand, for the sake of her, why Glen felt as though he had to lie. It wasn't like they were in a relationship or anything. Well, a sexual relationship, but that was about it.

Her mind raced back to the last time he'd licked her nana. She looked toward heaven again and thought, *Lord, please help me. Here I am in Your house thinking about some ding-a-ling.*

Patrice looked at the child and saw that she was smiling at her. She smiled back. *Yup, this is Glen's child, all right.* She tried very hard to focus on the service, and planned to deal with Glen later.

Chapter Ten

"This is really nice." Faye used her hand as a sun visor while looking across the water.

"It is, isn't it? It must be nice to take a sail every once in a while." Lo was sitting on a cooler, her legs crossed, and enjoying the breeze whipping through her hair. Patrice was beside her, but hadn't said a word ever since they'd left the church. Lo stared at her, hoping she would say something, but Patrice kept silent. She sighed. "What's wrong with you, Patrice? You are mighty quiet."

"Nothing. I've just been thinking."

"About?"

"You know, you getting saved." Patrice paused to study Lorene's face. "Let me ask you something, Lo. I'm glad you gave your life to the Lord, but are you going to act all holier-than-thou, trying to make us feel guilty when we want to do things that we know we really shouldn't? I mean, you're my girl and all, and I would really hate to see our friendship just fall all to pieces. You know, you have a new way of living. Lo, I don't mean any harm. I'm just not ready to give my life to the Lord. Shucks, He has restrictions."

Faye looked Lo dead in the face, waiting for a response. Even though she wasn't as open as Patrice, she felt the same way, since she had some things hanging in her closet that she wasn't ready to give up yet.

Lo sucked her teeth. "Naw, girl. Listen, I'm not going to preach Jesus every time you do something wrong. That's not my job. I can't sit here and judge you. I'm nobody's mama, Savior, or God. Shoot, I know for a fact that I'm going to mess up my own self. That's what God meant when He said we all have sinned and fallen short of the glory of God. All I know is that it's better to sin with God in my life than without Him. He knows we aren't perfect."

"Yeah, this is true, but at least you are at the next level," Faye responded.

"Look, y'all, I'm the same Lo. The only thing that has changed is, God is in my life. And if you really think about it, He is in yours too. The only difference is, I acknowledge Him. I'm going to try to be very conscience of what I do or say. Now, don't get me wrong. I still might cuss

Dwayne's hind parts out when I see him—trifling nigger."

They fell out laughing.

"But I might do it in a more appropriate way. I'm still asking the Lord to help with that. Anyways, I'm not going to make it uncomfortable for you. I love you. We can still go out every once in a while."

Patrice's smile was so huge, you could see her see teeth and tongue. That was the best news she'd heard all day. She gave her a high-five and said, "All right now! That's what I'm talking about. Don't be no dried-up Christian." She wrapped her arms around her friend.

Keith walked up behind them holding a silver tray with several glasses of soda on it. "Hey! How come I miss out on all the good stuff? Y'all over there looking like a Kodak moment."

"Don't be jealous, don't be jealous," Patrice said, reaching for a glass of soda.

"So, are you ladies enjoying yourself?" Keith held the tray out toward the other two.

"Yes, sir," Faye said, lifting a glass to take a sip. "By the way, Keith, who was that fine man playing the bass guitar today?"

Patrice placed her hand on her chest. "Ooo, girl! Wa'n't he fine? He can strum my strings anytime."

Faye giggled. "And after he strum yours, he can pluck mines."

Faye and Patrice laughed.

Embarrassed, Lorene said, "Y'all just don't have no shame, do you? Keith, please excuse these clowns."

Patrice scoffed, "Shucks, Keith know how we talk."

Keith chuckled. "Afraid she's right."

"I know I'm right." Patrice winked.

Keith looked at Lorene and smiled. Their eyes had locked for a moment.

Patrice noticed they were giving googly eyes to one another, so she made up an excuse to go, to give them a few minutes alone. "Keith, what is your mother doing? Does she need help with anything downstairs?"

"She's making some finger sandwiches," he answered, never taking his eyes off Lorene.

Faye rubbed her stomach. "All that food we ate at church, I don't need a finger nothing. I'm too full to even suck my fingers."

"Come on here, Faye, so the two lovebirds can have some private time."

It was easy to see Keith's embarrassment through the reddening of his fair-colored skin. Lorene, on the other hand, who was as dark and smooth as milk chocolate, easily covered her blush.

"Shut up, Trice! We're just friends," Lorene said.

"Mmm hmm. Ain't nobody blind," Patrice commented as she and Faye giggled their way to the lower deck.

When they got downstairs, they were pretty amazed at how nice the boat was. It actually looked like a small apartment, with a kitchen area, and a living room area equipped with a small entertainment center and facing the water. There was also a beautifully decorated bathroom, and a small office area with a phone and computer. After looking around in awe, the girls found Keith's mom and offered their assistance.

"Hey, Mrs. Simmons, do you need us to do anything?" Faye asked.

"Naw, babies. Y'all, just sit on down and relax yourself and enjoy the view. I'm getting ready to go up in a few minutes to try and catch some fish. What Keith call hisself doing? Sweet-talking Lorene?" she said, a knowing look on her face.

"Yes, ma'am," Patrice said, laughing at Mrs. Simmons' nosiness.

"Chile, you should've seen him this morning, telling me that y'all were coming to our church today. Every time he mentioned Lo's name, the boy's eyes lit up like fire crackers." She threw one hand on her hip and pointed at the ladies with the fork she held in her other hand. "He's head over heels for that chile."

Patrice and Faye burst into another round of laughter.

"Well, I ain't gon' bother them. I'll just try to do some fishing in the back of the boat."

As Mrs. Simmons tidied up the kitchen, Faye nudged Patrice. "So what's the deal about the little girl in church?"

Cutting her eyes at Mrs. Simmons, Patrice whispered, "I'll tell you later."

Another twenty minutes passed before Miss Simmons headed out with her fishing pole in tow. Finally Patrice had more liberty to talk.

"Girl, I wasn't going to tell you and Lo this, but I've been spending the night over Glen's place every once in a while."

"You what? You mean, after what he did to you?"

"Don't look at me like that. He did call me. I mean, how many rapists you know that call their victims?"

"That is not the point. Patrice, I'm convinced something is wrong with you."

"Will you stop? We just got finished talking to Lo about her judging us. Now here you go. Don't sit here acting like miss high almighty. You love a good strong dick too."

"Mmm. So it's good and strong? How many inches?" Faye said, quickly changing from a frown and reprimanding tone to an inquisitive tone accompanied with a sly grin.

Even though Faye laughed, Patrice had a serious look on her face. "Ho, don't mess around and get a beatdown in this here nice boat."

"Girl, I'm just playing." Faye dismissed Patrice's warning with a wave of her hand. "Finish telling me."

"Anyway, I saw a picture on Glen's coffee table of that same little girl that was in church today, but he said that his daughter lives in New Jersey with her mother."

"You lying."

"I wish I was. I swear it was the same child."

"Well, maybe she does live in New Jersey. You know, it was Friends and Family day. I mean, just because you seen her in church doesn't necessarily means that she lives here."

"Yeah, you're right. I know one thing. As soon as we go home, I'm going to give him a call and see if he tells me that she's still in New Jersey. If he says she is, I'll know who I am dealing with." Patrice sucked her teeth and rolled her eyes. "Girl, I can't stand a liar." Patrice knew within herself she had some nerve saying that because she was the queen of all lies and thieves. She had every intention of stealing at least fifty dollars by dancing the next day, thinking of a few new sexy outfits she wanted to buy for Glen to rip off of her.

Chapter Eleven

Patrice heard her mother getting ready to go to work. She looked at her clock on the nightstand and saw that it was midnight. Her mother worked the graveyard shift at a seafood factory. Patrice got out of bed to use the bathroom.

"Trice, I want that kitchen clean before I get home," her mother said from her bedroom.

Patrice rolled her eyes. "Ma, I have to go to work too."

"So what are you saying—Now that we both have jobs, the house has to stay nasty? Like I said, I want that kitchen clean before I get off."

"Mmm-hmm. I hear ya." Patrice flushed the toilet, and as she began to wash her hands, she saw her mother walk by the bathroom.

"All right, keep on getting smart with me. Don't let the devil fool you." Annie Ruth headed downstairs then stopped and turned around. "Don't forget, I want your choir to sing at the Revival tonight."

"I thought that was tomorrow night."

"No, it's tonight." Annie Ruth heard the taxi-cab pulling up. "All right, I'm gone. You have a good day."

Patrice got back into bed and yelled, "You too."

"Joy, joy, joy . . ."

The choir sang its heart out. They looked nice in their navy blue attire.

As Patrice was shaking the tambourine, she saw a man staring at her. Dressed in a black two-piece suit, white shirt, and a black-and-white designer tie, his hair was freshly cut, and his skin was smooth like a dark Hershey's bar. It was the bishop's nephew. She looked away and then looked back at him, and his eyes were still set on her.

After the church service, he walked toward her. "Hey, Miss Lady. It's good to see you again."

"It's good to see you too." Patrice smiled and gave him a hug.

"I love to hear you sing. You have a beautiful voice, Patrice."

"How did you know my name?"

"A man asks questions when he's interested."

Patrice blushed and looked down.

"So, where are you headed now?"

"Home."

"It's only ten o'clock. It's too early to go home. If you don't mind, may I take you out to get a bite to eat?"

"Wait a minute, I don't even know your name."

"Quinton," he responded, showing all his pearly white teeth.

Patrice thought, *Lawd have mercy, this man is fine. I can't be going out with this man. I'm with Glen now. Hell, then again, forget him. He's lying to me, so I don't have to be faithful to him. Besides, we haven't made any real commitments.*

"So, may I take you out?"

She glanced at her watch. "Hold on a minute. Let me inform my friends."

Quinton nodded.

Patrice found Lorene through the crowd. "Just so you know, I'm leaving with Quinton. I don't want you calling tomorrow, cussing me out."

"And just so you know, I wasn't going to cuss you out. I was going to choke you to death if you'd left here tonight without letting someone know." Lorene chuckled. "But I'm glad to see you learned your lesson."

Patrice smacked her lips. "Whatever."

Lorene gave Patrice a kiss on the cheek. "Trice, be careful. I love you."

"Love you too." Patrice pranced back over to Quinton. "Okay, we're good to go."

"Great."

Patrice and Quinton had a nice time dining together. They enjoyed each other's company. On the way home he held her hand, and Patrice started to get a tingling sensation between her legs. When he pulled in front of her apartment, he turned off the ignition and said, "I had a good time tonight."

"So did I. Too bad it has to end."

"It doesn't have to." He reached over and gave her a kiss, and she kissed him back. He began to rub her breast. Then he unbuttoned her blouse, lifted her bra, and started sucking her nipple, turning Patrice on.

He stopped. "I know what you're thinking."

"What?"

"Here I am, a man of the cloth, rubbing all over you."

"No, I'm not thinking that. Whether you a man of the cloth or not, you're still a man. And I know you have needs, and so do I."

He was amazed by her response.

She giggled. "Don't look at me like that. Come here." She kissed him on the mouth. Patrice wanted to invite him in, but decided against it because she knew her mother didn't have to work tonight. "Well, the night has to end, because I'm not alone." She looked at the apartment.

"Oh, you don't live alone?"

"No. Actually I'm still living with my mom."

"I see. Well, do you want to get a room?" He rubbed her breast.

Patrice's mind traced back to Peaches' words at the restaurant, and then she thought that it was too soon to have sex with this man. *Shit, I'm horny as hell right now, and apparently he is too.* "I thought you'd never ask."

On the way to work Patrice thought about her one-night stand with Quinton. *That was a waste of time. Who would ever think somebody that fine has a pencil dick? I hope I never see him again.*

She finally made it to work. It was her first time on the job working without the help of Christina or any other crew member.

Every time Patrice danced, she was a bit nervous doing so, although she considered herself to be a professional thief. She could steal the white off rice if she wanted to. Patrice would go to any clothing store, put two garments together on one rack, ask to try it on, and when she came out of the dressing room, one would be in her bag. From pocket books, to shoes, to undergarments, to two-piece suits, this girl had a full wardrobe and hadn't paid one red cent, always telling her mother and friends that someone had given whatever it was to her.

Patrice glanced at the menu board to see which combo cost the most. The roast beef combo was $5.96 plus tax, which would be $6.58. Patrice thought, *Okay, $6.58 times five is $32.90. Okay, that's not enough. I need to sell something else because my goal is fifty dollars, nothing less.* She calculated the price of another combo meal. A Hardee's big cheese combo was $4.99, plus tax. Four of them would total $21.96. "Ooooo, $4.86 more," she whispered to herself and began to dance, literally. Then she thought, *No wonder they call it* dance. *Stuff like this will make you dance when you know that payday is every day.*

On the way home, Patrice was as happy as could be, her pockets filled with cash. Looking out the window, She was smiling and thinking to herself, *This is not bad at all. I've been there for only two months and making close to $500.00* *tax-free money every two weeks.* Just thinking about it, Patrice danced in her seat again. When she saw a few folks on the bus looking at her, she played it off and started singing a song quietly.

"I'm getting ready to take a shower. Care to join?" Patrice asked.

"Mmm-hmm." Glen, still in heat, held her by the waist all the way to the bathroom.

Before bathing they made love again.

When exiting the shower, Glen looked at Patrice and said, "I love you so much."

Patrice smiled. *Yeah, right. If you love me, you wouldn't lie to me.*

"Hold on a minute. I forgot to get some towels." Glen opened the linen closets and pulled out some freshly washed white towels. "Here you go. I don't want water all over the floor."

"Thank you."

As she was drying her hair with a towel, she said, "Baby, let me ask you something. Remember I told you I got a new job a while back and you weren't enthused about it, can you tell me why?"

"I just—I don't know." Glen shrugged his shoulders.

"Yes, you do. Why?"

"I really don't feel like getting into that right now. I got other things on my mind."

"Oh, really? I couldn't tell. What's bothering you?"

"I'm just wondering how my daughter is doing," Glen said, putting on a pair of boxers.

"Oh, I see. Well, it seems to me that she's doing okay."

Glen stopped what he was doing. "What do you mean, it seems to you that she's doing okay?"

"It means I saw her in church Sunday and to me she is doing okay." Patrice looked him dead in the eyes, trying to interpret his reaction.

"What in the hell are you talking 'bout, Trice? You're saying you saw Tiffany? My daughter?"

"Yes, I saw Tiffany. Your daughter."

"Patrice, don't play games with me."

"Do I look like I'm playing *Family Feud*? I ain't playing games with you. I did see her. It was at the church I had gone to last Sunday."

"What church?"

"I told you already. We went to Keith's church in Smithfield."

"How do you know for certain that was my daughter? You know what they say—Everybody has a twin. That could have been someone that looks like my child."

"How many twins do you know with the same birthmark?"

Glen had a frown on his face. He placed his hand on his chin and stared at the floor as though he was looking at something.

"Glen? Glen."

He acted as though Patrice wasn't in the room.

"Glen. I thought you said she was in New Jersey. Glen!"

Glen slammed his fist on the dresser as hard as he could.

Patrice jumped and got up and ran to where Glen was standing. "Baby, what is it?"

At that moment Patrice was scared to death. Glen looked Patrice in the eyes. Those beautiful eyes of his looked like puppy dog eyes begging for a piece of bread. He took Patrice by the hands, and they both sat on the bed.

"Baby, please tell me what's going on."

Glen paused for a moment and then said, "Jessica must have moved here."

"Who is Jessica?"

"Tiffany's mother."

"Baby, what's going on? Could you please tell me why she's here and she's supposed to be in New Jersey? As a matter of fact, how did you end up in Virginia and you have, well, you thought you have a little girl that lived in New Jersey?"

"Baby, listen to me. I have nothing to hide from you. I just want you to hear me out, okay."

Patrice nodded her head.

"Remember I told you I go to see my daughter every chance I get?"

Patrice nodded.

"Well, that was a lie. I haven't seen Tiffany since I left New Jersey."

"So how did you get that picture of her?"

"My sister sent me the picture. She tries to keep in contact with Jessica, just to let me know how Tiffany's doing."

Patrice continued to listen.

"Before Tiffany's mother and I broke up, I found out that she had been cheating on me with some trifling nigga that was dealing drugs. At the time I was in college. I couldn't afford to buy her the things that she wanted. Apparently he could. I wanted to surprise her on Mother's Day and take her out to dinner and give her an engagement ring that I had been saving up for it for months.

"When I arrived at her mother's house, I saw a Mercedes Benz parked in the driveway. I knew it didn't belong to her mother, because her mother was driving an Escort at the time. Her mother worked at a telemarketing company, so I knew she couldn't afford a Benz. Her mother loved me so much, because I reminded her of her late husband. She told me that she knew that I would make a good husband to her daughter. She'd given me a key to her house and told me if I ever wanted to come over to see her grandbaby, I was more than welcome.

"I came in the house and heard the bed upstairs sounding like it was about to fall through the ceiling. I quietly went up the steps and walked softly towards her bedroom door. I'd be damn if this nigga wasn't pumping the hell out of Jessica. Her legs were flying everywhere. I was so shocked, I just stood there. Then finally the words came out of my mouth. 'Nigga, get your ass up!' I scared the hell out of the both of them. Then I jumped on his back and beat the hell out of him. Jessica was crying and trying to pull me off of him but before I knew it I slapped her. I'd never hit a woman before a day in my life. I scared myself, when I realized what I had done so I left, but not before threatening to take my daughter away from her.

"The very next day, a gang of brothers jumped me. One of the punks stabbed me in the leg. I believe he was aiming for my nuts. I heard the same nigga that was screwing my girl tell me, 'I wish you would try to take Tiffany away from somebody.' Then he kicked me in the stomach and spat on me and left me there to bleed to death. I was able to identify everybody that whupped my ass, except the one that stabbed me. As for the nigga that was screwing my girl at the time, I told the cops exactly where to find him, and they busted him red-handed, dope everywhere. He did some time, but she kept in contact with him by writing letters. He hired some big-time lawyer and only got five years. So far he's done three."

"Isn't that how old Tiffany is?"

"No. In the picture she's five. She just turned six a couple of days ago. When all of this took place, Tiff was only two."

"So he's getting out in two more years?"

"Exactly. You see, I was in Trenton at the time this mess went down. I moved to Virginia to get away from trouble. I know no one can hide from trouble, but those niggas weren't going to make it easy for me. Like I said, he still has a couple more years to do. Now when you said you saw Tiff in Smithfield, then I remembered that Jessica has an aunt that lives in Smithfield. She lives in a beautiful white house all by herself. In order for Tiff and her mother to stay there, she is probably making them go to church. This punk is serving time in Sussex prison. Jessica must be going to see him. I got to find out where she's staying and go get my child."

"Do you know where her aunt lives?"

"No. Not exactly I just saw a picture of the house in photo album."

"Baby, it's nine forty-five. I know you're not going this late."

"No, I'm not, but I'm going first thing in the morning."

"Do you want me to go with you?"

"Baby, no. You don't have to do that."

Patrice rubbed his face with the back of her hand. "I want to."

Chapter Twelve

It was close to 7:00 P.M. when Dwayne got a phone call from his man friend. "Hello," he answered. A sexy baritone voice said, "Hey, baby. What are you up to?"

"I'm not up to anything, Stephan. What are you up to?"

"Nothing. I was hoping that we can turn our nothings into something."

Dwayne knew what he was getting at. "So what do you have in mind?"

"I can show you better than I can tell you. May I come over?"

Dwayne smiled and licked his lips seductively, although Stephan couldn't see him. "Baby, you know you don't need an invite."

"That's good to hear. I'll be over shortly."

Dwayne was lying in his bed, dressed in a lime green negligee. He rubbed his nipples, pretending he had full, round female breasts. He smacked his lips and said to himself, "Gotta love that man."

He got up and sprayed air freshener all over the house. As he was doing so, he glanced at the picture of himself on end table in the living room, one in which he stood in front of what used to be his parents' house. In an instant he was transported back to his younger days.

"Dwayne! Dwayne! Get in this house, boy!" His father yelled from the front porch of their old wooden home, one similar to what you may have seen on *The Waltons*.

An eight-year-old Dwayne came running to the house, his clothes dirty from playing kickball all day. He loved playing kickball and dodgeball with his friends.

Gordon was holding the screen door open for Dwayne as he entered the house. "What did I tell you about playing in your school clothes? Look at you, with your filthy self! Go on upstairs and run you some bathwater. Miss Jackson is gon' be here in a little bit for your piano lessons. I'll be up in a minute to help you."

"But, Daddy, I'm big enough to take my own bath now," Dwayne whined. He hated when his father tried to help him bathe, especially knowing that he only helped when his momma was at the grocery store or at choir rehearsal.

Gordon raised his hand, threatening to knock the wind out of him. "Boy, don't you talk back to me! You do like I tell you."

Dwayne jumped back and ran upstairs with tears beginning to stream down his face. He knew what he was in for. Dwayne took his time running the bathwater trying to prolong the inevitable. He was relieved when several minutes had gone by and his father had not come up. Quickly he washed his body, but just as he was getting ready to get out of the tub, he heard the bathroom door squeaking.

"Where you going, boy?" Gordon asked, an evil grin spread across his face.

"I—I'm done."

"Naw, you ain't. Look at that dirt still on you. Get back in that tub."

Dwayne had a sad look on his face and did what he was told.

Gordon took the washcloth and soap and started bathing Dwayne, forcing his legs open. With perverted pleasure, he took his sweet time washing Dwayne's little penis, rubbing and massaging with both hands. He looked straight into Dwayne's eyes, as if he was waiting for him to moan with pleasure.

"Did you clean your behind good?" he whispered then licked his lips.

"Yes, sir." Dwayne's voice started cracking as the tears welled up.

His father stood him up and turned him around. "Let me check and see." He made the washcloth really sudsy and started washing the crack of Dwayne's behind.

Dwayne saw that his father had dropped the washcloth in the water, but continued rubbing his thick finger across his anus.

"Bend over," he directed, turning Dwayne to the back wall of the tub and positioning his son's hands against it.

Dwayne's eyes filled with tears as his father stuck his index finger in the boy's anus, and masturbated with his other hand. He slid his finger in and out of Dwayne's butt faster and faster, going up and down on himself at the same pace. Dwayne glanced behind him and saw that his father's eyes were shut tight, his mouth wide open, and he was panting as if he was in pain.

But Dwayne was the one in pain. He started crying silently.

After a series of shudders, Gordon stopped, got up from his knees, and told Dwayne, "Wash yourself up and get out this tub. Clean up this mess and get dressed."

***

The doorbell rang, bringing Dwayne back from the past. *Well, Dad, it's not a woman at my door. I hope you're happy.* Opening the door, he laid eyes on a tall, masculine-looking, dark-skinned brother with a bald-head. Dwayne batted his eyes like Betty Boop. "Hi, sweetness."

Chapter Thirteen

"City and state, please?"

"Smithfield, Virginia."

"What listing, please?"

"Yes. I'm looking for an *Emma Parker*."

"Thank you. Please hold for the number, and thank you for calling."

Glen was so anxious to get the number, the automated voice response couldn't come on the phone quickly enough.

"That number is 757-555-1870. Again, 757-555-1870. Thank you for calling. Good-bye."

Glen wasted no time dialing the number he'd memorized. He had been worrying about Tiffany all night long. He was so glad that Patrice had spent the night, because he kept having nightmares and waking up with sweat pouring from his forehead.

His tossing and turning prevented Patrice from getting any sleep at all. She did her best to console him through the night, until he finally got some rest.

When Glen awoke the next morning he looked at her soft, sexy body and said very softly to keep from waking her, "Poor baby, I kept you up all night." Although he intended his involvement with Patrice to be nothing more than a one-night stand, he found himself becoming emotionally attached. He enjoyed Patrice's company so much, sometimes he hated to see her go. He loved the way she made him feel inside and out.

He picked up the cordless phone and closed the bedroom door and went into the living room. The phone rang several times, but he didn't hang up. Someone finally answered the phone.

"Hello?"

"Yes. May I speak to Mrs. Emma Parker?"

"Speaking."

"Mrs. Parker, how are you doing? This is Glen Pearson." He hoped his name would ring a bell.

"Glen Pearson? Son, looka heya, if you callin 'bout some dental caya, health caya, or medic-aya, whatever you are callin 'bout, I don't caya for none of it. So if you would please take my name of ya callin' list, I'd 'preciate it."

Trying to prevent her from hanging up, he raised his voice a little and said, "No, no, no, ma'am!" When he realized that she was still on the line, he lowered his voice. "I'm calling to ask, is Jessica Michaels staying there with you?"

"Who is this again?"

"Glen Pearson. I'm Tiffany's father."

She was quiet for a moment then she said, "Ooooh! You dat nice college boy from Jersey. Yeah, Jessica's mother told me so much about you."

"Yes, ma'am. How is Ms. Mary doing?"

"Oh, she doin' good. She misses you terrible. She said you like a son she never had. She misses her grandbaby too. She cried some kinda bad when Jessica took her from there. I told Jessica if she stay heya wit' me she carrin' her hind pots to church. If you don't know what to do wit' your life, at least give it to the Lawd."

Glen could see that he wasn't going to get a word in edgewise. He was patient, letting Mrs. Parker ramble on. He understood they were lonely people and that when they finally got the chance to talk to someone they wouldn't let go. Even though he was glad to hear everything that she was saying, he wanted to find out about Tiffany. He patiently waited for a pause so he could jump right in.

"I'm sorry to hear that Ms. Mary is upset. Is Jessica there right now?"

"Naw, she gone to Sussex. She and a nice young lady. I believes her name is Sandy, Sondra, something like that. Yeah, she from anotha church, and they went togetha. She told me that she joined the prison ministry. It does my heart well to see her tryin' to git on the straight and narra.

Prison ministry? That lying-ass girl. She ain't ministering to nobody but that bum drug dealer boyfriend of hers. "Mrs. Parker, where is Tiffany?"

"She took her wit' her."

"Do you know when she'll be back?"

"Yeah, normally when she goes, she comes in round five thirty or so."

"Mrs. Parker, if you don't mind, may I have your address so I can pay Jessica and Tiffany a surprise visit?" *A surprise visit? That's what got me in trouble in the first place.*

"Naw, no problem at all. It will be nice to see ya."

She began to rattle off, but Glen couldn't find his notepad and pen he had in the drawers of the end table.

"Hold on a minute, Mrs. Parker, let me find something to write with." Glen found a piece of paper in the kitchen drawer and came back to the phone to get the address again.

"I'ma cook a nice supper for ya. Normally when Jessica gits in, she tryin' to leave and go someplace else. I'ma make her stay, but I ain't gon' tell her you comin', okay."

"Yes, ma'am. Thank you so much. Bye."

As soon as Glen hung up the phone, he heard the toilet flush. Soon after, Patrice walked in the living room wearing his tee shirt, eyes puffy and scratching her head. As she was getting closer, he asked, "Did you move my notepad and pen?"

"Yes, I had to make a grocery list. It's in the kitchen."

"Baby, you know how I am. I like to keep things in its proper place. That way, if I need it again, I don't have to tear the house up looking for it."

"Okay, you don't have to act like a big baby."

"I'm not acting like a big baby. I'm just trying to get you to understand I like things in order. Do you have to work today?

"Nope. I only work Monday through Fridays." Then she asked, "Who was that on the phone?"

Glen didn't say anything. He just smiled at her as she took a seat beside him on the couch.

"Baby, who was that on the phone?"

Glen jerked his head away. "Your breath stinks."

"Your mama."

Glen cracked up laughing.

"Baby, stop playing and tell me who you were talking to."

"Sweetheart, please go brush your teeth. Go find a piece of chewing gum, mint, or something. I can't talk to a beautiful woman with her breath smelling like horse manure."

Patrice playfully punched him in the chest. "You get on my nerves," she said, standing to her feet and heading back toward the bathroom.

After Patrice brushed her teeth and gargled with Listerine, she went back to bed.

"Trice? Trice? Come here, baby, so I can tell you who that was on the phone."

Patrice hollered from under the covers, "I don't want to know now." She felt Glen pulling the covers back. "Go on." She snatched the covers from him.

He pulled again.

"Go on, Glen. I'm tired."

Glen sat on the bed beside Patrice. "Well, since you don't want to talk to me, I'm not going to tell you I got the address where Tiffany is staying."

Patrice popped her head from under the covers. "For real?"

"Mmm-hmm."

"Oh, baby." She sat up and hugged him.

"Your breath smells good."

Patrice sucked her teeth. "Shut up. So why are we sitting here? Let's go get her."

Patrice was getting out of the bed, but Glen pulled her back around the waist and sat her on his lap. "Come here, girl. Where are you running off to?"

"Glen, come on. We got to go," Patrice said excitedly.

"Calm down. We have plenty of time to go get her. She's not going to be in until five thirty or so. It's only eight forty-five in the morning, a beautiful Saturday morning at that. Right about now, I am the happiest man living. I'm holding a gorgeous woman in my arms that loves me. I—"

"Hold on. Who told you that I love you?"

"Baby, don't you know that actions speak much louder than words?" Glen started kissing Patrice on the back of her neck then slowly moved his hand to her crotch.

"I want some honey from the honeywell."

"Boy, you are so nasty."

"I know."

Joined at the lips, they both laid back on the bed, while Glen moved on top of her. He knew exactly how to turn Patrice on, putting his wet tongue in her ear.

As soon as he did, her body went into shivers, and just like that, Patrice had her first climax. Glen thought to himself, *Uh-huh, the faucet is on.* He worked his way to her breast, licking in a circular motion as he slid his finger in her hot box. "Oh, baby, you are sooo wet," he whispered.

Patrice felt his shaft growing against her leg and reached for it. "Pleeease put it in me, baby," she moaned.

"Not yet."

Glen began licking at her navel as if it were her nana, while Patrice pulled on his stick. "Oh, baby, squeeze Jimmy. Yeeessss, squeeze it, baby." Glen rolled to his back. "Sit on my face, baby."

She did as he instructed.

"Turn around."

Patrice was now facing his feet. Before sticking his tongue in her honeywell, he stuck a couple of fingers in it first. She was so wet, she started dripping. "Oh, baby, you are so juicy. Juicy fruit. Baby, put Jimmy in your mouth."

Patrice frowned. *Oh, hell no. I ain't putting nothing in this mouth but bread, water, and a hot tongue.*

"Go ahead, baby."

Instead, Patrice grabbed the lotion on the nightstand and squeezed the bottle on his manhood. She started squeezing and massaging his manhood. After the lotion had saturated in his skin, she kissed and licked the sides of his penis.

That was as far as she would go, but Glen ate her nana like it was dessert. Patrice was going insane as he had his second and third helpings. His tongue was moving so fast, like an electric vibrator.

Finally she collapsed, but that didn't stop him. He kept going at it until there was no more milk in the bowl. He got up and flopped Patrice around on her stomach.

Patrice immediately had a flashback. "Please don't stick King Dong in me."

"I'm not."

He took that same bottle of lotion and squeezed lotion on her back then he massaged her back, her buttocks, her legs, and both feet, pulling each toe like a mother playing "this little piggy went to the market" with her toddler. Then he turned her back around so that she was lying on her back, and spread her legs so wide that she almost did a Chinese split in the air.

He stuck his finger in her coochie to see if she was wet enough to take him. No, she wasn't. He buried his head in her coochie again. He stuck his tongue smack dead in the middle of "the little man in her boat," and wiggled it with rapid speed. That turned her on. Patrice arched her back and started shivering. He then stuck his tongue in as far as it could go. "Aaaah . . . Patrice . . . you are so rich and sweet."

"Gl—Gl—Gl . . . Gleeeeeen . . . Gleeeeeen!" A big gush of hot juice came all at once outside of her.

Glen climbed on top of her and stuck his pipe right on the tip of her clitoris. He didn't move, but just stared at her like he was studying homework.

A hot tear streamed down the side of Patrice's face.

"Baby, are you all right?" he asked in a whisper.

She nodded her head slowly.

"Then why are you crying?"

"You make me feel so good and so loved."

Then before she knew it, he thrust himself in her hard, and fast as lightning, making her scream with pleasure. Patrice was so weak that she couldn't move. It was if he was making love to a human-size rag doll, but as soon she was able, she kept up with his rhythm.

In their heads they must have heard "Fantasy" by Earth, Wind & Fire, because they were going at that pace. The invisible DJ must have changed the song to "Boogie Fever" by The Sylvers, because they sped up.

In unison they both cried out in pleasure, arriving at a climax together.

Glen's heart was beating so fast, as he lay down beside Patrice. He said, "Girl, if you keep working me out like that, I can cancel my membership at the gym."

When she didn't respond, he saw that she was crying. "Baby, what's wrong? I didn't hurt you, did I?"

"No."

Glen pulled her close and started caressing her face. "Then, what's wrong?"

"Nothing's wrong. Everything is so right, and you are right. I do."

"You do what?"

Patrice sighed and then gazed into his eyes. "I do love you."

Glen couldn't believe she'd finally said those words to him. "Oh, baby, I love you too. Hot damn, I'm so happy! I'm going to get Tiff, I got a woman that's beautiful and she loves me, and I got a ten-thousand-dollar increase in my salary."

Patrice sat up quickly. "You got a what?"

"I just got promoted yesterday."

"Oh, baby, that is great news! We got to go out and celebrate!"

"That's what I'm planning to do as soon as I get Tiffany."

Patrice had a big grin on her face, but it soon turned into a frown. "Do you know what?"

"What?"

"It's a shame I been letting you pump the day-lights out of me for the past couple months or so and I don't know what you do for a living."

Glen started laughing. "That's why I'm crazy about you. As soon as I date a lady, she starts asking me, 'Where do you work? How much money do you make? What kind car you got?' " Glen's voice was high-pitched, trying to mimic a woman.

Patrice cracked up. "Don't talk like that."

"They do, babe. That junk gets on my nerve. It's not like that with you though. When we are together, you make me forget about everything. No drama whatsoever."

They were silent for a moment.

Glen squinted his eyes and stared across the room. Patrice could tell that he was in deep thought.

"And do you know what else?" He now looked at Patrice, touching her chin and turning it toward him. "The first night we had sex, I was testing you."

"You were what? Testing me? Well, did I pass or fail?"

"You failed."

"I failed?" Patrice couldn't believe what he was saying. As a matter of fact, she couldn't understand what he was saying.

Glen nodded. "Yup. Normally if I bring a woman home and she gives it up from the beginning, I'll drop her so quick. But the only reason I called you the next night, I could tell you didn't want to be here with me. And also, girl, your honey is so sweet, I had to get some more. The second time we were together, I had never in my life felt that way before. Girl, I've had plenty of imitation syrup, but you got that natural honey."

"So, in so many words, you gave me a make-up test? So I passed that, huh?

"With flying colors. Baby, your coochie IQ is so high, you can skip the next couple of grades and college. You have your master's in that department."

Patrice laughed. "Okay. What you're saying doesn't make any sense at all. If I can remember correctly, I told you I felt as though you crossed your boundaries. You then apologized, and now all is forgiven. But now you're feeding me a bunch of mess, talking about, you could tell I didn't want to be here with you. So you knew what you were doing that night?"

Glen saw that her laughter had turned into fury. "Baby, I'm not bullshitting you. See, let me explain something to you. Women I deal with will guide my hand to their private parts, and then to the bedroom, but you gave a little resistance. Although I felt as though you wanted me as much as I wanted you, you made me fight for it, and that turned me on. Like I said before, please don't think for a moment that I raped you."

"I'm not thinking that. I just wanted you to clarify your theory."

After some moments of silence, Patrice laughed again. "My coochie IQ is high. You are so nasty. Don't you want a woman that can bring more to the table, besides a bowl of coochie?"

"This may sound crazy, but no. Sweetheart, I want to take care of my woman. You may not know this, but that's every man's dream. That's why I was a little disappointed to hear about you getting a job. The only reason a man would have his woman helping him to bring home the bacon is because he can't hold it on his own. If he can hold it on his own and is still peeking in her wallet, he's greedy as hell. Just like women want to stay home and let their man take care of them, we want you to stay home and take care of our castle while we work hard to take care of family."

Patrice scooted into Glen's arms and rubbed his chest.

She felt so safe with him. He made her feel so good when he was inside her, but she felt even better with him in her heart.

"I've seen my mother work so hard to take care of me and my brother and sister that it was a shame. She worked at a hospital as a maid, cleaning up shitty sheets all day, then cooked at a restaurant all night. Because I was the oldest, I had to take care of my siblings the majority of the time. I made a promise to myself—My wife is not going to work like a dog."

"Lucky her."

"Lucky her? What? You don't want me to be your husband?"

"Baby, I like working. Now if you had told me this when we first met, it would have been a whole other ball game, but now I like what I do." *Getting free money, that is.* "On top of that, I'm too young to be thinking about marriage. Don't you think it's too soon to be talking about that?"

"Yeah, it's too soon, but it's not too soon to ask you to move with me—Will you?"

Patrice thought about her mother saying time and time again that she didn't support shacking up. She didn't want to disappoint her mother, but then again she had to live her own life. Maybe she could tell Annie Ruth that she was moving in with a girlfriend of hers. *No*. That wouldn't work, because when Annie Ruth called or came to visit she'd know it was a lie. She'd just tell her mother that Glen was visiting her a lot, and would only invite her over when he was at work. But, hell, then again it didn't really matter what she thought. Annie Ruth wanted Patrice to get a job and pay rent. Well, she'd done even better. She got a job and moved out.

"Okay, on two conditions."

"What's that?"

"Can I keep my job?"

"Baby, if you want to work, by all means work, but if you decide to quit, I will take care of you."

Okay, good answer. "Second, what do you do for a living?"

"I am the manager in the Engineering Department for the City of Newport News."

Patrice was impressed. "HNIC, huh? Come here, you."

As they were getting ready to go for round two, the phone rang.

"Hello?"

"Hi, Glen. This is Jessica."

Chapter Fourteen

"Ouch, Lo!" Lorene's client squirmed, trying to find comfort from the pain of having her hair braided.

"What? Am I braiding too tight?" Lorene gathered a pinch of hair from her kitchen table to start on the next braid.

"Hell, yeah!"

"I'm sorry. Shucks, I'm trying to make it last for at least two weeks."

Lorene's mind wasn't on doing hair anyway. Her thoughts were only on Keith. Before her client came, Lorene had just gotten off the phone with him. They'd made plans to go to the movies later on that evening, and Lorene was looking forward to it. Lorene had developed strong feelings for Keith, who'd been calling her every night, asking her how her day had been. He also brought her lunch every afternoon, since his lunch hour started a half-hour before hers, and would send her "Just thinking of you" cards, and roses to her job.

Lorene thought back to the day they'd gone to the carnival and it had poured down raining. She had ruined her sandals that day, and without hesitation, he offered to buy her new shoes. By far he was the nicest gentleman she'd ever dated.

Just before she could finish the last braid, the phone rang, and her father answered it.

"Hello?"

"May I speak to Lorene please?" It was Dwayne.

"Lorene, phone!"

Lo start grinning, thinking it was Keith.

"Hello?"

"Hello, Lorene."

Right away, Lorene said a silent prayer. *Lord, please help me not to cuss this man out.*

Now I know she heard me. "Hellooo?"

Lorene tugged on her client's hair again, and the young lady shrieked, "Oooouch!"

"I'm sorry." She tried to ease the pain by rubbing her client's head. "Hey, Dwayne."

"Honey, I know you want to cuss me out, and you have every right to, but let me tell you something. If you had something against me, we could have handled it woman to woman. For the sake of me, I couldn't understand why you had to call me out like that in front of the whole choir."

"Dwayne, hold on a minute." Lorene gave her client a hand mirror.

"Girl, this is so pretty, but you are sure heavy-handed. It don't make any sense."

"Girl, I'm sorry. I have a lot on my mind."

"That's all right." The young lady gave Lorene twenty dollars. "I'll see you in two weeks."

Lorene nodded her head and smiled as the young lady left.

"Dwayne, I'm back."

"Girlfriend, I was so pissed, I gave this dingy little boy that was begging me for some change twenty dollars to slice your tires. I was going to act like I had nothing to do with it, but I haven't been getting any rest at night. My conscience is eating my ass up. That's why I haven't been coming to choir rehearsal. I told Peaches to tell y'all that I was sick, but really I wasn't ready to face neither you nor the choir. So, Lo, please forgive me, girl. Wait a minute. Before you say anything, I want to let you know I just put a two-hundred-dollar money order in the mail today addressed to you to cover the damage."

Lo was getting heated all over again as he was confessing, but then all of a sudden she felt peace. "Thank you for calling, Dwayne. I really appreciate it, but do you know what? I ain't even mad at you. Not anymore that is. I was just as guilty as you. You're right. I should have come to you before making that outburst. Daddy always told me to think before I speak, but of course, I didn't take his advice."

Dwayne almost fainted. He couldn't believe Lo didn't rip him apart. He could hang with the best of them, but he wouldn't mess with Lorene, because the girl was crazy. The girl wouldn't harm a fly, unless the fly kept getting on her nerves. Then she'd swat the hell of it.

"Girl, what done got into you? Are you okay, sweetheart? Are you schizophrenic?"

Lorene snickered. "Nothing, boy. I mean, there ain't no need for crying over spilt milk."

"Oh no, girly. You didn't spill any milk. That was a gas leak. Lo, did you mess around and let the Lord in your heart? You must have because, giiiirl, this doesn't even sound like you talking. I know Jesus when I hear Him."

Lorene fell out laughing. "Boy, you are crazy, but yeah, you can say that."

"How come ain't nobody told me? If I would have known that, I could've kept my two hundred dollars and just ask for forgiveness."

"Boy, I am saved, not silly. So when are you going to cross over the other side and stop letting them men folks abuse you?"

"Girl, please. I love the Lord and He heard my cry, but I also love a good groan," Dwayne said, repeating the lyrics from the Richard Smallwood song, "I Love the Lord."

Chapter Fifteen

Glen, his attitude changing from good to bad, sat straight up and asked, "How did you get this number?"

"Ah, four one one?" Jessica asked in sarcasm, as if he had never heard of such a thing. "You haven't been calling me, so why are you calling me now? Is Tiffany all right?"

"Yes, she's fine. Listen, I'm sorry for what happened Glen, but I was hoping that we can patch things up, if not for us, at least for Tiffany." She was acting as though she was getting ready to visit her great-aunt Emma, but really wanted to move in with him so they could be one big happy family.

Jessica had no idea that Glen knew she was already in Virginia. He was getting sick to the stomach because he knew the girl was lying through her teeth. His only concern was trying to see his daughter and possibly gaining custody.

The real reason for the call was, Jessica had just left Sussex Prison and wasn't able to visit her boyfriend because she forgot her ID. So she asked Sandra to visit him for a while. When Sandra came back to the front, Jessica found out that her drug-dealing boyfriend wasn't getting out for another twenty years. The narcotics police had found more hardcore evidence against him.

T-Bo, the night before his arrest, had killed a fifteen-year-old girl who sold drugs for him. He found out that she was stealing his money to take care of her mother and younger siblings. Even his hotshot lawyer couldn't get him out of that one. But Jessica didn't care how he made his money; she wanted to live like the lifestyle of the rich and famous.

Now that she'd learned that T-Bo wouldn't be out for another twenty years, she was trying to come back to Glen for him to take care of her and Tiffany. She thought if she couldn't have five million, she'd settle for five thousand. It beats a zero.

She and Sandra had a lot of time to spare, so they drove to the mall, shopped, and ate out. Besides, she knew Aunt Emma wasn't expecting her until five or six. She wasn't ready to go home just yet, because her aunt would make her clean the house from top to bottom.

Glen didn't let on that he knew she was lying about coming to visit her aunt. Nor did he let her know that he'd be coming over. He just listened as she dug a hole for herself. "Whatever, Jessica. Really, I don't have anything to say to you."

"What do you mean, you don't have anything to say to me? What about Tiffany?"

"What about her?" he asked nonchalantly, but really his heart melted every time someone mentioned her name.

Jessica whined, "I mean, we could at least try to reconcile for her sake."

"Let me tell you something. In case you forgot, I didn't hear from you in three years. Three years, Jessica. I couldn't even come to see Tiffany without my life being threatened. *You* did that, Jessica. You could've prevented this whole thing from happening, but no, you wanted someone that poison people's system with crack, instead of a real man. Where is he anyway? Why are you trying to come back to me? Did someone finally kill his ass? I sure as hell hope so."

"Glen, baby," Jessica said, her voice trembling, "I just don't want to live that type of lifestyle anymore. I was wrong, and I am truly sorry. We need you in our lives."

Glen said calmly, "Look, let me ask you one more time—Is my daughter okay?"

"Yes."

"Okay, this conversation is over." He hung up the phone.

Patrice watched him as he began to rub his forehead. Then she began to rub his back. "Are you okay?"

"Yeah," he whispered.

"Come here." Patrice opened the covers so that Glen could lie back down. She wrapped her arms around him and they lay there silently.

Glen and Patrice were quiet during the ride across the James River Bridge. Glen was a little nervous because he didn't know what to expect. He looked at Patrice a couple of times and saw that she was just as nervous as he was. He took her hand, kissed the back of it, and held it to his chest.

Patrice didn't respond. She just kept staring straight ahead.

Glen was anxious to get to Mrs. Parker's house to see his baby girl, so stopping was the last thing on his mind. As he was getting closer to his destination, his heart started pounding a little faster.

He asked Patrice to look out for Farmers Road. When he saw it, he made a right turn, driving very slowly because of the dirt and rocks.

Finally, Patrice spotted the beautiful white house with black shutters. It looked like it was freshly painted and was surrounded by full green shrubberies in front of the huge porch, beautiful pink flowers lining each side of the red brick walkway.

Mrs. Parker must have had a gardener because she was too old to keepup the yard and house herself. Glen got out the car first then opened the car door for Patrice. He held her hand tightly as they walked to the front door. While ringing the doorbell, they heard a car driving up the dirt road. Glen squinted his eyes through his sunshades and realized it was Jessica.

Chapter Sixteen

Traffic was thicker than peanut butter. Dwayne hated going to the mall on Saturdays. He knew everybody and his or her mama would be out. He would normally go shopping in the middle of the week but decided at the last minute to buy a new suit from Gents Fashions. Although Jean and he had robes a different color from the rest of the choir, every time they were supposed to wear them, he would say, "I look too fabulous to be covered in a potato sack."

The boy could dress his butt off. Every Sunday he looked like he stepped out of a *GQ* magazine. Pinstriped doubled-breasted suits with cuffs in the pant leg, silk shirts with tie and handkerchief to match, nylon socks, and snakeskin shoes. The brother was fierce.

When he finally found a parking space and got out of the car, he noticed that he had parked beside Faye's mother's car. Even though Faye's mother let Faye drive her car from time to time,

Dwayne hoped this time it was Faye's mother in the mall, instead of Faye. He didn't feel like running into her, seeing that she called herself cussing him out for having Lorene's tires sliced. Although there was peace between Lorene and himself, Faye probably wasn't feeling it.

Sure enough, as he entered the doors on the Food Court side, he ran smack-dab into Faye. She was with a very muscular, bald-headed, brown-skinned man. Both of them were licking ice-cream cones and had several bags in their hands.

When she saw Dwayne, her facial expression changed from one of bliss to one that said, *Yeah, nigga, I know what you did.* "Hey, Dwayne. How are you doing?"

"Fine, and yourself?" He nodded his head nonchalantly.

"Dwayne, this is Bobby. Bobby, this is Dwayne."

Dwayne nodded and said, "How're you doing?"

"A'ight. How're you doing, man?"

Dwayne took a quick glance between Bobby's legs, a habit he just couldn't break, and then looked back at Faye. "I see you've done a lot of shopping. Did you buy me something?"

Faye's friend asked her for the keys to the car. "Here. I'll be out in a minute," she said, handing him her bags as well. "Naw, I didn't buy you nothing."

Dwayne didn't want her to bring up his foul behavior, so he tried to take control of the conversation. "You didn't tell me that Lo got saved."

"How could I? Ain't nobody seen nor heard from you in weeks. Here we are at choir rehearsal learning a cappella songs. Peaches told us that you weren't feeling well, but I didn't believe that mess. You just didn't want to take your *tass*-whipping like a man."

Dwayne knew he could chew and spit her out like a stale piece of gum, but he chose not to go there today. He just wanted to buy a new suit, go home, and possibly call his man over to take care of his sexual desires. "Look, Faye, dear, I don't feel like getting into it with you. I'm too tired. Besides, I already talked to Lo, and I also gave her some money to get new tires. She didn't tell you? I mean, I thought you were girls. Y'all talk about everybody and everything else."

"Yeah, she told me. You know, if she can forgive you, who am I? I got too much going on in my life to worry about you."

"Same here. So, like I said, there is no need to get into that."

Faye rolled her eyes then asked, "So when are you coming back to choir practice, or are you still sick?" She puckered her lips as if to say, *You weren't sick to begin with.*

"I'll be back Tuesday night. I have a new song to teach."

"Is it yours this time?" she said, unable to pass up the opportunity to tease him.

Dwayne rolled his eyes and said, "Bye, Faye," and walked away.

Dwayne was taking his time trying to find the right suit to wear that Sunday morning. He came across a plain black suit that reminded him of what his father used to wear. He pushed the suit to the side and continued to look, his mind wandering back to another incident in his past.

"Daddy, I got to use the bathroom," he said to Gordon in the middle of church service. They were sitting in the back pew. Dwayne was squirming, trying to keep from peeing on himself. He looked at his mother, who at the time was in the choir stand singing.

"All right, come on." Gordon grabbed him by the hand and took him to the restroom. While Dwayne was peeing in the urinal, his father was staring at his little penis, making him very uncomfortable. When he finished, he was shaking it, trying to shake off the pee.

"Boy, shake it good. I don't want you walking around here smelling all pissy." Gordon took Dwayne's penis and started feeling it for a while.

Dwayne couldn't believe he was doing this in the Lord's house. "Daddy, we have to get back inside. Mama is going to worry."

"All right, we'll do this some other time. Zip up your pants and let's go."

Some other time? Dwayne had had enough of his father's sick behavior. *Something has to be done about this, but how?*

The short white salesman broke Dwayne out of his thoughts. "This is one hundred percent wool. Do you care to try it on?"

"No, thank you. I'm looking for something softer. I need a light-blue, rayon material suit."

"Oh, right this way." He showed him a light-blue lined suit with a black vest, with embroidery on the collar, the front of the vest and the front of the coat. "Now this just came in yesterday."

Dwayne's eyes lit up. "This is me for sure. I'll take it!"

"Great. What size are we looking for?"

"Thirty-eight."

"Okay, I do believe we have it in your size." The salesman browsed through the rack. "Here it is. Let me get you to try it on, so we can alter the hem for you."

On his way to the dressing room, Dwayne glanced back at the black wool suit, thought again about his father, and mumbled, "I wonder which demon's dick in hell you're trying to fondle with."

Chapter Seventeen

Jessica couldn't believe her eyes. She unbuckled her seatbelt slowly and got out of the car then opened the back door to let Tiffany out, never taking her eyes off Glen. "What in the world is he doing here? Who is this heifer that he's with? Did Aunt Emma tell him I was here?"

Sandra was in the driver's seat and noticed Jessica's strange stare at this man. She asked Jessica in a low voice, as if Glen and Patrice could hear her, "Jessica, who are they?"

Jessica ignored her question and kept staring at Glen.

"Jessica? Are you going to be all right, or should I stay?"

Jessica had Tiff by the hand and bent over in the car window and said, "No. You can go. I'll call you later. Thanks, okay." Jessica started walking toward the house.

"Jessica! Your bags," Sandra called.

Just seeing Glen made her forget all about the new clothes in the car trunk. "Oh yeah."

Sandra popped the car trunk and got out of the car to help Jessica with her bags. Now that the trunk hood was hiding them, she felt more comfortable to talk. "Jessica, are you sure you're going to be all right? Who in the world are those people that got you acting all funny?"

Jessica kept her voice low because she didn't want Tiffany to hear her. "That's her daddy." She pointed at Tiffany, but Tiffany didn't notice because she was looking at Glen and Patrice.

Sandra's eyes almost popped out of her head, and her mouth was open wide enough to stick a whole sandwich in it. She covered her mouth then quickly dropped the hand that she covered it with. "What? You're lying!"

"Yes." She gave Tiffany a small bag. "Here, baby, carry this for mommy."

"Mommy, who is that?"

Jessica didn't acknowledge her question as she looked around the trunk to see if she had gotten everything.

"Well, who is that with him?" Sandra asked with a confused look.

"The hell if I know." Jessica squinted. "Wait a minute. Aw shit! Girl, you're not gonna believe this, but that is the bitch I saw in church."

"Girl, you better call me as soon as they leave." Sandra slammed the car trunk, got in the car, and slowly drove off, still watching her girlfriend and her surprise guest.

Jessica and Tiffany walked slowly to the porch. She gave Glen an evil eye. Before she could say anything, the front door swung open.

"May I help you?"

Glen cleared his throat. "Hello, Mrs. Parker. I spoke to you on the phone earlier today. I'm Glen, and this is my lady friend, Patrice."

Patrice smiled and gave her a nice-to-meet-you nod.

"Yes, yes." Mrs. Parker chuckled and hugged Glen like a long-lost son. "Lawd have mercy, all of y'all came at once?

That's good. I was afraid I wasn't gon' keep you coming as a secret from Jessi. Lawd knows I can't hold warda on a hot day. Come on in."

Glen held the door open for the ladies. Patrice let Jessica and Tiff go in first. As Jessica walked past Glen, he looked at her like he wanted to slap the taste out of her mouth, but he couldn't help but smile at Tiffany. He began to pick Tiffany up and give her a bear hug and kiss but stopped when he noticed she flinched and grabbed a hold of Jessica's leg.

As Patrice passed him, they both looked at each other with a ready-or-not-here-I-come face.

"I got some biscuits in the stove for ya. They nice and hot. Suppa will be reda in a minute. Take a load off. I'll call ya when it's reda."

Jessica and Tiffany went straight upstairs without looking back. Once Jessica went into her bedroom, she paced the floor thinking, *Damn, that man looks so good. His chest is all thick like he'd been working out. If that bitch wasn't with him, I woulda jumped his bones. But that's all right. I'm gonna make him mine, one way or another.*

Tiffany shot past her bedroom, making her way back downstairs.

"Wait a minute, Tiffany. You go down when I go down."

Patrice and Glen sat on the plastic-covered living room couch. Patrice rubbed her nose, not liking the odor that lingered in the house. Although she inhaled the aroma of the country homemade cooking, the odor of medicine and snuff didn't mix too well together. However, Mrs. Parker had nice furniture. The house had wall-to-wall plush red carpet with plastic runners all through the house.

"Baby, Tiffany is cute as a button," Patrice whispered to Glen. "How come you didn't speak to her?"

Glen smiled a little. He had his elbow on his knee and kept rubbing his chin. Patrice could see that he had a lot on his mind.

It bothered Glen that his own flesh and blood didn't recognize him. He hated Jessica by the minute. Why hadn't she told his baby girl about him? He wanted so badly to send pictures of himself to Jessica for Tiffany, but he didn't know her address. Even though he gave money to his sister for his daughter, he still wasn't satisfied. Glen felt a man should be able to take care of his children without the aid of someone else. He hated that he had to move away. If he didn't, Jessica's boyfriend had men ready to beat the life out of him. He wasn't having it. He wanted to survive for one reason, which was Tiffany. His father wasn't there for him, and he didn't want to put his daughter through the same thing.

"Baby, maybe I shouldn't have let you come with me."

"Why?"

"Because . . . just sitting thinking about how Jessica made my life a living hell makes me angry, and I might say something very ugly to her."

Patrice hunched her shoulders. "So?"

"I mean, words can turn into arguments. Then, next thing you know, arguments can turn into fights."

"Please. I wish she would jump this way. I'd have to set her soul free."

Glen snickered. "Babe, you're a little rough around the edges, ain't you?"

"I done told ya."

They laughed a little, trying to be relaxed in an uncomfortable environment.

"Who is Mrs. Parker cooking for? An army? At first my stomach had butterflies, but now it doesn't have anything in it and is growling something terrible."

"Yeah, I'm hungry too. The only thing I ate today was you." Glen chuckled.

"Do you know what? I'm going to rebuke that nasty demon in you."

They both laughed again.

"It does seem like we've been sitting here forever, doesn't it?"

"You ain't lying." Patrice glanced at her watch. "But it's only been twenty minutes."

"It seems longer than that."

"What's up wit' your girl? Is she scared to come downstairs or something? It doesn't take that long to put a couple of shopping bags away."

"She must be scared. Scared that I'm going to smack the hell out of her."

Mrs. Parker came shuffling around the corner with some house shoes that were too big for her.

"Jessi ain't come downstairs yet? What in the world is she doin'?" She looked at Glen and Patrice and waited for a response, as if they knew. "Well, the food is reda. Jessi! Tiffna! Come on down heya and eat!"

The dinner table was perfectly set, as if a caterer had done it. The mashed potatoes and gravy, string beans, corn pudding, collard greens, and hot buttermilk biscuits were on each side of the table in blue china bowls. The fried chicken and roast beef were in the middle on china plates. She mixed a little lemonade Kool-Aid in the sweet tea.

As they all took their seats, Glen said, "Mrs. Parker, you didn't have to go out your way and cook all this food."

"Aww, it's no trouble at all. I cooks like dis almost every day."

Now that the scent of the food was in Patrice's nostrils, she was glad that she no longer smelled the medicine and snuff. "It does smell and look good."

"Why . . . thank ya, baby. Yes, indeed. I'm so glad y'all could come. It's not every day I get some compana. It's good to talk to someboda other than myself every once in a while. You know, folks don't visit us old folks anymore. I thought it would be nice to have Jessi heya wid me, but she runs the streets more than cars. Well, does anyone of you care to say grace? Jessi, why don't you say it?"

Jessica hung her head a little, her eyes shifting at everyone from embarrassment because she didn't know how to pray. The only thing she knew how to say was, "Bless the bread, bless the meat, and bless this stomach, 'cuz I'm getting ready to eat."

"Lawd, gal, hurry up. We's hungry!"

Patrice remembered Glen praying so beautifully when they'd first met. She gently nudged him and mouthed, "Pray."

"I'll pray," Glen said. "Father God in the name of Jesus, thank You for blessing us for another day. You didn't have to do it, but You did, and for that we are grateful. Father, thank You for this food that Mrs. Parker has prepared for us. Lord, she has opened her doors to this lovely home and opened her arms of love and acceptance. And for that alone, Father, make provision for her. And bless those that don't know where their next meal is coming from. For we are truly blessed. In Jesus name we pray. Amen."

"Amen," they all said in unison.

Every one began to dig in. Tiffany was swinging her legs back and forth and humming a tune that nobody knew. She was tearing into a chicken leg. Children loved drumsticks.

Mrs. Parker started running her mouth again. It didn't bother her if no one spoke. She was just as happy as a lark that she had some company. Glen kept looking at Tiffany and smiled. He was so happy to see her. On the other hand he couldn't stand the sight of Jessica and didn't even bother to look her way. He was acting as if she wasn't in the room.

Tiffany was swinging her leg so hard that she started kicking the bottom of the table.

Jessica popped her hand a little and said, "Tiffany, stop."

"Tiffna, stop kickin' yo' leg like you crazy, girl. Act like you got some mannas."

In Glen's eyes, Tiffany couldn't do any wrong. It really hurt him that he had missed the past few years of her life. It was eating him up inside.

Jessica kept cutting her eyes at Patrice. *That bitch probably called herself trying to get close to Tiffany in church. I don't know who you think you are, but you better stay the hell away from my family.*

"So what's yo' name again, baby?" Mrs. Parker asked Patrice.

"Patrice."

"Patice?" Jessica mocked.

Bitch, don't make me slap you. "No, Patrice," Patrice responded in a low tone.

"Don't pay Jessi no mind. I swear the girl acts like she got lard in dem dere ears of hers." Mrs. Parker giggled. "You a pretta little girl. Yo' hair so pretta. That ain't no china hair, is it?"

Patrice chuckled. "No, ma'am."

"Yes, indeedy you some kinda pretta."

Patrice was feeling a little uncomfortable about Mrs. Parker's compliments, but when she noticed Jessica's look of envy, she felt better. "Why, thank you, Mrs. Parker." Patrice looked at Jessica again and thought, *Yeah, bitch, I look better than you with all that horsetail hair hanging off your head.*

"Glen, where you find this pretta young girl at?"

Glen didn't want to tell her at a club, so he just laughed.

"You know my hair was thick like that when I was younga. Girl, when you get my age, everything starts fallin' out. Hair, teeth, puffiness in yo' bosoms."

Everybody cracked up laughing. Even Tiffany covered her mouth and started giggling.

"Shucks, it's the truth. My late husband used to use whip cream, but when they start looking like pancakes, he started using syrup."

Everybody burst into laughter again.

Mrs. Parker really knew how to break the ice. But Glen wanted to change the subject, because that was a bit too much information for Tiffany, and for him as well.

"Mrs. Parker, you are hilarious. So how long have you lived here?" Patrice asked.

"Oh, it's been 'bout forty years now. My husband built this house."

"It's beautiful," Glen said, relieved that he got her talking about something other than her titties. He slyly looked at Patrice's breasts and then Mrs. Parker's and thought, *Is this is what I have to look forward to? Hell no. My baby is going to get breast implants when she gets old.*

Glen started making funny faces at Tiffany. She tried not to laugh, but she couldn't hold it in any longer. The sound of her laughter was like music to his ears. He made a face again, and this time she made one back.

Everyone laughed except Jessica.

"So, Mrs. Parker, do you have someone to upkeep your house, you know, to take care of anything that might give out on you, like plumbing, heating, or something like that?" Glen was hoping that she'd say no, so that he could find the time to do it, just to be closer to his daughter. Although he was planning on taking his daughter away from Jessica, he wanted her to know him much better first.

"Well, Robert Lee comes every so often. But he's been slackin' ever since he got himself another job. Don't blame him much though. It takes a lot to take caya of home nowadays. And I know I can't pay him what his job is payin' him. You know, being that I gets a social security check, I'm on a budget."

Bingo! Glen said, "I'll be happy to come on every other Saturday to check on things for you, if you don't mind."

"I can't pay you that much. I can only give you what I gave Robert Lee."

"Oh, no, ma'am. You don't have to pay me at all. I would just like to volunteer my services."

"Well, in that case, naw, son, I don't mind at all. You is just as sweet as you can be. No wonda Mary misses you so. Afta you leave tonight, I'm gonna miss you myself."

Jessica was glad to hear that he would be coming over also. She just had to get him back. She was going to do everything in her power to make that happen. She didn't know who the hell that stank whore was that he had with him, but it didn't even matter, because she knew she had something that wench didn't have—his child.

As they finished their meals Mrs. Parker told Jessica to help with the dishes.

Patrice said, "Mrs. Parker, thank you again for dinner. It was delicious. Would you like me to help you clean up anything?"

"No, ma'am. I don't invite guests over to clean. You just git outa heya and sit down and relax yo'self."

Glen started to grow on Tiffany in just that little time of their visit. She walked past Glen and Patrice and smiled.

He said, "Hey, pretty girl."

She responded, "You made me laugh at the table. You're funny."

"Who? Me? That wasn't me. That was my twin."

Tiffany laughed. "Na-uh, that was you. I learned a game. Do you want me to show you?"

"Sure. Why not."

"You got to stand up."

When Glen stood, Tiffany reached out her left hand and took hold of his left, then her right to his right, and sang, "Here we go zodiac, zodiac, zodiac. Here we go zodiac all night long."

As Tiffany continued the song, Patrice said to Glen, "You've caught on well. Looks like you've done this before."

Glen mouthed, "Shut up," and Patrice burst into laughter.

Tiffany continued, "I'm gonna wear my dress above my knee and shake it, shake it, shake it, to the one I see."

Glen eyes widened. "Hold, hold, hold up! I'm not wearing any dresses now."

Tiffany and Patrice burst into laughter.

"My mommy's boyfriend said the same thing." Tiffany laughed.

"Oh, yeah?" Glen asked

"Yup, he's in jail. We went to go see him, and then we went to the mall. Do you like my new shoes?" Tiffany stuck out her foot to show off her pink-and-white Reebok.

"Yes, they're pretty just like you," he commented. Glen was heated, but he didn't show it.

Then they played beauty shop. Glen was her client. She put a doll baby on Glen's head, and the doll's hair hung off the side of his head. She said, "All done."

Glen was acting like he was so excited. "Let me see, let me see."

She held a make-believe mirror in front of him.

"Ahh. My goodness! This is fabulous, darling. How much do I owe you?"

"One dollar."

"Oh no, darling. I have to give you five dollars." Glen pulled out a five-dollar bill and gave it to her, and her eyes brightened up as if she was at a candy shop.

Patrice said, "What do you say?"

"Thank you." She gushed before taking off toward the kitchen yelling, "Mommy! Mommy! Look what I got!"

"Where did you get that from?"

Tiffany went to the doors of the living room and pointed at Glen. "From that man."

Glen looked at Tiffany with much love, and then his eyes started filling up with water. It really bothered him that she didn't refer to him as daddy.

Patrice said, "Baby, can you help me get something out of the car?" She didn't want Glen to break down crying, so she used that as an excuse to get him out of the house.

As soon as they got outside, Glen began to weep, and Patrice held him.

The evening had slipped away, and it was now 9:00 P.M. Glen picked up Tiffany, and kissed her neck and blew on it, imitating the sound of a fart.

Tiffany burst into laughter. She really enjoyed Glen.

When he put her down, she followed him. She thought he was getting ready to leave. "Bye," she said.

"I'm not leaving yet. I have to talk to your mother first. Wait a minute." Glen looked at Tiffany with suspicion. "Are you trying to get rid of me or something?" he asked.

"No. You can spend the night if you want. Auntie Emma has two more bedrooms upstairs. You can sleep in one of them."

Jessica was sitting at the dining room table and heard Tiffany's offer. "Miss thing, you don't pay any bills. How are you going to offer somebody a room?"

You shut the hell up. Obviously, you don't neither, you leech! Glen thought. Every time Jessica opened her mouth, he cringed. "No, thank you, sweetheart, but Mr. Glen is going to his own place tonight, okay," he said sweetly to his daughter.

"Are you coming tomorrow?"

"No, but you will see me next Saturday, okay."

"Okay."

"Tiffany, go get ready for bed," Jessica said.

"Yes, ma'am."

Patrice gave Mrs. Parker a hug and said, "Mrs. Parker, it was nice to meet you."

Mrs. Parker gave Patrice a sad look, hating to see her company leave. "Don't rush."

"Wish we didn't have to, but I have to get ready for church tomorrow."

"So, Patrice, will you be attending our church tomorrow, or your own?" Jessica asked. "That's if you have your own."

"No, I will not be attending Mrs. Parker's church." Patrice paused. "And, yes, I do have my own church that I will be attending."

Jessica tried to laugh it off.

"What you talkin' 'bout, Jessi? Patrice, you came to our church before?"

"Yes, ma'am. Keith had invited me and my friends."

"Keith Simmons? Lawd have mercy. That is a nice young'un. Well, you know you are more than welcome to come again if you like."

Patrice smiled.

"Go on and take some of det food home witcha. Lawd knows, we ain't gon' eat it all."

They followed Mrs. Parker into the kitchen to take home a couple of plates.

"Thank you again for having us." Patrice headed for the door after hugging Mrs. Parker for the second time.

"Oh, no problem. Come again, heya?"

"Yes, ma'am," they said in unison.

Patrice looked at Glen. "Ready?"

"Baby, give me a minute. I want to talk to Jessica about Tiffany, okay."

"Do you need some assistance? 'Cause I've been itching to slap her for a while now. I'm trying to respect Mrs. Parker's house, but she's making it hard, baby."

Glen chuckled. "Naw, I've got it, but thank you." He kissed her on the cheek.

"No problem." Patrice headed to the car.

Mrs. Parker wanted to give them their privacy and went in the den, which was in the back of the house.

Glen went to join Jessica at the dining room table. He was getting ready to give Jessica a few choice words, so he kept his volume down. "You know I been waiting to say this all evening—You make me sick. I can't stand your lying ass. I wanted to cuss you out when you called me, but I wanted to see how deep you were going to bury yourself. You know damn well you were already here in town and going to make-believe that you were on your way. You didn't even have the decency to tell Tiffany about me, after all I'd done for your ungrateful ass. I have every right to let Mrs. Parker know that your trifling tail ain't join no prison ministry, but I don't want to make it hard for Tiffany. But then again, maybe I should say something, so she can kick your ass out in the street and Tiffany would be able to stay with her daddy."

Jessica gave him the evil eye. "Are you finished?"

"Hell no. I just need to pause for a moment before I jump across this table and choke the hell out of you." Of course, Glen said that out of anger, knowing he wouldn't touch her.

Jessica chuckled. "I'd like to see you try it."

With evil eyes they stared at each other.

"First of all, I would like to know who in the hell was that heifer you brought in my aunt's house uninvited."

"Uninvited? Tramp, you don't call the shots when it comes to inviting someone. And how the hell do you know if she was invited or not? If I can remember, your stanking ass was at Sussex visiting your joke of a boyfriend. And, further-more, she's not a heifer—you are. She's more of woman than you'll ever be. You know what, I don't want to hear what you have to say, because you ain't going to do nothing but lie anyway. I just want to know when can I come get Tiffany."

"What do you mean, get Tiffany? Nigga, you're not taking her!"

"Jessica, don't sit here and make it hard for yourself, because you know I can make it hard for you."

"Listen, you motherf—" Jessica caught herself when she saw Tiffany looking at her.

Tiffany didn't know what they were talking about, but she could feel the tension in the room. "Mommy, I forgot to kiss you goodnight." She went to Jessica, and they gave each other a kiss. Tiffany smiled at Glen and said, "You are more funner than Daddy T-Bo. Mommy, can he be my daddy instead?"

Glen was flabbergasted, his body temperature rising as high as the clouds. He just stared at Tiffany with a frown, then at Jessica, hatred in his eyes. *No, this bitch ain't letting my daughter call that trifling nigga her daddy.*

Jessica's face read, *Yeah, so what? What are you going to do about it?* Then she corrected Tiffany and said, "It's more fun."

Glen still was staring at Jessica with evil eyes. "I believe she asked you a question. I believe you should answer her, Jessica."

"Baby, go on upstairs and go to bed."

Glen hit the table with his fist and raised his voice. "Damn it, Jessica! Answer her!"

Jessica and Tiffany jumped. Jessica stood to her feet and took her daughter by the hand, "Come on, baby, let Mommy tuck you in."

As she walked by, Glen grabbed Tiffany.

"No!" Jessica screamed as she attempted to pull Tiffany away from him.

Glen pushed her back with one hand.

"Mommy!" Tiffany cried.

Mrs. Parker yelled from the den, "What's goin' on in dere?"

"Nothing, Mrs. Parker! Sorry to disturb you!" Jessica's eyes were filled with fear.

"Tiffany, sweetheart, your mother doesn't want to answer your question," Glen said in a much calmer voice, staring at Jessica. "But it would be my pleasure to answer it for you." Then he looked at his daughter. "First of all, don't be scared, okay. I want to let you know that I would never hurt you. Do you know why?"

Tiffany, her arms wrapped tightly around Jessica's waist, shook her head from side to side as tears trickled down her face.

"Because I love you. That's why." He smiled, hoping to make her feel more relaxed. Glen knew that children could sense whether or not grown folks are real or phony. His heart melted when she smiled back. He then pulled Tiffany gently, as she loosened her grip on her mother.

Glen sat her on his lap. "Baby, do you want me to be your daddy?"

She nodded.

"Well, guess what? I am."

Chapter Eighteen

After Keith said the opening prayer, Jean told the choir, "Listen up, everybody. Dwayne has something to say."

Dwayne slowly walked and stood in front of the choir, looking as though he'd lost his best friend. "I would like to this time apologize to you all for my unacceptable behavior. I asked the Lord to forgive me and Lorene"—He bowed his head to Lorene as if he was giving her honor—"Now you. I know I did a terrible sin against Lorene. I'm not going to make an excuse for what I've done, but this just lets me know that God took on flesh and became man so He can die for our sins. And by Him doing so, that took away the burden of sin that we so heavily carry, and He holds us in His arm like a true father should hold his child so that we can have a pure relationship with Him if we follow his way." Dwayne was speaking in a preaching tone, thinking about how his natural father treated him.

Oh, please! Patrice thought. *Why is it that you know so much what God has done for us, but yet you don't seem to understand something simple like God made Adam and Eve, not Adam and Steve? People kill me trying to pick stuff out the Bible that suits them. Live by the whole Bible, not just some of it.* She wasn't feeling Dwayne, and didn't even care to look at him. They may have forgiven him, but she wasn't about to.

Dwayne saw Patrice looking at her fingernails, staring at invisible dirt. Then he said, "And if that's not good enough for some of you and you have not sinned, by all means, please cast a stone."

Patrice looked up and saw that Dwayne was staring directly at her. Her face had a soft expression, as if to say, "He's right." She looked toward heaven and thought, *Lord, what can I say? Who am I to throw a rock? But then again I don't care. Like I said, if he's coming in here preaching the Word, then live by it.*

Oh Lord, our Lord, how excellent is Thy name Oh Lord, our Lord, how excellent is Thy name in all the earth

The sopranos sang out their part as Jean had taught it. When she asked them to repeat what she just sang, she noticed Patrice didn't open her mouth for a single note. "Did you get it, Patrice?" she asked. "Do you need me to go over it again?"

"Oh no, I got it."

"Okay, I'm gonna need everybody to sing, to make sure they got it." Jean stared hard at Patrice.

Patrice sang along this time, but it was hard for her to concentrate. She was thinking about the nights she spent with Glen and also wondering, was he okay at Mrs. Parker's house. Normally Glen would spend his Saturdays relaxing, but now he was mowing Mrs. Parker's lawn and doing a little house maintenance. It's not that she was worried about him nor didn't trust him; the fact of the matter was, she didn't trust Jessica.

On the way home last Saturday night, Glen had told her everything that was said and done in the dining room at Mrs. Parker's home. She tried to convince him to turn around so she could cuss Jessica out, but of course, she was only selling wolf tickets.

The thought of Glen going over to Mrs. Parker's made her miscalculate her register a couple of time this past week. Her goal was to make much more than what she was stealing already. She thought she needed to dance a little harder.

After leaving work, instead of going home, she would just stay at Glen's place until he came home. She hadn't moved in with him quite yet. She was still trying to decide whether or not that was something she really wanted to do, although she felt like she practically lived with him, since she had a key to his place, which he'd given to her the very next day after asking her to move in.

Since that night she'd watched Glen call Mrs. Parker's house, asking several times to speak to Tiffany. Sometimes Mrs. Parker would answer and hand Tiffany the phone. Other times Jessica would answer then lie and say Tiffany was asleep.

"Jessica, put Tiffany on the damn phone!" Glen huffed.

"I said she's asleep, dammit."

"It's mighty funny, she's asleep every time you answer the phone."

"Look, I told you she's asleep. I don't know what else to tell you."

"All right. Well, I'll come wake her up myself then."

Then she would put Tiffany on the phone.

As much as Jessica wanted to see Glen, she knew there was no way she would ever get the chance to be with him because of Patrice. She saw the love in his eyes when he watched Patrice at the dinner table. She remembered that same look of love that they'd once shared. She knew she couldn't compete.

Faye hunched Patrice, forcing her to refocus on the choir rehearsal. Without moving her lips, she said, "Where did Jean get this tone-deaf cow from?" She kept her eyes on the new girl, who had on a pair of black slacks and a white jacket with black polka dots. The new girl was trying to lead this beautiful song by Richard Smallwood.

Patrice cracked up laughing inside. She wasn't going to help the girl or suggest anything, because the last time she remembered doing that, Jean started power-tripping, saying, "I want everyone to listen to me when a song is being taught. Don't depend on the person beside you, because they may be singing the wrong note themselves."

Patrice felt that Jean only said that because she was intimidated by what Patrice knew. Ever since then, Patrice didn't care if they sounded like howling dogs, she wasn't going to help anyone anymore. As she watched the girl make a fool out of herself, she said to Faye without moving her lips, "Girl, you are retarded. Cows don't sing."

Patrice, Faye, and Lo were professionals at holding a complete conversation without their lips moving, because they'd spent so much of their time talking about folks at church while the service was going on.

"That's what I'm trying to tell you."

They both laughed without moving any facial muscles. They cut their eyes at Lo, who sat in the alto section, on the other side of the tenors.

Lo sat up slowly and looked at the both of them then sat back just as slowly. Her actions said it all—the girl sounded horrible.

The new girl stopped singing and looked at Faye and Patrice, who were giggling.

"What's wrong with y'all? Y'all need to stop," Jean said.

Patrice continued to laugh out loud this time, trying to apologize through her laughter, but no one could understand her. Her laugh was contagious, causing the entire choir to burst into laughter. The choir didn't mind hurting somebody's feelings if they couldn't sing.

Jean rolled her eyes and shook her head.

"Honey, I'm sorry, but when you sang the *mooooon* and the stars, I'd visualized the cow jumping over the moon," Peaches said while laughing.

The choir screamed with more laughter. The new girl smiled from embarrassment.

"I ain't lying, Peaches, I thought the same thing too!" Faye said, cracking up, and the laughter continued.

After rehearsal Patrice, Lorene, Faye, Peaches, Keith, Dwayne, and the new tenor, also Jean's new lover, Reginald, gathered around Jean's car. They enjoyed each other's company so well, often lingering around after practice.

Dwayne still felt uncomfortable around the crew, but he tried extremely hard to fit in again. He thought it was already bad enough trying to be accepted by society and didn't want to experience the same feeling from his friends.

Most of the group had welcomed him back, but it was a struggle for Patrice. After he'd made that statement about casting the first stone, their friendship was just not the same.

Lorene glanced at Dwayne. "Keith, excuse me for a minute. Dwayne, can I speak to for a moment?"

Dwayne nodded.

Patrice shot Dwayne a nasty look, hoping Lorene had some more curse left and give him a piece her mind.

"Jean, what in the world were you thinking, letting that girl lead that song? That was a shame and a pity. I was embarrassed for her," Faye said.

Jean sucked her teeth. "No, you weren't, not with all that laughing y'all were doing. Y'all love to embarrass people. Besides, you know I don't discriminate."

"Yeah," Peaches added, "but you shouldn't tolerate such nonsense."

Jean smiled. "Well, the poor girl probably won't even come back anyway."

"Where in the world did she come from anyway?" Patrice asked.

"She heard us sing at Mount Calvary and wanted to join."

"Mount Calvary?"

"You know, the church where Minister Thompson was eyeing you?" Peaches said.

The group then hummed in unison. They all knew it was something going on between Patrice and Quinton, especially after seeing them leave church together a while back.

Patrice snickered and said, "Y'all need to quit. I ain't *studden* him."

"You mean, 'studying'?" Jean asked.

"Oh, so now you're an English teacher as well as choir director?"

"You're funny. Anyway, I thought y'all were an item now," Jean commented.

"Oh, hell no." Patrice started to speak in first person. "Patrice drives an eighteen-wheeler, not a Tonka toy truck."

Everyone laughed.

"Your ass is so nasty. Yeah, I heard about that eighteen-wheeler you are driving from time to time after nine." Peaches sneered.

Patrice circled her hips as if she was grinding against an invisible man and said, "And you heeeeard right."

Mostly everyone laughed, and so did she. She noticed a disappointed look from both Keith and Lorene, realizing that they were the only two in the bunch trying to live right. Quickly, she attempted to cover her antics by lying. "Naw, naw, I'm just playing."

Keith cleared his throat and said to Lo, "Are you ready?" He had planned to spend the rest of the day with Lorene.

"And where are y'all going?" Faye asked with a big grin.

"You are so nosy, but if you must know, we're going sailing."

"Ooooo! I want to go. Y'all, Keith's momma got a fierce boat," Faye said, snapping her fingers.

"No, you can't go. I can't take you everywhere," Lorene said.

"I didn't want to anyway," Faye said, her nose in the air as if she smelled a bad odor. Then she giggled, which let them know she was just joking.

"Well, good people, it's been nice. Dwayne, my man, I really enjoyed what you'd said in there. He gave Dwayne a brotherly hug. "Stay encouraged, my brother."

"Thanks, man," Dwayne answered in a manly tone.

Everyone finally made their departure.

Dwayne rode with Peaches. Peaches started the ignition, and all you could hear playing on his radio was "Sweet Dreams" by Eurythmics.

Dwayne didn't get in the car just yet. He was waiting for the opportunity to speak to Patrice privately and caught her as she was getting in the passenger side of Faye's car. "Patrice, may I talk to you for a moment?" he asked from behind.

Patrice rolled her eyes before turning to face him. "Lord have mercy. Wait a minute, Faye," she whispered then turned in Dwayne's direction and said, "Yes," looking at him directly.

"Look, I don't know what your problem is, but I would like to let you know, I don't have to answer to you or no one else. The only one I have to answer to is God. I did damage to Lo, not you. She was willing to put this all behind her, so it doesn't really matter if you do or not. I would appreciate if you would stop huffing and puffing and blowing the house down every time we get together."

"Dwayne, what are you talking about? I don't have a problem with you."

"Patrice, let me tell you something. When you become the type of individual like myself, I not only have a man's discernment, but a woman's intuition. Honey, it's one thing when you lie to others, but you need to stop lying to yourself."

"Listen, Dwayne, let me tell *you* something that, obviously, you do not know. Lo almost had a nervous breakdown that night you decided to be Jack the Ripper on the girl tires. It's very hard for me to accept that. It's easy to say, 'I'm sorry.' That don't mean nothing. How sorry are you really? I don't like when folks hurt people I care for."

"Patrice, I really can't go back and erase what I did. What do you want from me?"

"I just want you to leave me the hell alone," Patrice stated calmly.

"Girlfriend, we have to get beyond this point. I'm just going to pray for you," Dwayne said, before walking to Peaches' car and getting in.

Ha! Pray for me? You better pray for your own self, you damn faggot. Patrice rolled her eyes and got in the car.

"Girl, what did he say?" Faye inquired.

"Trying to feed me that same bullshit about forgiveness."

"*Buck* him," Faye huffed.

Chapter Nineteen

Keith was really enjoying Lo's company. They had the yacht to themselves. After they arrived just where there was no land in sight, he locked the helm. He gazed into her eyes. "Are you enjoying yourself?"

Seated comfortably beside him, she smiled and answered, "You know I am."

"I'm glad." He nodded

"Keith, can I ask you something?"

"Yes."

"Why me?"

Keith chuckled. "Why you?"

"That's not funny. And, yes, why me? I mean, it seems like you're taking interest in me. I tried to think it was platonic, but something is telling me it's much more."

"I don't know. It was just something different about you."

"I know. I was quick to cuss an old lady out," Lorene admitted shamefully.

Keith chuckled again. "But if you cussed her out, it would've been for good reason," he teased. "Come on, let's go inside."

He held her around the waist gently, as she strolled inside the cabin. Lorene sat on the soft cream couch positioned in front of an oak table that had a wine rack underneath. He went in the nook, opened the cabinets, which matched the oak table, and pulled out goblets. He took a seat beside her and pulled out the ice bucket and a bottle of sparkling apple cider then filled their glasses.

"Where were we?" he said softly.

"Again, why me?" Keith chuckled. "There you go laughing again." He gazed into the sea. "Well?"

He took a sip from his glass then looked directly into Lorene's eyes. "You speak truth. Mmm-hmm, you tell like it is. I saw a diamond in the rough. I noticed your girls are wild. I pay close attention to those little remarks being made when a man walks by. 'Oh, child, he can ring my bell anytime. I'll not only answer the door, I'll open it wide.'"

Lorene giggled. "That's them for you."

"I also notice you don't feed into it, and if they get out of hand, you lay them out."

"Yeah, that's me." Lorene laughed.

"So, I said to myself, if she can speak truth without God, I know she'll be true with Him. That's why."

Lo was touched by his answer and instantly felt an attraction that caused moisture between her legs. Ashamed, she tried to change the atmosphere. "Okay, can you answer this question?"

"What's that?"

"A man of your status, why do you even bother to put up with the choir's nonsense? We are a handful, a handful of mess, that is."

They laughed.

"I'm serious. How does that saying go? Birds of a feather flock together?"

"Yes, that's how it goes, but do you know what? Jesus didn't hang around the Scribes and Pharisee. How can they hear without a preacher, and if they are not shown, how can they see? Look at the change that has come over Dwayne. I know he hasn't given his life wholeheartedly, but it's a step. That couldn't have happened if sinners were hanging with sinners only. Somebody got to be in the midst speaking the truth. I'm believing God for the choir, Lo. If we all don't give our lives to Jesus anytime soon, I'm hoping that one day we will."

"Why do you keep saying *we*? You are saved."

"Actually I'd said, *we all*. Besides, sweetheart, I haven't arrived. We are all sinners saved by grace."

"This is true."

Silence hung in the air.

A smile crept across Lorene's face. "Keith, this is really nice. I—"

Keith placed his hand on her chin, turned her toward him, and landed a passionate kiss on her full lips. Immediately, Keith was convicted, as lustful thoughts bombarded his mind.

"See, I'm sinning already. Now I got to ask the Lord to forgive me."

She grazed his lips with the tip of her finger. "You're fine."

"I love you, Lo."

Before his desires could take over, he hopped to his feet. "Maybe we should be getting back."

Chapter Twenty

Glen was sitting as his desk, staring at a picture of Tiffany. He had taken it off of his coffee table and brought it to work with him. At first it was too painful to have the picture at work. He was hardly able to concentrate on what he needed to do. Now that he'd been going over to Mrs. Parker's every Saturday to do a little maintenance and to play with his daughter, he could now look at the pictures with sweet memories. He loved her so much. He had plans to take her shopping, to amusement parks, traveling and much more. Even though it had only been a few years, he felt as though he had to make up for lost time.

Glen's new promotion kept him busier than his old job. He had been employed by City Hall for three years after moving to Newport News from Trenton. He can remember it like it was yesterday.

***

An older gray-haired African American interviewer said to him, "I see here that you received your B.S.E. degree."

"Yes, sir." Glen was more nervous than a turkey one week before Thanksgiving.

"Mmm-hmm. Well, we no longer have the position you're seeking. However, we do need an administrative assistant. You can type at least fifty words a minute, right?"

Glen couldn't believe what he was hearing. Yes, he did want the engineer position that was in the Sunday's ad. The job description was to plan, design, produce, maintain and operate. He thought maybe he'd have a good chance, because this was what he'd gone to college to do. He did, of course, know how to type as well. He would be satisfied with any position that they gave him, just as long it paid much more than what he was receiving at his current telemarketing job, which was a couple of dollars just above minimum wage. But he still had hopes of becoming an engineer manager one day. All he knew was that he needed a job with better pay, and fast.

"Yes, sir, I can."

"Well, good. How would you like to start first thing tomorrow morning?"

"Yes, sir," Glen said, showing his bright white teeth.

"All right. I'll see you at eight A.M. sharp."

"Thank you, sir. Thank you so much." Glen shook his hand and left.

After serving so faithfully on his job as an admin assistant for three years without missing any days from work, he was now the manager of the engineering department. It wasn't easy. He remembered the countless times he spent working with the former engineering manager, Mr. White.

Normally it would take receiving several promotions and constantly climbing the corporate ladder to become an engineering manager, but like the saying goes, 'It's not what you know, it's who you know.' Mr. White suggested that Glen take his position after he retired. Now he managed the design, consulting, computers, development and production, manufacturing, and electrical departments and loved every minute of it. Of course, he had people that worked under him to help manage these departments, but when it was all said and done, Glen had the last say.

Here he was, sitting in a corner office with a view of the Chesapeake Bay. He especially loved the view at night when he stayed over to make sure he hadn't left any task undone, and tonight was one of those nights. Watching the view made him think of Patrice. Just like he planned on making Tiffany happy, he wanted to make Patrice happy as well and take her to Las Vegas, where the nights are filled with lights.

He was informed that there would be new hires next week. He wasn't the one that did the hiring, but he had to make the final decision when it came to someone being hired in his department. He reviewed the resumes before him.

"Looks good. Mmm-hmm. How impressive," he said to himself. "Looks good. Okay." He called his administrative assistant. "Debra, call Mr. Donald Purnell for an interview."

Glen was very pleased to see this young man had had such long service at his previous jobs. He was also impressed by the duties he'd performed. Just the way the resume was put together said a lot, but what really caught his eye was, Donald was from Trenton, New Jersey. Glen thought it really shouldn't have mattered where he was from, but just the whole package alone made him decide to have Debra give him a call.

"Sure will. Anything else I can do for you, Mr. Pearson?"

"No, thank you. Oh, Debra."

"Yes, sir?"

"Thank you again for staying after hours. I appreciate it."

"You're quite welcome."

Glen was glad to have Debra as his assistant. He saw the same drive in her that he once had when he was an admin assistant. She also resembled Patrice, but he had no thoughts of Debra being anything else, besides being his assistant. He knew what he had at home.

Glen shivered, just thinking of Patrice loving him the way she did. He couldn't ask for anything better. He couldn't wait until she moved in with him, because sometimes he hated coming home to an empty apartment.

"Mr. Pearson, Patrice is on line two."

"Thank you. Were you able to get in contact with Mr. Purnell?"

"Yes, sir. I scheduled him to come in at nine A.M. for an interview."

"Great. You can call it a night. Again, thank you, Debra."

"And, again, you're welcome. Good night."

"Good night."

Glen pushed line two. "Hey, baby."

Patrice wiped the sweat from her brow. "Hey, yourself. When are you coming home?"

"Oh, so you're at my place?"

"Yes, I am," Patrice sang.

"Good. I was hoping you would be. I miss you."

"Aww, I miss you too. Which leads me back to my question. When are you coming home? I'm cooking dinner tonight."

Glen shuffled through the papers on his desk. "Well, in that case, let me hurry up. I should be there around seven thirty or so, depending on traffic."

"Okay. I love you."

"I love you too."

Traffic was indeed backed up. There was no way Glen was going to make it home by the time he'd predicted.

He finally made it home at exactly 8:40 P.M. As he'd entered his apartment, the aroma of fried chicken brought a wide grin across his face.

Patrice greeted him with a kiss.

"Baby, you got it smelling all good in here."

"I thought you said you were going to be here around seven thirty. Had me over a hot stove sweating like a Negro slave and you weren't here to eat it."

"Trust me, I'm going to eat it."

Patrice pouted. "But it's all cold now."

Glen kissed her on the cheek. "That's what the microwave is for."

"Don't get smart."

Glen chuckled. "I'm not getting smart."

Glen loved Patrice's little attitude. He found it humorous. He couldn't wait until she moved in. Strange, but he looked forward to lover's spats, believing that if you don't go through anything, it's not worth it. He was ready to take on and conquer any challenges they had to face.

"Whatever. Just wash your hands and go eat."

Glen smiled and softly smacked Patrice on her behind. "Yes, ma'am."

Not only did Glen wash his hands, but he also slipped into something more comfortable. After entering the kitchen he saw Patrice starting on the dishes.

After the microwave rang, Patrice then placed his plate in front of him. Along with fried chicken, she had cooked macaroni and cheese, and sweet peas.

Immediately he dug right in. He noticed Patrice didn't have anything to say. Normally she would always initiate the conversation between them. Then he thought, *What better time to ask.* "Baby, when are you going to move in? You're always over here anyway. You have a key. What's the holdup?" Glen sucked on his chicken bone.

"Well, since I'm over here all the time, it shouldn't really matter if I move in."

Glen felt like he'd lost the battle before it even got started. "You're right, but, sweetheart, I love you and I want to share my life with you. I don't want to keep picking you up from your mama's house. You can stay here with me."

"I know but . . . ." Patrice was trying to think of an excuse not to move in with him. She really wanted to, but she was straddling the fence. She didn't want to let her mother down, yet she didn't want to disappoint Glen either. She found the perfect excuse. "You don't have enough closet space. Baby, I have more clothes and shoes than J.C. Penney's." She wasn't exaggerating.

"Okay, this is what I'll do. I'll put my things in the living room closet, and you can have the bedroom closet."

This man is persistent. She tried to think of another excuse but couldn't. *Disappoint Ma or Glen? Hell, I'm going to please myself.* A sly smile on her face, Patrice said just above a whisper, "You'll give up your closet space for me?"

"Yes."

"I'll move in." She winked.

"When?"

Patrice sighed. "I don't know. Probably sometime next weekend. I'm not sure, but I think we have a singing engagement this weekend. Wait, it's gonna have to be on a weekday, because I do remember we're singing next Saturday and Sunday."

Glen thought, *Yes, I won the battle.* He got up and kissed Patrice very affectionately. "You won't regret it. Do you need any help moving in?"

"No, I'll be all right. Mmm, let me see." Patrice rubbed her chin. "I'll just move in next Friday. That will give me time to pack up everything. I'm sure Millie wouldn't mind if I get off an hour early."

Glen gently rubbed his fingers through her hair. "Are you sure you don't need any help?"

Just the thought of working and moving made Patrice tired already. Then she sighed. "Mmm . . . nah, I'll be all right."

"Well, take me to work that morning and you can use my car to do what you got to do."

Patrice kissed him on the cheek. "Thank you, baby."

"You're welcome." Glen rubbed his stomach. "By the way, dinner was delicious, baby."

"Thank you." Patrice suddenly remembered that Glen was late coming home. "Wait a minute, you're not off the hook that easy."

Glen frowned with confusion. "What?"

"What took you so long to come home?"

"I'm sorry. I had to finish some paperwork before tomorrow. Baby, it's not easy being a manager. I have more responsibilities now."

"I hope you handle your business well, like other things." Patrice's eyes roamed Glen's body and focused on his crotch.

He covered himself with his hands, as though he didn't have anything on. "And you say I'm nasty. You're the one."

"You love it."

"Sure do." He gathered her in his arms and nuzzled her neck.

"But, seriously, I have an open slot for an engineer and I could use some new talent. I ran across a young man that I feel can do the job. His resume was pretty impressive, but I'll see what he's made of in the interview."

"Oh, I see."

"Here, let me help you with that." Glen grabbed the dish towel, dried the dishes, and put them away.

"Thanks. So, what kind of talent are you looking for?" Patrice didn't have the slightest idea of what he was talking about, or getting ready to say.

"I need someone in the electrical field."

"What do they have to do? Fix lights?"

"Naw, it's a little bit more than fixing lights. Electrical engineers design, develop and test, you know, stuff like that."

After they finished up the dishes, she and Glen went in the living room and sat on the couch. Every night their normal routine was watching *The Jeffersons*, but they were too involved in their conversation to pay attention to the sitcom.

"Ah shucks, you do have a lot on your plate, don't you? So do you think that he's the man for the job?"

"Pretty much. His resume was set up very nicely, and guess what else? He's from Jersey."

Patrice shrugged her shoulders. "And?"

"I mean, it's seems strange that someone from Jersey has moved here and applied for a job at City Hall."

"I don't see anything strange about that. Isn't that what you did?"

"Yeah, you're right. It's no big deal. It's just coincidental, I guess. Well, enough work talk. So how's my baby doing tonight?" Glen snuggled close to Patrice.

"Uh-uh, back up. We're having a decent conversation here."

Glen chuckled. "Okay, but let's talk about something else. I don't want to start bringing my job to my residence."

"Okay, that's fine. Hmmm, let me think." Patrice looked at the ceiling. "What can we talk about?"

"I know what we can talk about. Answer this question for me—Why aren't you in school?"

Patrice knew what he meant and tried to be funny. "I already graduated."

"Okay, let me rephrase the question—Why aren't you in college? I can tell you have a sharp mind. You're not only beautiful but also smart."

"What gives you that impression?"

"Let's just say, a brother knows these things."

"Well, thank you, but what would I go for? I don't even know what I would major in."

"I think you would do well in social science."

"Wait a minute, I thought you said you didn't want your wife to work. If I go to college, that means I'm looking for a career."

"I don't want my wife to work, but we're not married."

Patrice frowned. "Excuse me?"

"Oh, you can dish it but can't take it. I kind of remember having this conversation with you, and you said you wanted to work at Hardee's, remember? Now hopefully someday I will make you my wife because, Patrice, ain't no doubt about it, I'm in love with you. But if anything was to happen to me, it will be nice to have something to fall back on."

"What is this? Are you changing on me? You just finished saying how you hated the fact that your mother had to work like a dog, and now you're talking about having something to fall back on? I'm not getting this, Glen," Patrice shot, becoming frustrated.

Glen began to take offense with her tone. "Yeah, my mother did work like a dog. She worked her body to death. I'm not trying to have a fight with you, Patrice," he calmly stated. "What I'm saying to you is, you can do something with your mind, get paid for your mind. But, like I said, if something was to happen to me, you'll be able to hold your own. Baby, you don't have to work. I'll take care of you. I'd take care of you now, but you insist on working at Hardee's. But I would like for you to go to school."

Patrice was silent. She didn't want to be pressured into going to school. Although she'd graduated with honors, she had to struggle to get the grade. Once she'd graduated, she knew that was it for her. She started pouting. "Glen, I don't want to go to school."

Glen kissed her on the forehead. "Okay, at least tell me why you hate school."

"I didn't say I hated it."

"Well, tell me why you don't want to go."

"Because"—Patrice sighed—"I don't finish anything. I can have a great idea, go for it, get tired of it, and quit. That's a way of life for me. Do you really want to know why I haven't moved in yet?"

Glen lifted his brows, awaiting a response.

"Well, really it was two reasons. One, my mother is against shackers, and the other is . . ."

"What, sweetheart?"

"Glen, all I ever wanted is to get married and live happily ever after. I know it's foolish, but every little girl dreams that. I guess I am too young, huh? I'm still having childish dreams. Lo always tells me that I need to grow up. She's right. I—"

"Hey, Patrice."

"What?"

"You're jabbering."

"Am I?"

"Yes, you are. What was the other reason?"

"I'm afraid of losing you. Baby, from what I understand, men like you don't come around that often, and if they do, they are spoken for. I see the love in your eyes when you talk about Tiffany, the way you care for people like Ms.

Mary and Mrs. Parker, and most of all, you loving me. Let's be real. People that live together, don't make it. They start having fights and find out some things that they don't particularly care for. You're going to see the real me, and I'm going to see the real you. I hear my momma say all the time, 'Why buy the cow if you're getting the milk for free?' I must admit at first I was in it for the thrill and had no idea that I was going to fall in love with you. Like I said, I do want to get married, but again, every time I start something, I don't complete it. Baby, I'm afraid the relationship will go unfinished. I know I'm jabbering and what I am saying doesn't make any sense, but this is how I feel."

"Come here." Glen pulled Patrice in his arms, and she rested her head on his chest.

"Listen, it's easy to love someone or something. It's like buying a car new. When you see the car in the lot, you're all excited and probably say to yourself, 'I love that car. I got to have it.' And this is true, you do love it. The real question is, Do you trust it? You don't know whether or not that car is going to break down. That's why people buy warranties. So on that note, baby, I want your trust. I need for you to trust me, and most of all, yourself. Stop giving up on things so easily. Don't give up on us before we even get started, okay."

Patrice didn't respond.

"Patrice, look at me."

She slowly gazed into his eyes.

"Okay?"

Patrice slightly shrugged her shoulders.

"Listen, this is what I'm going to do."

"What's that?"

"This may sound a little corny, but I'm giving you a warranty, meaning, after we live together for a while, if I break your heart, I will repair it at no cost."

She laughed a little. "Yeah, that is corny."

"Well?"

"Okay."

Chapter Twenty-one

As Patrice sat on the swing at the park, the children were all around her playing on the sliding boards, monkey bars, and the merry-go-round. They were all having a ball, including Patrice. In the midst of the laughter, she saw in the distance a tall, handsome man impeccably dressed in a white silk shirt, white slacks, and a white pair of shoes, standing there watching her.

Patrice heard a scream. She turned her head to the left and saw a child crying because he fell and scraped his knee.

She then looked back at the man and noticed that he didn't move, and his eyes stayed focus on her. Out of nowhere, she saw a pit bull barking very viciously and charging after her. She knew the ferocious animal was going to eat her alive.

Before the dog got within ten feet of her, the man pulled out a silver gun and shot it to death. When Patrice heard the gunshot, she woke up in a sweat.

"Are you okay?" Glen said groggily. Patrice had awakened him with her loud moaning.

"Yes, I was having this dream, but it seemed so real. I was sitting in the—" Before she could finish her sentence, she heard Glen snoring. "Glen!"

"Hmm?"

"Wake up. I was telling you about my dream."

Glen glanced at the clock. "Baby, can you tell me later? I got to get up in two more hours." He draped his arm around Patrice and nestled into his pillow.

Patrice looked at the clock. She didn't realize it was 4:30 in the morning. "All right," she said with a defeated sigh.

She drifted back to sleep and dreamt the same man stood watching her with a smile on his face. Awakened with a start, she glanced over at the clock, which read 5:45 A.M.

She eased out of bed, trying not wake Glen, showered, and got dressed early, knowing she had to take him to work. She thought about the conversation they'd had two weeks ago about her moving in, when suddenly she heard the alarm. Although Patrice had been staying with Glen every night since then, the time had come for her to move in completely.

After his morning shower, Glen trod to the kitchen, where he found Patrice spooning leftovers into a plastic dish, preparing his lunch. He seated himself in front of a plate of grits, eggs, and toast, and listened to Patrice share her dream or, as she put it, her nightmare.

"So what do you think it all means?"

"I don't know, baby. I'm not a dream interpreter. I have crazy dreams myself and can't understand them." She sighed. "Tell me about it. Well, I guess I should dismiss it." "Baby, don't let it bother you. We all dream crazy stuff sometimes." "Yeah, you're right."

"Do you want to take me to work so you can use the car to get your things, or do you want to wait until I get off?"

"I can take you. It shouldn't take long to put my things in the car before going to work. The only thing I have to bring is my clothes, shoes, and personals. What time will you be home today?"

"Ah, you sound so sweet calling this your home," he teased.

"Keep on. I'm going to change my mind." Patrice shoved a bag with his lunch inside toward him as he rose to his feet.

He grabbed her in his arms and planted a sloppy kiss on her cheek. "You know I'm just playing with you."

She pushed him away. "Move, Glen."

Glen slapped her on the behind.

"That's it. I'm not moving in."

"Oh yes you are, too." He chuckled as he grabbed her again and began tickling her.

In a fit of giggles, Patrice struggled to free herself from his grasp.

"Yes, you are moving in. Take back what you said."

"Stop, Glen! You're going to be late for work," she managed to say through her laughter.

"I don't have to clock in like you do. Say you will."

"Okay, I will!" She gave in, bringing the torture to an end. "You get on my nerves." She pouted.

"I love you too."

It was payday. Hardee's didn't pay their employees on Friday. Patrice had already stolen five hundred dollars, so along with her check, she had six hundred and eighty-nine dollars and fifty-two cents. Patrice thought, *Not bad for only forty hours in two weeks. Humph, I'm making more than you, Lo. You can talk about my little shift all you want.*

Patrice didn't want to spend the money she'd stolen until she received her check. The members in the choir knew she'd be broke until payday, so she didn't want them to start asking her questions about having money.

She couldn't wait until later on that night. Normally, she and the girls would go to the Milky Way club on Wednesday nights, when ladies got in free before 9:00 P.M. Patrice knew that Faye would go, especially since she didn't have to pay. She wasn't sure that Lorene would go, though, because she'd been spending a lot of time with Keith. Every time she had the chance to call, Lo wasn't home. And if she was home, Keith was there with her watching movies and eating popcorn.

"Well, if y'all are willing to go, drinks are on me tonight, ladies," she said to herself.

While Patrice was getting ready to clock in for work, Millie walked up behind her with a new employee, a young white girl with blonde hair, blue eyes, and pearly white teeth. It threw Patrice for a loop because all the employees at Hardee's, except Millie, were black. The few times there had been a white employee, he or she was usually poor white trash. But this girl was pretty, and reminded Patrice of Hayley from *All My Children*.

"Patrice, this is Leslie. Leslie, this is Patrice."

"Hi." Leslie extended her hand to Patrice and smiled.

"How are you doing?" Patrice shook her hand weakly. There was just something about this girl that she didn't trust.

"Patrice, I want you to train Leslie in drive-thru," Millie said.

That wrecked Patrice's whole day, and would set her back at least fifty dollars. She didn't need anyone over there spying on her. "Okay," she said to Millie. Patrice was upset that she couldn't dance today. It's not like she really needed the extra money, seeing that Glen was actually taking care of her. Nonetheless, she was used to getting free cash.

"Is it hard?" Leslie asked Patrice.

"No, it just moves pretty fast during lunch rush." Patrice's tone was low and unfriendly.

"Are you okay?" Leslie, her head cocked to the side, looked at Patrice.

"Yeah, just a little tired." Patrice really wanted to say, "Stop talking to me, please. If something was wrong, it's nothing you can do about it, Barbie!"

Patrice wondered what shift Leslie was going to work. Christina worked 4:00 A.M. to eleven, and she had the eleven to 3:00 P.M. shift. "So, Leslie, what will your shift be?"

"Six A.M. to eleven. I can't work on Thursdays and Sundays. I go to Christopher Newport College and I have morning classes. The rest of the days, I have classes starting at noon. On Sundays my parents make me go to mass with them. We're Catholic."

Girl, I asked you one question. This ain't no interview. You already got the job, damn! Patrice thought, glad to hear that the two of them wouldn't be working together. But Christina would be pissed.

"How about you?" Leslie asked.

"Eleven A.M. to three P.M., and off on the weekends," Patrice said bluntly. *Now that's how you're supposed to answer a question. Maybe I should train you how to do that.*

Chapter Twenty-two

"Jessi, where's you goin?" Mrs. Parker watched as Jessica stood in the bathroom, curling her hair.

"Over my friend's house. She's picking me up in about ten minutes." Jessica hated that she had to rely on someone to take her here and there. She would've gotten a car by now, but she kept failing the written test at DMV. It was so discouraging that she stopped trying.

"You know we got church tonight."

"I know. We are going to church."

Jessica had no plans of going to church. She had a couple of packages to deliver for T-Bo. Even though he was in prison, he still had a lot of authority on the outside. With the snap of his finger, he could have someone killed if he wanted. His business was still running, and Jessica was one of his top employees. A lot of times she had to take Tiffany with her, because there were times Mrs. Parker wasn't in the mood to baby-sit, leaving her with no alternative.

"Well, since you goin' to church, you leave Tiffna heya wid me. You know that boy calls her every day. I want her to be heya when he calls. We'll meet you at church."

"No. I'm taking her with me. He can talk to her some other time." Jessica knew it was crazy to risk taking her daughter. *Tiff will be all right.*

"All right, Jessi, you actin' like the devil. I don't want no mess 'round heya betweens you two. Y'all think I'm crazy. I know you tryin' to keep that boy from speakin' to that young'un. You don't find too many fathers these days tryin' do right wid their chi'rens.

He got a "miss beauty queen." He can make another child. Jessica dared not talk smart to Mrs. Parker because, even though Mrs. Parker was an old woman, she would knock the wind out of her. Mrs. Parker didn't play.

"Aunt Emma, he can talk to her after church. I'm not trying to keep her away from him."

"You a lie, and the truth ain't in ya. Look atcha nose, it's just a-growin'. Girl, don't you know I was born one day, not yestaday? I been around a long time. I can smell mess a mile away, and you's a mess, Jessi. Now, like I said, if you go, go, but that chile is stayin' heya wid me."

Jessica couldn't argue with her. Besides, she was glad Mrs. Parker decided to keep Tiffany, because she really hated to take her when dealing drugs. She really didn't have to deliver the packages tonight anyway. The only reason she was going to leave was to spite Glen, because she was very jealous of his newfound relationship.

The last time Glen was there, Tiffany was in her bedroom watching cartoons, and Mrs. Parker was crocheting in the den. Jessica waited for the opportunity to entice him, wearing some daisy dukes and a tube top, while he was trying to fix the broken floor tile in the upstairs bathroom.

"Mmm-mmm-mmm . . . I see you still know how to use those strong hands."

Glen didn't acknowledge her, and just kept on working as if no one was in there with him.

She squatted down, spreading her legs. "Is there anything I can help you with?"

"Did you wash? You can help me by bathing. Girl, get up. I enjoyed my lunch. I don't want to throw it back up," Glen said, trying to hurt her feelings.

Jessica was offended. "I don't stink! You know you want to take a good sniff of this." She gently rubbed her crotch.

Glen didn't bother to look at her.

"Ahh, come on, baby." She got up and started massaging his shoulders. "I know you're still mad at me, but I can make it up to you." She rubbed his chin.

"Jessica, get the hell off of me! You can't make anything up to me. The only thing you can do for me is get the hell out of town and leave Tiffany here with me."

"That ain't happenin', captain. You can forget it, but you can see her every day if you want, if you come back to us and leave that tramp alone."

"Jessica, please stop begging for a butt-whipping. And, furthermore, I don't have to come back to Tiffany, because I never left her, just you. You make me sick to my stomach, so get out."

After that incident, Jessica tried her best to keep Tiffany away from Glen.

Tiffany looked forward to talking to Glen every day. She had gotten attached to him, and Mrs. Parker took notice. One Saturday when he came over, Mrs. Parker wouldn't allow him to do anything else but spend some time with Tiffany, knowing she was the real reason why he'd volunteered to help around the house to begin with.

Glen enjoyed himself playing beauty shop, Candy Land, and hide-and-seek with Tiffany. One time they'd made a mess everywhere on the kitchen table with Play-Doh, making hats out of the colorful substance.

"Daddy?"

Hearing Tiffany call him *Daddy* was music to Glen's ears. "Yes, sweetheart."

"That's not how you make a hat. You're doing it wrong."

"No, I'm not." Glen pretended to pout.

Tiffany giggled. "Yes, you are. You're supposed to do it like this." She took a small portion of yellow Play-Doh and stuck her thumb in the middle to shape it into a bowl. She then flattened a blue piece and placed the little bowl in the center. "See." She smiled.

"Man, that's a lady hat." Glen crinkled his nose. "I'm making a baseball cap."

Mrs. Parker came in the kitchen. "Lawd have merca. Who gonna clean up this mess?"

They both looked at her and then at each other and started smiling devilishly, as if they were reading each other's mind.

Glen jumped to his feet and playfully grabbed Mrs. Parker. "Get her, Tiff!"

In a burst of laughter, she tried putting the clay hat on Mrs. Parker's head.

"Get on away from me now! Y'all stop playin' around!" Mrs. Parker fussed, but she was laughing, and seemed to be having just as much fun as Glen and Tiffany.

Tiffany laughed. "Auntie Emma, you make me laugh."

"Well, thet's good, 'cuz in a minute um gon' make you and your daddy here clean this mess up." She giggled. "Y'all want some of this cake heya I made?"

"Yes, ma'am," they said in unison. "Come on, Tiff, let's get this Play-Doh off the table before you get in trouble."

"Me? You too!" Tiffany smiled.

He whispered, "Yeah, you're right. It looks like Ms. Parker can beat up a man like me."

Mrs. Parker heard him. "You got thet right."

They burst into laughter again.

Once Mrs. Parker saw they'd cleaned up, she placed the three plates of cake on the table. "So what y'all plans for the rest of the day?" she asked.

Glen shrugged his shoulders.

Tiffany blurted, "Oh, Daddy, can we go to Chuck E. Cheese?"

"Chile, you don't mind spendin' money thet you ain't got, do ya?"

Tiffany beamed. "I got some money in my piggy bank."

"I don't know, Tiff. Don't you want to stay here and watch a movie or something?"

"No. Can we go pleeease?"

Glen looked at Mrs. Parker.

"Don't look at me. She's askin' you."

"Well, okay, let's go. Mrs. Parker, do you want to come?"

"Naw, sir! Them chirens ain't gon' drive me up the wall. Y'all gon' have fun."

The very next day, at exactly 5:30 P.M., the phone rang. Tiffany ran to it, the biggest smile on her face, and yelled, "Hi, Daddy!"

Jessica cringed, saying to herself, "I hope T-Bo's plan works."

Chapter Twenty-three

"Hey, you." Lo wrapped her arms around Keith as soon as he stepped foot across her threshold. "Hey, yourself." He kissed her on the cheek, and hugged her just as tightly. "What are you doing here on a Wednesday night? Aren't you supposed to be at church?"

"What? I can't come see you on a Wednesday night? God ain't going to get mad at me for coming here instead of going to church, is He?"

Lorene playfully pushed him. "Don't get your briefs all in a bunch. I didn't mean it like that. You know what I meant. I prefer that you be here anyway." She pulled his head down to her own and gave him a kiss.

Mesmerized, Keith didn't say a word. His glance reflected adoration, with a hint of lust floating back and forth between her lips and eyes.

"Lo, who is that at the door?" Lorene's father asked from the den.

"Come on in, so you can meet my father." She pulled Keith by the hand.

"Oh, snap! He's here? He's never here when I come to visit you."

Lo smiles. "I know."

"What a minute, baby," Keith said, pulling back and peering down the hallway. "Does your daddy own a gun? He might be waiting to shoot me for coming after his daughter."

"Will you cut it out?" She laughed.

Keith sighed and looked up at the ceiling.

"It'll be okay, trust me." Lorene took Keith's hand and led him to the den, where her father was seated comfortably in a recliner, reading the newspaper. Folding up the paper, he shot a glance at Keith over the rims of his eyeglasses. "Daddy, this is Keith. The one I've been telling you about?"

"How are you doing, son?" her father said with a nod of his head.

"Fine, and yourself." Keith walked over and respectably shook his hand.

"Just fine. Have a seat."

Keith sat on the couch, opposite a floor-model TV with a nineteen-inch TV on top of it. Lo sat down beside him then locked their fingers together.

"What are you telling my daughter that got her cheesing so hard when she talks about you?" Rev. McCall started.

Keith was a little intimidated by his deep, raspy voice and the authority that Rev. McCall released with every spoken word. "Uh, only good things, sir."

"Oh yeah? What do you do for a living, son?"

"I work at Ford Motor Company, sir." Keith withdrew his hand from Lorene's and clasped his own two together.

"Oh, you do pretty good for yourself then?"

"Yes, sir."

"Lo tells me you loves the Lord." Rev. McCall rested his folded hands on his round belly as he studied Keith's face.

"Yes, sir, with every part of my being." A smile crept across Keith's face at just the thought of God's goodness.

"That's wonderful. You from these parts?"

"I live in Smithfield, sir."

"And you come all the way out here to see, Precious, huh?" Rev. McCall cut his eyes lovingly at his daughter.

Keith looked at Lo and answered without taking his eyes off her. "Yes, sir, she's worth it."

The questions went on for another fifteen minutes, until Lorene finally cut in and let her father know that she and Keith were going in the living room to talk.

"That wasn't so bad." Keith smiled

"I told you, and you panicking for nothing." She laughed.

"That's not funny. I didn't know what to expect."

"Aww, it's okay," she said, rubbing his chin.

"You didn't tell me your nickname is, Precious, precious." As she rubbed his chin he kissed her finger.

"Don't even go there. He's the only one that calls me that, and if you even try, I will not talk to you for a week."

"Well, I better not take that chance, because I couldn't bear the thought of not talking to you one day, let alone a week." Keith kissed her on the cheek. "Listen, the reason I came over tonight was because I want to take you to the beach."

"The beach? I thought it closes at sunset?"

"Naw, they have something special going on tonight. They're having different groups to sing, and dance, and later on they're having fireworks."

"Really? You're not planning on swimming, are you?"

"No, ma'am. I don't feel like being ate up by jellyfish tonight."

"You are so silly. Okay, let me tell my dad we're leaving."

In minutes they were seated in Keith's car, headed to Buckroe Beach.

Once Keith parked, he let Lorene out of the car. Holding hands, they strolled down the sidewalk toward the sand and waves.

The night was beautiful. Stars were shining brightly in the sky. Children ran up and down the beach. Folks lay sprawled across the sand, listening to people singing on the waterfront stage. Lorene and Keith really enjoyed the view. With their arms circled around each other's waist, they walked along the seashore. They stopped, and Keith stood behind her and held her around her waist.

"Mmm, this is nice," Lorene cooed.

"It is, isn't it?"

Then she turned and faced him and stared into his eyes. He stared back in silence with much love. Then Lorene finally said, "Keith, I love you."

He didn't respond. He just smiled. Then he said, "Stay right here. I'll be right back."

Leaving Lorene sitting on the sand, Keith approached a group of kids building a lopsided sand castle. After a few minutes of nearly silent conversation, he dug into his pocket and pulled a few dollar bills, handing one to each of them. Then he came where she was and sat behind her, making it so that she was sitting between his legs. Again, he held her around her waist.

"Keith, what are you up to?"

"You'll see." He kissed her on the back of her neck.

Seconds later the kids trotted over to Lo full of giggles. "Hi, Miss Lorene," they sang in unison.

Lorene smiled, though confused. "Hi."

At once the children got on their knees and started writing in the sand with a stick. One wrote Will, another wrote You, another wrote Marry, and the last wrote Me. Still giggling, they looked at Lorene for a response.

Flabbergasted, she spun quickly to face Keith, who was now holding an open ring box. In the lighting from the open stage the diamond flickered beautifully. It was a dazzling ring with diamonds made in solid fourteen-karat yellow gold. Although anxious, Keith remained expressionless as he waited for a yes or no.

Lorene got up and covered mouth with her hands. It was so wide, a fist could have easily fit inside. She kept looking at the ring, then at Keith, back and forth.

He got up and walked up close by her and asked, "Baby, I know we haven't been seeing each other a long time, and I know this is a bit sudden, but I know this is right. It feels so right. I know how I feel about you in my heart. Every time I'm with you, it beats twice as fast. Every time I see you pull on of those pretty curls on your head, it sends chills down my spine. Every time I hear you laugh, I feel strength. Every time I hear you cry, I feel a piece of my heart ripping. Every time I see you, I see me. So, baby, I'm asking you again." He bowed down to one knee. "Will you marry me?"

Lo dropped to her knees to embrace Keith and excitedly whispered, "Yes."

The children screamed and jumped for joy. Keith and Lorene kissed each other and as if on cue, the fireworks began to burst in the air.

Chapter Twenty-four

Even though it was in the end of June, today was a perfect day to move because it was only 80 degrees. Patrice was hoping it wasn't going to be one of those hotter-than-fish-grease days. With the last of her things crammed into the back seat of Glen's Mustang, she headed off to pick him up from work. As she drove she almost ran the red light, thinking about Leslie, the new employee. Patrice knew that, by Leslie working the six to eleven A.M. shift, she would notice Christina dancing in drive-thru. Patrice didn't trust Leslie.

The honk of a car horn jarred her attention back to her driving, and she slammed on the brakes. "Oh my Lord, if I wreck this car, Glen is going to kill me, if I don't kill myself first," she said to herself.

While the light was still red, she tried looking in her purse for Christina's telephone number, to warn her about Leslie. As soon as she dug her hand in her purse, the light turned green. "Why is it, every time you want to do something the light turns?"

Patrice found a parking space close to the entrance of Glen's job. She looked at the clock on the dashboard, which read 4:55. "Good. I got five minutes before he gets off. Hopefully I can find her number." She searched inside and out, and still no number.

Patrice lay her head against the head restraint. She suddenly remembered putting Christina's telephone number in her wallet. Hastily she looked, and there was the tattered piece of paper with the number on it. "Yes. Girl, I sure hope you are home."

Glen came to the car smiling. "Hey, baby." He greeted her with a wide grin.

Patrice got out of the driver side to allow him to drive. Still thinking of her potential loss of stolen income, Patrice's response was bland. "Hey."

"Baby, what's wrong?" Glen noticed right away that she had something on her mind, and that, whatever it was, it was worrying her.

"Nothing." She tried to dismiss it, but her puckered lips and crinkled forehead told a different story.

"Yes, it is. What's wrong? Did you have a bad day at work today? Did you get into it with your

mother or friends? Did I do something? Tell me,
What's bothering you?

"It's nothing you can do about it. I'll be okay."

"Patrice?"

"I'll be okay, so drop it!" she barked.

"Okay, I'll drop it."

The rest of the ride home was silent. Glen
didn't really like Patrice's attitude at the moment, but he figured she'd come around sooner
or later.

When they arrived home, without speaking,
Glen helped Patrice get the rest of her things out
of the car. He had expected to inhale the aroma
of a waiting meal, but the only sense that was
engaged when he opened his front door was an
unsightly mess of clothes, shoes, books, and
various other odds and ends spilling out of boxes
and onto the living room floor. Trying to ignore
what he saw, he took quick steps toward the
kitchen, hoping that there would be something
he could at least warm in the microwave. When
he found nothing, he felt his frustration rising,
but tried not to let it show.

"You didn't cook anything?" he asked Patrice
in a low tone.

"Glen, what do I look like? Your maid?" Patrice planted her hands firmly on her hips as she
waited for a response.

Glen was a little puzzled by her reaction. *It hasn't even been one day*, he thought to himself. He didn't want to start a fight, since he didn't know what he was fighting about.

"Do you know what? I'm just going to get something to eat right now because this apartment is too small for me, you, and your attitude. He grabbed his keys and left.

As soon as he pulled off, Patrice called Christina. Watching out of the living room window for his return, she quickly pushed the number into the handset of the cordless phone.

"Hello?" a child answered.

"Hello. May I speak to Christina?"

"Chris!" the child yelled in Patrice's ear.

"I'ma slap the hell out of you if you keep playing with me!" Christina barked. "Who is it, Tasha?"

"Oun know."

Patrice heard someone breathing on the phone. "Hello?" She crinkled her forehead. It sounded like a wild bunch of children at a daycare in the background.

"Hello?" Christina said, sounding out of breath.

"Hey, Christina. This is Patrice. What in the world is going on over there? It sounds like a jungle gym. And who are you gonna slap the hell out of? Don't make me call Child Protection Services on your ass." Patrice giggled.

"Hold on a minute. Hang up the phone!"

After someone hung up, Patrice was able to hear much better.

"Girl, you might just have to do that. My nappy-ass head li'l brother is running around the damn house with my bra on. Li'l faggot."

Patrice laughed.

"That shit ain't funny. I'ma bring them over there and let you watch these bad-ass kids." Christina slapped the back of her little brother's head as he quickly ran by her. "Girl, hold on a minute. I got to go my room for some peace and quiet." Christina saw one of her siblings on her bed watching TV. "Get out." She slammed her door shut. "I'm back."

Still hearing the ring in her ear, Patrice then asked, "And who was that screaming in my ear?"

Christina shook her head. "Sorry about that, chile. That was my big-head little sister. She's five going on twenty-five."

"Oh, look, I can't talk long. I got to tell you something before my boyfriend gets back." Patrice once again looked out the window.

"What?" Christina reached for the comb on the dresser.

"Girl, Millie hired a new girl today to work in drive-thru." Just the thought of Leslie made Patrice worry.

"And? So what? That ain't no big deal," she said as she was combing her hair.

Patrice began to panic. "Yes, it is, girl! She's going to be working your shift and find out about our dance."

"Girl, please?" Christina patted her hair in place. "You need to calm your ass down. I told you about the dance, didn't I? She may want a piece of the action too." She started switching her hips from side to side.

"I don't think so, Christina. This chick is white, and pretty at that. She's up to something. I could feel it."

Feeling frustration approaching, Christina huffed, "Whatever! I don't care if she looks like Farrah Fawcett. She ain't going to stop a good thing."

Regretting that she'd made Christina upset, Patrice said in a calm tone, "Christina, just be careful, okay."

"Girl, it will be all right. I trusted you, didn't I? Besides, I got to do what I got to do to get out of this house. My momma is worrying the hell out of me with all these stankin'-ass kids."

"How many sisters and brothers do you have?"

"Three brothers and two sisters, and all of them are under the age of thirteen. If I'm not working, she is trying to make me babysit. I got to get out of here, chile. I saw this nice apartment uptown, and the rent is reasonable. On top of that, I got to pay my pimps."

"What in the world—"

"Bills, girl. All of my pimps' names are bills."

Patrice started laughing. "Well, if that's the case, he's pimping me and everybody else."

Christina smacked her lips. "Which bill is pimping you? Girl, I wish I had it as good as you."

"You got that right." Patrice then took note of all the mess on the floor. "Girl, I got to clean up, anyway. I may not have a pimp, but my man does. So, really, I know where you coming from. You got to take care of Mr. Bill."

"That's what I am trying to tell you. So I can't worry about this new chick right now."

There was a brief silence.

"Anyway, what do you mean, you got to clean up? I thought Glen kept his place up to par."

Patrice pulled herself away from the window and tried picking up a few things. "He does. I just moved in with him today."

"Dag, you don't sound too happy about it."

Patrice was searching for space in the coat closet for her books. "I am, but, girl, he's starting to get on my nerves already."

"Already?" Christina crinkled her forehead.

"Yeah, but I've been staying here for the past two weeks. Besides that, I'd spent the night quite frequently."

Christina nonchalantly stated, "Oh, well, y'all just got to work it out."

Patrice mumbled, "Well, actually he didn't do anything. This Leslie thing was bothering me, and here I am taking it out on him."

Bam! Bam! Bam!

Christina was startled by the loud knock on her bedroom door. "What in the hell? Girl, hold on!" Christina forcefully opened her door. "What!"

"June Bug is in the bathroom tryin'a smoke toilet paper again!" Tasha yelled.

"I'ma beat the—Girl, let me go before the house get burn down, but don't let that shit mess up your relationship. We'll be all right. Bye."

Patrice heard a click then the dial tone. She had become so wrapped up in her conversation that she didn't hear Glen pull up. When she heard the keys jingling at the door, she tried to hurry up and put the phone back on the handset, not wanting Glen to think she wasn't cleaning up while he was out.

Glen entered just in time to see Patrice hang up the phone. "I hope whoever that was helped you with the issue you're dealing with right now," he said still aggravated about her unexplained attitude.

"Whatever, Glen. Did you bring me anything?" Patrice glanced at the KFC bag and drink that Glen held in his hands.

"Patrice, didn't you get off early today? You had time to fix you something to eat. If you didn't feel like cooking, you could have brought you something home from your job. And, furthermore, you knew I was going to get something to eat, you should have asked for something before I left."

"You don't have to get nasty about it." Patrice rolled her eyes. "I made plans anyway to hang with my girls tonight. I just got paid today, and I can treat myself and them for a bite to eat."

This made Glen even more furious. "How are you going to make plans without telling me anything about it, Patrice?"

"Glen, the last time I checked, I'm a grown-ass woman. Damn, do I have to let you know everything I do?"

"Yes, you do! That's just common courtesy when you're living with someone. You just don't make plans without letting anyone know."

"I just told you!"

"Yes, now you're just telling me! You made plans, Patrice. This wasn't a spur-of-the-moment thing."

"Look, you ain't gon' get me all worked up and angry before I get out." Patrice picked the phone up again and started dialing Faye's number, as she and Glen engaged in a staring contest. Patrice could see fire brimming in his eyes, but that didn't intimidate her at all.

After Patrice heard someone pick up and said hello, she knew it was Faye. "Hey, girl, do you still want to go out tonight? . . . I'm tryin'a find something to put on now . . . Yes, darling . . . Let's go to the Milky Way. You know it's ladies night tonight . . . uh-huh . . . uh-huh. Girl, you don't have to worry about that. The drinks are on me . . . What do you mean, I can't afford it? . . . Ha, ha, ha, you ain't got to joke my wages . . . Well, you know it's the least I could do, since y'all always looked out for a sister."

Patrice continued looking at Glen with an expression that said, "Yes, I'm going and there's nothing you can do about it."

"You have to pick me up. Glen is not going to let me use his car . . . I don't care how mad he get. He don't own or control me! His daughter's name is Tiffany, and my birth certificate says *Patrice*," she said, rolling her eyes away from him.

At this point, Glen was no longer hungry. He placed the food on the kitchen table and continued to listen.

"Call Lo and see if she wants to go, if not, that's fine . . . Be here at eight . . . All right, see you then." Patrice hung up the phone and headed toward the bedroom to start getting ready.

Glen followed her, staring in disbelief. "The Milky Way, Patrice? You're not actually going, are you?"

"Move, so I can find something to wear." She rummaged through a pile of clothes on the bed, and then looked in the closet. "When are you going to move your stuff out of here so I can hang up my clothes?"

Before Glen could respond, the phone rang, and he answered it. "Hello . . . Faye, can you call her back? We're talking right now."

Patrice snatched the phone from him and covered the mouthpiece. "We're not talking about anything, you are." She rolled her eyes at him. "Hey, girl . . . She wants to go? . . . Oh, so you're picking both of us up? . . . Good. Don't be late, Faye . . . uh-huh . . . okay, bye."

Glen was now more hurt than heated. "Baby, you just moved in here with me and now you're going to disrespect me like this?"

"Look, Glen, I don't want to be cooped up in the house the entire time playing wife. I told you from the beginning, I'm too young for that. I want to go out and have fun with the girls every once in a while. Is that all right with you?"

"I have no problem with you hanging out with your girls every once in a while, but I do have a problem with you not telling me in advance, and I do have a problem with you going to the Milky Way. Hell, any club for that matter!" Glen shook his head and mumbled, "Damn, you haven't even lived here a full twenty-four hours yet and now you feeding me some bullshit."

Patrice was trying to make out what he was saying. "What?"

Glen sighed. "Don't even worry about it."

"Okay, I apologize for not telling you before now, but what is the big deal about going to the clubs? That's where I met you."

"That's what I'm trying to say, Patrice. Niggers go to the club to see who they're going to take home to pump the hell out of!"

"So what you are saying is, I was just a piece of meat for you to pump the hell out of?" She folded her arms across her chest.

"I'm not going to lie. Yes, but then I fell in love. It doesn't always happen that way, and you know it."

"I'm not going to club to be picked up by men, Glen. I'm going to hang out with my girls. That's it!"

"How do I know that?"

Patrice looked at him in disbelief and said, "What the he—Look, I don't know who the hell you think you talking to, but I am not Jessica. Now if you can't trust me, then why in the hell am I here?"

"I've been asking myself that same question ever since I got home."

Patrice couldn't believe they were having this conversation, but after all, she did provoke it. She wanted to apologize and erase everything that happened, her pride wouldn't let her. Besides, she was mad as hell, especially after Glen's last statement.

"You know what? This was a bad mistake. When I get back, I'm moving out," she announced, right before slamming the bathroom door and jumping into the shower.

Chapter Twenty-five

The Milky Way was packed, and for once there were more men there than ladies. Patrice wore a black sexy mini dress that was cut out in the back, and high-heeled sandals that strapped up at the ankle, which she'd shoplifted from Club Fashions in the mall. Faye wore a black top that laced up the front to hide or show more cleavage, a pair of jeans accented by black seams, and a pair of uniquely designed black leather boots. Lo had on a soft blue tank top, a black skirt trimmed with blue lace, and a pair of plain black pumps.

As normal, Patrice, Lo, and Faye had to show their ID's. As long as you were eighteen and older, you could get in. But if you were going to drink, you had to show proof to the bartender that you were at least twenty-one. Seeing that Patrice and Faye were nineteen, and Lorene was twenty, Patrice knew how to get around that. She would always get an older person to buy the drinks for her.

That's exactly what she did, once she entered the club. She saw an older female friend and told her what she wanted. Patrice asked the girls what they were drinking.

Faye ordered the Long Island ice tea. She assumed Lo wanted her usual, which was rum and coke, but she settled for just coke instead. Patrice ordered tequila sunrise for herself. They found a round table seated for four in the middle of the dining area.

Patrice smiled. "So what's up, y'all? It's been a while since we went out."

"I know, right," Faye responded.

As they began popping their fingers and dancing in their seats, Faye blurted, "Oh, y'all, guess what happened on the bus Saturday?"

Lorene contorted. "What bus?"

"Oh, I didn't tell y'all my church had to go to North Carolina?"

Patrice said, "Hell naw, you didn't tell me. You know I like bus trips. I could have went with you. What did y'all go for?"

"The choir had to sing. It was a last-minute thing anyway. So let me tell you what happened. I overheard Sister Lisa telling Sister Veronica that she had to sing at another church next Sunday, and she was asking Sister Veronica to help her out. Sister Veronica told her she charges one hundred dollars to sing."

"What? Who in the hell do she think she is?" Patrice huffed.

"She was playing, right?" Lorene inquired.

"Girl, that's what I thought, until Sister Veronica said she'd write up a contract. So at that moment I turned around and looked her dead in the face and saw that she didn't crack a smile."

Patrice said, "I must admit, the girl does have a nice voice, but damn, that's ridiculous."

"Hold on, let me finish telling you," Faye cut in. "So Sister Lisa said, 'Now, Veronica, I don't know how you're gonna take this, but whether you be cool or come out of a bag on me, you see, it really doesn't make any difference. But it's only fair to let you know that your voice is not all that.'"

They burst into laughter.

Lorene continued laughing, holding her stomach. "No, she didn't start quoting 'Woman to Woman' by Shirley Brown, did she?"

"Girl, I cracked up laughing when she said that," Faye commented.

Patrice added, "I'm glad she did. That don't make no damn sense. If she was all that, her ass wouldn't be on the church bus going somewhere to sing. She'd be on a damn tour bus."

They laughed again.

"Lo, I couldn't believe you came out tonight, being that you're trying to live right. Not only that, you kicked us to the curb now that you have Keith in your life," Patrice sneered.

"Don't even try it. I told you that I would still hang out with y'all sometimes. And as far as Keith and I, we believe in giving each other space."

"But, *bam*, is this the first time that y'all had any space between you?"

"Come on, y'all," Lorene said. "You know how it is when you're trying to get to know someone, and, Patrice, I know you ain't talking. All you and Glen do is rock the boat."

Patrice rolled her eyes."Please . . . that boat has been anchored."

Faye asked, "Meaning?"

"He's tripping. He didn't even want me to come tonight. He acts like he can't trust me. We got into it. When I get back, I'm moving out. So, Faye, you have to wait until I gather my things. I'm going back home with Ma. No, that's all right. I'm going to Ma's house when I leave here. I don't even want to see him tonight."

Faye was relieved. "Whew! You scared me there for moment."

Patrice gave a confused look.

Faye told her, "When you said, 'That boat had been anchored,' you had me thinking that you're getting tired or bored with having sex with him and, girl, I want you to be happy in that department."

"Oh, hell naw, girl. I'll never get tired or bored with that 'wonder thunder.'"

Lorene and Faye burst into laughter.

"But for real, though, Patrice, you're being selfish once again."

"How is that being selfish, Faye?"

Faye rolled her eyes and looked at Lorene. "Lo, will you please school your girl."

"Did you let him know you were going out tonight?" Lo asked.

"What is this about letting folks know stuff? He ain't my damn daddy!"

"No, but he is your man," Lo explained. "Wouldn't you want him to show you the same respect? You know me, Patrice. I don't particularly care for people living together without getting married first anyway, but you're going to do what you want to do. You made that choice. You chose to live with him, and since you did, y'all have to come to some type of agreement when you're going to do things without each other. You coming here without his okay is not right."

Patrice became annoyed. "Well, did you tell Keith you were coming here tonight?"

"Don't get an attitude with me, and yes, as a matter of fact, I did. But if he had any problems with it, I would have told y'all I would try going some other time. Also, you seem to be forgetting one thing—we're not shacking."

"She got you on that one, Patrice." Faye smirked and then glanced at Lorene. "But what did he say when you told him that you were hanging out with us tonight?"

"Have fun."

"Give me a break! Suppose he did have a problem with it? Girl, he don't own you," Patrice said, still frustrated.

Lo covered her mouth with her left hand and slid it very slowly to her chin, to make sure Faye and Patrice caught sight of her ring. "Yes, he does."

"Oh my God!" Faye screamed. "No, you don't have a heavy rock on your finger!"

"Ooo, Lo, that is gorgeous!" Patrice said.

Lo wore a wide grin. "That's why I wanted to come out tonight. I wanted to celebrate this shining star and no more single life."

Patrice pouted. "I'm jealous."

"Don't be," Lo smiled.

"I'm serious, Lo. How come you caught a fish and haven't been fishing?"

"I told you time and time again, men are like dogs. They love a chase. If you see a big dog charging after you and you don't run, he don't want you. If you run, of course, he's going to keep running after you until he bites the you-know-what out of you."

Faye started to laugh. "Lo, I'm not used to you avoiding cuss words."

"I know, girl. I'm trying my best to stop. It gets hard sometimes. Now back to you, Patrice. You need to run, but first you got to make up with Glen. After you've made up, leave on good terms, and run like he—see, I told you it gets hard sometimes."

They all laughed.

After Patrice calmed down from laughing, she caught on to what Lorene had said. She frowned. "But wait a minute, Lo. I don't recall you ever running from Keith."

"Come to think of it, she hasn't, Patrice. Lo, sweetie, what you did is not called running. That, my friend, is trotting."

Patrice scoffed, "Shit, she didn't even trot. You never showed Keith any rejection."

"Okay, okay, you got me there, but I don't give my hind parts up as soon as a relationship starts."

"She's got a point there, Patrice."

"Faye, shut the hell up! I'm tired of you hopping from one side to another. Either you're for me or against me now, shucks!"

Faye burst into laughter.

"All right, Lo. Congratulations, girl. I'll call you," Faye said, after dropping Lorene off.

"I'm happy for you, Lo. I'll call you too," Patrice said.

Faye waited until Lorene was in the house safely before driving off. "That ring was fierce, wa'n't it?" She glanced over at Patrice then focused back on the road.

"Yes, ma'am. I'm glad it's Keith. He is so nice. She couldn't ask for anything bet—Faye! Watch out!"

A car from on the other side of the road crossed the median and was heading straight for them. Faye froze in complete fear, but the car came to a screeching halt and was just an inch away from colliding into Faye's.

Patrice was holding her chest and breathing heavily to the point of hyperventilation, and Faye was in total shock.

A drunken man got out of the car and staggered to Faye's side of the window and said, "Did

I scare you, honey?" His words came out slurred, and drool ran down the side of his mouth. His eyes were bloodshot red, and it looked and smelled like he peed on himself.

"You damn right, you scared us, you drunken bastard!" Patrice shouted from the passenger's side, practically lying in Faye's lap to look the man in the face.

"I ain't talking to you, witchee-poo."

"We ain't got to talk, but I will get out this car and kick your drunk ass!"

"Sshh. Be quiet and let the lady talk," he slurred.

"I'm all right," Faye finally forced from her lips.

"Okay, sweetie."

At that he turned and stumbled back to his car.

"Faye, you need to cuss him out, get his license plate number, and press charges. Do something. Don't let him get away with that. Is there a pen in your—"

"Patrice."

"Glove compartment? You sitting there looking retarded! You need to be writing that fool's license plate number down and report that sorry muthaf—"

"Patrice!"

"It don't make no damn sense, his black ass out here this time of night tryin'a kill somebody! I ought to follow his ignorant ass."

"Patrice!"

"What?!"

"I just want to go home."

On the way home, they were both quiet.

When Faye pulled up in front of Glen's door, Patrice held her hand and said, "Faye, call me when you get in," but Faye didn't call.

Chapter Twenty-six

Glen had been miserable all night. After Faye had picked Patrice up, he tried eating the meal he'd purchased from KFC but couldn't. He didn't have much of an appetite. He tried waiting up for Patrice so he could apologize to her, but he didn't hear when she came in because he was fast asleep.

When he got up this morning, he thought that she didn't come in at all, because he was in the bed alone. Come to find out, she was knocked out on the couch. He wanted so badly to wake her up to make amends, but he decided not to. He just watched her sleep. She was so beautiful to him.

Before leaving for work he picked her up, laid her on the bed, and kissed her forehead. He had to make it right, because everything was going so well in his life. He didn't want to screw it up now.

Now at work, he found it nearly impossible to concentrate. He was supposed to introduce himself to the new hires. He told his secretary to postpone it until the following day, not wanting anyone to see his sour attitude.

All he did was think about Patrice. He really loved her. He reflected back on the time he was looking forward to occasional disagreements, but after their little quarrel, he had to eat his words. He just wasn't a confrontational type of guy.

He ended up leaving work at midday. He would have left much sooner than that, but he had some work that absolutely needed to be done before the end of the day.

His ten-minute drive home felt like sixty minutes. When he pulled in front of the door, he didn't get out just yet because he wanted to finish listening to the song playing on the radio, "Since I Lost My Baby" by Luther Vandross. After the song played, he went into the apartment.

When he opened the door, he saw that Patrice had rearranged the apartment. The kitchen table was in the middle of the living room floor. She had pulled the end tables and coffee table in the kitchen, so there would be enough room to make love without bumping into anything. On the table were candelabra with five lit candles, a chilled bottle of red wine with two goblets, and china plate settings. The plates were filled with

Cornish hens, cabbage, and corn on the cob. The stereo was tuned to the jazz station and playing very softly.

But what really surprised him was seeing Patrice sitting at the table in a silk black gown that showed her cleavage, and a matching robe outlined with black lace. She had on furry-heeled bedroom slippers, and her hair was pinned up, leaving some hanging in the back. She looked sexy.

The only words that came out of Patrice's mouth were, "I'm sorry."

Glen then apologized to her. He blew out the candles, picked her up, and took her to the bedroom, and they ate dinner later.

Chapter Twenty-seven

Christina woke up at 8:00 A.M. She was excited about having the entire weekend off. Normally she worked on Fridays, Saturdays, and Sundays, but badly needing an escape from her mama and siblings, she'd requested the weekend off two weeks ago to go to Georgia with her boyfriend Alvin. While packing her clothes, she heard the telephone ringing. "Chris! Telephone," June Bug hollered.

"I got it. Hello?" She answered with a smile, expecting it to be Alvin.

"Hello, Christina. This is Millie."

Christina could hear her siblings playing in the background. She yelled, "Hang up the phone!"

After a few seconds of clatter, the background noise was silenced, and there was silence on the line.

"I'm sorry. Who is this again?"

"Millie. I'm sorry, Christina. I know I gave you this weekend off, but I really need you today."

"Millie," Christina whined, "you know I'm getting ready to go out of town today."

"I know, but I only need you until Patrice gets in. You can go at eleven o'clock. The breakfast rush is hectic right now, and the only person I have in here is this new girl, and Miss Wilma is in the back cooking."

"Where is everybody else?"

"Everybody called out today. See, this is why I hate when y'all get paid, 'cause y'all don't like to come in."

"Excuse me? I come to work when I am supposed to, so you can drop the 'y'all' stuff." Christina didn't feel like dealing with Hardee's today.

"I know, and I apologize. I'm just frustrated right now."

"How come Patrice can't come in early?"

"She's not answering the phone. Christina, please come in? If you come in and work from nine to eleven, I'll let you come in next Friday two hours late with pay."

"A'ight," Christina said reluctantly. "We're not leaving until around two anyway. I'll be in." *At least I'll get the chance to meet Leslie today and possibly make a quick twenty dollars.*

A half hour later, Christina pulled into Hardee's parking lot and saw that Millie wasn't joking. Cars were backed up a mile away. A few more employees had arrived, but they were from a different Hardee's. She glanced at the drive-thru and saw Leslie. Patrice hadn't exaggerated. She was a beautiful white girl, but the poor child was struggling. There were spilled drinks all over the counter, order tickets were out of order, and she looked frantic as she tried to run and get the customers' food.

Christina, however, was used to this kind of chaos. After clocking in, she pulled her uniform hat over her head and said, "I'll get the order. Just tell me who gets what next."

"Thanks," Leslie responded with a weak and humble smile.

Sure enough, Christina sped the line up in a matter of seconds. After everything had finally slowed down, she went in the back to get a pair of headsets, and then she introduced herself. "Hi, I'm Christina, and you are?"

"Leslie." She smiled again, this time with an expression of friendliness.

"Is this your first day?"

"This is my first day working drive-thru by myself. I was trained on Wednesday."

"Oh, do you like it?"

"Mmm-hmm. It's a challenge, but that ol' rotten-teeth lady get on my nerves already. She's hollering at me like I've been here for one year instead of three days."

Christina started laughing. "She's always like that. You'll get used to it. And don't pay her any mind."

Leslie looked at Christina's shoes. "Oooo, girl, you got the new Nike's. They're the bomb! Where did you get them?"

Christina was a little astonished that this white girl talked like a sister. "A & N. They were on sale."

"I can't wait until I get paid, because I have to go and get me a pair."

Christina thought, *Why is Patrice all in an uproar? But just in case she's a spy, I'll keep her busy until I make twenty bucks.* Hearing a beep in her headset, she responded to the customer in drive-thru. "Welcome to Hardee's. May I take your order please?" She covered the mouthpiece. "Leslie, do me a favor and restock the condiments. You know where everything is, right?"

Leslie nodded then immediately headed to the storage area. "Yeah. Do you want me to get the napkins and cups too?"

Christina nodded her head to Leslie. She said to the customer, "Okay, you said gravy and biscuit and a small cup of coffee?"

bothering at me b/c I've been here for one year instead of three days."

Christine started laughing. "She's always like that. You'll get used to it. And don't pay her any mind."

"... you got the new Slice's Tic ... to the touch if you didn't cut them."

Chapter Twenty-eight

Patrice and Glen lay in the bed cuddled in each other's arms, not wanting to get up for any reason. However, they had to eventually get up and go to work. They'd heard the phone ring around 7:45 in the morning, but they ignored it.

"Baby, thank you for dinner last night. It was delicious."

"And thanks for the appetizer," Patrice said with a sly grin. "It was very delicious."

Glen chuckled. "No, I should be thanking you. That was breakfast, brunch, appetizer, lunch, dinner, and dessert, baby. That was the works!"

Patrice laughed. "You are so corny."

"Try *horny*."

"Will you stop with the rhyming?"

"Okay, I'll stop but, baby, let me tell you. You never cease to amaze me. Every time we make love, it's an adventure."

Patrice was quiet.

"What's wrong? And please don't say nothing. That's how we ended up fighting yesterday."

Patrice thought about everything that Lorene had said to her last night. She loved Glen, and even though she told him that she was too young to get married, deep down within, she wanted to be his wife. She'd be twenty in four months, on November 13. She figured that it would take another year or so for her and Glen to get engaged, make wedding plans, and actually walk down the aisle. By that time she'd be old enough to say, "I do."

"Baby, I'm still moving out."

"What? Why? I thought we made everything all right."

"We did, but if you love me like you say you do, and I know I love you, we can't afford to argue then make up over and over again. We will never get the chance to grow. We'll just be going around in circles, and I don't want that. And I know you don't. Do you?"

On the inside Glen pouted. *Dag, I don't want you to go. Let's make this work. Let me apologize.* "Baby, I'm sorry about yesterday. If you want to go out with the girls, by all means go. We don't have to fight about anything."

"It's not about hanging out with the girls, and yes, we will fight. That's what couples do. If you don't go through nothing, it's not worth having."

Glen laughed to himself and shook his head.

"What's so funny?"

"It's almost like we have the same minds."

"What do you mean?"

"Believe it or not, I was thinking the very same thing just before you moved in. I was kind of looking forward to the fights. Now that we're actually fighting, it doesn't feel too good."

"I know, right?"

"So, you think it's best that you move back in with your mother, huh?"

"I would prefer somewhere else, but my momma's house will have to do, because I don't want to sleep on park benches."

"Can I make love to you one more time before you move out?" Glen began to kiss her in the mouth.

Patrice pulled back. "No, you and I have to go to work, and you're already late."

"Please. I told you I don't have to clock in. I'm on salary."

"Well, I do have to clock in, and I get paid by the hour. So, if you don't mind, please get up and take a shower."

"You're telling me to stop rhyming. Listen to you."

"I guess I'm a poet and didn't know it."

They laughed as Glen pulled away from her arms, leaving her alone in the sheets.

Chapter Twenty-nine

Mr. Bates in Human Resources escorted the new hires around the Newport News City Hall. They stopped momentarily in front of Glen's office.

"Mr. Pearson, this is Donald Purnell. He'll be working in electronics in the engineering department. And this is Cindy Featherstone. She'll be working in the Municipal Code Corporation as the support specialist," Mr. Bates said, referencing a distinguished-looking black gentleman, and a short white woman, her face covered by thick lenses that were much too big for her petite face.

Glen extended his hand for a handshake to each new employee. "Welcome aboard. Nice to meet you."

"Thank you," they said in unison.

Glen thought Donald looked familiar. He tried to place where he'd seen his dark, smooth skin, thick, round lips, slanted eyes, and wide nose.

Donald replied, "It's nice to meet you, Mr. Pearson. Say, didn't you go to New Jersey State University?"

"Yes, I did attend there. I graduated in nineteen eighty."

Donald said excitedly, "Okay! I thought you looked familiar. We went to school together. I've seen you around campus."

Glen couldn't remember seeing Donald on campus. He shrugged it off and said, "Oh, all right. It's a small world, isn't it?"

"Indeed, it is." Donald continued smiling.

Glen focused his attention on Ms. Featherstone. "Ms. Featherstone, MCCI is looking forward to having someone as bright as you."

Her eyes crossed a bit when she laughed. "I sure hope so."

It was almost lunchtime, and Glen was getting ready to make an escape, to satisfy his hunger. He heard the doorknob turn.

"What are you doing here?"

Glen was surprised to see Patrice walking in his office with a picnic basket. She wore a close-knitted dress that clung to her body and showed cleavage, and high-heeled pumps. He then focused his attention on the men in the hallway ogling at Patrice's firm, shapely buttocks just before she shut his office door. She not only brought the whiff of fresh fried chicken in the building, but a stunning sight to the men's sore eyes.

"Baby, you can't be coming by here unannounced and make me whip somebody's ass." He kept his eyes at the closed door, as if he could see the men through it.

Patrice placed the basket on the desk. "I'd called in. Faye and I had breakfast, and she let me use her car to bring you lunch."

Glen wasn't amused.

She walked around the desk where he was sitting and sat on his lap. "Aww, don't be like that," she cooed, gently rubbing his face. "I know who I belong to." She kissed him affectionately.

Glen's manhood started to stiffen. He pulled himself from the kiss. "Baby, I'm serious. You can't come here making me horny as hell on my job. It's not appropriate, especially not wearing something seductive like this." He gently touched the dress across her thigh.

Patrice was a little disappointed that Glen wasn't too happy to see her. "Dag, Glen. You can sure mess up a good thing. I thought maybe you would be enthused about my surprise visit, and appreciate lunch being brought to you for a change."

"I am, baby. You just have to prepare me for the visits. I just don't want people to get the wrong impression about my professionalism. I take my job very seriously, and I want my office to be respected."

Patrice dropped her head in defeat and sighed. "Let me go. Enjoy your lunch."

As she was getting up, Glen stopped her. "Hold up. Baby, I'm sorry."

Patrice swiftly looked at him astounded. "Okay, Dr. Jekyll, where did Mr. Hyde go?"

Glen chuckled. "I had that coming, didn't I? No, really, seeing men gawking at my lady triggered my jealously. I have to work on that." Glen tenderly rubbed her hair and kissed her cheek. "Girl, you're fine as hell."

Patrice smiled. Then she exhaled noisily. "I'm sorry. I'll warn you next time. But tell me this, do you want someone that don't nobody want but you? I know, I don't. Shucks, I love when other women check you out."

Glen gave thought to what she was saying. "That's a good point. I've never looked at it like that." He looked at the door again. "Look on, brothers, look on. This beautiful woman is mine. Let's eat, baby."

***

Glen was finished for the day. He put the stack of papers in his briefcase, and just before turning off the lights, he glanced at the basket in the corner by the window that Patrice had left in his office several weeks ago. A smile came across his face as he reminisced about Patrice feeding him the meal from Chic-A-Sea as if he was a one-year-old child. Although Glen still wished that Patrice was living with him, he was a true believer in absence makes the heart grow fonder. He hadn't seen her in three days, and the anticipation of being with Patrice tonight made him speed up his pace.

Just as he was getting into the elevator, he saw Donald jogging toward him. Ever since Donald had mentioned his college to him, Glen showed kindness, asking him to join him for lunch. Glen took pleasure in their conversation as they harked back to their college curriculum. Once he felt comfortable in Donald's presence, Glen was able to talk about other things besides school.

"Mr. Pearson, hold on."

Glen held the elevator door for him.

"Thanks, man."

"You're welcome. So how are things so far?"

"It's going pretty well." Donald panted, trying to catch his breath. "Whew! I got to exercise. The desk is making me lazy."

They chortled.

"So, you don't remember seeing me around campus, huh?"

"You do look familiar, but, man, it was so many people there. I don't even remember seeing myself."

Donald chuckled and nodded his head. "You're right about that. Say, Mr. Pearson, I'm just moving in the area. What do these Southern folks do for fun on a Friday night?"

"The usual. You have the clubs, bar, dining, and movies."

"If you don't mind me asking, what do you do?"

Glen hesitated, but after having the chance to build a rapport with Donald, he thought otherwise. "No, not at all. I normally spend time with my little girl or my beautiful lady friend, but she's crying that we need space."

"Oh yeah? That was your lady that pranced in here about a month ago?"

Glen nodded then smiled.

"No disrespect intended, my brother, but she's hot."

Glen continued to smile, remembering the conversation he and Patrice had in the office. "Thank you."

"But you know I could never understand that. They say we don't spend enough time with them, and when we do, they say they need some 'me time.'"

They laughed as the elevator coasted to the ground floor.

"That's a woman for you, man." Glen sighed.

"I know it's not proper procedure for staff and new employees to mix, but what do you say we hang out tonight, you know, get a couple of drinks? Maybe I could find me a beautiful lady friend."

Donald was absolutely correct, staff and new employees shouldn't mingle. Glen didn't want to give the impression that he was giving Donald or anyone else special privileges. The rules apply to everyone—Do your job or get fired, plain and simple. But then again, that whole theory was thrown out the window after the other employees saw Glen and Donald eating lunch together at various times. Besides, it wouldn't hurt if he had a hanging partner. Patrice does, so why shouldn't he?

"All right, man, that's cool. Let me give you the directions to the Fort National Base Club. The bar and honeys are off the chain. That's where I met mine. But if you're going to swing with me outside the workplace, you have to call me *Glen*."

Chapter Thirty

Keith had talked to Lorene on the phone until 2:00 A.M. Sunday morning. He just couldn't get enough of her. She made him feel so alive. He loved her because she walked in integrity. Keith felt complete with her. He loved her like Christ loved the church and gave Himself for it. And so he was glad he went to the next level with her. He'd asked Lorene to come to his church with him, but since she had to sing a solo at one of her father's engagements—Rev. McCall was the guest minister at one of the local churches—he asked to go with her.

It surprised Lorene for Keith to ask, because he didn't miss his church for anything. When the choir had engagements on Sunday mornings, they had to get a backup drummer.

Lorene rode with her father to church. When they arrived, her eyes lit when she saw Keith sitting at the end of the third pew. She lightly tapped him on his shoulder, and he got up and let her in.

Why do men always feel as though they have to sit at the end of the pew? Lorene whispered in his ear, "How did you beat us here?"

Keith whispered back, "Drove very fast."

They smiled at each other then focused their attention on a woman who had approached the sanctuary podium to give the weekly announcements. She wore a huge metallic gold hat that looked like it was going to fall off her head at any second, a green two-piece suit with gold buttons on the blazer, and gold pumps that looked like she'd need the jaws of life to get out of.

"Good morning, saints. So glad you came to join us on the beautiful day the Lord has made. I'm now going to read to you the weekly announcements. Okay, let's see, uh"—She put on her glasses, which was connected to a silver chain around her neck—"We are going to, uh, have a, uh, fish fry on free—I mean Friday. We need to raise some money for the, uh, building fund."

Between her stumbling over her words, fumbling with her glasses, and looking like a decorated Christmas tree, the announcements turned into what seemed like a stand-up comedy routine.

Keith laughed a little. "What in the world? How long is this announcement going to take?"

Three teenagers who sat in front overheard Keith and glanced back. Lo was trying her best not to bust out laughing, which caused tears to stream down her face.

She continued, "We are having a shut-in on, uh, next Friday night fo' the, uh, sick and shut-in. We believe in praying for the saints around here. Amen."

The congregation said, "Amen," in unison.

Keith kept nudging Lorene, making her laugh even more.

"Choir 'hearsal on Tuesday, Bible study on Winzday, and the missionary meeting on Turs-day."

Keith whispered in Lorene's ear, "Girl, you know I love you, missing my church service for somebody that reads worse than my six-year-old nephew."

Lorene smiled and playfully hit him on the leg. "That's not nice."

"I know, but it's the truth." And then Keith thought, *I sure hope Lo's daddy can preach to make up for these "mispronouncements."*

After the announcements, they received the offering. While the money was collected and counted, people started going to the bathroom and talking to each other, like they were at a social gathering. Keith couldn't understand how folks could go to the movies and sit there for two hours or more in complete silence, but couldn't hold their water in church.

Keith was missing his own church terribly. He knew he was in love, because he was willing to make that sacrifice to be with Lorene instead of going to his church. Then he noticed that Lorene kept looking around the church, as if she was in search of someone.

When what seemed like intermission was over, a minister came to the podium and introduced the speaker. "Church, I am here to introduce the speaker for the hour. Eugene McCall was born in New Orleans, Louisiana. There, he attended Washington High School. After graduation, the Lord led him to Dunimas Christian College, where he received his master's in theology with honors. After college he married Miss Ginetta Travis, and remained her loving husband until her passing. They only have one child, Miss Lorene McCall, and today he calls her *Precious*, because when he sees her, he has precious memories of the late Ginetta McCall."

Lorene's eyes widened. She whispered to Keith, "I didn't know that."

"After you hear a selection from the choir, you will hear from no other than Rev. Eugene Mc-Call."

The choir sang a poor rendition of "Oh Happy Day," the lead singer wailing off-key. In Keith's opinion, it sounded as if the entire choir had missed 'hearsal. You could tell they were so proud of their performance, because every choir member had a big grin on their face.

After the choir sang, Rev. McCall came to the podium. His deep raspy baritone voice made the speakers tremble. "Praise God."

"Praise God," the congregation replied.

Rev. McCall dropped his head and started to laugh. "Let me ask you something. When someone tells you to clap your hands, what do you do?"

A voice from the back of the church responded loudly, "Clap your hands."

Rev. McCall pointed in the direction the voice came from. "Say it again, brother. I don't think they heard you."

"Clap your hands!" the brother said much louder this time.

"You are absolutely correct. Can you all please demonstrate? Okay, now clap your hands," Rev. McCall commanded, and everyone readily obeyed.

"Good, good. Now, everyone, if you please, stomp your feet."

Everyone started to stomp their feet.

"Very good. You are catching on. Now this time I'm going to tell you to praise God. Are you ready? Praise God!"

A few folks yelled out a hearty, "Hallelujah!" while others shouted, "Glory," and other words and phrases of praise.

Rev. McCall continued, "By George, I think you got it. Come on, come on, that's it. Give Him the praise!"

The congregation continued to cry out in praise, while Lorene's father opened his Bible in preparation of bringing forth his sermon. "Yes, He is worthy and without Him we could do nothing but fail."

A few members of the congregation said, "Amen."

"I give honor to my Lord and Savior Jesus Christ. I thank God for being here. Hopefully you will receive what the Lord is going to tell you this morning, but before He does, I would like my beautiful daughter, whom I have with me today, to sing a selection." Rev. McCall found that he could preach better when the song that was sung before his sermon was anointed, and the choir that just rendered the selection most definitely wasn't anointed with olive oil, but Pennzoil.

Everyone began clapping their hands as Lorene walked to the front of the church, and although Keith had never heard his fiancée sing, his chest became swollen with pride.

She lifted the microphone from its stand. "Truly, it's a blessing to be in the house of the Lord once again. Before I go any further, I would like to ask a dear friend to bless us with his gift of music."

Someone came from the back of the church. The young man touched Keith's shoulder as he walked by. It was Dwayne. She had previously asked him to come to her father's engagement. Dwayne felt that was the least he could do. Lorene and Dwayne greeted each other with a smile as he made his way to the piano and began to play softly.

"If it hadn't been for the Lord on my side, I don't even want to know where I'd be. Truly, He is a wonderful Father which art in Heaven, and I thank Him for blessing me with an earthly father." She turned around and smiled at her dad. "He is a man of integrity, and he doesn't mind telling you the truth, whether it hurts or not. People say that I am like that." She looked at Keith. "Well, I guess the apple don't fall too far from the tree."

A few people chuckled after that comment.

"And all this time he has been calling me Precious, I had no idea I was reminding him of mom." She looked at her father again and said, "I love you." She turned to the congregation. "This song that I am about to sing is for me. Now that I have given my life to the Lord and have a true relationship with Him, I've found out that He is my best friend. So again it is for me. Now if you get something out of it, praise God, but I have to minister to myself before ministering to you."

The church said, "Amen," in unison.

Dwayne started to play the intro to the old-time hymn, "Jesus Is All the World to Me," and Lorene began singing. When the lyrics flowed from her lips, Keith started to get goose bumps. Lorene had an incredible range, and sang with power and conviction.

The parishioners began screaming and crying to God. Some silently swayed from side to side, waving hands, others rocked back and forth, mouthing, "Thank you, Jesus." It was so moving that a warm tear trickled from one of Keith's eyes. He could tell she was singing from the bottom of her heart, because she shed several tears herself.

As she came to the end of the song, she held one note so long, the praises of the people were rushing toward heaven. After she sang her last word, Dwayne continued to play a reprise, as Lorene lifted her hands and offered her own praise, when she began her fancy footwork in a dance. While her feet and legs moved swiftly going up and down but the rest of her body was as stiff as a board, automatically several members of the congregation stepped in the aisle.

Keith got up from his seat and went directly to the drums. He asked the drummer, could he play. Immediately the drummer got up and then Keith grabbed the sticks, adjusted the seat, and went for it. Putting a hurting on the drums, he and Dwayne knew how to feed from each other when it came to playing together. People began to praise God in their own way.

A man began running around the church as if he was in a marathon. While another lady hollered out, "Thank you, Jesus," rubbed her hips, making her dress go up, exposing her girdle. Another man arched his back so far, he neared a perfect backbend. Then there was another lady shaking her head so hard that her hair became a wild and seemingly unruly mess, but when she stopped, her hair went right back in place.

Rev. McCall started singing, "Yes, Lord," to calm everyone down from shouting and tearing the place up, and soon Lorene and Keith found their way back to their seats, while Dwayne remained at the piano.

Rev. McCall started his sermon. "You know, a lot of preachers ask the congregation, 'Do you have your Bibles?' Now I'm not going to ask that question, because I know we didn't go to school without our books. So, on that note, I'm going to tell you to turn your Bible to Ephesians 4:9 through 12." He read the scriptures. "Tell me something—Why do we take the time to come to church? Is it because we love to get together to praise God, or because the Bible tells us not to forsake the assembly of others? Why not forsake the assembly of others? I mean, we can look at sermons on TV now. Somebody help me. Why do we come to church? Is it because we love to hear the choir sing, the musicians play? Why do we come? We get up early in the morning to put on our prettiest dresses and our finest suits. I heard one lady tell me she comes to church because the church is a spiritual hospital, and that there is sickness in us that only God can heal. Well, that was a good answer, but He is God. He could do that while you are sitting in your living room. You know, people are funny. They give their hearts to the Lord and forget all about the ones that haven't yet. I was under a pastor one time and every time I would have a friend that he didn't know anything about, the first question he would asks me is, 'Is he or she saved?' What in the world? Jesus didn't save us to preach to save folk."

Keith nudged Lo. They glanced at each at other, remembering the conversation that they'd had on the yacht.

"What would I look like telling a mathematician that two plus two is four? He or she would think I was crazy."

Everyone laughed.

"You know, I worked on my job for many years, and there was a lady that worked with me who wore thick cinnamon crunch pantyhose, only wore skirts and dresses, never pants, and had hair nappier than sheep's wool. She carried a Bible that was the same size as what you'd find sitting on the coffee table of folks' homes."

Everyone cracked up.

"This woman wouldn't talk to anyone who didn't look like her. Rumor had it that her husband left her. I can't say I blame the man. I don't want to take a woman on my arm looking like I am helping the elderly."

The congregation laughed again.

"Now I'm not trying to tease her, but the point I'm trying to make is, it shouldn't matter what you are wearing, what matters is, you are fishing for souls. He said, 'Go therefore and preach to all nations.' You ain't got to growl at them like us preachers do, but preaching simply means proclaiming the gospel. Tell folks about Jesus. Which leads me back to the question, Why do we come to church?" He paused for a moment. "Let me help you with that. The church is a training center. The Word says, 'For the perfecting of the saints, to teach you, for the work of the ministry. He said, 'The works that I do, that you may do also, and greater works you will do,' meaning, He did the job by Himself. Now if one man can do it, surely we all can do it together as a whole. 'For the edifying of the body of Christ,' meaning, when you do this, your mind will be kept in perfect peace. With God all things are possible. When you seek Him first, all things will be added unto you. He just wants to know, Do you love Him? And when you show Him that you love Him, He will love you back. How many of you want God to love you back? I heard a man once sing, 'It's so good loving somebody and somebody . . .'"

"Loves you back," the congregation added.

"Mmm-hmm, y'all know the song."

The congregation laughed.

Rev. McCall continued, "He not only loves you back but He got your back." At this point, his preaching became mixed with singing.

Immediately Dwayne moved to the organ, playing and following every note Rev. McCall hit. Several people stood to their feet encouraging him to go on.

"You see, saints, we don't come here to show off our fashions, to hear the choir sing, or to socialize with each other. We come here so God can teach us, for He is a great teacher. The singing and dancing, and seeing folks shout, and seeing your best friend are complimentary gifts. That's free. Oh yeah, that's free. He wants to teach you how to act, when to act, what to say, and when to say it, what to do, how to do it. He's teaching us how to fish. He wants everybody to go to heaven. I said Heeeee wants every. I said eeevery . . ."

The congregation once again started to give God an undignified praise.

". . . booody to gooooo to heaven. Hell was made for the devil and his angels, not us. So learn something, saints.

Study to show yourself approved unto God. A workman need not be ashamed."

Everyone heard a repetitious stomp, only to see someone dancing again. Dwayne accompanied the individual by playing, and then the congregation joined in by clapping their hands to the beat.

Once everything settled down, Rev. McCall was able to say, "Now it may be someone in here and this is your first time coming to school and you would like to enroll, meaning, if you want to give your hearts to Him today, you are more than welcome to do so at this time."

As a few churchgoers made their way to the altar for prayer, Lorene joined her father up front and began soulfully singing a simple praise of Hallelujah.

After church, Lorene, Keith, and Dwayne stood in the sanctuary talking. Several times they were interrupted by people exclaiming to Lorene that she sang very beautifully.

A short man with a small crater face, a big nose, and with teeth hanging out of his head said to Lorene, "Sweetheart, I know the Reverend is some kind of proud of you. It's a wonderful thing to have a young daughter doing the Lawd's business. And God has really anointed you brothers to play like that. Y'all need to come here more often. It's about time we had a lively service. Y'all come again, hear?" He shook each person's hand and walked away.

"That was nice of him. At least somebody complimented me today. Folks act like we are mud pies, when somebody can put a whipping on a song with their voice, even though they didn't sing a cappella. Give us some type of credit." Dwayne laughed.

"You know they mean well. Besides, it ain't even about that," Keith said.

"I know," Dwayne lied. "I'm just playing." He did want people to tell him every once in a while that he did a wonderful job.

Keith focused his attention back to Lorene. "How come you never told me that you can sing like that?"

Lorene smiled. "I thought you knew. You hear me sing all the time with the choir."

Keith frowned. "You're right, with the choir. You've never led any songs."

Dwayne said, "I told Jean the girl could blow. I don't why Lo isn't leading anything."

"Y'all stop making a fuss. I told her I didn't want to lead anything." Lo sighed. "Too many times people try to compare me with Patrice. Patrice is the one that has the banging voice."

"Yeah, but you can tell Patrice sings like she's at the Apollo. She's not trying to give God no type of glory. She is always somewhere showing off," Dwayne huffed.

Keith and Lorene just listened as he ranted.

"I mean, every time Jean and I listen to new songs for the choir, she'll come out of her mouth, 'Oh, I bet Patrice can beat that down,' " Dwayne said, mimicking Jean. "She needs to realize that we are the Love, Joy, Peace and Deliverance Community Choir, not Patrice and the LJPD singers. You know what I'm saying?"

Keith raised his eyebrows, slightly tilted his head, and gave a you-got-a-point look. Lorene however didn't show any expression, not wanting to appear bias.

"I'm sorry, but Patrice gets on my last nerve anyway." Dwayne rolled his eyes then sighed. "Well, look, I have to go. Peaches is going to meet me at my mother's house for dinner. Do you want to come? My momma can cook a mean meal."

"No, thank you. I'm taking Lo to my place to meet the rest of my folks."

Dwayne squealed, "The rest of your folks? You mean you put that stone that the builders rejected on her finger and your family don't know her yet?" Dwayne's eyes briskly looked back and forth at the two.

Keith and Lorene chortled.

"Man, come on, only cowards take his lady to his family to get an approval." Keith gazed into Lorene's eyes. "I don't need them to help me make a decision."

"I know that's right," Dwayne said. "Well, I guess the next time I'll see you will be at choir rehearsal."

As Dwayne rushed off, Lorene yelled, "Thank you again for playing for me. You know you are the best."

He swirled around. "No problem, sweetie. I'll talk to you soon."

She turned to Keith and smiled. "You didn't mention to me that you wanted me to come over your house today."

"Oh, I'm sorry. Did you have any plans?"

"No, but I've already met your mother."

Keith playfully rolled his eyes to the back of head. "For real?"

"Shut up." Lo laughed.

"Seriously, I really want you to meet the rest of my family. Everyone is coming over for dinner today, and I want them to meet their newest family member." He rubbed her chin with his thumb and index finger.

"All right, boy. Respect the Lord's house."

Keith was startled when he saw Rev. McCall walking toward them. He was coming from the pastor's study, where the board of trustees gave him a monetary love gift.

"Sorry, sir."

"Don't be. I'm just messing. I know how it is to have a beautiful lady like this. I had one myself."

Lorene blushed. "Daddy."

"What is y'all youngsters getting ready to do?"

"We are going over Keith's house for dinner."

"Well, have fun. I'm going to Piccadilly with a few of the ministers."

Lorene glanced at the bunch that was waiting for him. She saw a nice-looking woman in her forties in a white two-piece suit and a pair of pointed, taupe-colored three-inch-high pumps. Her designer pantyhose featured a rose on the ankle. Underneath her arm she held a clutch purse that matched her shoes. She peeked over at Rev. McCall from beneath the wide-brimmed hat that covered her unmistakably dyed coal-black hair.

"Daddy, who is that?" Lorene asked without moving her lips.

He turned around and glanced at the woman, who in return glanced at him with a sexy smile. "Oh that's Sister Evelyn Smith. She's the bishop's daughter. She got the hots for me." He grinned devilishly.

"Ah shucks now. Go on, Reverend. You still got it, huh?" Keith said playfully.

Rev. McCall said with that same smile on his face, "I done told ya."

Keith joked further by saying, "Lorene, how come you didn't tell me that your pops is a player?"

Lorene stretched her eyes in slight offense. "Because he's not. Daddy, don't put any ideas in his head."

Rev. McCall only laughed. "Son, she don't know. It's just a man thing." He and Keith slapped hands.

"All right, keep it up." Lorene rolled her eyes at the two special men in her life.

"We need to get on out of here. We're holding up these folks from cleaning the church. Precious, do you need any money?"

"She'll be fine, sir. I have her," Keith said before Lorene could answer.

"I tell you, boy, you're a man after my own heart."

Chapter Thirty-one

Dwayne headed to his mother's one-story two-bedroom house. She and Dwayne had moved there from Holly Springs, Mississippi when Dwayne was only thirteen. After his father died, she wanted to get away from the place and be closer to her own mother. Once her mother was laid to rest, she had no one besides Dwayne, whom she cooked for every other Sunday. That was their way of maintaining their bond. Even though his sexuality did have a way of bothering her just a bit, Mrs. Mitchell had nothing but unconditional love for her son.

She stood in the kitchen, checking on her chicken and dumplings, and succotash. She had also made homemade biscuits and fresh lemonade with sliced lemons the way Dwayne liked it. Mrs. Mitchell was so involved with preparing the meal that she didn't hear Dwayne and Peaches come in the kitchen.

"Mmm, Mother, you sure do got it smelling good in here!"

She spun around in astonishment. "Lawd, will you look here? Dwayne, you are mighty sharp today, son."

"Thank you, Mother."

"And, Peaches, you are looking right jazzy yourself."

Peaches beamed. "Thank you, Mother Mitchell."

"Dwayne, see if you can find something in your room to put on while you eat. Get something for Peaches too. I can't have you boys messing up your fine wear."

"Yes, ma'am."

"Dwayne, just get me a shirt," Peaches requested.

Dwayne went into the bedroom that his mother still referred to as his room. She'd left everything like it was before he moved out. Dwayne even had some old clothes from when he was in high school that he was still able to fit in. He opened the closet to get a hanger for his suit, and to find something relaxing to wear while lounging around the house. Pushing past several garments, he came across his prom suit. It was a black suit trimmed with blue silk stripes down the pant leg. The suit took him back down memory lane.

***

Escorting his date, Raquel, who'd worn a blue silk dress that matched his suit, they took to the dance floor when the band began playing Michael Jackson's "Thriller."

"Dwayne, you sure can dance your ass off," Raquel said flirtatiously.

Dwayne smiled. "Thank you. You're pretty good yourself."

Mmm-mmm-mmm! Look at the bulge between them thighs. Feeling aroused, she said, "Dwayne, let's go somewhere quiet so we can talk."

Thank you. I am so bored. "That's fine with me."

As he began to lead the way to the exit, Raquel stared at his butt. *I'm gonna talk, all right— when I scream your name.* When he turned down the street where she lived Raquel said, "Dwayne, I took the liberty of renting a room. Let's go there to talk."

Lord have mercy. Girl, I'm ready to take your ass home, he thought. Nonetheless, he drove to the motel.

When she felt he wasn't moving fast enough, she pulled his hand and guided him to the room. She tried kissing him, but he was reluctant. Then she turned on some music and began stripping, but her erotic teasing did nothing for him. She even went as far as rubbing her butt against his manhood, but got no response.

Dwayne was embarrassed. He tried to do what other men do, but he couldn't. "Raquel, I don't feel too well," he lied.

"What's wrong with you?"

"I don't know. I think it was something in the punch or food. All of a sudden my stomach is feeling queasy. I think I'm going to call it a night."

Raquel became frustrated. "Dwayne, I'm not ready to leave. I already paid for the room. You can just lie down awhile until the pain goes away."

"No, I'll feel better at home." Dwayne saw that Raquel was disappointed. "Um, are you going to be all right here by yourself?

Hell no! I need some dick. I'm not wasting my money. I'll just go back to the prom and find somebody else. Maybe Damon will give me some tonight. She mumbled, "No, you can just take me back to the prom."

The next day in school she told everybody that he was a faggot, because men didn't turn her down.

Dwayne didn't even try to dispute it. He didn't know if he was one or not. All he knew about sex was what his father had taught him by force. Every time he walked down the hallway, the students would snicker. And the snickering and laughter continued into his college years, where he mainly stayed to himself, until he met Tracey.

Dwayne was at a block party, sitting alone. He saw a guy watching him. He smiled a little and turned his head in the opposite direction. Before he knew it, the same guy was beside him.

"How are you doing?" he asked.

"Fine," Dwayne replied.

"My name is Tracey, and yours?" Tracey smiled.

"Dwayne." Dwayne felt the sincerity in his smile and smiled back.

Tracey glanced at the vacant seat beside him. "Do you mind if I have a seat?"

Dwayne nodded, and Tracey slowly took a seat.

"So, Mr. Dwayne, tell me, why are you sitting here by yourself looking like you lost your best friend?"

Dwayne vaguely shrugged his shoulders.

"You don't talk much, do you?"

"I do when I have something to say."

The rest of the evening Tracey continued trying to break Dwayne's shell. Dwayne was actually enjoying his company, but he didn't know Tracey's intentions.

On the way back to his room, Tracey told him, "Hold up. I'm going that way."

Shortly after that, he and Tracey became the best of friends. Then lovers.

After a night of wild sex, Dwayne suddenly began to cry profusely. Both concerned and confused, Tracey coaxed him into sharing what had him so upset.

Tracey hadn't noticed before, but Dwayne had been an emotional wreck all day. It was the sixth anniversary of his father's passing, and he was haunted by his memory, and the details of his death.

Dwayne told him everything about his father messing up his life. He told him that some white kids had found his father's body on Halloween night. Apparently the kids wanted to have a spook party in an old house where a witch doctor used to live. They were putting pumpkins in the yard and found some fingers sticking out of the ground, like mushrooms.

Next thing you know, it was broadcast all over the news. The police questioned his mother about it. She told them nothing, because she knew nothing. She couldn't take all the talk and stares of the town people, so she moved out of town to be close to Dwayne's grandmother.

Dwayne just cried and cried. Tracey wrapped his arms around him, trying to console him. After Dwayne pulled himself together, he looked at Tracey.

Tracey rubbed his chin. "Baby, it's going to be all right. I need you to do me a favor and stop worrying yourself sick, okay."

"I'll try," Dwayne mumbled.

"Tracey is here for you now." He gently rubbed Dwayne's lips. Then he kissed him in the mouth.

Dwayne kissed him back. That was the first time he felt true love.

"Dwayne! What you doing back there?" Mrs. Mitchell yelled. "Come on and eat."

Chapter Thirty-two

Keith had so many questions for Lorene that he didn't know where to start. For one, he wanted to know more about her mother. She'd never said anything about her. He knew that she had to be a wonderful lady, especially after what Rev. McCall said about her. He also realized that she looked nothing like her father. Her father's love for her said a lot about her. You didn't find too many fathers loving their daughters like that.

On the way to his mother's house he saw that Lo was very silent, but yet she had a pleasant look. "What's on your mind?"

"I had absolutely no idea that was the reason he calls me that."

"Sweetheart, can you tell me a little something about your mother?"

She sighed a little. "To be honest with you, I don't know too much about her myself. Well, as far as her personality goes, because she died when I was two years old. The only thing I remember about her is, she used to tickle me a lot just before going to bed, and make me say my prayers."

"Why did she die?"

"Daddy told me that she had low blood. Her blood sugar kept dropping, causing her brain not to work properly. Daddy said he would always try to make her eat and drink something, because she would go without food for days. At first he thought that she was fasting, until she had a light stroke. Then she had to start taking insulin. He said she hated it. He would beg her to take it, because we needed her, but she wouldn't." Lorene paused for a moment. "Well, from what I understood, she did, but it was too late. She had another stroke and died."

"So, how did you deal with it?"

"How did I deal with it? What kind of question is that? I was only two. I can't remember." Lorene was a little irritated.

"I'm sorry, baby. I didn't mean to upset you."

"That's okay."

Keith heaved a sigh. "I mean, people just don't realize how blessed they are. I mean, if anything was to happen to my mother, I don't know whether or not I would survive."

"You would. You have me."

He kissed the back of her hand.

Lorene sighed. "Now as far as daddy dealing with it, it was rough. Even today he makes a big fuss about me not eating. He always says I need to put some meat on my bones." She tittered. "At the time I just don't be hungry."

"Now you got me worried. You do eat on the regular, don't you?" Keith looked at her from the corner of his eye.

"You're trying to be funny." Lorene laughed. "You know I eat on a regular, Keith."

"Oun know. You might be trying to keep it from me or something."

"Will you shut up, talking that foolishness," she said playfully.

Keith laughed.

After a moment of silence during the ride, the conversation resumed.

"Keith, what happened to your father?" Lorene asked, turning the tables.

"He fell off a ladder while working on the ship in the shipyard and broke his neck. We were little too, my sisters and I. It wasn't easy, but God has taken care of us."

They were silent for the rest of the ride.

Several cars filled the driveway and lined the streets in front of Mrs. Simmons' home. He had a time trying to find a parking space but finally parallel parked in front of a neighbor's house a few doors down. He opened the door for Lorene. He noticed she was a bit nervous, because her hands were sweaty.

He laughed. "Now it's your turn to be tortured."

"That's not funny." She giggled. "I introduced you to one person, not the whole clan."

"Just like you told me, it will be all right."

Hand in hand, they strolled up the sidewalk and to his mother's four-bedroom two-story brick house.

"You ready?" he asked as he inserted his key in the lock.

Lorene nodded as she held on to his arm.

He smiled at her then quickly pecked her lips. "Let's go then." He turned the knob and yelled, "Hello! Where is everybody?"

Mrs. Simmons had a beautiful home. A long hallway led to a sunken living room, just past the dining room. The dining room had two entrances, one from the hallway, the other, from the kitchen. A bar surrounded by a set of swivel stools divided the kitchen and the living room. From the living room a portion of the second floor balcony could be seen. Her bedroom was downstairs on the left of the house, and above the garage was a "frog," meaning, family room over garage.

"We use this room as an escape to a quiet place if the house is full of people."

Finally he led Lorene to the deck, which took up the whole backside of the house. Keith peered through the glass door before sliding it back, and pointed out to Lorene who everyone was. There were his mother, two sisters, a little boy, a young gentleman that looked to be one of his sister's age, and two older men. Mrs. Simmons had her back turned, cooking steak on the grill.

Suddenly Lorene felt less than confident. All of them were red like Keith. No one had a rich mocha complexion like her.

No one had noticed them standing there, until Keith pushed the door open, announcing their arrival. Everyone just looked at them like they weren't expected.

Keith said, "What a brother got to do to be noticed around here? Y'all didn't here us come in?" he barked with a smile.

Mrs. Simmons turned from the grill where she forked a few steaks around. "Lawd, I was hoping y'all were going to make it. Hey, baby." She walked over to Lorene, and they exchanged kisses on the cheek.

"How are you doing, Mrs. Simmons?"

"Girl, you got that pretty ring on your finger. You can skip the formalities. You can call me the same thing Keith calls me—Ma."

Lorene smiled. "That's going to take some getting use to."

"I know, sweetie, but you will." Mrs. Simmons laughed. "Keith, stop being rude and introduce your future wife to the family."

"I'm trying to. You come spitting on folks' face, calling it a kiss, and yapping off at the mouth first thing." He chuckled.

"Yeah, you better laugh 'cause you ain't too old to get your hind parts whipped," she joked, swatting at Keith's behind with a spatula.

He laughed. "Everybody, this is Lorene McCall, soon to be Lorene Simmons." Lorene couldn't help but notice his family's unenthusiastic response. "Lorene, this is my oldest sister Marie, next to the oldest, Carrie, and her little boy, Marcus."

In unison his sisters said a snooty, "Hello," as if they were beauty queens. Marcus was too busy worrying his grandmother for a hotdog to speak.

Keith continued, "This is Carrie's husband, Jerome."

Jerome smiled. "How are you doing?"

Lorene was glad to see a warm smile. "Fine, and you?"

Jerome continued to smile and scanned his eyes up and down at Lorene, until he caught his wife's reprimanding eyes.

"And these old potatoes are my uncles, Uncle James and Uncle Wilbert."

"Boy, who you calling an old potato? I'll take my fist and put it dead in your eye," Uncle Wilbert scolded.

Lorene giggled.

"Don't pay them any mind, baby."

"Nice to meet you." Uncle James extended his hand for a handshake.

"Yeah, it is nice to meet her, and it will be nice to get rid of him, always running off at the mouth. Keep on. You're going to be gummy like me "cause I'ma knock all of them out." Uncle Wilbert pointed to his dentures.

Keith couldn't hold back his laughter. He grabbed a yard chair for Lorene. "Here you go, baby. Take a load off. Care for anything to drink?

"Diet soda, if you have it. If not, anything will be fine."

"Girl, you don't need no diet soda, skinny as you is. Let's get her some sweet tea." Mrs. Simmons pulled Keith by the arm.

As soon as Keith disappeared into the house, Marie and Carrie dove in on Lorene. "So where did you meet Keith, Lorene?" Marie started.

"I sing in the choir he plays for."

"And you tried snatching our little brother as quick as you saw him, huh?" Carrie asked, turning up her nose as if she smelled something foul.

"No, actually he snatched me."

Carrie rolled her eyes. She already didn't like Lorene because of her dark skin and coarse hair. Carrie and Marie were very light and had straighter hair. They didn't need to relax or press it, just wash, dry, and go. Even though Lorene's hair was thick and had Shirley Temple curls, she had to maintain that by going to the hairdresser every two weeks. But Keith's sisters both had bad skin, and had more acne craters than a land mine.

Marilyn opened her mouth to spit more venom but quickly changed her mind when she saw her brother getting ready to step out of the deck again, but he seemed to be held up, perhaps by talking to his mother.

Feeling highly uncomfortable, Lorene willed Keith to come on out, but he only stood in the doorway, holding two glasses, and moving his lips conversationally. Then he suddenly moved away. Right away, Lorene decided to go inside to see what was prolonging him. She got up and said, "Let me see if Mrs. Simmons needs anything."

"Hmph!" one of the sisters scoffed behind her back, but Lorene didn't stop.

Mrs. Simmons was sweating over the hot stove. She opened the oven to pull out a pan of

hot macaroni and cheese, and blew out a puff of
air when the heat met her face. "Whew!" she exclaimed, fanning herself with a potholder.

Lorene stepped closer to assist her. "Ma, let
me get that." She took the potholders from Mrs.
Simmons' hands. It felt strange saying *Ma*, because the last time she'd used that word she was
two, and she couldn't remember saying it then.

"Ahhh, listen to her calling you *Ma*," Keith
teased.

She turned around after placing the hot dish
on the counter and saw Keith leaning against the
wall. "And where have you been?"

"I'm sorry, baby, but the bathroom was calling
my name."

She squinted her nose. "Nasty."

He shook his head from side to side. "Nature."

"Don't even start no lovers' quarrel 'round
here," warned Mrs. Simmons. "Keith, call everybody in the house so we can eat. I'm hungrier
than two elephants."

"Yes, ma'am."

Everyone came in, sat in the dining room, ate,
talk, and laughed. Like every family, they talked
about the good old days. Mrs. Simmons had Lorene cracking up, talking about the things Keith
used to do when he was little. She told them
about the time she took him to the doctor when

he was three years old. The doctor gave him a big piece of jaw-breaker candy. The candy was so big, it made Keith look like he had the mumps.

The nurse told him, "You're going to get lock-jaw."

Keith didn't say anything. He just looked at her with a frown on his face.

She said it again, "You're going to get lockjaw."

Keith thought the nurse said, "I'm going to knock you in your jaw." So, he told her, "I'ma knock you in your jaw."

Everyone hollered. Marie and Carrie just smiled a little. They weren't saying much at the table.

As plates were emptied, refilled, and emptied again, mostly everyone began to move toward the den to watch TV. Carrie and Marie cleared the table and prepared to clean up.

"Ma, where is the dish detergent?" Lorene geared up to help.

"It's under the sink on the left, but I don't want you in here getting in my way." Mrs. Simmons puckered her brow. "Go on with Keith, 'cause I don't want him starting no mess with Wilbert."

Keith took her to the frog. Taking a seat on the futon, he grabbed Lorene's hand. "So, what do you think?"

"Think about what? Your family?"

"Yes." He chuckled with an expression that said, *What else could I be talking about*?

"Your Uncle Wilbert is hilarious, and so is your Uncle James. You know I love your mother. I think I'm going to like calling her Ma, although it's new to me. Your brother-in-law is nice too. Little Marcus, well, let's just say, kids will be kids." Lorene paused, measuring her next words carefully. "Now, your sisters, they don't like me."

"What makes you say that?"

"I can just tell."

"They don't mean any harm, that's just their way. They just have to warm up to strangers. You'll get used to them, and before you know it, y'all will love each other like sisters for real."

Although far from convinced, Lorene replied, "I guess you're right."

"Do you want to watch a movie?"

"Yeah. What you got?"

Keith walked over to the TV stand and rambled through a collection of videotapes. "Let's see, we got *Rambo*, *Rocky I* through *V*, *Body and Soul—*"

"Ooo, I love that movie. Put that one in."

"*Body and Soul*?"

Lorene nodded with a smile.

Keith slid the tape into the VCR then sat close to Lorene again, draping his arm around her shoulders, and she lay her head on his. Quietly they began to watch the movie.

When Syreeta and Billy Preston began singing "With You I'm Born Again," Keith and Lo looked in each other's eyes and gazed lovingly, as if the song was written just for them. Their desire for each other didn't have to be spoken.

As Billy sang, Keith couldn't help but pull Lorene into his arms and kiss her passionately. His hands found their way to her full thighs, while her hands traveled up his chest then caressed his face. It didn't take long for their temperatures to rise, and reluctantly, they pulled away from each other to come up for air.

"We got to hurry up and get married, because I'm on fire right now, and this futon is about to become a bed," Keith whispered.

"I'm burning up too. Let's go, because I don't want us to do anything that we will regret later."

Keith nodded his head in agreement then led Lorene back downstairs.

Chapter Thirty-three

Once Glen got out of the shower he heard the phone ringing. "Whoever that is have to wait. I'm not dripping water all over the place." After drying himself, he heard it ring again. "Hello?" "Good morning," Patrice sang. "Good morning. How are you doing?" "Fine, and yourself?"

"Other than missing you, I couldn't be better." Although Glen was pleased to hear Patrice's voice, he didn't have much time to talk to her and quickly tried to find out the reason for her call. "What's up, baby?"

"May I use your car today? I want to go shopping."

Trying not to drop the phone while he clothed himself, he said, "You're not going to work?"

"Yeah, I want to go when I get off."

Glen wanted so badly to see Patrice. "Why don't you wait till I get off so we can go together? I can stand for some new ties," he said, trying to decide which tie will go better with the cream shirt he had on.

No! I don't want you to see me stealing, she thought.

"Baby, I can't wait that late to go, because Ma wants me to rearrange her bedroom later on this evening," she lied.

"Oh, okay. How is she doing, by the way?"

"Fine."

"That's good." Glen glimpsed at the clock and sighed. "Okay, it's seven twenty now, so be ready in twenty-five minutes."

"Okay, I love you."

"Love you too."

Patrice saw Glen through the kitchen window as he pulled up, and immediately went outside and hopped in the car. She reached over and gave him a kiss.

Glen noticed she still had on her nightclothes. "I told you to be ready."

"I am. I don't have to be dressed this early."

"Patrice, suppose something happen between here to work? Girl, you better start wearing something decent when you leave the house."

She waved it off. "Please . . . it'll be okay. I'm coming straight home."

After pulling up in front of City Hall, Glen reached over and gave Patrice a kiss again. "Baby, please be back at five."

"Sure thing."

She worked her regular shift. Hardee's had a buy-one-get-one-free special. Drive-thru was so busy, she had to have some help, but that didn't stop her from dancing.

After her shift was over, she counted her drawer. It was one hundred and forty five dollars over. She danced. As she hurried to stuff the money in her bra, she saw one of the cooks, Miss Wilma, coming in to work, walking as if she was in a lot of pain. Patrice shoved her empty till toward Millie and stopped to talk to Miss Wilma before leaving.

"Miss Wilma, what's wrong with you?" Patrice prepared herself for an earful because Miss Wilma was the type of person that always sang the blues and didn't mind singing for whoever would listen.

"That husband of mine, he's so mean to me. I told him that I didn't feel like going to work today, and he said you better get your ass up and go to work. You know, we got bills to pay. I told him that my stomach was hurting. Then he punched me in it and asked, did it feel better?"

"Miss Wilma, you need to call the cops on his trifling ass."

"Naw, I'm pretty used to it by now. Besides, that wa'n't nothing but a love tap."

Patrice felt so bad for her. Here it was she had a man that told her she didn't have to work and treated her like a queen, while Miss Wilma's man acted like he's a hard taskmaster whipping a runaway slave.

"Well, if you need anything, let me know."

"Okay, sweetie, you have a good one."

Patrice left and drove straight to the mall, headed for Montgomery Wards. She was happy to see it was very busy. That way the sales associates would be distracted. She saw a designer dress on sale for only fifty dollars, which she didn't plan to pay. She spoke to the dress as if it could actually hear her, "I'll be back for you. Let me find something that matches."

Leaving the dress, she browsed through the jewelry department, where she spotted a silver necklace and earrings set. She picked it up and acted as though she was looking for another set of jewelry. Coughing and bending over, Patrice skillfully dropped the jewelry in her purse. Then she picked up another set before heading to the shoe department, where she found a pair of high-heeled black sandals priced at forty dollars.

Normally she would put each shoe underneath her arms if she was wearing a coat but it was summertime. So instead of stealing the shoes outright, she switched the price with a less expensive pair, bringing the price down twenty dollars.

Satisfied with her accessories, she went back to the woman's wear and put two of the same dresses on one hanger and asked the sales associate if she could try the dress on. When she went into the dressing room she hurried up and put one dress on underneath her clothes and came out with the other dress in her hand. She told the sales associate that it didn't fit. She paid for the shoes and told the cashier that she changed her mind about the jewelry.

Right before leaving, she heard someone yell, "Miss!"

Patrice's heart stopped. *Oh shit! Oh shit! Oh shit!* She couldn't think quickly enough. She wanted to run like hell but decided against it because she knew it was all over.

The security guard ran toward her. "You dropped your keys." He smiled.

Patrice almost fainted. She was barely able to say, "Thank you."

Once she got in the car, she pulled tissue from her purse and wiped the sweat off her forehead.

Then she did her calculations. "Let's see, I stole $145.00 from Hardee's and I went shopping and got a $50.00 dress, $40.00 shoes for only $20.00, and $35.00 jewelry set. I saved $105.00. And I made $20.00 from working today. Mmm, let me see, that's $290.00 I made today and only spent $20.00. That's pretty good for one day's work."

She smiled all the way to Glen's job, planning to take him to dinner with her extra cash.

Chapter Thirty-four

"Jessica, put her on the damn phone. I'm tired of messing with you!" "I'm serious. She's asleep right now," Jessica responded nonchalantly.

"She ain't 'sleep! She always waits until I call her! Now put her on the phone before I come over there and smack your ass!"

"Glen, calm down. The girl is 'sleep. I ain't lying." Jessica glanced out the window into the backyard, where Tiffany was trying to learn to hula-hoop. If she had anything to do with it, Glen would never see Tiffany again.

Glen slammed the phone down in Jessica's ear; he knew she was lying. Right away, he called his lawyer friend, John Henderson, to find out what he had to do to get full custody of Tiffany. Glen listened very attentively, and jotted down John's advice. After listening to John, and learning that the process would take some time, he became very angry, because he wanted his daughter as soon as possible.

And to make matters worse, Patrice wasn't there with him tonight to help him cool off. His way of cooling off was dipping his stick in Patrice's honey. Frustrated and looking for relief, he called her. While waiting for someone to answer the phone, Glen couldn't help but to rub his manhood.

"Hello."

"Baby?"

Patrice smiled. "Hey."

"I need you tonight."

"Nope."

"Please? Damn, Patrice, I haven't seen you two weeks. I need you, baby."

Patrice sighed. "Glen, what did we talk about?"

"We talked about not living together until the time is right. We didn't say anything about not getting our freak on."

Patrice was hot for him too, but she had to run like Lorene told her too. So she lied and said she was on her period.

"Why you didn't tell me that in the first place?"

"Because I love to hear you beg." She giggled.

"You are not right." He pouted.

"I know, but I still love you."

"I love you too." Glen continued rubbing his testicles. It felt like they were about to explode. He whined, "Come on, baby." He began to squeeze his loaded organs. "Well, since you're on your period, can you at least su—"

"No! I'm not going to suck your dick!"

"A'ight. I'm sorry. Dag, you don't have to get hostile."

She smacked her lips. "I got to go. Ma wants me to scratch her scalp for her."

"You mean to tell me you rather scratch dandruff out your momma's head instead of make love to me?"

"Bye, Glen."

"A'ight. Love you."

Glen had to do something. He just couldn't sit around the house. Maybe he should just drive to Mrs. Parker's house. As much as he wanted to hear from his little girl, he wasn't up for the drive.

Then he thought about giving Donald a call. They'd hit it off very well the other night at the club. Donald ended up leaving with a fine woman. When he saw Donald earlier at work they'd talked very briefly. Donald told him he was going to see his new lady friend tonight, hoping she was willing to spread those telephone poles. The girl he met was five feet, eleven inches. Good God Almighty, the girl got legs like the Twin Towers.

Glen said to himself, "I know he's riding that giraffe." And so he thought he shouldn't bother him. *Maybe I should give Debra a call.* "What the hell am I thinking? I can't cheat on my baby." Defeated, he got in the shower and look at his limp, wet penis and said, "Okay, buddy, I guess it's just you and me tonight." Taking his manhood into his hand, made slippery with soap, Glen did the job himself.

Donald had been talking to Lisa ever since he'd met her Friday night at the FNB Club. He'd asked her to dance and found that she could move her body like a professional gymnast. He thought, *If she can move like this on the dance floor, what in the world can she do in bed?* He was willing to find out tonight and jumped at the invitation to go up to her apartment when he took her home. Absorbing the décor of her home, he concluded that black and gold must be her favorite colors. He was trying to be a gentleman, to sit and talk with her, but after their first glass of wine, she made her move.

"I want to sex you up."

Donald stretched his eyes in both surprise and lust. "Do you?"

Lisa started to undress right there in front of him, peeling away her blouse slowly, her tongue hanging out of her mouth.

"You don't want to do this in your bedroom?" Donald asked, his erection growing in his pants.

"Oh, we will."

She stood in front of him completely naked and started to undress him, but he anxiously undressed himself.

He easily slid inside her, once she guided him to her spot. "Dag, baby, did you squirt a whole bottle of lotion in you?" he asked, referencing her wetness.

She ignored his question and began riding him like she would a black stallion. Then she got up and lay on the floor, opening up her long legs for him to enter.

Donald did just that. Deep inside of her, he started rotating his body in a circular motion like he was stirring a pot of soup. Then he put her legs over his shoulders and started to speed up. Donald had those long legs flying every which away, running into her like a freight train.

"Ooooo, Donald! Yeessss! Ah! Ah!"

"Yeah, baby, yeah, baby. Does it feel good to you, baby?"

"Yes!" She felt the freight train come to a slow halt.

"Aw, man, that was good, baby! You know what you are doing!" Donald hollered, flopping down beside her.

Lisa turned her back to him and kept silent.

Donald put his arm around her waist and asked, "What's wrong with you?"

She shook her head from side to side.

"Don't even try it. Don't lay here acting like you didn't want to do this. Y'all women are a trip. You give your goodies away all early and expect us to respect you in the morning."

"You can leave now."

Donald didn't want to do that. He was living at a cheap motel, which was siphoning his money every week. His plan was to get a woman with her own place, give her a couple of dollars to help out with the rent, and get all the free coochie he wanted. Although he didn't respect Lisa, he didn't want to go back to the roach motel, so he had no other choice but to sweet-talk her.

"Baby, you know I'm just playing. Shoot, as good as this stuff is"—he stuck his hand in between her legs from the behind—"I don't have any choice but to respect you, with your pretty self."

"Then why did you say that then?"

"I just wanted to see where your head is at. A man knows a good woman when he sees one." *You ain't one of them.*

She turned to him with a half-smile. "You think I'm a good woman?"

"Yes."

"Ahh, you are so sweet. Come here." She planted a kiss on his lips.

After Donald and Lisa showered together, they went into the living room to watch TV. Then she went into the kitchen for a minute and returned with a bowl of butter pecan ice-cream.

Taking a seat beside him, she began to spoon-feed him the ice cream, but noticed that his mind seemed to be elsewhere. "What are you thinking about?" She wiped the corner of his mouth.

Donald's face was expressionless. "This guy on my job."

"Who? Mr. Pearson?"

He broke out of his trance. "Yeah. How did you know?"

"I saw him with you at the club."

"Do you know him?"

"I know *of* him. I've seen him from time to time on the job." Lisa was done with the ice-cream and made her way back into the kitchen.

"What job? You work at City Hall too?" He yelled making sure she heard me.

"Mmm-hmm. I'm the City Treasurer's administrative assistant."

Get out. I'd stroke a gold mine. Oh, I know I'm going to keep you around. Talking about killing two birds with one stone, you could kill three—providing shelter, satisfy my sexual needs, and help destroy Mr. Glen Pearson. "How come we never seen you?"

Lisa returned to the couch. "Because my office is way in the back. I hardly ever get to see anyone."

"Small world." Again Donald went back into his trance.

She nudged his leg with hers. "Why are you thinking about him?"

He was silent.

"What, Donald?"

"Can you do me a favor? Naw, that's all right. I don't want you to jeopardize your job."

"What?"

"Never mind. Sorry I brought it up." Donald could really use Lisa's help in bringing Glen down, but how?

Glen called Patrice after getting off work. He was able to talk her into coming over for a few hours where he planned to seduce her. When they arrived at his apartment, he had Patrice wait in the hallway for just a minute while he lit several candles all over the bedroom.

Patrice saw the romantic glow as soon as she stepped foot inside. "What is this?"

"I want to have a romantic evening with my girl. Is anything wrong with that?" He took her by the hand and led her down the hallway.

"Glen, this is nice, but I'm not in the mood," she said, withdrawing her hand from his.

"Patrice, are you cheating on me or something?" he asked point-blank.

"Glen, why are you asking me that stupid question? You still don't trust me, do you? I told you, we need to chill out awhile."

He came closer to her and wrapped his arms around her and started kissing her on her face and neck. "I understand that but, baby, I need you. I need to be inside of you. I need your love."

The softness of Glen's sexy lips was beginning to make her moist and weaken her defenses. *That damn Lo. It's easy for her to say run. She doesn't know the benefits of stopping to take a water break.*

Reluctantly, Patrice pulled away, but Glen did the very same thing he did the first night they'd met. He began forcing her to the bedroom.

"Glen, I said no!" she shouted, shoving him back toward the living room.

Glen was utterly confused by Patrice's actions. "What the hell is your problem?"

She looked at him with evil eyes, sat on the couch, and buried her head in her hands.

Glen sat down beside her and started rubbing her back. "Baby, I'm sorry, but can you please tell me why we can't make love every now and then?"

Patrice wiped away a tear as she sighed and looked at him. "I'm tired, Glen. I'm tired of giving myself to every Tom, Dick, and Harry and then end up being alone. I love you, I really do. I want you to be in my life the rest of my life, but that's not going to happen if I keep giving you free milk."

Glen pulled her into his arms, leaned back on the couch, and rubbed her shoulder. "Baby, I asked you, did you want me to be your husband. You're the one who said that you were too young."

"I know, but just because I'm too young don't mean I should keep giving myself to you until I'm old enough."

Glen knew she was right. He really loved Patrice. Something had to be done. He was so caught up in his thoughts that he didn't even realize that Patrice had gone to use the bathroom.

Moments later she came around the corner completely naked. Immediately Glen's manhood began to stiffen. He hadn't seen Patrice's flawless body for so long that he continued to stare, starting at her feet and working his way up toward her face. Then he realized that her eyes were blasé.

"This is want you wanted, right?" she said just above a whisper.

Glen got up and guided her to the bedroom, reached into the closet and grabbed his bathrobe, and put it on her. He kissed her forehead. "Not like this."

Chapter Thirty-five

Glen had an appointment with John Henderson, a family attorney, to discuss getting Tiffany for good. He was tired of playing phone tag with his daughter. Besides, Jessica wasn't really providing for her, Mrs. Parker was. He wanted a real family and was determined to get it. He'd come to this conclusion after talking to Patrice last night. He really wanted her in his life too.

John was on the phone with a client. He saw Glen at the door and waved his hand for him to come in.

"All right, man. I need you to take care of that as soon as possible... Okay . . . Okay. Take it easy." He hung up the phone. "Glen, my man, how's it going?" John got up and shook Glen's hand.

Glen blandly responded, "It's been going good."

John gestured for Glen to have a seat on the plush sofa beside the office door. "So, did you manage to take my advice since the last I talked to you? Because I see a bit of disturbance on that handsome face of yours." John rubbed his chin. "You know, we can't let nothing stress the countenance."

Glen was able to muster up a laugh. "Man, you are still crazy."

"You know it." John reached for his coffee mug. "Talk to me."

"Man, it's crazy. I need you to tell me what I need to do to get my baby girl ASAP."

"Well, that's what I'm here for. You know, a lot of fathers never get full custody because they never ask for it. So, at least, you're heading in the right direction. Well, first you have to go to domestic relations and file a petition. They want to know what kind of custody you are seeking."

Glen quickly responded, "Full."

"The court is going to serve—you said her name is Jessica?"

Glen cringed at the sound of her name. "Yes."

John chuckled. "That bad, huh?"

Glen sighed. "You just don't know."

"And I don't want to know. Got enough drama of my own. Well, they are going to serve Jessica a notice." He sipped his coffee. "Mmm, that's good. I'm sorry. Where are my manners. Did you want a cup?"

"Naw, I'm a'ight."

"Okay. Now if she doesn't show up for court, the court will delay the case. However, if she does, they're going to ask her, does she have any opposing comments."

Glen leaned back. "Like what?"

"I don't know. That all depends on what kind of skeletons you got in your closets. And if you do have some bones in there, man, she's going to tell them anything and everything to drag you through the mud."

The phone rang. "John Henderson . . . ah . . . let me call you back I have a client right now . . . all right . . . bye." He continued, "First, let me ask you, are you paying child support?"

"Yes."

"Good. Is it court-ordered, or do you pay her voluntarily?"

"Voluntarily."

"Checks or cash?"

"Checks. They were being sent to her in Jersey, but after she moved here, I understand that her mother sends it to her. Jessica probably changed her address at the post office by now."

John grimaced as he listened attentively to Glen. "Now, whose mother you sent the checks too?

"Jessica's mother, but what I'm saying is, I was sending the check to Jessica, but her mother is sending it to her."

"I see. Well, you do have the check receipts, correct?"

Glen nodded.

"Mmm-hmm. So, what you are saying is, you are paying child support without court order?"

Glen nodded.

"Man, this looks good." John smiled then leaned back in his swivel chair. "Well, so far you are on the up and up on things, huh?"

"Absolutely."

"Good. Next, you have to make sure that you have a suitable place for your daughter to live in. Do you live in an apartment or house?"

"A one-bedroom apartment."

John frowned again. "Move. Get you a bigger apartment or a house. Do you have a lady friend that you may be sharing the place with? Because if you do, move her out."

Glen was glad that Patrice had already moved out, sparing him the trouble of trying to get her out now.

"Let me ask you something. I know I said just a minute ago that I don't want to know your drama, but do you think Jessica is an unfit mother?"

Glen thought about the various times he had been over to Mrs. Parker's house. He came up with nothing. He shrugged his shoulders and shook his head. "Not that I know of."

"Well, I'm going to say this only because you are my dog. If you can get some concrete evidence that she is unfit, trust me, you're in there for sure."

Without hesitation, Glen bought a newspaper and began searching the classified for real estate. He was pretty sure he had a good chance of winning custody. He'd planned on getting a house one day, but he never anticipated getting one this soon. Now that he had two beautiful girls that he wanted so much to take care of, he had to do what needed to be done.

A home in Yorktown caught his attention, one with a master bedroom that featured a bathroom, sauna, and two walk-in closets, and three other bedrooms. Glen knew Patrice wouldn't have to complain about closet space, with all the clothes she owned. Besides a kitchen, dining room, and living room, the house also had a fireplace, a playroom, a utility room with washer and dryer, an attic, a basement, and a pool. He circled it and gave the owner a call to make an appointment to view it. Then he thought he'd call Patrice and ask her to ride with him.

***

Glen smiled, surprised to see Annie Ruth open the door. "How are you doing, Annie Ruth?"

"Fine, and yourself? Come on in." Mrs. Russell continued cutting potatoes at the kitchen table. "Patrice! Glen's here! Have a seat, Glen. Ain't no telling when she's coming down. These young girls today act like they are getting ready for ball when they know their man is coming."

Glen chortled. "You got it smelling some kind of good in there. What are you cooking?

Annie Ruth laughed. "Pork chops, and fried potatoes and onions. You are welcome to stay for dinner."

"I may take you up on the offer."

"It will be ready in another hour. Where y'all headed?"

"Mmm, I don't know. I haven't seen my baby in a while. I just want to take her for a ride."

"Your baby. Y'all are something else. Ain't no babies 'round here. I'm not warming milk and changing diapers." She giggled.

"You know what I mean. You have never called Mr. Russell *baby*?"

"Now, Glen, I like you. Don't mess around and get cussed out."

Glen burst into laughter.

Patrice finally came downstairs. "What are you laughing at?"

"Your mama is a trip. I'm getting ready to get cussed out." Glen continued laughing.

"Why? What did you do?"

"I'd ask her, did she ever call your daddy *baby*."

"Yeah, you are looking to get the black smacked off you. Don't bring his name up, for God's sake. She despised him. I still don't know how I got here today."

They all laughed.

Glen gave Annie Ruth a hug. "I'm sorry. Is the dinner offer still open?"

She scoffed. "Yeah, I guess. Just don't mention the enemy name no more."

"I promise. We'll be back."

Glen opened the car door for Patrice, and then he grabbed a bag out of the trunk. Once he was in the car, he gave it to her. Inside was an I-miss-you card.

"Aww, thank you, baby."

"So how have you been doing?" Glen kissed the back of Patrice's hand.

"I've been doing okay." She smiled while looking out the window.

"I missed you, you know." He kissed her hand again and caressed it.

Then she looked at him and whispered, "I miss you too." She focused her attention out the window once again. "May I ask, where are we going?"

"Mmm, nowhere in particular. I just want to take you for a ride through the county."

Patrice crinkled her nose. "Do you mean *country*? Talking about a lot of trees, good gracious."

"What? You don't like the country?"

"Of course, I do. What I meant is, the trees are so beautiful, and it's so peaceful."

Glen was glad to hear her say that. "Would you do me a favor and get that yellow piece of paper in the glove compartment for me?

Patrice rambled through the papers. "Got it."

"What's that address on it?" Glen studied the houses as he drove by them.

"Forty-seven Ivy Neck Road. Whose address is this?"

Glen acted like he didn't hear her question. "Let's see . . . forty-one . . . forty-three . . ."

"Glen, where are we going?"

Glen still ignored her. "Forty-five... forty-seven." He pulled in front of the two-car garage. "We're going home."

The house had dark yellow sidings, and a large porch in front and back.

Patrice's eyes beamed. She yelled, "Are you serious?" She didn't wait for his response. She hurried and got out of the car then circled the house.

Glen tried to follow her, but she was moving too fast.

She then asked, "You bought this?" and ran to the front porch.

Glen chuckled then joined her. "Not yet. I wanted to see if you liked it first."

"Do I like it? Baby, I love it!" She kissed Glen passionately. Still overly excited, she peeked in the windows. "Let's go in. Do you have a key?"

Glen laughed. "Calm down, Patrice. No, I don't have a key. I made an appointment with the realtor for tomorrow, and then we can go inside, okay, but right now I need you to calm down."

"Okay, okay, okay, I'm calm." Patrice smiled, showing all her teeth. She looked up at the house at the beautiful windowpane, and then ran off the porch, jumped up and down and then screamed, "Ahhhh! I'm sorry, baby. I can't calm down! I love it!"

Before Glen knew it, she took off, running around the back again. Glen shook his head and sighed. "Lord have mercy."

Chapter Thirty-six

Glen and Patrice took off so they can meet the realtor at 2:00 P.M.

They finally had the chance to see the inside of the house. The first thing they noticed when they opened the door was the shiny hardwood floor. After exploring the rest of the home, and finding out the owner didn't exaggerate with the detailed description, Glen's mind was made up.

"So are you ready to become a homeowner, Mr. Pearson?" the realtor asked.

Glen smiled at Patrice. She had that same beam in her eye from yesterday.

"I believe I am." Patrice kissed Glen affectionately, the kiss lasting quite some time.

"Uh, do you guys need a moment alone?"

They looked at the realtor and burst into laughter.

"We're sorry. As you can see, my lady is overwhelmed."

He smiled, "Yes, I see. Well, let's get started on this paperwork."

After Glen signed his last signature, the realtor said, "Congratulations."

Patrice smiled the entire way Newport News. When she saw that he was taking her to her mother's house, she said, "I want to stay with you tonight."

"Are you sure?" Glen didn't look at her.

"Yes, I'm very sure."

Patrice was so happy about the house that she wanted to celebrate with Glen, and so she gave in. She thought that since he'd been patient with her, she'd let him fulfill his sexual fantasy with her.

"Damn, baby, if I would have known you can do magic like that in bed, I would had bought a house along time ago. I need to make a doctor appointment so he can check my heart because it hadn't slowed down yet."

She cracked up laughing. "Shut up. You are so crazy."

"Coochie like that will make a nigga crazy."

Laughing still, she hit him with the pillow. "I'm getting in the shower. Care to join?"

"Hell no. I'm trying to get this heart rate to beat at its normal pace." Glen lay on his side and closed his eyes.

Patrice started singing in the shower. After she was done and returned to the bedroom, she found Glen in the same position she'd left him. He appeared to be asleep. She tried to maneuver around the room quietly without disturbing him.

Glen slowly turned his head toward her. "You have a beautiful voice, baby," he said just above a whisper.

"You scared me. I thought you were dead." She giggled. "But thank you."

He finally managed to pull himself out the bed. "Whew! I needed that rest." He smacked Patrice on her behind. "You're bad, girl! Make a brother want to press charges against you for attempted murder."

She laughed. "Baby, did I leave my black shoes over here?"

He chuckled. "Which pair? You have so many."

"The ones that criss-cross around my ankles."

Glen looked behind the bed and pulled out a pair of shoes. "These?"

"Yes, thank you. I want to wear them to church tomorrow night." She put the shoes by her purse to take home.

"You got to sing?" Glen rummaged through the dresser drawer to find a pair of briefs.

"Yup."

"I got to give it to you, you sound good. Does the whole choir sound as good as you?"

She smiled. "What kind of question is that? Besides, you've heard me sing before."

"I know, but not like that. You know a lot of people that sing in the choir really can't sing."

"And how would you know? When was the last time you stepped foot in somebody's sanctuary?"

Glen wanted to get back at her for that comment. He took the talc powder and squirted it all over her.

"Boy!"

He cracked up laughing and ran to the bathroom and locked the door.

"Oh, I am going to get you back! Now I got to take a shower all over again. Get on my nerves!"

Glen kept laughing.

"Uh-huh, go on, get your laugh out. I am going to see how hard you laugh when I pay your butt back."

He calmed down a bit and turned on the shower. He unlocked, crack the door slowly and then peeped around the corner looking for Patrice, to see if she was ready for her vendetta. "Patrice! Don't play."

She pushed the door slightly, knocking him back. "Boy, ain't nobody thinking about you. Move so I can take another shower. You get on my nerves, with your big head self."

Glen chuckled. "Which one?"

Patrice playfully rolled her eyes. Glen got in first then took Patrice by the hand to help her in.

"Glen, I didn't tell you this when we first met, but I sing with the Love, Joy, Peace, and Deliverance Choir."

Glen's eyes stretched wide. "You're lying. For real?"

"Yup."

Glen crinkled his brows. "All this time, why didn't you tell me before now?"

"I don't know. I just didn't think that much of it."

"Is Jean still directing and Dwayne playing?"

"Yup."

"Damn, it's a small world. What about Elisha, Monte, and Vicky?

"No, I think all the people you sang with are gone."

"Humph, well, tell Jean and Dwayne I said hello."

Patrice frowned. "Do you know what? You have heard me sing, but I have never heard you sing before."

"Would you like for me to sing for you?" Glen gently rubbed her back with the washcloth.

"Yes, that would be nice."

"What would you like to hear?"

Patrice turned to him. "Anything."

Glen began singing "The Closer I Get to You," originally performed by Roberta Flack and Donnie Hathaway. Patrice was amazed by what she heard. Not only was her man fine, but he could sing the song much better than Donnie. He started out singing Roberta's part, and Patrice started singing Donnie's part. After singing so beautifully together, they gazed into each other's eyes.

Patrice finally said, "I love your voice, but most importantly, I love you."

They kissed, and continued to bathe in the silence.

Patrice asked, "Did you talk to Tiffany today?"

"No. I did call, but Mrs. Parker told me she's with Jessica. She said something about, she had to drop off a package for someone and she'd be right back."

"I didn't know Jessica had a car."

"She don't. She uses her friend's car while she's at work."

Glen and Patrice showered, taking turns washing each other's back. When they were done, Patrice wanted to make love again. But she didn't want to give Glen another heart attack.

As they entered the bedroom, she hid the talc powder from him. Then she started brushing her long, wet hair.

That turned Glen on.

She saw him staring at her in the mirror. "What are you staring at?"

"You. You are so beautiful."

She turned to him and planted a kiss on his lips. "Thank you. Baby, let's go out tonight."

"Baby, you know it's a work night. Where do you want to go?"

"Fort National Base Club. We don't have to stay out late. We can invite some of our friends. You've never met Lo and Faye, have you?"

"I've spoken with them over the phone."

"Well, you have to meet them. They are the best. Did you have anyone you would like to invite?"

"Not really. Well, I can invite Donald. Do you remember the guy I was telling you about?"

"Yeah, so you two have gotten well acquainted?"

"We went out last Friday to FNB."

"What? And you didn't tell me?"

"I forgot."

"Well, did you at least have fun?"

Glen was surprised at her response. He thought she was going to go off because he'd gone without her. "Yes, I did."

"What's up with that look? You're shocked that I'm not mad because you went to the club? Baby, I trust you. Always remember that."

"I keep falling in love with you." He gently rubbed her hair.

"I know. So let's give everyone a call."

Everyone showed up, Patrice, Glen, Lorene, Keith, Faye, Bobby, Christina, Alvin, Lisa, and Donald. Since it was Patrice's idea, she introduced everyone, and Glen introduced Donald and Lisa. After they were seated, the waitress came and took their orders. While she scribbled their drink requests on a small pad, the DJ started to play "Juicy Fruit" by Mtume, which made Glen grin. The song made him think about the time he and Patrice made beautiful music together.

Faye screamed, "That is my jam!"

It must have been Patrice and Christina's song too, because they were the only ones popping their fingers and dancing in their seats.

Faye began singing, "*Do what you want, I don't care, I'll be your lollipop . . .*"

Patrice joined, singing alto, and Christina sang soprano, "*You can lick me everywhere.*"

Everyone at the table laughed at the three, including themselves.

Patrice yelled, "Christina, I didn't know you had singing skills, girl! You got to join our choir."

"Hell, I didn't know you sing in the choir. But one thing we do know we have in common, we can dance our ass off!" Christina and Patrice laughed at their little secret.

"That's what's wrong with y'all now," Lorene commented. "You're being licked too much."

"Don't knock it, until you try it, girl. Don't knock it, until you try it." Patrice popped her fingers and stuck her tongue out.

Donald slapped Glen on the back. "You're taking care of business, ain't you, bro?"

Glen smiled. "Got to."

Christina nudged Patrice. "Patrice, which one you were telling me about is getting married?"

Patrice pointed at Lorene. "Lo."

"Lo, let's see the rock, girl," Christina yelled across the table.

Lorene raised her left hand, spread her fingers wide, and stuck her tongue out. She leaned on Keith, who had his arm around her shoulder.

Everyone hollered, "Ahhhhhh."

Bobby took a sip of his Hennessy. "Better you than me, dog."

"What are you trying to say?" Faye asked, taking offense.

"Naw, what I am saying is, for any relationship to work, you got to be able to see the real deal with each other and accept it. Baby, you fine, but I don't think I can handle you waking up beside me looking like somebody's grandma, wearing big cotton drawers and a flannel nightgown, with rollers in your head."

"Okay, you're talking junk now. Don't come begging for some tonight," Faye said with puckered lips.

The brothers said in unison, "Ooooohhh!"

"Slow your roll, partner," Alvin said. "Don't mess up a good thang."

Donald cringed. "I just can't stand a needy woman. Every time you turn around, she got her hand out. Damn, get a job."

"I don't know, man. I like to supply my woman's needs." Glen lifted his glass to his lips and took a gulp before continuing. "I want her to rely on me."

"Man, you a fool. She's going to have you running around like somebody lost their damn mind. The only thing she does is sit her ass at home, and we work like slaves. No, no. Christina, you better keep your job, baby," Alvin said.

"Whatever," Christina huffed. "The only reason you guys feel that way is because you broke."

The girls laughed.

Keith added, "I don't feel that way. I'm with Glen. If she wants to work, that's fine, but I'm not going to ask her how much money she has, so we can pay this light bill."

"Then again, I see what Donald is saying. I mean, if you come into a relationship acting all needy, you're going to expect your partner to do everything, and when they can't, you're going to be disappointed. That's why we are called helpmates, not God," Faye said.

"Well, I wish you the best." Lisa picked up her glass to Lorene and Keith. "All I ask is, don't try to change each other after you get married. Accept each other for who you are."

"Here, here!" Patrice picked up her glass too, and they all followed.

They continued enjoying their evening with food, fun, dancing, and laughter.

Donald was at the bar ordering another drink when he saw Glen headed toward the men's restroom. He kept his eyes on Glen until he disappeared behind the door. While taking a sip of his drink he glanced at Patrice at the table enjoying herself. Then he made his way to the restroom. As he walked in, he saw Glen at the urinal.

Glen looked up. "What's up, dog?"

"I was about to ask you the same thing," Donald said, unzipping his pants.

"What you talking about?"

"Man, Patrice is looking hot tonight. You're really handling your business, ain't you?"

Glen smiled. "Well, we have established that, but yeah, you know how I do. My baby is looking sexy tonight. Hold up, look who's talking. You got a hot one too, or should I say cold one, because she is most definitely a tall glass of ice water."

"She's all right. You have the beauty of all beauties. I bet she can put a hurting on you." Donald smirked

"You ain't lying. I almost had a heart attack before coming here."

The men chuckled.

"Man, when we're connected, I feel like I'm at a hot-chocolate factory. Willie Wonka wish he had candy that sweet."

They laughed, washed their hands, and went back to join the others.

Glen sat by Patrice, wrapped his arms around her, and leaned in for a kiss. Then he jumped into a lively sports discussion with Keith.

Patrice, all the while, couldn't help but notice how much Donald was staring at her.

Chapter Thirty-seven

Leslie had been working for Hardee's for several months now. She came to work crying the blues. Business was very slow, so she had time to tell Christina she needed money to pay her insurance. She scratched her head. "Christina, I just can't afford to have my license suspended."

Christina squealed, "Girl, you got to pep it up. You can't be walking around looking pitiful all day." She refilled the cupholder.

Leslie wiped the counters. "I'm just going to get a second job working at the strip bar or something." She pouted. "If I have to, I will sell some pussy until I get the money I need."

"Girl, shut the hell up, talking that damn foolishness! Look, if I tell you something, you can't be sharing it with nobody else. And the only reason I'm gonna tell you is because I halfway like you," Christina said, pretending to fuss. She finally broke down and let Leslie in on the dancing, telling her the very same thing she told Patrice.

Leslie got excited and said she was going to do it too.

Now that Christina let the cat out of the bag, she danced right in front of Leslie, showing her how it's done. "It's easy as stealing candy from a baby."

Leslie whispered, "You aren't scared that you might get caught?"

"No. Look at it like this. They're throwing away a lot of food every day, and every once in a while, we give out free food to our family and friends. Girl, Hardee's is not going to miss this money."

Leslie beamed. "Are you serious? How long have you been doing this?"

Christina scoffed, "Ever since I've been working here."

"Wow! I really do need the money, but I'm too scared to do anything like that."

"And you ain't scared to sell your pussy? If you get caught, your ass is going to jail and you might end up with VD."

Leslie didn't flinch.

Christina smacked her lips. "Look, there's nothing to be afraid of. Well, I've shown you how to do it, so now it's up to you."

Leslie was still a bit frightened.

"Girl, just give it a try. When the next customer drives up, just don't ring up the order.
When they give you the money, pretend like
you are putting it in the drawer, ball the money
up, and walk to the front like you are looking
for something, and then put the money in your
pocket. That way, you don't have to wait until
your shift is over to count your drawer. Instant
withdrawal, baby." Christina wiggled her body
in the latest dance move. Christina explained it
a little different from Patrice. This way was the
quick version. Then she thought, *I got to make
sure I show Patrice the latest dance move.*

When the headphones beeped, Christina let
Leslie take the order, and Leslie stole the money.

Patrice was looking around for the handsome
man in the white attire. She looked left, right,
and even behind her, but he wasn't there. She
picked a couple of daisies from the field, and
when she looked up again, there he stood before
her. Initially she was afraid, but after he smiled,
she felt comfortable and opened her mouth to
make conversation. Before she had the chance
to get a single word out, a pit bull came charging
after her.

The man did it again. Out of nowhere, he took out a silver Magnum and shot the dog before it got too close to her. She woke up when the phone rang.

"Hello?" Patrice's voice was raspy.

"Hey, Patrice, I need you to help me with my bridal shower," Lorene said.

"You call me early in the morning for a darn bridal shower?" Her clock read 7:15 A.M.

"It's hard to catch you lately. You're always hanging with Glen. By the way, are you still running?"

She sighed and turned her head trying to get comfortable. "Girl, please . . . I have to stop and rest sometimes."

"All right, Trice. You remember what I told you. You are so hard-head."

Patrice yawned. "Well, at least we don't do it much like we used to."

"Anyway, I need you to get the invitations and decorations."

"When?" Patrice asked, dozing off.

"ASAP. I want to have it in three weeks. That way I can give people enough notice so they can shop."

Zzz!

"Patrice, wake up!" "Okay, okay, I hear you," she mumbled. "Trice, don't say okay and take forever getting it done."

Patrice became alert. "Okay! I have to do a little shopping anyway today, so I'll get it while I'm out."

"Thank you, love."

"Mmm-hmm. Bye."

As soon as Patrice hung up the phone, it rang again.

Dag! Is my number on one of those TV advertisements or something? "Hello?"

"Hey, baby. How are you?" Glen asked, while looking for a pair of socks.

"Fine." Patrice yawned again.

"I asked, 'How are you?' not for a description."

Patrice smacked her lips. "Glen, what do you want?"

"What's wrong with you?"

"I'm sleepy, and Lorene called before you did, talking about some bridal shower."

"Oh, well, you can go back to sleep. I just wanted to know, are you coming over to keep me company tonight?" He glanced at the bed, remembering his last sexual encounter with her.

"I don't know. We'll see."

"A'ight then. Get you some rest. I'll talk to you later. Love you."

"Love you too," she said, before going back to sleep.

Patrice's alarm went off at the regular time, but she still ended up oversleeping. She was a little heated that Lorene and Glen had broken her sleep.

She had to be to work at 11:00 A.M., which meant she had to be on the 10:30 bus. She wasn't going to make it, so she called Millie to let her know she'd be thirty minutes late.

While waiting for her bus at the transfer station, she saw Miss Wilma getting off the bus going in the opposite direction. *What in the world? Where is Miss Wilma going? She is supposed be at work.* "Hey, Miss Wilma!" Patrice yelled.

Once Miss Wilma made her way to where Patrice was seated, Patrice asked, "Are you just getting off work? I thought you were off today."

"Chile, I took Renee's shift today."

"Don't she work four to ten? How did you get to work? I know the bus don't run that early."

"Miss Millie picked me up this morning. Whew! Lord knows I am tired and needed this day of rest, but we can use the extra cash."

"I know that's right." Then Patrice thought, *Your husband is probably beating the hell out of you and the only place you can find peace is at work.*

"You're late, ain't you?"

"Yes, ma'am. I overslept."

"Yeah, I've done that before. Girl, they got a mess down there at the job today."

"What mess?"

"Girl, Christina got arrested today."

"What! Why?" Patrice acted as though she didn't know what was going on.

"Millie wasn't letting folks use the phone. You can't go home early, and if you do, you are fired. She's counting all the cashiers' money, and Christina's drawer was over one hundred dollars and some change."

"You're lying!"

"Wait, let me tell you. You know that Leslie girl? Well, she was in the back with a lie detector device, and all of us had to answer some questions."

I knew it, I knew it, and I knew it. That white winch is a detective. "So she's a cop? What kind of questions did she ask?"

"Stuff like, 'Did we have any felony charges? Did we ever take food or money from the business? Um . . . Have we seen anyone or know anyone else who may have taken food or money from the business?' You know, stuff like that. You know, I heard them talking in the office when I was making biscuits, and I heard Christina's name, your name, and a few others."

Patrice's heart skipped a beat. "I don't know why they're mentioning me. All I do is come to work, mind my business, and go home."

"So, just to let you know, Millie is running a tight shift today. The cashiers don't know what's going on because, like I said, you can't use the phone or go home early."

Patrice wondered if Christina ratted her out.

Miss Wilma's bus pulled up, and she told Patrice, "I'll see you tomorrow."

Patrice said to herself, "Oh no, the hell you won't. I'm quitting today." She got on the same bus she got off and went home.

Chapter Thirty-eight

Donald eased his way right into Lisa's place. He knew her weakness was sex, so sexing her up was his way of getting what he wanted. Every time he spent the night with her, he would leave clothes and other personal belongings behind, until there was nothing else left at the motel. After some passionate lovemaking, they lay in bed talking about their previous get-together with the gang, particularly Glen. "I can't stand that nigga."

"Who? Mr. Pearson?"

"No, Glen. He doesn't deserve to be called mister anything."

"Why do you hate him so much?"

"Glen just think he is all that. I knew him from back in the day. And, on top of that, he's acting like he don't remember me, and I know damn well he does."

"That's not a good reason to hate him."

"Baby, you just don't know. I wish there was some type of way I could destroy him."

"It's that serious?"

"Like I said, you have no idea how serious it is. Do you have any ideas how I can put him out of his misery?"

"No way. I don't have any vendetta with this man. You're not getting me into this." "Come on, baby." Donald started kissing her neck and rubbing her thighs. "Think of something for big daddy."

"Oooo, stop. You know that's my weak spot. Okay, okay. What's in it for me?"

"Me."

"Oh no. I already got you. You have to come up with something a little better." "Okay. What about ten gees?"

"Ten thousand dollars? You're banking like that?"

"Let's just say, the person who I work for banks like that." Lisa looked at Donald, trying to read his face to see, was he saying what she thought he was saying. He looked at her very seriously. "What about embezzlement?" Donald nodded his head very slowly. "And do tell."

"You know I work for the City Treasurer. Well, all the money that comes in for any reason, whether it's fund-raising, city projects, or miscellaneous checks for employees, comes to me first. I also have access to everyone's account, even yours."

"Oh, really?"

"Really. I can make it so it looks like Glen is taking money from different accounts."

"Aw, man, I think I'm in love." Hearing this sort of information got Donald's adrenaline flowing. He pulled Lisa into his arms and began stoking the fire once more.

Chapter Thirty-nine

Jessica had to deliver a pound of cocaine to one of her buyers tonight. She called Sandra and told her to pick her up around eight o'clock. Mrs. Parker had gone to the mothers' board meeting, leaving her and Tiffany in the house alone. She started to leave Tiffany home by herself because she was asleep, but the last time she did that, Tiffany woke up and tried to pop some corn in the microwave and nearly burned down the kitchen. The house was so thick with smoke that Mrs. Parker almost had a heart attack when she came home from one of her church meetings. Jessica told her that she did it. Not wanting to take that risk, she pulled Tiffany out of bed and brought her along.

Jessica and her girlfriend pulled up in front of a low-income complex. The grounds that were supposed to have thick, green grass had dirt instead, and the doors to the apartments were smudged with dirty handprints, some of the windows busted out.

A skinny man dressed in a clean white tee shirt, a brand-new pair of blue jeans, and a pair of Converse tennis shoes walked out to the car. Because his breath smelled like burnt dookie and he had a gold tooth in the front, the entire neighborhood called him Tookie. "You got it?"

"Do you have it?" Jessica shot back, referring to the money.

He handed her a fistful of rolled bills, and in return she thrust him a package.

Tookie noticed a pair of eyes watching him from the back seat. Sticking his head in the car window, he saw Tiffany. "Hey, sweet young thang."

Jessica yelled, "Tookie, get your stinking-ass breath out of my face! You got your junk, so go on about your damn business!" She rolled the window up and said to Sandra, "Let's go."

"Mommy, what was in that bag you gave that man?"

"None of your business. I told you to stop asking so many questions, with your fast butt."

"Jess, you got to stop bringing her with us."

"I can't leave her by herself. What am I supposed to do?" Jessica looked at the money.

After getting her share of the money, the majority of it would go to T-Bo. She put money in his kennel every week. The rest of it would go to the operational manager of his business, who was supposed to hold on to it until T-Bo got out. But since his sentence had been increased, they tried smuggling the money into the prison. T-Bo even had guards working for him.

T-Bo felt that Tiffany belonged to him, and that he should take care of his woman and daughter. So he wanted to get Glen out of the picture.

Jessica planned on getting out of her aunt's house very soon, wanting to get herself and her daughter away from Mrs. Parker and, even more so, from Glen. She had saved up enough money, and now she had to think of something to tell her aunt about how she came up with the money.

Chapter Forty

Last night Patrice's dream was a little different. She was sitting at the same park, but this time the man was nowhere to be found. She even got up and began to search for him to no avail. Not long after, the same pit bull along with a German shepherd came running her way, their vicious teeth showing, and slobber coming from their mouths. She screamed and started running, but they easily gained ground on her. The German shepherd bit her ankle.

Patrice woke up with a scream, caught her breath, and then glared at the clock, which read 8:20 A.M. She was used to getting up and going to work, but now, since she no longer worked at Hardee's, she had a lot of time on her hands.

Millie kept calling her to ask when she was coming to work, but she pretended to be her mother, saying, "Patrice is not at home." Then she talked her mother into changing the telephone number, and never stepped foot in Hardee's again. She had one more check coming from Hardee's, so she called the night manager and told him to mail it.

Patrice knew Glen would take care of her, but she liked having her own money, and didn't want to go to him for every little thing. She was also hoping that Glen would hurry up and finalize the purchase of the house. She really wanted to move in with him, so they could live comfortably.

Glen allowed her to use his car so that she could get some shopping done for Lorene's bridal shower. After dropping him off at work, Patrice went into Kmart. She was gathering things for the party in the shopping cart then headed to the women's apparel section to find a gift. She dropped the most expensive negligee she could find on the rack, dropped it in the cart, and pushed it to the flower department, where there were no hidden cameras. She shoved the negligee in her purse then headed to the registers to pay for the other items.

When she was just about out of the store, a man leaving the store ahead of her turned around and held up a badge. Another person ran toward them, and they both carried Patrice to the office in the back.

The man told Patrice, "Do you have something that belongs to us?"

Patrice shook her head. "No, I do not."

The man showed her a video of her stealing the negligee.

They must have put a camera there lately, because that was the part of the store where she always stole merchandise.

The man looked at her purse.

Patrice took out the negligee, and said nothing. Then they made her wait in the office for a while. She figured they had called the cops and were waiting for them to come and take her downtown.

While Patrice was waiting in the office, she started singing "Holy One, I'm Never Gonna Let You Down" by Tramaine Hawkins.

When she sang the last note, the man came into the office and told her, "We're going to let you go this time, but don't ever come back in here again. If we ever catch you in here, we'll press charges."

After that episode, Patrice made up her mind that she was never going to steal again.

Lorene was excited about tonight. She'd told Patrice that she wanted her party to be held at Mrs. Simmons' place on Thursday night instead of Friday because she and Keith had made plans to leave tomorrow evening at 6:00 P.M. to go to Disney World for the entire weekend. (Originally, she wanted to have it at her house, but she thought it would be better to have it there because it was very spacious.) Keith had received two free tickets for listening to a salesperson trying to sell him a timeshare. He'd made it seem as though he was interested, but in actuality he wanted the free tickets they'd promised him just for coming. He and Lorene wanted to go on a pre-honeymoon.

Patrice and Faye were able to get there much sooner than Lorene and her guests, so they had a lot of time to decorate very nicely with pink and white balloons, streamers, and place mats, leaving a small gift bag there for each. Patrice set up the counter to look like a salad bar. She had a cake on the counter with white frosting, and a bikini shaped in pink frosting on top. It also read "B2B," short for bride-to-be. B2B was also printed on the pink and white napkins.

Faye made a mini bar on the other side of the counter, where she was mixing gin and some tropical fruit in the blender.

Carrie and Marie arrived first. They'd been out shopping. Of course, they let themselves in.

Faye smiled. "Hello. How are you doing?"

They just stared as though Faye smelled bad.

Patrice noticed their snobbish behavior. "No, we don't think that we're too cute to speak."

"Excuse me?" Carrie asked.

Patrice huffed, "I didn't stutter."

Mrs. Simmons came out of the downstairs bathroom. "Hey, y'all. Patrice and Faye, these are my girls, Marie and Carrie."

"Nice to meet you," Marie said weakly, only because her mother was present.

When Marie and Carrie went upstairs, Faye, her nose turned up, looked at Patrice, as if to say, "Why are they acting all stuck-up?"

Patrice was already in a foul mood because she'd seen a bad red dress at JCPenney's that she wanted so badly to steal, but was now too afraid. "I am not the one."

Within the next hour everyone else showed up, including the girls from the choir and some of Keith's cousins, and Lorene arrived a little after everyone else.

When the party officially got started, Lorene had the time of her life. Patrice made everyone pick out a suggestion from a shoebox filled with sex tips. Patrice got the tips from a book she'd bought from Frederick's of Hollywood. They played a few games, gave out door prizes, gave gifts, ate, and just had a good time.

At least, they thought they were having a good time, until they heard a knock at the door. Patrice answered it.

The tall, chocolate, handsome man asked, "Is Keith home?"

"No," Patrice responded.

"Good," Faye screamed then turned on the stereo, blasting Marvin Gaye's "Sexual Healing."

The handsome gentleman started stripping and dancing in front of Lorene.

Mrs. Simmons yelled, "Lawd have mercy! Baby, mama don't have any cash right now, but will you take a check?" She wasn't a big Bible-toting, you're-going-to-hell-if-you-don't-live-right Christian, but believed in having fun.

Soon the ladies got up to dance with him, stuffing money in his bikinis. Lorene laughed and laughed, having a ball. When the song came to an end, Lorene had to wipe the sweat from her face.

Wanting to refresh her makeup, she headed for the frog to get her purse, telling everyone, "I'll be back." On her way up the stairs she heard voices coming from behind the frog door, which was cracked a little. Instinctively, she walked closer to the door to listen.

"What in the world was Keith thinking when he asked dark chocolate to marry him?" Marie said.

"I ain't lying," Carrie said. "What kind of kids are they going to have? Spook-a-boos?"

Both women laughed.

"I hope their hair take after our side of the family, because I'm not claiming nobody's nappy-ass-head kids whose hair look like steel wool," Marie said, continuing to laugh.

"Stop it, Marie. You know you should be able to relax their hair."

"Girl, if their hair look anything like their mammy's, it won't be able to relax. It will always be nervous."

"Did you see how skinny she is? She'll stagger on a windy day."

Lorene's eyes began tearing up. She burst in the room and looked at the both of them with hatred, and immediately the laughing ceased. They knew from her expression that she'd overheard them.

"Excuse me." Lorene kept her eyes on both of them as she reached for her purse.

When she came downstairs, tears were streaming down her face. She told Patrice and Faye that she had to go, and everyone fell silent.

Mrs. Simmons rushed to her aid. "What's wrong, baby girl?"

"I'm sorry, Mrs. Simmons."

"Uh-uh, it's *Ma*. And what are you sorry about? "

"Mrs. Simmons, thank you for everything, but I have to go. Jean, please drive me home."

"What in the hell happened?" Patrice then looked up and saw Marie and Carrie looking down.

One at a time, everyone began to leave, but Faye and Patrice stayed behind to clean up, and to get Lorene's things for her.

Right before Patrice left, she walked over to Carrie and Marie and said, "I really hope you two didn't hurt my friend, because, if she tells me that you did, you are going to see demons come marching in and your ass is mine like a glass of wine. Believe that."

Faye heard what she'd said and added, "And when she's done, it will be my turn." They both went to the kitchen and kissed Mrs. Simmons good-bye, leaving Keith's sisters stunned and intimidated.

Chapter Forty-one

"He needs to be working. It'll be good for him."

"Honey, he's too young to be thinking about work. He needs to do his schoolwork, and just have fun, like children are to supposed to do. He'll have his whole adult life to worry about a job."

"Like I said, it'll be good for him. I got my first job when I was eight years old, shining folks' shoes and mowing lawns. He's twelve, practically a man. He ain't gotta come crying to us, talking about he wants some money for this and that. Now if Mr. George needs some help out there on his farm, and he's willing to pay him, he needs to go."

"What about his homework and his piano lessons?"

"Hell, he ain't going to be out there every day. He only needs him three days out of the week."

From upstairs in his room, Dwayne heard his parents arguing about him working. Although his mother was dead set against it, Dwayne didn't mind going to help Mr. George. That would give him some time away from his father. Maybe after coming home from working in the garden, his father would see that he was tired, and leave him alone.

"Dwayne!" his mother yelled. "Come here!"

Dwayne came down the steps and bounced his eyes back and forth between his parents, their facial expression looking as if they were getting ready to punish him.

"Dwayne, your father says that it would be a good idea if you go help Mr. George with his farm. I think you should worry about your school, piano lessons, and play. Now, son, you don't have to, if you don't want to go work for him. It's up to you."

Dwayne's eyes brightened up, and without hesitation, he blurted, "I want to!"

Dwayne was coming home from Mr. George's place. He was a good ways down the road when he saw his mother getting in her car to leave. He didn't feel like dealing with his father. He thought, maybe his father wouldn't mess with him, since he was too tired, but he didn't want to take that chance. He turned around and went back to Mr. George's farm, requesting more work.

"Boy, you ain't worn-out yet?"

"No, sir."

"Naw, you get on to the house, so your folks won't worry about you."

"They're gone. I just saw them leaving as I was heading home."

"Oh, yeah? Well, I still ain't got nothing for you to do right now, but you can stay for a spell until they come back. I'm getting ready to eat me some suppa. You can join me if you like."

"Yes, sir, thank you," Dwayne said, relieved.

Dwayne sat comfortably at Mr. George's house for another two hours. Then he heard a knock at the door, and fear came over him all at once, knowing it was his father.

He hurried to the bathroom to stall for more time and pressed his ear to the door.

"Come on in. You finally came back, eh? Yeah, your boy told me you and your wife stepped out for a while."

"Stepped out?"

"Yeah, I already fed him, so he should be a little worn and ready for bed."

"Well, I know you are too, so I'm just going to take him on home and get out of your way."

"Dwayne! Your paw out here!"

Reluctantly, Dwayne came out of the bathroom and looked into his father's eyes. He could read them very well, and they were saying, "I'm going to tear your ass up when we get home."

"Son, tell Mr. George thank you for letting you stay until we got back." His father knew it was all a lie, but he didn't let Mr. George on.

"Thank you again, sir." Dwayne hated it when his father instructed him to say thank you, as if he was some little three-year-old.

"You quite welcome. See ya tomorrow."

As they were leaving, Dwayne's father turned around and said, "Oh, Mr. George, about tomorrow, you can send him on home on time. I'll be there."

During the walk home, Dwayne's father didn't look at him or say one word. When they got home, Dwayne asked him for his mother.

"Don't worry about it. Just go on up there and get your bath and go to bed."

Dwayne had gotten used to his father's routine, and he hated every minute of it. He tried to hurry and take his bath and get it over with. He started to yell and tell his father, "Come on, I'm ready," but in all reality, he wasn't going to do such thing.

Surprisingly after he'd finished bathing, his father hadn't come up. He couldn't believe it. Quickly Dwayne went to bed and just stared at the ceiling, wondering what was wrong with his father. It wasn't like him not to take advantage of his mother being away. *Where is she anyway?* he thought. She should have been home by now. Then he remembered that she'd volunteered to overnight with the mother of the church, who was very ill and couldn't do things on her own, and her usual caregiver was out of town.

Oh, man! Dwayne thought. *I can't stay here with him.* Consumed with worry, Dwayne was unable to sleep and kept looking at his clock on the nightstand.

Three hours passed before Dwayne concluded that his father wasn't going to bother him tonight, and he finally dozed off.

Dwayne suddenly woke up and felt cold hands on his behind.

His father got into his bed with him. "We stepped out for a while—That's pretty good, son. I didn't know you had it in you."

Dwayne began to sweat. He didn't cry like he used to because he'd become accustomed to the abuse.

His father rubbed his anus with something greasy, something he'd never done before. He'd always messed with him in the tub, but that was about it. Then he poked his finger in his rectum. "Mmm, you are a liar now, huh? Get up! Get in the bed on your knees and bend over!"

Dwayne was afraid, but did as he was told.

His father slapped his butt for every word he was saying, "Boy . . . don't . . . you . . . know . . . better . . . than . . . to . . . lie!" Then he went to Dwayne's nightstand for more Vaseline. Standing behind Dwayne, his father sodomized him, poking him in the anus until Dwayne screamed in pain.

Dwayne had been thinking about his father during his lunch break at the shipyard. He was pulled away from his memory when he heard the whistle blow, indicating that lunch time was over.

As he made his way to his workstation, his foreman barked, "Mitchell, you got a call in the office."

"This is Dwayne speaking."

"Mr. Mitchell, this is Nurse Adams. We're calling to let you know that your mother had a massive heart attack. She's in CCU at Riverside Hospital."

Dwayne dropped the phone and just stood there in shock.

His foreman noticed the immediate change in his demeanor. "Mitchell, are you okay?"

Struggling to hold himself together, Dwayne fumbled to place the handset back on the receiver. "My-my mother, she had a heart attack. I-I got to go."

"Do you need somebody to take you to the hospital? You don't need to be driving all shaken up like that."

"I'll be all right."

"No, you won't. I'm going to take you, and that's that."

Within the hour, Dwayne jumped out of the Toyota Tundra's passenger seat, blurted a few words of thanks to his foreman, then rushed through the hospital doors and to the patient information desk.

"Excuse me? Can you tell me which room Ms. Betty Mitchell is in, please?"

"Just a minute, sir," she answered politely. After striking her keyboard and glancing at the screen's search results, she asked him, "Are you her son?"

He nodded quickly. "Yes."

"Room 312," she said, handing him an access card.

He took off running to the elevator. Once he got to her room he saw several tubes in her nose and an IV in her arm. Instantly, he broke into tears. His gasping awoke her from her not-so-restful sleep.

She looked at him with weakened and sickly eyes and motioned for him to come near.

Dwayne pulled a chair up beside her and began to gently rub her hand. "I don't believe I'm going to make it."

Her voice was so very faint, he had to lean in really close to understand her. "Yes, you will, Ma. Please don't say that." Dwayne's tears were flowing heavily.

"It's okay, son. I'm ready to go." She closed her eyes with a pained expression, but peeled them open slowly. "I need to tell you something that I was going to take to the grave with me but decided against it. You deserve to know the truth."

Dwayne dropped his head, not wanting his mother to see that he was still crying.

A forced cough burst through her lips before she added, "Son, I knew what your father was doing to you."

Caught by surprise, Dwayne suddenly looked up and into her eyes.

Dwayne's mother nodded her head slightly. "I saw a lot of hurt in your eyes when you were a boy. I was thinking it was them young'uns in school messing with you, but when I saw you telling little Susan off, the child that was always bullying somebody, I knew that couldn't be it. Every child in the school and neighborhood respected you." Her smile quickly faded, and she seemed to drift off to sleep.

Needing to hear more, Dwayne said softly, "Ma."

"I'm still here, baby, just a little tired." She paused to take a deep breath. "I noticed your father always wanted for me to leave, saying he'd watch you. Son, I used to be so tired working and doing different things for the church that when I came home I automatically went to sleep.

Some nights I'd feel your father stirring around and moving in the middle of the night but never paid it no mind, until one night I had to get up and use the bathroom. Your father wasn't in the bed with me, but I heard your bed squeaking."

Dwayne hung his head in shame.

"Look at me, son. It's all right." She paused momentarily to look at Dwayne, love in her eyes. "I peeked in your bedroom door and saw your father doing ungodly things to you. I almost had a heart attack right then, but I didn't, because I knew that something had to be done about it." She drifted off again.

This time Dwayne didn't call her, because he was too overwhelmed with everything he'd heard so far.

She strained to get his name out. "Dwayne?"

"Yes, ma'am, I'm here."

"I went back into bed as if nothing had happened, but my heart was broken, and I was devastated. I was supposed to go to work and to choir practice the next day, but didn't. I wasn't going to take my eyes off him. He was trying to get me to go, but I insisted on staying home. That night I begged him to drive down Shaddy Road with me."

Dwayne thought, *Not Shaddy Road. Not a ghost himself will go down that road.* Old man Slim, a known witch doctor, lived down that dark roadway, and after he'd died, it was rumored that anyone who dared to go down that road would meet his or her demise and would never be seen or heard from again. Even on a sunny day, it was too dark and gloomy.

"He wouldn't go at first. He called me crazy, but I told him that old man Slim had a box full of money from people buying some healing potions. I told your father I knew where it was buried. Big-mouth Sally saw him hide it there when she bought some herself, and made me promise not to tell anyone. He still wouldn't agree to come with me, but I kept on whining and told him I wasn't going anywhere else until I got that box full of money. He was scared, but he finally came on.

"We took a shovel with us, and I kept digging a hole in the ground, while he sat on a tree stump looking as scared as a cat in a room full of bulldogs. It just so happen, I hit a rock with the shovel and told him I found it. He jumped up and ran over to finally help me dig it out the ground, and that's when I took and hit him upside the head with the shovel with all the strength I had in my body." Her hand tightened around Dwayne's fingers as she remembered the strength she'd garnered through her pain, devastation and desire for revenge.

"Once he fell, I kept on beating him until he was dead. I continued to dig the hole, and that's where I buried your father."

Dwayne felt a gamut of emotions run through his body all at once—Shock, horror, fear, confusion, disbelief, pain, and others he couldn't identify.

"I'm sorry, Dwayne. I didn't know he was so sorry. Do me a favor?"

"What's that?"

"Son, be a man. Every time you let these men folk abuse your body, think about the pain that your father has caused you and I. Especially you."

Son, be a man. Everytime you let these men talk about your body, think about the pain that your father has caused you, and I. Especially you.

Chapter Forty-two

The entire ordeal from the night before kept playing in Lorene's head over and over again. On the way home, Jean kept asking Lorene what happened, but she just looked straight ahead, occasionally wiping tears from her eyes.

When Jean dropped her off, she told her, "I hope you'll be all right, Lo. I'm worried about you."

Lorene said, without looking at her, "Thank you. I will. Drive safely."

When Lorene entered the house, her father called her in the den.

"Yes."

"Precious, Keith has been calling—" Rev. Mc-Call saw that Lo had been crying—"Baby, what's wrong?"

"Nothing."

"Lorene Denise McCall, don't sit here and lie to me. I asked, what is wrong with you?"

"Daddy, it's nothing you have to worry yourself with. I'll be all right. I'm getting ready to go to bed."

"Don't you want to talk to Keith?"

"No. If he calls back, just tell him I went to bed."

Keith kept calling. He was so worried about Lorene. He wanted to know what happened, and to make sure she was all right. He wouldn't let Rev. McCall rest, until he talked to Lorene.

Rev. McCall had to calm him down the very last time he called. "Son, the last eight times that you called I told you that Lorene went to bed. Now, I know that's not good enough for you. There have been times when she's been dead to the world but as soon as she knew that you were on the phone, she's resurrected. I'm not going to say that she is 'sleep, but I do know that she's in bed. Now, son, I don't know what happened tonight that made my Precious cry, but I do know this—You were created for her. God knew you before you were placed in your mother's womb. He knew that you and Lorene would one day be joined together. Of course, I'm her father and she's my seed, but she will be bone of your bone and flesh of your flesh. It's your job to find out what's bothering her and do something about it. Of course, God is her Protector, but He has chosen you to be her shield. It's late right now, and I don't want you to come over here in the middle of the night. But, first thing tomorrow, you need to console your woman. I know what I'm talking about, because I had one that was just like her, and I'll give anything to have her back. Now you get yourself some rest and let us do the same. She'll be here tomorrow, and you can talk to her then."

The next morning, Lorene sat on the recliner looking out of the window at her father. Once again, he was loading up his car with luggage, having to preach at a Holy Convention out of town. Many times, Lorene looked forward to having the entire house to herself, but for once, she truly wished that he didn't have to go.

The phone had been ringing all morning, but Lorene ignored it, knowing it was Keith. She couldn't talk to him just yet. After hearing his sisters last night, she figured that it would be best that they slowed their relationship down a bit. Better yet, they would be better off not getting married at all, not wanting to cause any problems between him and his family.

Feeling the onset of a headache, she took the phone off the hook and then trudged back to her bedroom to sleep off the slight pounding in her head.

Lorene had been resting for nearly an hour when there was a knock at the door. She looked at the clock on the wall. It was 9:00 A.M. She was reluctant to answer the door because she knew it was Keith. Nonetheless, she walked slowly to the door to open it. She gazed at him with sad eyes and then opened the door wider so he could come in.

Keith had a look of worry on his face. "Baby, talk to me," he said, focusing on her eyes.

Lorene just sat back down on the recliner. Keith followed and knelt beside her, but Lorene stared at her lap.

"Baby, please talk to me," he pleaded softly.

"I changed my mind," she said, her voice cracking.

"Change your mind about what? Us?"

Lorene wanted to say yes, but she was in love with Keith. In a way, she didn't want to lose him over some foolishness. Then again, it hurt so badly, she didn't want to go through with it. "About going to Walt Disney."

"Okay, we can go some other time, but can you at least tell me why you changed your mind about going?"

Lorene was silent.

He got up and pulled her up so he could hold her in his arms. "Listen, I love you, and when you are hurting like this, it makes me hurt too. But, at least, you know the cause of the pain. Will you please tell me so we can deal with it together?"

Water began to fill Lorene's eyes. Keith kissed each one of them to keep them from falling. Lorene finally said to Keith with a raspy voice, "I love you too, but I can't marry you," buried her head in his chest, and burst out crying.

Keith grasped hold of her shoulders and pushed back so he could look directly in her eyes. "Whoa! What did you just say?"

"I can't marry you," she mumbled with lowered eyes.

Keith sat down on the couch then pulled Lorene onto his lap. "No. You have to talk to me, Lorene. You have to talk to me right now."

Lorene looked into his eyes and saw a man that she never saw before. Keith's look was so serious, he could have made the devil think twice before bothering him.

"Lorene, baby, I need you to talk to me," he repeated once more with a finality that suggested to Lorene that she could no longer hold back her thoughts.

Lorene slid off his lap and sat beside him. She inhaled deeply, blew out the same breath of air that had just filled her lungs, then proceeded to tell him all that she'd overheard his sisters say.

When she finished and looked at her fiancé, she saw anger. Keith was so mad, his eyes had turned blood-red. He sat very quietly for a long time.

Finally, Lorene broke the silence. "Keith, please say something."

"Lo, are you planning on marrying me or my sisters?" He bit into his bottom lip.

"You."

"Do you love me or my family?" Keith raised his eyebrows as he looked directly at Lorene.

"I love your mother and—"

"Lo, you know what I mean. Do you love me or my family?"

"You."

"Are you relying on my family to protect and provide for you, or are you relying on me?"

"You."

Keith gently grabbed Lorene's face and kissed her with all he had within him.

She had never tasted his whole tongue before. The longer they kissed, the hotter she became. She wanted Keith badly. Her sweetness began to throb, and Keith's manhood started to swell.

"Tell me that you love me, Lo," he panted in her ear.

"I love you."

He kissed her again. "Tell me that you need me."

"I need you."

He kissed her again. "Tell me that you want me."

"I want you, Keith."

He kissed her again and again. "Tell me that you'll marry me, Lorene." He nudged away a single tear from her eye.

She didn't answer right away but yearned for more kisses.

He pressed his lips against her neck, jaw, and then her mouth. "Will you, Lo? Will you marry me?"

Lorene was extremely moist. "Yes. Yes, Keith." She traced a finger across his jawline and looked straight into his eyes. "I'll marry you."

Unable to further bridle his desires, Keith peeled back her robe and began nuzzling her breast. Lorene didn't stop him. She only guided his head.

Keith unfastened her bra and sucked her nipples, causing her to moan with pleasure. Lorene slipped her hand between Keith's legs and massaged the bulge pressing against his pants.

She tried unzipping his pants, but the zipper was stuck, and he quickly undid it for her.

In an instant she fully shed her robe and pulled her bra away from her body as she lay back on the couch. Keith wasted no time kissing every inch of her beautiful brown skin, his fingers tugging at her panties.

Lorene stood to make their removal easier then lay naked on the floor as Keith undressed himself, standing over her. She couldn't keep her eyes off his huge, smooth penis. He lay beside her and randomly planted more kisses, while his fingers explored her vagina.

Wrestling against the pleasure she felt, and her moral beliefs and convictions, Lorene looked into Keith's eyes. "We're supposed to do this on our wedding night."

"We can stop if you want," he huffed, although he truly wanted her.

Slowly she rose from the floor and held out her hand to him. "I don't want to stop." She guided him to her bedroom and, for the first time, allowed him to make love to her.

Lorene stroked Keith's chest. "God is mad at us. We were supposed to wait until our wedding night."

"Believe me when I say that our wedding night is going to be just as special. But you're right. I'm sure He is upset with us, but to be honest with you, He's been mad for quite some time now."

"What do you mean?"

"He said, if you've lusted in your heart, you might as well have done it, sure enough. Girl, every night, I do this to you in my heart and mind."

Lorene swatted his arm playfully. "Keith!"

"I'm serious, baby. You make a brother scream, but that's okay. He is just and faithful to forgive us. Not that we should take advantage of His grace, but what's done is done now. Besides, we'll be legal in a couple of weeks, although a couple of weeks is too far away. I want to marry you right now."

"We're practically already married." She laughed.

Keith laughed with her then planted a kiss on her forehead. "I guess you're right." They lay silently in each other's arms, until Lorene looked up at him and realized the wide grin on his face. "What are you smiling about?"

"Let me ask you something—Are you a virgin?" "Mmmm, let me be honest and say no."

"No?" She rubbed his loins with a sly smile. "Not anymore." After a second round, Keith and Lorene showered together. And Lorene decided that she wanted to go to Florida after all.

Chapter Forty-three

"Baby, I'll wait in the car." Lorene folded her hands in her lap. "No. I want you to come in with me. You don't have to hide from my wicked sisters."

"Baby, I don't want any trouble."

"It's too late. They already started, and I'm going to finish it." Keith was hot. "Now please, Lo, come in with me," he insisted.

Lorene did as he asked, and they held hands as they entered the house. Marie and Carrie were in the living room watching a movie. Keith stormed to the TV and turned it off.

"What the hell is your problem?" He figured, since he had sinned already today, he might as well go all the way.

"What are you talking about, Keith?" Marie asked innocently, although Lorene's presence should have given her some indication.

"I don't know who told you two that you were Miss Americas, but you are not. Beauty is skin-deep, but ugly is to the bone, and right now, I'm looking at two of the most ugliest-ass beasts that I have ever seen in my life. You two get on my damn nerves, always putting people down, but you ain't no better than nobody else."

Mrs. Simmons heard Keith cussing out his sisters in the living room and rushed from her bedroom to see what was going on. "What in the world is wrong with you, Keith?"

"Fakey and Flakey said some terrible things about Lorene at the bridal party last night!"

"Oh, really? What did you say?" Mrs. Simmons, her hands on her hips, looked at her daughters, waiting for an answer.

Keith didn't give them a chance to say anything. "They talked about your future grandchildren and about Lorene's skin color!" Nor did he take his eyes off his sisters. "Let me tell you something—You better apologize to her, or you will no longer have a brother! Family is by force, wife is by choice, and guess what? I choose Lorene! Y'all walking around here with your nose so far up your ass that you got a dodo ring around your nose."

Normally Mrs. Simmons didn't tolerate her children fighting, let alone cussing. She didn't care how old they were. This time she was so disgusted with Carrie and Marie, she let Keith eat them alive.

"You're so stupid! You need to study your history. The only reason you are red is because a white master raped our ancestors! That ain't nothing to be so proud of that you have to put down folks' true color."

Marie looked at Lorene and then Keith and finally spoke up. "Keith, I'm sorry."

"I know you are sorry, with your sorry-ass self, but I don't want your apologies. You need to be saying that to Lo! And, Carrie, you better not even part your lips at me. You need to be worried about your husband and your child. Your own husband can't even stand you, and your son doesn't pay you any mind. So you two better leave Lorene the hell alone!" Keith was so mad he could bite nails. He took Lorene by the hand. "She is going to be my wife, whether you like it or not. If you hurt her again, I'm going to hurt you. That's a promise!"

The two sisters sat motionless, not sure if they should take the chance of moving. Keith looked at Lorene and said, "Baby, come on."

Lorene followed him as he stormed into his room and slammed the door behind them. He sat on his bed and buried his head in his hands. Lorene eased over by him and put her arms around his neck, trying to calm him down, and he held her around the waist.

When he calmed down, he looked toward heaven and said, "Lord, I really blew it today. First, I had sex with my fiancée, and then I cussed my sisters out and didn't show any respect to my mother. But, to be honest with You, Lord, I'd rather sin with You than without You. I can't make this journey alone. I need Your help and Your guidance. Lord, I am like David when he said, 'I am just a worm.' I am a worm, Lord. I am not worthy of anything, but You are. You are truly worthy. I thank You for Your grace and loving kindness. Lord help me with these things, in Jesus' name, Amen."

Lorene felt a warm tear come down her cheek and she said, "Amen."

Chapter Forty-four

Ms. Mitchell was dressed in a pink lace dress with a white rose pin on the right. Her skin was much darker than when she was alive. She had on a jet-black bob wig that looked too big for her small head. Her casket was soft gray with silver bars on the side, and silver lining on the inside, and was surrounded by several flower arrangements.

Dwayne sat on the front pew with other distant family members and friends. While everyone cried and moaned, he sat there looking like he was mad at the world. His focus was on his mother.

Just before LJP&D Choir sang, a lady came to the podium to read sympathy cards to the family, but Dwayne was barely able to concentrate. The woman opened the last card and began to read aloud:

"I can tell you that it's going to be okay But how would I know? I never experienced this day I can tell you that's she's in a better place

Holding the Savior's hand and accepting his warm embrace But how would I know? I can only hope that she is It's not my call or will, but His But this I do know, I know this indeed You can count on me anytime you need A pal, buddy, and a friend you will find Dwayne, just know that I love you till the end of all times. Again, I love you, Patrice Russell."

Dwayne finally took his eyes off his mother and glanced around the room for Patrice. Her eyes were red and full of tears.

The choir stood, and Patrice took the microphone and began to sing:

"What a friend we have in Jesus All our sins and griefs to bear What a privilege to carry Everything to God in prayer"

Even though the song was just a hymn, LJP&D Choir tore the song up all to pieces, performing it exceptionally well.

Tears began to flow from Dwayne's eyes, and the family's cries expanded.

After Patrice led the song, she lifted her hands toward heaven and gave God praise, something Dwayne had never seen her do. It let him know that she'd sung from her heart, not her talents.

There was someone else in the congregation who'd never heard Patrice sing like that. Her rendition actually touched Glen's heart.

After laying Ms. Mitchell's body in its final resting place, several people returned back to the church's fellowship hall to offer their condolences, and also to enjoy a meal close to what they'd generally have at Thanksgiving.

Every member of the choir lined up to offer encouraging words to a sorrowful Dwayne, including Patrice, who stood last in line. Although Glen was by her side, she asked him to allow her and Dwayne to speak privately.

"No problem, baby." Glen then excused himself and went to chat with Keith and Lorene.

Patrice turned her attention toward Dwayne and grabbed his hand. "When you said, 'We have to get beyond this point,' I never thought that it will be here. Dwayne, I'm sorry. I am so sorry that you lost your mother. I knew you had a close relationship with her. But what I am truly sorry for is treating you the way I have." She dropped her head in shame for a second, but then forced herself to look Dwayne straight in the eyes. "The truth of the matter is, regardless of what our past differences have been, I love you."

With a tearful smile, Dwayne embraced her. "I love you too, girl. You know that. And thank you for singing today."

"It was the least I could do, Dwayne."

Dwayne could see the sincerity in Patrice's eyes.

"Call me if you need anything," she offered, before rejoining Glen.

Dwayne nodded.

Exhausted emotionally and physically, Dwayne took a seat in the quietest corner he could find. As if the grief he felt wasn't enough, his thoughts were also consumed with all the packing he'd have to do at his mother's house.

As he glanced around the fellowship hall, he noticed that people were beginning to trickle out. Through the crowd he thought he saw a familiar face slipping out of the door. Bobbing his head to see around moving bodies, there was no mistaking who he'd laid eyes on. It was Tracey.

Immediately, Dwayne jumped to his feet and attempted to move toward him, but was side-tracked by a heavyset woman who attended his mother's church.

"We sho' gon' miss Miss Betty and dem pretty hats she used to wear." She took Dwayne into her full bosom, against his will, and nearly squeezed the life out of him.

"Yes, ma'am," he responded respectfully, his eyes darting wildly to see where Tracey had gone.

"Matta fact," she said, "what you plan on doing with them hats and thangs? 'Cause you know me and yo' momma was 'bout the same size."

"I, umm, I," Dwayne stuttered, having not really heard what the woman had said, "I'm sorry. Please excuse me." At that he darted toward the door, giving mini hugs along the way to those who grabbed at him. Finally he'd made it outside, but it was too late. There was no sign of Tracey.

The funeral attendant rested a hand on Dwayne's shoulder. "Are you going to be okay getting home, young man?"

Startled, Dwayne jumped. "Uh, yeah. Thanks."

"Again, my condolences."

The church woman waved and called out to Dwayne as she bustled out of the fellowship hall's doors, "Don't forget me, baby!" and headed to her car in her turned-over heels.

He walked back inside to say his final farewell for the evening, sorely disappointed that he and Tracey hadn't had the opportunity to speak. Fishing in his pocket for his keys, he stepped quickly to his car and pulled off.

As he pulled up to his home, his heart stopped when he saw Tracey emerging from a spotless black BMW.

Tracey strolled up to Dwayne's car and opened his door. "Hey," he said with a pleasant smile.

"Hey," Dwayne whispered, his mind instantly flooded with the memories of the many nights he and Tracey had spent together.

"I know it's been a long day, but do you mind if I come in?"

"Sure."

With measured steps and no words spoken, they headed for Dwayne's front door. Even in his time of sorrow, he longed for Tracey. Weakened by his memories, Tracey's presence, and the scent of his cologne, he'd really missed him.

"Have a seat," Dwayne said when they entered the apartment.

Tracey sat on the couch, and Dwayne sat close to the end.

Dwayne said calmly, "It took my mother's passing to see you again?"

"Baby, please don't start. You know the company I worked for sent me to the other side of the world. I wanted so many times to see and talk to you, but couldn't."

"Tracey, that's a poor excuse. You could have at least gave me a ring every now and then."

"Look, the only thing I can say at this point is, I am sorry. Dwayne, I missed you terribly. It's really nothing I can do about it now, so let's focus on now. Now I am here."

Indeed you are, looking all sexy in those black pair of slacks, tight shirt, and your thick hair in a ponytail. He didn't want Tracey to know that he was only having good thoughts of him, so he turned his head away.

Tracey slid close to Dwayne and started rubbing his head.

"Stop," Dwayne whined, moving Tracey's hand, although he really didn't want him to stop.

To his disappointment, Tracey did as he was told.

"So how are you holding up? Are you going to be okay?"

"I'll be fine."

The room was silent, and Dwayne avoided eye contact. But he couldn't hide the bulge in his pants.

"Come here, Dwayne. You know I still love you."

Dwayne wasn't going to refuse Tracey a second time. He leaned on his shoulder and allowed Tracey to caress him then looked into Tracey's eyes and was instantly drawn into a kiss.

Tracey didn't need much else. Right away, he stood to his feet and gently pulled Dwayne and led him to the bedroom.

With every step Dwayne took, he could hear the voices of his parents resonating in his head. First, his mother's deathbed words: "Son, be a man." Then his father's voice: "Boy, you ain't never going to amount to nothing. You'll always be my bed slave, and don't you ever forget it."

Tracey let his hands freely roam Dwayne's body, as he undressed him.

But there was a war churning inside of Dwayne. All of a sudden he felt like that little boy that his father had abused for so many years. No longer did he sense and feel Tracey. In his mind, it was his father who was stripping him of his clothes, his dignity, and his manhood.

Dwayne suddenly drew back and scrambled for his clothes. "I can't do this," he blurted, his eyes reflecting confusion and shame. "I just can't do this."

Tracey took a seat on the bed and stared into Dwayne's eyes. "What's wrong, baby?" he said softly.

Dwayne looked at him with sadness. "Tracey, thank you so much for coming by to check on me. I'll be fine, and you have to leave." Without hesitation, he dashed from the bedroom and headed for the front door to properly see Tracey out.

Respectfully Tracey followed, but stopped to study Dwayne's face before leaving. "I'll always love you, Dwayne," he whispered. "Always. If you change your mind later tonight, tomorrow, or whenever, you know I'll come running." He leaned in to kiss Dwayne.

Dwayne quickly turned his head away. "Good night, Tracey."

Tracey bit into his bottom lip as he stepped outside. Before he could turn back to say anything further, Dwayne had already closed the door, and was crying profusely on the other side. Hearing his sobbing, Tracey thought about giving Dwayne a few minutes to compose himself, but then he thought better of it and headed to his car. "I'll give him some time," he said aloud to himself.

Tracey tried calling Dwayne and leaving messages on several occasions, but Dwayne never responded.

Chapter Forty-five

Lately Donald had been spending more time in the computer lab than at his workstation. He was to turn in his assignment to operational management in another hour, but he was on the computer sending messages to Lisa, who had informed him that the city had raised twenty-five thousand dollars at a big fundraiser a week earlier. When she got the opportunity, she then transferred ten thousand dollars to Glen's account, and then later sent a coded message to Donald telling him what she'd done.

"Good. Everything is going as planned," he whispered to himself.

Ms. Featherstone had taken notice of the frequent times that Donald was missing from his desk and moseying around other departments where he had no business. She knew an employee in his field didn't need much time in the computer lab, which was the only place in the entire building where the computers were synched together. Sneakily, she watched when he entered and left the lab, then trekked behind him to try to determine why he'd been there.

Glen kept glancing at his watch for the last fifteen minutes. He couldn't wait until it was time to leave City Hall, to spend quality time with his favorite ladies. When he pulled out his car keys from his blazer, he noticed the shining new house key on the ring. He smiled and said, "New house, new beginnings."

Immediately he jumped in his car and drove to pick up Patrice, and then headed to Smithfield to get Tiffany. The three went to Captain George's Seafood Restaurant. He was excited and really had something to celebrate.

Tiffany pointed at the seasoned shell shrimp. "Daddy, I want some of that."

"How do you know you will like it?" Glen asked.

"You have some on your plate."

"That's because I like it. I'll just put two on your plate, and if you like it, we can come back for more, Snagglepuss?"

"Okay." Tiffany gave her daddy a toothless smile.

Glen and his two favorite girls looked like the perfect family in their evening wear. Glen had on a navy blue suit with a black pleated shirt and black shoes. Patrice, her hair in a French roll, had on a navy blue spaghetti strap dress that showed off her curves, high-heeled sandals to match, and dangling silver earrings, with matching necklace. Tiffany had on a white dress accented by light blue rose appliqués, and a navy blue satin sash that tied in a bow in the back. And light blue tights and black patent leather shoes covered her legs and feet. From her neck down, she looked adorable, but her hair was a wild, tangled mess.

"Little girl, Miss Patrice is going to get Miss Lorene to braid your hair. We can't have you walking around here looking like you're an orphan."

"Leave my baby alone. I think she looks lovely," Glen lied, nudging Patrice under the table, and smiling at Tiffany.

"Thank you," Tiffany said, grinning from ear to ear.

"You're welcome. So how was daddy's girl today?"

"Fine. Me and Aunt Emma played, and I watch TV. Then me and Mommy took a brown package to this man."

Glen stopped chewing and looked at Tiffany with confusion, then at Patrice. "Baby, what did you say?"

"Me and Aunt Emma pla—"

"No, sweetheart. What did you say about a brown package?"

"Mommy gave a brown package to a man. I don't like him. He don't brush his teeth."

"What kind of package, baby? Do you know what she puts in it?"

"No," she answered, grinning as she shook her head.

"Is it like a dinner package? Do you smell food coming from it?"

"No, Daddy," Tiffany answered as if that was the most ridiculous thing he could have said. She put her fork down and began to talk with her hands. "It's like about this big"—she held her hands a few inches apart—"and it smell funny." She crinkled her nose, exposing the gap created by her missing front teeth. "Every time I ask Mommy what is it, she always say, none of my business and then tell me to stay out of grown folks' business. One time when I asked her, she slapped me."

Instantly, Glen's blood began to boil as his appetite dissolved. He had planned on having a delightful evening with Patrice and Tiffany, but now his mind was filled with worry. He had to stop procrastinating and go on ahead and hire a PI.

The very next day, he went to Results Investigation and explained the situation to Dan Williams, a highly trained and experienced investigator, and stroked him a check. In return Dan told him that he'd get on it right away.

Chapter Forty-six

October had come before anyone knew it. Glen was settled in the new house. Patrice couldn't deny him when he asked her a second time to move in with him. The house was far more comfortable than the apartment, because now they had the luxury of escaping each other by going to another room.

While Patrice sat in the den trying to make plans for her birthday party, Glen was in the study, calling Dan to see what was going on with the investigation. Dan assured him that he need not worry about a thing, and that everything was under control. Glen went in the den to see what Patrice was up to.

"Hey. No updates?"

"No. I wish he would hurry up. I want nothing more to have my baby girl here with me."

Patrice said calmly, "I know. Something is bound to happen. You got to stop worrying yourself to death."

"Yeah, you're right. So what are you doing?

"Trying to make an invitation list for my birth-day."

"Oh yeah. It's just around the corner, isn't it?" Glen plopped down beside her and glanced at the list of names she'd written down.

"I know you haven't forgotten."

"Baby, I'm sorry. I just been so consumed with Jessica getting her behind caught, I can hardly think about anything else." Glen closed his eyes and licked his lips, as if savoring the sweet taste of victory.

"Okay, you're off the hook this time."

"Thank you." Glen took the list from her. "Who do you have so far?"

"So far, just the choir members I hang out with, and Donald and Lisa. Oh yeah, I forgot all about Alvin. Poor thing, I know he misses Christina."

"Yeah, I feel for the brother. I'm glad you didn't get tied up in that stealing mess."

"I know, right?" Patrice thought, *If only you knew*. "Oh well, did you have anyone you want me to include?"

"No, not really. You know the only person that I hang out with is Donald and sometimes Keith. Keith and I don't really have a choice in the matter but to hang out, being that you and Lorene are Siamese twins."

"Green is not your color."

"Huh?"

"Green with envy." She laughed. "You know you can't have me all to yourself."

"I'm not envious. I have a buddy, Donald. Have Keith and Lo set a date yet?"

"As a matter of fact, they did. They're getting married on June the first, next year. The theme is 'New Beginnings.'"

"Awww, how sweet."

"It is." Patrice wanted to ask him if there were plans for marriage in their own future, but she didn't want to pressure him. Besides, she was just happy being with him and having him taking good care of her. Glen had opened a bank account in her name and gave her major credit cards. She couldn't have been more contented.

"Where are you talking about having this party?"

"If the weather permits, I want to have it on Keith's yacht. If not there, then here. And I want everyone to wear cream or off-white." To Patrice those colors symbolized safety, and with the bad dreams she'd been having for several months now, safe was definitely what she wanted to be.

In addition to that, the man in her dream that would come to her rescue always wore white.

"Mmm, that's different. Why those colors in particular?"

After she explained, Glen nodded then got up and went in the kitchen to fix him something to drink. He yelled to Patrice, "Have you talked to your mother lately?"

"As a matter of fact, I talked to her just before you came home from work."

"How is she doing?"

"Okay. You know she misses me."

Glen came back in the den. "I miss you too." He sat his drink down, leaned toward Patrice, and began planting kisses.

And one thing led to another.

Jessica received a phone call from Tookie at approximately 6:45 P.M. Mrs. Parker had already left for church. For once she'd planned on going too, until she received the phone call. Tookie told her he had a guy that needed 500 grams of heroin.

Jessica knew that was well over a half of million dollars. Blood rushed to her head, just thinking about her cut of the money. She'd never had a sale so large before and couldn't wait to finish the deal and tell T-Bo about it. Then on second thought, she said to herself, "Hell, I'm telling him nothing. All of that money is going in my pocket." For sure she'd be able to get away from Glen, Mrs. Parker, and T-Bo.

She could have kicked herself for not sending Tiffany with her aunt. There was no way she could take her on this deal. Figuring she wouldn't be gone long, she made Tiffany a sandwich and gathered several snacks and took them to her room and left her home by herself.

"Mommy's gotta go somewhere real quick, okay, baby."

"Okay, Mommy," Tiffany answered, although her eyes instantly filled with fear at the thought of being home alone. "Suppose a monster tries to come get me?"

"Well, baby, if you stay in your room and watch this video," she said, sliding a Disney movie into the VCR, "no monster would be able to find you. He would just think that someone left the TV on. I brought you all kinds of good things to eat so you won't have to come out of the room at all."

Tiffany whined, "Suppose I have to pee?"

"Let's go take care of that now." Jessica walked Tiffany to the bathroom, turning on every light along the way.

When she got Tiffany settled back in her bedroom, Tiffany said, "Can you leave the hall light on?"

"Of course, baby."

Shortly after that, Jessica took the phone off the hook, just in case Glen tried to call, and was on her way to collect her money.

"I can't wait to tell Theresa this," she said to herself.

Jessica had met Theresa at a party about two months ago. Theresa was drunk as hell and ranting about how she was going to kill her ex-husband for taking her child away from her. Jessica felt her pain, because she was in the same predicament, being harassed by threats from Glen to take Tiffany from her care. Jessica had calmed her down, and since then, they'd become good friends. There would be times they would go riding together, go to house parties, and just sit around the house talking about anything and everything. Sandra would hang out with them too, but she ended up moving out of town. Now it was only Jessica and Theresa.

She recalled a recent conversation with Theresa about making some real money. Theresa had said to her, "Girl, I get tired of nickel and diming. I need some real dough. I was thinking about working at the strip club or maybe selling my twa-twa or dealing drugs. I don't care, as long as the money is right."

"Now I can see your trifling ass selling your tail and being a striptease, but selling drugs—naw, you can't handle that," Jessica told her.

"Who can't? Yes, I can, and I'll snort it too. As a matter of fact, I need a little bit right now."

Jessica had her doubts but was willing to put Theresa to the test. "Come on. I know where we can get some."

Minutes later, they pulled up to an old warehouse a couple of miles down the road. Jessica rang the bell in code and was soon met by a tall, heavy man with wavy hair. They went in, and Jessica exchanged words privately with the man for a few seconds. He left the small waiting room, came back with a pound of heroin and dropped it in Jessica's hands.

Without saying another word, the two ladies left and rode in silence until they were a good ways from the warehouse. Finally Theresa said, "So I see you got it like that, huh?"

Jessica didn't say anything. She just took a glimpse at Theresa and poked her lips, as if to say, "I sure do."

"Girl, I knew it was something about you I liked. I hit the jackpot."

When Jessica saw how excited Theresa was she knew she could trust her. "Honey chile, that's not the best part. I deal too."

Theresa's eyes almost popped out of her head.

"Yes, baby, I make twenty-five hundred a week."

"Get out of here! So what do a sister got to do to get a piece of the pie?"

"Yeah, that's my nigga." Jessica came back from her trip down memory lane.

Theresa had been driving her to her drop-offs when Sandra couldn't do it, but now that Sandra was out of the picture, she and Theresa were a regular Thelma and Louise.

"Girl, can you believe it? Five hundred grams! I'm in the money!" Jessica screamed.

"No, *we* are in the money, because I know you're going to give me a cut, 'cause gas ain't free!"

Jessica wasn't planning on giving her one red cent, but she said, "You know I got you." Jessica knew she couldn't get away from not offering her any money. "Come get me in twenty minutes."

"You ain't taking Tiffany, are you?"

"Hell no. Just in case somebody acts retarded, I don't want my baby getting hurt."

"You're right about that. I'll be there in a few minutes, girl."

Jessica and Theresa met Tookie and a tall dark-skinned guy with a small dreadlocks and goatee. Theresa opened the trunk, and Jessica took out the suitcase full of heroin.

When Tookie reached for the suitcase, Jessica held on to it tightly. "Wait a minute, I ain't never seen you around here before." She eyed the second man suspiciously.

"Look, I don't have time for this shit. I can take my money somewhere else." The man dismissed Jessica with a wave of his hand and began to walk off.

Both Theresa and Tookie started cussing Jessica out, asking if she was crazy.

Jessica had her eyes fastened on the man, wanting to see just how far he'd walk. Just when the man was about to get into his car, Jessica yelled, "Wait!" and waved him back over.

He strolled back casually to the trio and stared at Jessica with evil eyes. Not intimidated, Jessica returned his stare.

"You can do business with me. I just have to make sure that you're legit."

The man handed Jessica the briefcase full of money, and she made the swap.

When she and Theresa got back in the car, she screamed, "Yeah! Yeah! We're in there, baby!"

Theresa was silent for a moment.

Then Jessica asked, "What's wrong with you?"

"Well, Jessica, actually *you* are in there—prison, that is." Theresa held up her badge. She was an undercover cop working for the Smithfield Police Department Narcotics Bureau.

Jessica tried to slap her but came to a dead halt when, in an instant, Theresa pulled and cocked her gun. Then suddenly a group of officers swarmed around the car from out of nowhere, each one with a drawn gun aimed at Jessica, who burst into tears.

"Get out the car, and lay on the ground," Theresa ordered, once she saw one of the cops stood ready to take Jessica down. "Thanks, Took," she said out the window to Tookie, who was standing by.

When Glen told Dan about the stinking-breath man that Tiffany described, the police easily found Tookie and took him down for questioning. They offered him a deal if he would help to catch Jessica, which he readily agreed to. Jessica was charged with drug trafficking, child endangerment, and abandonment. After Theresa had talked to Jessica on the phone earlier, she called someone to come to the house and look after Tiffany, and Glen was immediately notified.

Chapter Forty-seven

With Jessica serving twenty-five to thirty-five years in prison without parole, with no opposition, Glen took full custody of his daughter and right away changed her last name to his own. Glen felt bad that her mother had to serve hard time in prison, but he knew that Patrice would make up for that loss. Now that he had his baby, he planned on proposing to Patrice and presenting her with an engagement ring on her birthday.

Glen was in his office, calling different jewelers, trying to price rings, until he saw his boss, Mr. Lee, at the door.

"Glen, may I speak to you for a moment?"

"Yes, sir. Do come in."

"Something that was brought to my attention was a bit of disturbance to me. I see here"—he showed Glen a sheet of paper—"that your account is well over fifty thousand dollars."

Glen took a look at the paper. He frowned and said, "I don't know how this could have happened, sir."

"Oh, really?" He looked at Glen with squinted eyes of disbelief. "Glen, maybe you should come with me."

Glen looked at him with confusion and before he could count to three there were policemen standing in the doorway. They arrested Glen on suspicion of embezzlement and were taking him to the police precinct for questioning.

Ms. Featherstone stood nearby watching the entire ugly scene unfold. Right before the group of gentlemen stepped into the elevator, she said, "Mr. Lee, can I speak to you for just a moment," she asked tugging on the sleeve of his suit jacket.

"Not now, Ms. Featherstone."

"Sir, this is important. It's about Mr. Pearson."

He studied her face briefly. "Wait just a minute, officers," he said to the policemen. He then turned to Ms. Featherstone. "This better not be a waste of my time. Follow me."

Behind closed doors, Ms. Featherstone shared her suspicions that Glen had been framed, but since she had no proof, Mr. Lee dismissed her theory and went forward with having Glen removed from the premises.

Hours later, Glen was allowed to go home, but he had to appear in court in two weeks, and he no longer had a job. He decided not to mention a single word of what happened to Patrice, hoping that his lawyer would be able to bring a quick resolution to the entire situation without anyone having to know anything.

Optimistic, but angry, Glen made himself feel better by going out to Kay's Jewelers and purchasing Patrice a fourteen-carat white gold cut diamond engagement ring. He refused to let the embezzlement allegations ruin his bright future with Patrice and Tiffany. Glen sat in the mall admiring his purchase, and thinking of how incredibly blessed he was. He had a new home, a beautiful fiancée, and most of all, possession of his daughter. Lost in his thoughts, he sat until the mall closed.

It was 9:45 P.M. when he got home. Tiffany and Patrice were already in bed. He knew it was way past Tiffany's bedtime, but found it odd that Patrice was in bed already.

Tired from today's drama, he decided to crash too. He tried not to awake Patrice when he got into bed, but when he crawled beneath the sheets, he noticed that she had on his favorite red silk nightgown. *She is so beautiful.* Unable to resist, he slid close to her and put his arm around her waist.

"Hey," Patrice said groggily.

"Hey," he whispered.

She turned around and tried examining his face in the dark. "What's the matter?" she asked, detecting a tone of defeat in his voice.

"Nothing. Just tired."

"You had to work late?"

"You can say that."

"Well, baby, don't work late tomorrow. It's my birthday, and I need you here with me."

Glen wanted to say, "I'll be here on time, seeing that I no longer have a job," but instead he said, "I won't."

Chapter Forty-eight

"All right, we're here," Lorene stated. "What do you want us to do first?" She and Faye arrived at Glen's house ready to decorate for Patrice's birthday party. Tiffany was rambling through the bags and pulling out everything. "Oooo, this is pretty. I want to help."

"She is so cute, Patrice. Look at you, being a mother," Faye teased.

"Shut up." Patrice rolled her eyes at Faye then looked at Tiffany. "Okay, you can help, but first you got to make sure your room is clean, okay."

"Okay." Tiffany scampered upstairs to her bedroom.

The phone rang and Patrice was quick to answer. "Hello . . . Hey, Mrs. Parker . . . Yeah, I just sent her upstairs to clean up her room . . . Yes, ma'am, she's adapting very well . . . Yes, ma'am. Okay . . . Did you want to speak to her? . . . Okay, hold on.

"Tiffany, telephone!" Patrice waited until she heard Tiffany pick up an alternate handset before hanging up.

"Okay, getting back to y'all. Why are you asking me what do I want you to do? I want you to hook this place up like I did for your party," she exclaimed looking at Lorene.

"Yeah, but you're an expert when it comes to putting parties together," Lorene whined.

"Girl, stop acting like a baby and start decorating the place."

Lorene and Faye were trying their best to decorate, but they were having a difficult time. Patrice was busy trying to decorate herself without worrying about them. She then thought about her reccurring dream and decided to share it with her friends.

"Y'all, I been having dreams about a man in white watching me. He is fine, and I'm a little girl in the dream. Every time a dog tries to attack me, he pulls out a gun and kills it. Sometimes it's been two dogs."

"That's strange," Faye said.

"I thought so too. And last night I dreamed the same dream, except this time it was several dogs coming at me. He takes that same gun and kills every last one of them."

"Well, Patrice, maybe that is the Lord watching over you, and while the enemy is trying to attack you, God is protecting you. Have you ever thought about that?" Lorene asked.

"You know, to be honest with you, I haven't."
Fear came over her all at once, and she had a
blank stare on her face.

"Are you okay?" Faye asked.

Patrice tried not to let her imagination run
away with her. "Yeah, I'm fine."

She saw that Lorene and Faye were still struggling with the decorations and stared with crinkled brows.

"We're serious, Trice. We don't know what
we're doing," Faye said.

"Lord have mercy. Y'all are a trip. Lo, you blow
up the balloons with that helium pump over
there. Pick out the white ones only. Faye, I want
you to put some confetti on the bar, just a dash,
and line the goblets up in a row."

"Where are you going to put the white rose
garland?"

"In all of the doorways," she told Faye. "I have
a cream lace tablecloth packed up somewhere.
Once I find it, Lo, I need you to put it on the coffee table and let it hang off the sides. Lord, help
me deal with 'Dumb-Dumb Decor.' "

They laughed.

All of a sudden Patrice felt a little dizzy and
began to lose her balance.

Lorene and Faye immediately stopped what
they were doing and ran over to her.

"Girl, are you all right?" Lorene asked, her voice laced with concern.

"Yeah, I'm all right," Patrice said weakly. She then looked at her stomach and rubbed it. "You're really making me go through some changes."

Lorene and Faye looked at each other, their mouths wide open and their eyes almost popping out of their sockets.

"What!" Faye screamed.

"Oh my God!"

"You lying!" Faye said.

"I wish I was."

"What does Glen have to say about it?" Lorene asked

"I haven't told him yet. I wanted to wait until tonight at the party."

"Awww," Faye cooed. "We're the first to know."

"You weren't supposed to be. That was by accident."

"Wait a minute, I thought you weren't going give him any until he asked to marry you?"

Faye looked at Lorene. "She didn't take your advice, Lo. She's supposed to be running."

Lorene rolled her eyes and smacked her lips. "Chile, I didn't take my own advice. I had to stop and rest myself," she said, blushing.

Now it was Patrice's turn to open her mouth and stretch her eyes. Faye did as well.

"Patrice, what are y'all looking scared about?" Tiffany had come back downstairs and noticed their faces.

"Sweetie, your auntie Lorene got her some cookies."

They laughed.

"Auntie Lorene, may I have some cookies?"

"These type of cookies are for grown-ups, baby," Patrice answered.

They laughed again.

"Tiffany, sweetheart, can you do me a favor? Can you go upstairs and watch TV for a little bit? I and Auntie Lo and Auntie Faye have to talk. I promise, when we are done, you can help with the decorations. You probably know how to decorate better than these two, but I'll call you. I promise, okay."

Tiffany pouted. "Okay."

Patrice watched Tiffany until the coast was clear. Once it was, she looked at Lo and put her hands on her hips. "What in the world?"

"I know. Don't even preach to me but, girl, like Keith said, 'What's done is done,' and, honey, he did me right. I understand why y'all don't run. That junk feels good." Lorene leaned back in the chair and touched her chest.

"I can't believe I'm hearing this. Do you, Faye?"

Faye eyes were still stretched. "No way."

"So give us details," Patrice ordered, taking a seat on the sofa beside Lorene.

Lorene told them everything. From the time Keith stepped his foot in the door up until they left for Disney World.

"So did y'all do the do at Disney World too? Oh, oh. Go on, Faye. I'm a poet." Faye smiled.

"No, we are going to wait until we're married."

Lorene laughed before giving her response. "Girl, you're crazy, but no, we didn't do it. We just lay in the bed in nude and caressed each other. We told ourselves we weren't going to do it anymore until we're married."

"You might as well have given the man some. That fish ain't fresh no more, heifa. Humph, all I got to say is that you have more willpower than me because, if Glen is poking that pipe behind me, I'm going to open wide." Patrice chuckled.

"You ain't lying! Honey, chile, if I'm going to be in the magical world with my man, you better believe I'm going to rock his." Faye stood in the middle of the floor, her legs gapped open, bouncing as if she were riding on the back of a horse.

They all were bursting at the seams with laughter.

Chapter Forty-nine

Glen had been roaming the streets all day. He knew he couldn't keep doing this every day. He was trying to think of a way to tell Patrice, but couldn't. He'd watched two movies, dined alone, and now he was window-shopping in the mall. He was browsing in JCPenney's when he ran into Donald.

Donald was shocked to see Glen, and was mad as hell to see him walking free. He thought for sure they had sent him upstate. He wanted Glen locked up. "What's up, man? Are you all right? I heard what went down in the hall today." Donald acted as though he was concerned.

"Man, it's a big mess. I ain't a thief, and the sad part about it is, they know this. But that's all good, though, because my mother used to always say, 'What's done in the dark will come to light.' I'm sure my lawyer will get to the bottom of this. My thing is, right now, I don't know what to tell Patrice."

"You mean, she doesn't know yet?" Donald told himself that he had to put that on his to-do list. He was planning on calling Patrice and asking her where Glen was, because he hadn't been at work.

"Naw, man, I ain't trying to burden her with that. I promised her that I will take care of her and I don't want her to go all off in a frenzy."

"I feel you on that one, bro. Lisa trips off of little stuff too." He laughed, hoping that Glen would too, but he didn't. He cleared his throat. "So what are you going to do?"

"Just take it one day at a time, man, one day at a time."

They talked more about a few other things.

"Oh yeah, did you get the invitation to Patrice's birthday party? If so, I hope you and Lisa are coming."

"Yeah, yeah, we're coming for sure. She's going to have it on the boat in Smithfield, right?"

"Naw, man. I'm sorry. So much has been happening lately, I forgot to call you and tell you that she decided to have it at our home."

"Oh, that's cool. To tell you the truth, I get seasick."

"I know what you mean."

Glen quickly gave Donald his address, and then slapped his hand in a shake. "I'll see you tonight."

Chapter Fifty

Dwayne visited his mother's gravesite today, bringing new flowers to replace the old ones. He sat there for a moment, and the tears began to flow. Then he began talking to his mother like she was actually sitting in front of him.

"Ma, how are things going? I'm sure the Lord is taking care of you. Can you please ask Him to look after me? Ma, it's hard. You probably already know, but Tracey came to your funeral. Ma, I really love him, I'm not even going to lie. I almost gave myself to him, Ma. On the same day you were buried, at that. You will be proud of your son to know that I didn't."

Dwayne's voice was cracking, and he wiped away the tears and stopped crying. "Thank you so much for loving me and accepting me for who I am. I know it wasn't easy. While other sons were bringing home beautiful women to their mothers, I was bringing other men. I'm sorry,

Ma, for hurting you. I know I can't take it back, but I can try to do something about it right now. Ma, I'm so tired. I'm tired of the hurt and pain. I can't bear it any longer. Before, you made it all easy, but now that you're gone, I can't do this anymore. Ma, I want the Lord in my life. I know He has thrown me away, but, Ma, you are close neighbors to Him. Please talk to Him and ask Him, will He consider coming into my life. Ma, every night I hear you tell me, 'Son be a man.' Now I'm trying to do just that. I know it's not going to be easy, but please have patience with me."

Dwayne was silent for a moment, and he began to cry again.

"Do you know what else, Ma? I'm not mad at you for killing Daddy. Please don't carry that guilt and shame in a glorious place. Even the Lord had wrote in His word, there will be a time to kill, and a time to heal, a time to break down and a time to build up. So, Ma, you had to do what had to be done. If you didn't kill him, he would have ended up killing me. Just to let you know, I am healed. I'm fine with everything now. Yes, I do miss you terribly, but I'm okay. I've come to the conclusion that I have to tear down these walls of homosexuality. I'm hitting one brick at a time, but believe me, it's coming down.

And I will begin to be the man that you and the Lord desire me to be. I know it had to be my desire first. It is my desire to do just that."

Dwayne gently touched the flower petals as if he were touching his mother's face. Then he stood and began walking slowly to his car. He looked back at the grave for a moment then he got in his car and drove home. He had to get ready for Patrice's party.

Chapter Fifty-one

Everybody that Patrice invited came to her party dressed in white, off-white, or cream as she'd requested. She looked extremely elegant in her cream tube blouse, with the front looking as though a big scarf hung around her hips. She wore a long sheer cream flowing skirt that tied at the waist on the side. She purposely forfeited a slip, wanting to show off her shapely legs underneath. She had on low-heeled thong sandals and her toes were freshly done in a French pedicure as well as her nails. She let her hair hang on her shoulders and looked absolutely gorgeous. Glen wore cream permanent press slacks paired with a sheer cream muscle shirt revealing his wife-beater underneath and his muscular pectorals. With a pair of cream Stacy Adams on his feet, the brother was divine.

When the guests arrived, they put their gifts on the table that Patrice had set up in the living room. Every one was amazed at how the place was decorated.

Lisa asked Patrice, "Did you hire someone to do the décor?"

"No, ma'am, I did it myself."

"Well, darling, this is magnificent. You have to give me one of your business cards so I can call you when I need some help with my party planning."

"Well, I don't have any business cards, but you're more than welcome to call me."

"Okay, great." Lisa smiled.

"But you know what? That's a good idea. I'd never thought of that. I have to make a note to buy some." Patrice patted Lisa's hand softly and walked to her next guest. She gave Peaches a hug. "Peaches, I'm so glad you made it. I thought you would have to work."

"I did, but I called out sick." He coughed into his fist then patted his chest, before they both burst into laughter.

"Aww, Dwayne came to my birthday party," Patrice said, as if she was talking to a two-year-old.

Dwayne kissed her cheek. "Happy birthday, precious."

Overhearing her father's name for her, Lorene interjected, "That's my name. Don't be calling nobody else that."

"So are you doing okay?" Patrice asked Dwayne.

"Yes. I visited the gravesite today. I really felt my mother's presence."

"Know that she will always be with you right here." Patrice pointed to her own heart.

Someone tapped Patrice's shoulder. "Excuse me, beautiful lady."

"Oh my goodness, Alvin." Patrice gave him a hug. "I'm so glad you could make it."

"Yeah, same here. You and Glen have a beautiful home."

"Thank you. So how is everything?" Patrice searched his eyes, looking for information about Christina.

"Everything will be all right. From what it looks like, she is only going to serve a year, being that this is her first offense."

"That will pass before you know it. Try to keep your head up."

"Oh most definitely."

"Well, enjoy yourself."

He nodded.

Glancing around the room for Glen, she spotted him standing by the bar talking to Donald, his eyes fixated on her. She smiled and mouthed, "I love you."

Glen winked in response then moved to turn the stereo down. Crossing the room, he gathered Patrice in his arms and held her at the waist. "Everyone, may I have your attention, please."

In a few seconds, the guests had quieted themselves and turned their attention toward Glen and Patrice.

"I would like to take this time and thank everyone that came to my baby's birthday party. Of course, it's tradition that we sing to the honoree." He looked at Keith and gave him the cue to dim the lights.

Then Lorene came from the kitchen with yellow sheet cake with white frosting. Around the edge of the cake was white frosting tulips with the green stems. Protruding from each tulip was a candle. The wording on the cake read: *We love you, Patrice. Happy Birthday*. Glen counted to three and the group began to sing the birthday song.

"Baby, I hope you have a plenty more that you will share with me. I love you so much. It's not just me that loves you, but... come here, Tiff."

Tiffany broke through the crowd in a white party dress and a head full of Shirley Temple curls. When she made it to her daddy, he picked her up in his arms and said, "Tiffany loves you too."

"Aww," the guests sang in unison, some of them applauding.

Once Glen put Tiffany down, he lowered himself to one knee, pulled the engagement ring from his pocket, and said, "And because we love you"—Tiffany got on her knees as well—"will you marry us?"

Completely elated, Patrice joined them on the floor and wrapped her arms around the both of them. "Yes." She kissed Tiffany on the cheek and gave Glen a long, everlasting kiss. "Yes, Glen! I'll marry both of you!"

Everyone one started clapping, but even when the clapping ended, their lips were still locked together.

Donald cleared his throat. "Dag, man, can we get back to the party?"

"I ain't kidding," Keith said.

Tiffany pushed Glen's arm. "Daddy, stop. You're embarrassing me," she said, evoking a laugh from the guests.

Glen pulled away from Patrice and looked at Tiffany with a no-you-didn't look. "Okay, I'll stop embarrassing you. It's past your bed time anyway."

"Can I have a piece of cake first?"

"Yes, but when you finish, I want you to go to bed."

"Are you going to pray with me?"

"Yes, ma'am, and tuck you in like I do every night." He pecked her on the forehead.

Keith looked at Glen's collection of tapes and found the Commodores. A few seconds later, "Brick House" blared through the speakers and couples began to dance. Since Dwayne and Peaches didn't have a date, they were in the corner popping their fingers, switching their hips better than a woman.

Faye and Bobby danced with their wine goblets in their hands. Faye raised her glass in the air and yelled at Patrice and Glen, "Y'all about to run out of the good stuff."

Glen stopped dancing and said, "I got some more."

Patrice saw Tiffany licking her fingers from the cake and swaying her little hips from side to side. "Look, baby," she said, nudging Glen and motioning toward Tiffany with her head. "I think you better get her to bed. I'll get the wine. Where is it anyway?"

"In the basement."

Patrice kissed Tiffany good night and told Glen to hurry back. Then she made her way to the basement. She glanced through an assortment of bottles, reading the labels, not quite sure what to bring up. Hearing footsteps on the way down to join her, she yelled out, "Baby, I can't find it."

"I'm sure it's down here somewhere."

Startled, Patrice gasped, realizing that it wasn't Glen, but rather Donald, who'd made his way to the lower level of the house. She took a quick look at him and continued her search. "Donald, what are you doing down here? You're missing the party."

"The party is down here," he snarled.

She quickly looked at him and saw that his usually friendly eyes were now filled with hate. Right away she became frightened, but hid it from him. "I can't find anything good. They're just going to have to drink punch."

She tried to take quick steps toward the stairs, but Donald grabbed her tightly from behind.

"Where are you going, pretty young thing? It's your birthday, and I want to give you a nice gift." Donald, breathing heavily in her ear, lifted her dress.

Patrice began to cry softly. "Donald, please don't do this. People are going to start wondering where I am."

"Not if we make this quick. You know you're so sexy. You smell sooooo good."

Patrice tried to pull away from him but couldn't. He was definitely too strong. She could feel his manhood growing behind her as he rubbed her hard between her legs.

Her mind raced back to when she and Glen first had sex. She realized, that wasn't rape, but this was. She pleaded, "Donald, please don't do this. Please, please," her tears flowing rapidly.

The pleading made Donald grind even the more. "Yeah, baby, that's it. I love when a whore begs."

Chapter Fifty-two

"God, thank You for the food I eat, the clothes I wear, and the shoes for my feet. Thank You for the roof over my head, and thank You for this nice warm bed. God bless Daddy, Patrice, Grandma, and Aunt Emma. And God don't forget about Mommy. I don't know where she is. I can't find her, and she won't call me. Please watch over her like Daddy and Patrice watch over me. Amen," Tiffany ended. "Good night, Daddy." She hugged Glen and gave him a kiss.

Touched and impressed by her prayer, Glen couldn't help but ask, "Where did you learn to pray like that?"

"Patrice."

Glen's smile quickly faded. "Baby, I want to tell you something. I don't want you to be upset when I tell you because I want you to know that I am here as well as Patrice, and your Aunt Emma."

"What about Grandma?'

"Yes, she's here for you too, but she lives rather far away. Listen, sweetie, you might not see or talk to Mommy for a long time."

With a saddened face, Tiffany asked, "Why?"

"Because, sweetheart, she lives with the bad people now. Your mommy did some very bad things. Remember she was giving that man a brown package?" Tiffany nodded slowly.

"Well, what was in that package was bad powder that makes people sick and sometimes die. She wasn't supposed to do that. The policeman said that it's against the law to do that. And when you do things that the policeman tells you not to do, they will put you where the bad people are."

Tiffany sat silently, trying her best to understand her father's words.

"But I want you to know that you'll be okay because you're with me and Patrice now."

"Well, since Mommy is gone, can I call Patrice *Mommy*?"

Glen smiled and kissed Tiffany on the forehead. "She would love for you to call her that." He wrapped the little girl in his arms and kissed her once more. "Good night baby girl."

"Good night, Daddy," she replied, snuggling beneath her comforter.

Glen rose from her bedside, tiptoed out and closed her bedroom door behind him. He jogged down the stairs to rejoin the party, where everyone was still in the middle of cutting the rug. His eyes scanned the room. "Lo, you seen my baby?"

"Last time I saw her was when she was getting more wine." Lo barely looked up at Glen as Keith twirled her into his arms.

"Thanks." Glen went to the doorway that led to the basement. "Trice! Trice!" When she didn't respond, he started to close the door, to look elsewhere for her, but just before he did, he heard something hit the floor in the basement, drawing him downstairs, where he found Donald holding a gun to Patrice's head, her eyes bloodshot red from crying.

Shocked, Glen stood frozen for a split second. "Man, what are you doing?" He tried to speak in a calm voice, although he actually was overcome instantly with rage.

"You can't see what I'm doing? You're dumber than I thought. You are determined to ruin folks' lives. You can't take a simple warning and leave Jessica and Tiffany the hell alone like we asked you too."

Suddenly Glen realized why Donald had looked so familiar. It wasn't from the college campus that he knew him. This was the man that stabbed him in the leg several years ago.

Donald could see that it was all coming back to Glen. "Oh, now your ass wants to remember. Oh, it's too late now, nigga. I was just about to get me some of this sweet pussy you talk so much about. You made it sound so enticing, I thought I should try some."

Furious, Glen charged at Donald, but came to a dead stop when he heard the click of a gun.

"Try it. Just try it. You'll see this gorgeous whore in a red dress instead of a white one."

Patrice couldn't help but be reminded of her dreams. Donald must have been the pack of dogs, and the man in white was God. Then she weakly cried out, "Jesus, oh Jesus, please, Jesus."

Just then, the basement door opened, and someone began coming down the stairs. Donald shot his eyes upwards, trying to see who it was, giving Glen the perfect opportunity to push Donald's hand away from Patrice's head. And Patrice was able to break free, while Donald and Glen wrestled for gun.

Seconds later, Keith was shot. He stumbled down the last few steps then collapsed on the basement floor.

Patrice let out a shrill scream. She could hear that the music had stopped as the guests began to rush to the entrance of the basement.

"Call the ambulance!" Lorene blurted through her tears, seeing Keith covered in blood at the bottom of the stairs. Suddenly she began to get dizzy and lose her balance, nearly fainting, and Dwayne, who stood behind her, was able to catch her from falling down the steps.

Still struggling with each other, Glen hit Donald in the temple of his head, instantly dropping him to his knees, and blood squirted out like a water fountain. And Glen continued to beat on him, kicking him in his head and side.

Patrice didn't want Glen to stop beating him; she wanted Donald dead, but then she heard a small voice say, "Stop him." Initially, she hesitated, but when she heard the voice again, she ran over to pull Glen away from Donald's limp body.

Instinctively, Glen pushed Patrice away, causing Patrice to lose her balance and stumble backward into a fall.

"Oh my God, the baby!" Faye screamed as she rushed to Patrice's side.

Those words brought Glen to an instant stop.

Chapter Fifty-three

Keith, Donald, Patrice, and Lorene were taken to the hospital. Preliminary test were run on Patrice to see if she and the baby were all right, and luckily, they were just fine. Patrice was put on bed rest for a couple of days.

Lorene was fine as well, but couldn't stop worrying about Keith, who was in the Intensive Care Unit. He had been shot in the lower part of his stomach. The bullet pierced his liver, causing both internal and external bleeding, which the doctors had a hard time stopping. He was connected to machines to monitor his heart, blood pressure, and respiratory rate. He was even connected to a ventilator.

Keith's family along with Lorene was in the visiting room when the doctor came in. He was looking at some medical reports. He lifted his brows to scan the faces in the waiting room. "Is there a Katherine Simmons in the room?"

Terribly shaken, Mrs. Simmons didn't respond right away, but Carrie spoke up on her behalf. "This Katherine Simmons, our mother."

"I need to speak with you for a moment." Seeing how upset she was, he suggested that someone come with her.

"Ma, do you want me to go with you?" Marie asked.

"No, I'll be fine," she said, her voice hoarse.

"No, you're not. I'll come with you," James offered.

"Are you her husband?" the doctor asked.

"No, I'm her brother."

"Come with me." The doctor led the way to a small room.

When they disappeared behind closed doors, Carrie began pacing back and forth. "See, you can't be around black niggers! They ain't nothing but trouble!" She looked at Lorene with evil eyes. "I should have known something like this was going to happen, hanging around black-ass spooks. Shit! He always reading the Bible. Didn't he see that darkness can't comprehend the light?" Once again she looked at Lorene.

Lorene stared, waiting for Carrie to finish venting. When she saw that Carrie didn't have anything else to say, she simply bowed her head in a silent prayer. "Lord, I would like to ask for

Your forgiveness. I am truly sorry for what I am about to do. Lord, I'm trying to tame my tongue, but now it's time to attack."

Lorene lifted her head up slowly, her narrowed eyes dead set on Carrie. "Look, you ignorant, wannabe-white, ugly-ass bitch. I'm tired of you running your mouth. The only thing that looks decent on you is your clothes. Those big red spots on your face look like a fatal decease. Every time I see you, I want to puke. Whoever told you that dark-skin people are second-class to you was a damn fool. If the KKK sees you walking in the woods alone, they would hang you on a tree and burn your ass, too. Which, at this point, would be perfectly fine with me." Lorene got up from where she was sitting and stood directly in front of Carrie's face. "Now my fiancé has already warned you once, and you don't have any more chances. I'm going to kick your high-yellow ass if you disrespect me one more time." Lorene paused, staring intently at Carrie. "Please jump, so I can do it right now."

Carrie didn't move. Neither did Marie nor Uncle Wilbert.

"I didn't think so." She turned around, went back to her seat and began gazing at the TV as if no one was in the waiting room with her.

Mrs. Simmons had the power of attorney and decided that Keith be maintained on a life-support machine, instructing the doctors to do all they could to keep him alive. She made a brief and somber announcement when she returned to her family. "The doctor said Keith can only have two visitors at a time. We've already been in to see him."

Carrie and Marie looked at Lorene and mumbled a few words, insisting that she go first.

As Lorene entered his room and saw him connected to the various machines, she couldn't hold back the tears. She sat in a chair, rubbed his hand, and stroked his hair. Closing her eyes, she asked the Lord to forgive her again for letting Carrie get the best of her, and then she asked the Lord to bless Keith.

"Baby, please try to fight this. I can't make it without you. You've become a part of me, and if you die I will too. Please fight. Hold on, baby, you'll be okay. You will." Lorene felt his hand twitch.

"I am fighting," he whispered. "I'm fighting, Lo."

With a slight smile, Lorene leaned in to kiss his cheek.

Keith smiled back. "Now that's the best thing I've felt since I been here."

Chapter Fifty-four

Glen and Patrice tried visiting Keith but were informed that only family members could see him. Nonetheless, they joined the family in the waiting room.

"Hey, Patrice. How are you?" Carrie greeted.

Patrice didn't know what to say. Carrie had thrown her for a loop. *Who in the world set her soul free?* Then Patrice smiled and answered her own question. *Lo.* She must have tasted and seen that Lo will whip her tail. "I'm fine. Thank you for asking. Where's Lo?"

No sooner than she'd asked, Lorene entered the waiting room full of smiles. She was glad to see Patrice and Glen. Not that she didn't have support from her future mother-in-law, but the more friends, the merrier. "He's getting better. We talked briefly."

Marie and Carrie went in to see Keith, while everyone else sat in the waiting room talking for a while.

Patrice and Glen finally said their good-byes and gave Mrs. Simmons and Lorene a hug and left.

On the way home, Glen held Patrice's hand and kissed her palms. It was his normal routine whenever she rode with him. "Are you okay?" he asked.

"Yes."

"Some birthday party, huh?"

"Out of this world."

"I really feel bad for Keith. He is such a cool guy." Glen shook his head. Then he said, "Baby?"

Patrice just stared out the window and didn't respond.

Glen looked back and forth between her and the road. "Baby?" he asked a second time, tapping her thigh.

"Huh?"

"When were you going to tell me that we were having a baby?"

"At the party. Everyone was lavishing me with gifts, so that was supposed to be my way of giving you a gift tonight." She chuckled, shaking her head. "But then Donald happened. Baby, I had no idea he was a snake in the grass. If I did, I wouldn't have put you or Tiffany in harm's way."

"I know you didn't. I'm just glad that son of a you-know-what is locked up."

"If it weren't for you, he would've been locked up in hell. I was going to kill him, babe."

"I know you were. That's why I had to stop you."

Glen brought his hand to her belly and rubbed it. "Our baby." He smiled. "The doctor did say the baby was fine, right?"

"Look at you worrying. Yes, the baby is fine." She smiled. "I just have to rest a couple of days. I don't want to end up putting a strain on the baby, behind stress."

"And I'm going to make sure that you get it. By the way, what are we having?"

"I don't know and don't want to know until I deliver."

When they finally pulled up in the driveway, Faye peeked through the window. She and Bobby had stayed at the house to watch Tiffany. When she saw that it was Glen and Patrice, she opened the door and waited for them to come in the house. She couldn't wait for them to answer her fifty questions.

"Is Keith okay? Are you okay? Where's Lo? How is Mrs. Simmons taking it?

"Calm down, Faye. I and everybody else are doing fine," Patrice assured her.

"Where is Lo then?"

"She's at the hospital. I don't believe she's going to leave Keith's side."

"How is Tiffany?" Glen asked.

"That little girl sleeps like a *bam* stone."

Bobby huffed. "You need to learn how to cuss."

"You need to mind your bizness," Faye said, cutting her eyes.

Patrice shook her head and wondered how the odd couple were always fighting but couldn't do without each other. Then again she remembered Faye commenting that Bobby knew how to handle all of her booty.

"Y'all thank you for watching her. I'm going on ahead and crash for the night," Patrice announced, beginning to climb the staircase.

"You mean, *morning*." Faye glanced at her watch. It read 4:00 A.M. "Poor thang, you didn't even get a chance to open your gifts."

"I know. I just have to open them later on today and send everyone a thank-you card."

"All right. We'll let y'all get some rest. See you later."

After Faye and Bobby left, Glen stuck his head in Tiff's room to see if she was all right. Once he saw that she was sound asleep, he trotted to his own room. He sat on the bed staring at Patrice as she undressed, focusing on her stomach. "Baby,

I know you get tired of me telling you this, but you're so beautiful."

She strolled over to him and hugged him tightly. "No, I'll never get tired of you telling me that."

"I don't want to marry you nine months from now. I think we should get married as soon as possible."

"Why do you say that?"

"Several reasons. Number one, I know you don't want to walk down the aisle with your stomach as big as a beach ball. Number two, I want our child to have my last name. It's kind of a hassle to go through a lot of legal papers to have your child's name changed, like I had to do with Tiffany."

Patrice grinned. "Well, it looks like I have to make some quick wedding plans, huh?"

Later on that morning Patrice had the same dream, except this time, there were no dogs.

Chapter Fifty-five

Glen got a call Monday morning from Mr. Lee requesting to see him as soon as possible. Glen didn't fell like dealing with a bunch of foolishness. He wanted to tell him, "Look, you already fired me, so can you please leave me the hell alone." He found himself, however, headed for the office with several thoughts racing through his mind. He thought, *A man could only take but so much without losing his mind.*

In a month or so, he'd been fired, and betrayed by a man he thought was his friend, but turned out to be his worst enemy, trying to rape his fiancé and kill both of them. Then he found out he was about to have another baby.

Now if he didn't find a job soon, he wasn't going to be able to take care of his family. And on top of that, his soon-to-be pregnant wife was a little stressed out from her best friend's fiancé getting shot and barely hanging on by a thread.

A change had to take place soon.

When he entered the building, Mr. Lee met him at the door and led him to the eighth floor. Then he guided him directly to the conference room. There sitting at the table were Lisa, Ms. Featherstone, Mr. Mathis, who was the City Treasurer and Lisa's boss, and a security guard, along with a policeman standing at the door.

"I know things have been pretty rough for you, but I'm glad you decided to come to speak with me today."

Not in a mood to make conversation, Glen just nodded his head silently.

"Have a seat, Glen."

Glen seated himself slowly, wondering what this was all about.

"Glen, we brought you here to apologize for the loss of your job. There were some misunderstandings on our behalf. I had a talk with Ms. Featherstone. The information that she shared with me made me decide to do some investigation. I must say that we have falsely accused you of embezzlement, and for that we apologize.

"You may have known Lisa Wright, who was the administrator for Mr. Mathis, the City Treasurer. Our records show that you were not here on August 15th, and security doesn't have you on the roster for that day. On that particular day money was drafted to your account—this is where Miss Wright comes in. Ms. Featherstone brought it to my attention that Mr. Purnell had been spending a lot of time in the computer lab. Although that is not a crime, she had her suspicion, because Mr. Purnell did not work in a department that required lab time. The records show that he was talking to Miss Wright. Again, messaging someone is not a crime, but what made our antennas go up was, Miss Wright would come to work on Saturdays, when she wasn't supposed to be here. We audited her computer and found that she was drafting money in your account. She claimed that Mr. Purnell had offered her a substantial amount of money to have you fired. Which is why she is now fired.

"So, to put it all in a nutshell, you fired me under false pretenses. You didn't look into it before firing me." Glen's blood was beginning to boil. "Here I am sitting at home for close to two months without pay because of these allegations."

Mr. Lee pulled out paperwork. "Glen we can not apologize enough. That's why we have a peace offering drawn up. If you don't want to come back to work for us, we can understand. However, if you do, we will add ten thousand dollars to your salary and pay you for your lost time."

That was a nice peace offering, Glen thought, but he was pissed behind the whole ordeal. "Make it twenty."

Mr. Lee and the other board members agreed. He finalized the offer on paper, and both gentlemen and other involved parties signed it.

Glen would report back to work bright and early the following Monday morning.

Chapter Fifty-six

Keith was doing much better. He was able to sit up on his own and go back and forth to the restroom, but he had a ways to go before he'd be released from the hospital. He'd just finished his breakfast the nurse had brought in for him and had a lot left over. He hated hospital food. Lorene would always make something healthy and delicious from home, or bring him things from his favorite deli.

"Merry Christmas," Lorene said to Keith when entering his recovery room. She had a bag full of Christmas presents. It was fun shopping for him, but she was looking forward to them shopping together. As she walked closer to him, she noticed the sad look on his face. "What is it? Are you okay? Do you need me to get the nurse?"

"I just wish I was out of here so I can be with you even more. I didn't plan to spend my Christmas like this."

Lorene rubbed his shoulder then his cheek. "Baby, no one makes plans to be in the hospital, but look at it this way—we will have plenty more Christmases and other holidays to spend together. I just thank God that you're alive. If you'd slipped away from me, I don't know what I would've done."

"I guess I need to be counting my blessings, rather than sitting here crying, huh?"

"It's nothing wrong with crying every now and then. It's healthy."

"Come here." Keith kissed Lorene in the mouth. "I love you."

"I love you too." Lo said, showing all thirty-two.

Keith looked at the bag full of presents. "So what do we have here?"

Lorene pulled out one gift at a time. "Here you are."

Keith opened the box that was wrapped in blue metallic paper and a white bow in the middle and held up the black rayon sweater. "Oooo, this is nice, baby. Thank you."

"There's more." She pulled out another box wrapped the same as the first.

Keith opened it then covered his mouth with a fist. "Oh, snap!" He was happy for his Calvin Klein blue jeans.

Lorene smiled. "I knew you would like them."

"Baby, I love them. They fit so well. I tried them on a while back in October in the mall."

"Okay, well there's more." She gave him a box wrapped in red paper with Christmas trees on it and a gold bow in the corner. Inside was a pair of black suede cats with rims made of black leather. "Baby, you are spoiling me."

"I just believe in sowing good seeds so I can reap good things."

"If you keep sowing seeds like this, you shall reap a harvest of blessings."

The very last thing Lorene gave Keith was a small box from a jewelry store. He looked at the box then at Lo. "What's this?"

"Just open it and see."

When Keith finally had the box open, he saw a gold ring band that had diamonds in it. "Baby?" he said, stunned.

"I thought it would be nice if a man can get an engagement ring for once. So this is to let people know that you're spoken for, before the wedding day."

He reached out for her, and they kissed passionately. He looked at his hand as Lorene slid the ring onto his finger.

"I'm so ready to get out of here, Lo. I want to go shopping and buy you some nice things. To top it off, I don't believe I would be out of here before the first of January. Even if I did, I'd still have to make arrangements for our wedding. This is just one big mess."

"Baby, I told you we can worry about that when you are out of here. It will be soon."

"Yeah, but not soon enough." He looked at Lorene and could tell that an idea was brewing in that pretty head of hers. "What's on your mind?"

"Let's get married on January the first."

"Baby, didn't you just hear what I said? I'm not going to be out of here by then."

"Yes, I heard you, but what I am saying is we can get married right here. My pastor can join us together in holy matrimony, Daddy can give me away, and our friends can come and witness it," she said excitedly.

"No, we can't do that. I know you women love to have big weddings, and now you're talking about a sick-and-shut-in wedding? Oh, no. Besides, we already made plans to be married June first."

"Baby, I don't care about that. Think about it, our theme is 'New Beginnings,' right? Well, what better day to get married than the first of the year? Honey, my concern is being your wife for the rest of my life. We can have a big wedding and reception later."

"You would want to do that?"

"Most definitely. Wouldn't you?"

"I wouldn't have it any other way."

Lorene grinned from ear to ear.

Just then, Mrs. Simmons came in the room along with her daughters. "Merry Christmas, sweetie." She kissed Keith on the cheek, and her daughters did the same.

Carrie and Marie even went to Lorene and gave her a genuine hug and smile. Lorene almost fainted. Lorene then focused her attention back on Mrs. Simmons. She too had a bag full of presents. Actually she had three bags full. Carrie and Marie were each carrying one.

"Baby, I took the liberty to do your shopping for you," said Mrs. Simmons.

"How did you manage to do that?"

"While I was cleaning out your room, I saw your Christmas list lying under the bed."

"Yeah, and our names weren't on it," Carrie said, referring to herself and Marie. "But we don't blame you though. We've been acting like bi"—Carrie caught herself from cussing in front of her mother. She again looked at Lorene and smiled.

Mrs. Simmons gave one of the bags to Lorene. The other bags of gifts were from her and her daughters to Keith and Lorene.

Lorene opened her gifts that supposedly came from Keith, giving him a kiss for every one she opened—a Louis Vuitton pocketbook, a black leather jacket, a pair of boots, a herringbone gold necklace, and a pair of gold hoop earrings.

Chapter Fifty-seven

Patrice stood in the kitchen cooking Christmas dinner. She had invited her friends from the choir over. She felt as though she had to do something to make up for the tragedy that happened on her birthday. She also invited her mother and Mrs. Parker, who Glen and Tiffany had gone to pick up an hour earlier.

She made a roast turkey, candied yams, corn pudding, smoked ham, fried chicken, cabbages, collard greens, potato salad, and macaroni and cheese, and her mother helped her through a batch of yeast rolls, which came out golden brown.

While she set the table, her mind went back to her shopping experience at Montgomery Ward the day before. Glen had given her his credit card and told her to use it as she pleased.

She was in the jewelry section trying to decide what to buy Glen when she ran into Bishop Thompson's nephew, Quinton.

"How are you doing?" he asked, smiling.

"I'm fine, and yourself?"

"Umph, umph, umph. Yes, you are fine. Are you still singing so beautifully?"

"I try."

"You know you can come sing for me anytime." Quinton stepped a little closer. "I ain't talking about singing for me in church neither." He licked his lips and looked at Patrice's breasts.

If you don't step back, you pencil-dick monkey . . . Patrice laughed softly and said, "Do you know what? I'm engaged. I became an instant mother, and now I'm three months pregnant. So you might as well put your tongue back in your head because it's too late to get this sweetness ever again." *Thank you, Jesus.* Her eyes dropped to his crotch then rolled away. She laughed again and said walking away, "Merry Christmas Rev. Thompson."

Patrice saw a silver Timex watch she wanted to give Glen. She thought about stealing it. She was just about to stick it underneath her arm, but then she thought about how God had always had her back in spite of her wrongful ways. She would never forget how He protected her from Donald. So, instead of stealing the watch, she put it in the shopping cart to purchase it.

As soon as she started to leave the jewelry section, she noticed someone watching her. It was Leslie. Patrice gave her an evil look. Leslie did the same.

Patrice didn't want her to think for a moment that she was intimidated by her. Really she was. Patrice hurried up and purchased her items and left the store.

Patrice heard Glen coming in the house, talking to Annie Ruth and Mrs. Parker. He told them to have a seat and make themselves at home. He and Tiffany came in the kitchen where she was.

"Hey, baby." He gave her a peck on the lips.

Tiffany saw the Duncan Hines cake mix on the table. "Oooo, can I lick the mixing bowl when you are done?"

Glen asked, "What do you know about a mixing bowl?"

"Auntie Emma makes cake all the time, and she lets me lick the bowl."

Patrice told her, "Yes, you can lick the bowl, but you have to put it in the sink when you are done."

"Yes, ma'am. Are you going to make it now?"

"I was hoping Ma will make the cake." Patrice made her statement loud enough for her mother to hear from the living room.

Annie Ruth yelled back, "I hear you in there. I'm a guest, I'm not supposed to be cooking."

Glen went to Annie Ruth. "Mother Russell, please bake the cake. Patrice made a cake one time and it was all lopsided. It doesn't matter who does it, you or Mrs. Parker."

"Forget you, Glen! I'm not going to cook anything else for your ungrateful butt."

"Baby, you know I'm just teasing you."

"Mmm-hmm, yeah, right. But it was lopsided, wasn't it?"

Mrs. Parker said, "We ain't havin no lopsided cake for Christmas, so let me git on up and fix this heya cake."

Tiffany yelled, "Yea!"

Just before everyone came, Glen and his family opened their gifts. Tiffany was ecstatic to see her huge dollhouse and bicycle. Glen gave Mrs. Parker a deep burgundy two-piece suit, and Annie Ruth a navy blue two-piece suit. He knew they would appreciate it, since they went to church all the time.

He opened his gifts and saw that Patrice had good taste in clothing. She gave him two shirts and two pairs of slacks from Gents, the watch, several pairs of socks, and a black pair of Stacy Adams.

Patrice pouted when she didn't see a gift under the tree for her.

Glen noticed and asked, "Do y'all want to see Patrice's gift?"

Everyone looked confused.

He took Patrice by the hand and told everyone, "Follow me." He guided them through the kitchen and opened the side door that led to the two-car garage.

When Patrice saw her brand-new blue Dodge Caravan with a big red bow tied around it, she screamed with excitement. She kissed Glen and ran to her new van to check out the interior.

Later on, once again everyone showed up for Christmas dinner, except Lorene. She was spending her Christmas with Keith. They laughed and had a good time just enjoying each other's company.

Patrice went to get the cake that Mrs. Parker had made, which was sitting on the counter. In doing so, she had to walk by the basement door. Her mind flashed back to her birthday. She was so glad that Donald's behind was in jail for good.

Chapter Fifty-eight

"Open up." A big nasty-looking white nurse was trying to feed Donald some "applesauce" in the infirmary.

Glen had really messed him up. His two front teeth were missing, and he had no feeling in his face. His left eye looked as though someone had stuck a knife in it. *Some way to spend Christmas*, he thought. Donald had plenty of regrets, but of course it was too late. His court date wasn't until that following February, but things didn't look good for him. He was being charged for attempted rape, attempted murder, and setting up Glen for embezzlement, and was going to spend the rest of his life in prison.

The nurse had to change his bedpan and clean him up. The entire time she was doing so, she was trying to give Donald her sexy bedroom eyes. She rubbed his face and said, "You are a cute one." She then started to play with his penis.

Donald was having a fit. "Get your damn hands off of me, you big bucket of lard."

"Honey, I don't think that you are in a position to tell me what to do. Looks to me I'm going to have a good time riding this black pole." She put a *Do not disturb* sign on the door and locked it. She then showed Donald porn magazines.

He knew what she was up to, so he closed his eyes. "Open your damn eyes before I stick this needle in your ass."

He knew she was serious as a heart attack, so he did as he was told.

After seeing a couple of pages Donald's penis was hard as a rock. Her eyes were gleaming with joy. She pushed the button on the side of the bed to make it low. She climbed on top of him and did what she said she was going to do—ride the black pole.

After she was done she said, "You are better than my husband. Look like I'm going to pull some long shifts from now on."

Donald cried like a baby. He never thought in a million years he would be raped by "Herman the She-Munster."

Chapter Fifty-nine

Patrice was so nervous. She had on a beautiful white sleeveless gown embroidered with white pearls, and long white gloves with the fingers cut out. She didn't pin up her hair. "How do I look?"

"You look beautiful."

"Even with this big beach ball in front of me?"

"Yes, especially with your beach ball," Lorene cooed, rubbing Patrice's stomach. "Aww, look at my little niece growing so fast." Then she looked in the mirror trying to touch up her makeup.

Lorene was now Mrs. Lorene Denise Simmons. She and Keith were married for three months now. She had on a white gown with wide laced straps on her shoulders. It was trimmed in small pearls at the bottom. Both of the girls' trains were twenty feet long.

On this glorious morning Lorene would be walking down the aisle along with her best friend to meet their soon-to-be lifetime partners.

"Lo, tell me the truth. I'm serious. How do I look?"

Lorene sighed. "You just asked me that. Stop worrying about the beach ball. The way the dress is made, it's covering it up very well. Girl, you look good to be six months pregnant, so stop tripping."

"Okay, okay. Lo, can you believe this? You and I are getting married on the same day."

"I know. When I suggested the idea of us having our ceremony on the same day to Keith he was acting a little selfish. He wanted everyone to focus on me, rather than you and I."

"Are you serious? Girl, I ain't mad. Glen felt the same way. But, you know, a little pouting goes a long way," Patrice said with a sly grin.

Lorene mirrored her grin. "Doesn't it?"

They paused for a moment and then burst into laughter.

"Are you two okay in here?" Regina came in to check and see if there were any last-minute touches that had to be made. She was the wedding coordinator. Only eighteen, the girl handled her business like she'd been doing it for years.

"We're fine," Lorene said.

"Okay, be ready in five more minutes." Regina closed the door and went back into the sanctuary.

The wedding processional began. Dwayne played softly while the bridal party entered. Bishop Thompson, Keith, and Glen came in from the side door of the sanctuary. Reginald and Bobby lit the candelabras, one on either side of the church.

After lighting the candles, they walked down the aisle to escort the mothers. Bobby escorted Mrs. Annie Ruth Russell, and Reginald escorted Mrs. Parker and Ms. Mary to their designated seats. After they were seated, the men rolled out the white paper down the aisle.

Jean came down the aisle with Reginald, Faye came with Bobby, and Carrie came with Jerome. Then Glen's sister and brother; Sharon and Boone came down the aisle together.

Normally one side will have all bridesmaids and the other, groomsmen. This time it was two couples on each side. Marcus came down the aisle with a soft baby blue silk pillow that held the rings. He stood in between his Uncle Keith and Glen.

After they stood in their positions, it was Tiffany's turn. She had on a pretty soft blue dress with a lace shawl. She wore white gloves, white socks, and white shoes. Her hair was parted in a ponytail up top, and the rest of her hair hung low. She had baby's breath in her hair. She threw down the blue flower petals on the paper. When she was done, she stood by Faye.

Everyone stood when they saw Rev. McCall standing in between the beautiful brides. He escorted both of them down the aisle. Patrice's father was deceased, but she always felt as though Rev. McCall was her father too. Patrice and Lorene didn't want the traditional wedding march, "Here Comes the Bride." Besides, it was two brides instead of one. So instead they had Dwayne play "We've Only Just Begun," by Paul Williams and Roger Nichols.

They were now in front of the church, ready to take their vows. When Bishop Thompson asked who was giving these beautiful brides away, Rev. McCall said, "I am." and took a seat up front.

When they exchanged vows Patrice and Lorene sang a song to their husbands. Patrice took the high, and Lorene took the low. They sang "Endless Love" by Lionel Ritchie, with a twist, because normally the song is sung by a male and female. But Patrice and Lorene sang beautifully. They both had Keith and Glen crying, and a few others.

It was time for the grooms to kiss the brides. It was as though Keith and Glen made a bet on who could kiss the bride the longest, because they wouldn't let up.

Tiffany pulled on Glen's coat and said, "Daddy, you are embarrassing me again."

Glen finally came up for air and looked at Tiffany. "Sorry."

Everyone laughed.

Bishop Thompson had the newlyweds face the audience and says, "Ladies and gentlemen, I now present to you Mr. and Mrs. Keith Simmons, and Mr. and Mrs. Glen Pearson."

Epilogue

When Tamika had awakened, Tiffany yelled, "Mommy, the baby is crying,"

Patrice was downstairs warming her bottle, knowing she'd be up in a few minutes. "Okay, sweetie, I'll be up in a minute."

Once the bottle was ready Patrice went upstairs in the nursery and fed little Tamika the bottle. She called Glen at the office.

"Mr. Pearson."

"Hey, baby."

"Hey, how's everything?"

"Fine. I'm running just a little behind schedule. Tiffany is still here. After I feed Tamika, I'm going to take her to school."

"Let me speak to my little pumpkin."

"Glen, she can't talk."

"I want to hear her cooing."

Patrice put the phone to Tamika's ear.

"Hey, little sunshine. How's daddy's baby?"

Tamika didn't coo. She was too busy trying to drink all of the milk. Glen smiled when he heard her sucking the bottle and taking breaths in between.

"Glen, I called to let you know you have to be home on time today. I have to meet with a client about planning a party, and I have class at eight o'clock tonight."

Patrice had taken Lisa's advice. She wasn't only a party planner, but now she'd decided to take courses in it. After the Donald incident, she opened her eyes to what Glen was saying awhile back. She needed to be able to do something to take care of her and their children, just in case something ever happened to him. At first she was planning on just making a little cash for decorating and planning parties for her clients, but she wanted to have a better understanding of dealing with people in the business world, and also become a certified planner. So far, her business was doing very well.

"I will. Are you planning on having another birthday party this year?"

"Heck no, not after all that drama last year."

"Well, how does dinner and a movie sound?"

"It sounds great."

"Good. I'll see you at five thirty. I love you."

"Love you too." Patrice thought about calling Lorene before she left but decided against it. She was just wondering how her friend was doing. But she had to get Tiffany to school. It's just that she didn't see Lorene that much anymore, now that she had got out of the choir.

Lorene and Keith were doing exceptionally well. Keith had bought a house in Smithfield, and Lorene was three weeks pregnant. She also had a mother now. Rev. McCall married Evelyn Smith.

Faye and Bobby were still together. He was now the owner of a fitness gym and Faye, a teller at a local bank. Bobby called Glen the other night, talking about settling down. Glen told him, "Go for it. Faye's a good girl."

Occasionally Dwayne still thought about the horrible things his father had done to him. He still missed his mother terribly.

One Sunday evening he had to play for a youth concert. He noticed that the youth director from a visiting church kept eyeing him. After church he stepped up to Dwayne to introduce himself.

Well, to make a long story short, Dwayne is in love again.

Readers Discussion Questions

1. Patrice was raised in the church. She knew the Bible like the back of her hand. She knew you could have a better life if you give it to Jesus. A lot of folks can live better lives but yet want to live like the devil. Why?

2. Glen chose to run from his problems, instead of facing them. He had already identified the brothers that beat him very badly. He felt as though his life was threatened. Would you have run?

3. Patrice had warned Christina about Leslie. Why didn't Christina listen?

4. Lorene was very forgiving after finding out the truth about her tires. Would you have done the same thing?

5. Lorene had not been living for God as long as Keith had. Keith should have known better than to fornicate and swear. Do you think he was really saved, or was he being a hypocrite?

6. Jessica already had enough money to dodge but yet she stayed around hoping that she and Glen would reunite. Why go through that?

7. Donald had plans of taking Glen out. Why go through the mulberry bush instead of killing him when he got the chance?

8. Dwayne felt as though his manhood was taken from him by his father. Boys have been molested by their fathers for centuries. Do you think all men turn into homosexuals after being molested?

9. Dwayne's mother didn't want to die without telling him the true story. Have you ever done anything so drastic that you think you would take it to the grave?

10. The saying goes, the apple doesn't fall far from the tree. Do you believe that Tamika

is going to grow up and have her mother's old attributes?

11. Do you think that Jessica deserves a visit from Tiffany every once in a while?

12. They say two wrongs don't make a right. Do you think Donald is only getting what he deserves?

13. Dwayne is in love again with another brother. Is it possible for a gay man to ever turn straight?

14. Old habits are hard to break. Do you think that Patrice will ever steal again?

15. Donald gave some real good loving to Lisa. Do you believe you would ever do anything to jeopardize your job, just to keep your lover in your life?

16. Keith's sisters couldn't stand Lorene because she was too dark? Have you ever felt that way about someone, or do you know someone that feels that way about someone?

Notes

Notes

Notes

ORDER FORM
URBAN BOOKS, LLC
78 E. Industry Ct
Deer Park, NY 11729

Name: (please print):_____

Address:_____

City/State:_____

Zip:_____

QTY	TITLES	PRICE
	16 On The Block	$14.95
	A Girl From Flint	$14.95
	A Pimp's Life	$14.95
	Baltimore Chronicles	$14.95
	Baltimore Chronicles 2	$14.95
	Betrayal	$14.95
	Black Diamond	$14.95

Shipping and handling-add $3.50 for 1st book, then $1.75 for each additional book.
Please send a check payable to:
Urban Books, LLC
Please allow 4-6 weeks for delivery

ORDER FORM
URBAN BOOKS, LLC
78 E. Industry Ct
Deer Park, NY 11729

Name: (please print):_____

Address:_____

City/State:_____

Zip:_____

QTY	TITLES	PRICE
	Black Diamond 2	$14.95
	Black Friday	$14.95
	Both Sides Of The Fence	$14.95
	Both Sides Of The Fence 2	$14.95
	California Connection	$14.95
	California Connection 2	$14.95

Shipping and handling-add $3.50 for 1st book, then $1.75 for each additional book.

Please send a check payable to:

Urban Books, LLC

Please allow 4-6 weeks for delivery

ORDER FORM
URBAN BOOKS, LLC
78 E. Industry Ct
Deer Park, NY 11729

Name: (please print):_____

Address:_____

City/State:_____

Zip:_____

QTY	TITLES	PRICE
	Cheesecake And Teardrops	$14.95
	Congratulations	$14.95
	Crazy In Love	$14.95
	Cyber Case	$14.95
	Denim Diaries	$14.95
	Diary Of A Mad First Lady	$14.95
	Diary Of A Stalker	$14.95

Shipping and handling-add $3.50 for 1st book, then $1.75 for each additional book.
Please send a check payable to:
Urban Books, LLC
Please allow 4-6 weeks for delivery

ORDER FORM
URBAN BOOKS, LLC
78 E. Industry Ct
Deer Park, NY 11729

Name: (please print):_____

Address:_____

City/State:_____

Zip:_____

QTY	TITLES	PRICE
	Diary Of A Street Diva	$14.95
	Diary Of A Young Girl	$14.95
	Dirty Money	$14.95
	Dirty To The Grave	$14.95
	Gunz And Roses	$14.95
	Happily Ever Now	$14.95
	Hell Has No Fury	$14.95

Shipping and handling-add $3.50 for 1st book, then $1.75 for each additional book.

Please send a check payable to:

Urban Books, LLC

Please allow 4-6 weeks for delivery

ORDER FORM
URBAN BOOKS, LLC
78 E. Industry Ct
Deer Park, NY 11729

Name: (please print):_____

Address:_____

City/State:_____

Zip:_____

QTY	TITLES	PRICE

Shipping and handling-add $3.50 for 1st book, then $1.75 for each additional book.

Please send a check payable to:

Urban Books, LLC

Please allow 4-6 weeks for delivery